Despite the tu... Bouchard legacy, ... to son, from mo... ...daughter, endures, while the shifting sands of history play mighty havoc with the lives of men, as the South is torn asunder and thrown back together again . . .

In *Trials of Windhaven*, Luke and Laure discover a greater closeness during their most bitter trial to date, as their joyous life together takes dramatic turns. Ben Wilson, the gentle Quaker doctor who lost his wife, Fleurette, to a sudden illness, travels to a Creek village in Oklahoma to practice medicine and finds love, while Laurette Douglas in Chicago learns a lesson in forgiveness the hard way. Andy Haskins leaves Windhaven Range to visit Luke—and Joe Duvray, Lucien Edmond's righthand man, becomes deeply involved with a young woman whose father is fast becoming Lucien's enemy.

From Lucien Bouchard's first proud struggle to build Windhaven Plantation, to the ravages of the Civil War, which helped destroy it, from the family's westward move to Windhaven Range, to the rebuilding of Windhaven Plantation, this tumultuous saga continues to unfold the dramatic story of the Bouchard family, their lives and loves, their triumphs and tragedies.

OVER 3.5 MILLION COPIES SOLD

The Windhaven Saga:

WINDHAVEN PLANTATION

STORM OVER WINDHAVEN

LEGACY OF WINDHAVEN

RETURN TO WINDHAVEN

WINDHAVEN'S PERIL

TRIALS OF WINDHAVEN

TRIALS OF WINDHAVEN

Marie de Jourlet

PINNACLE BOOKS   LOS ANGELES

TRIALS OF WINDHAVEN

An original Pinnacle Books edition, published for the first time anywhere.

Produced by Lyle Kenyon Engle

First printing, March 1980

ISBN: 0-523-40722-X

Cover illustration by Bruce Minney

Printed in the United States of America

PINNACLE BOOKS, INC.
2029 Century Park East
Los Angeles, California 90067

Dedicated to Mary Eileen,
Audrey, and Jeanie

Acknowledgments

A writer's sources can be both documentary guide and inspiration, particularly in constructing an historical novel. Mine, throughout this Windhaven series, have been both and more, resulting in lasting friendships with historians even from a distance. Once again, I wish to express my gratitude to Joseph Milton Nance, Professor of History, College of Liberal Arts, Texas A & M University; Mrs. Evelyn M. King, Assistant Director of Special Research, Sterling C. Evans Library, Texas A & M University; Rosanne McCaffrey, Research Coordinator, New Orleans Historic Collections; James R. Travis, University of Alabama Press at Tuscaloosa; and Mary H. Barton, Carrizo Springs, Texas.

My most appreciative thanks go also to Lyle and Marla Engel and Philip and Leslie Rich, of Book Creations, Inc., for their contributions of suggestions and their furnishings of bibliographical materials which were invaluable. Special thanks are due to Fay Bergstrom, tireless and helpful typist-transcriber, whose concern with and suggestions for this manuscript rivaled the dedication of an editor. She is one of the all-too-rare workers who sees beyond the mechanics and acts as a critical reader—which keeps an author honest!

Marie de Jourlet

TRIALS OF WINDHAVEN

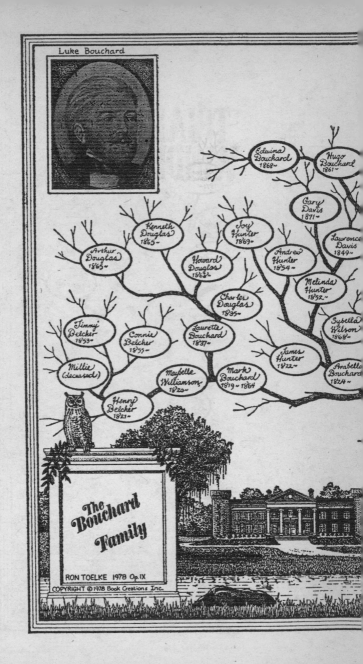

Luke Bouchard

Edwina
Bouchard
1868~

Hugo
Bouchard
1861~

Gary
Davis
1871~

Lawrence
Davis
1849~

Kenneth
Douglas
1865~

Joy
Hunter
1869~

Arthur
Douglas
1863~

Howard
Douglas
1863~

Andrew
Hunter
1854~

Melinda
Hunter
1852~

Charles
Douglas
1835~

Jimmy
Belcher
1853~

Connie
Belcher
1855~

Laurette
Bouchard
1837~

Sybella
Wilson
1868~

Millie
(deceased)

James
Hunter
1872~

Maybelle
Williamson
1820~

Mark
Bouchard
1819~1864

Arabella
Bouchard
1874~

Henry
Belcher
1821~

The
Bouchard
Family

RON TOELKE 1978 Op.IX

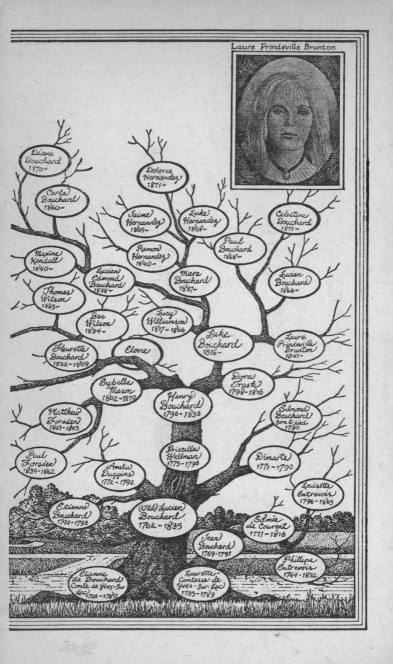

Laure Prindeville Brunton

Diane Bouchard 1870~

Carla Bouchard 1860~

Dolores Hernandez 1871~

Celestine Bouchard 1871~

Maxine Kendall 1840~

Jaime Hernandez 1869~

Luke Hernandez 1868~

Paul Bouchard 1868~

Lucien Edmond Bouchard 1838~

Ramon Hernandez 1840~

Lucien Bouchard 1866~

Thomas Wilson 1869~

Mara Bouchard 1837~

Ben Wilson 1834~

Lucy Williamson 1817~1866

Luke Bouchard 1816~

Laure Prindeville Brunton 1841~

Fleurette Bouchard 1832~1869

Elone

Dora Trask 1798~1816

Sybella Mason 1802~1870

Henry Bouchard 1796~1836

Edmond Bouchard born & died 1790

Matthew Forsden 1803~1865

Dimarte 1771~1790

Paul Forsden 1839~1862

Amelia Duggins 1772~1792

Priscilla Wellman 1775~1796

Louisette Entrevois 1796~1865

Etienne Bouchard 1791~1793

(Old) Lucien Bouchard 1762~1835

Edmée de Courent 1771~1816

Jean Bouchard 1759~1791

Phillipe Entrevois 1764~1832

Etienne de Bouchard Comte de Yves-Sur-Lac 1726~1789

Laurette~ Contesse de Yves-Sur-Lac 1735~1789

PROLOGUE

On October 18, 1869, bright sun dappled the creek and, beyond it, the Nueces River, which flowed near Windhaven Range. It was a joyous morning indeed for Luke Bouchard, who felt more youthful and strong than ever despite his fifty-three years, as he sat at the long dining-room table of the ranch house, holding his son Lucien.

The three-and-a-half-year-old boy had been kidnapped by men whom his father's enemy, the ruthless Henri Cournier, had hired for the purpose. They had ravished Luke's young wife Laure, and stolen little Lucien from his home, Windhaven Plantation, in faraway Lowndesboro, Alabama.

The child had been spirited off to New Orleans and from there Cournier's valet, Roger Benson, and a gently bred young woman who had been forced to become Benson's wife because of her late brother's gambling debt to Cournier, had attempted to take him to California.

Fortunately, previous to the kidnapping, Luke Bouchard had taken two recognizable chips from the great turquoise talisman given to him by the Comanche chief, Sangrodo, and set these chips in two tiny necklaces. These were worn by little Lucien and Luke's younger son, Paul, who was one year old. When a hunting party of Penateka Comanches had come upon Roger Benson and his wife and killed them, they discovered little Lucien in the wagon. Recognizing the turquoise chips as belonging to Sangrodo, one of their braves had ridden across the Mexican border with the child to find the Comanche chief's stronghold. Sangrodo himself had returned Lucien safely to Windhaven Range.

Luke Bouchard meanwhile had gone to New Orleans and confronted Henri Cournier with the confessions of the men who had raped Laure and kidnapped the child. Though severely wounded, he killed Cournier. In so doing, he

1

ended, finally, the vendetta of a family that for many years had been determined to destroy the Bouchards.

The hatred on the part of the Courniers reached back to the time of the French Revolution, when Luke's grandfather, Lucien, had come to America. Old Lucien's childhood sweetheart, Edmée de Courent, had decided to marry Lucien's older brother, Jean. The pain caused by her decision, as well as his outrage at her suggestion that they become lovers after her marriage, had prompted Lucien's departure to the New World.

Upon his arrival in America, Luke's grandfather sold his horse to a banker. With the money, he bought supplies and a pack horse and traveled to Mobile, and from there to Econchate, then the stronghold of the Creek, later to become Montgomery, the capital of Alabama.

At the outset of the French Revolution, Jean de Bouchard and Edmée went to Haiti, to run a sugar plantation. There Edmée flirted with the grandfather of Armand and Henri Cournier. When one of her husband's servants denounced her to his master, she tried to save herself by declaring that Auguste Cournier had forced her to submit to him. Jean de Bouchard called Auguste Cournier out and severely wounded him in a duel. The embittered Creole had urged his grandsons to avenge the dishonor that a Bouchard had brought upon his family.

A generation before the kidnapping of Luke's son, Edouard Villiers, Armand Cournier's cousin, had come to Windhaven Plantation ostensibly to court Arabella Bouchard. In reality, he wished to marry her in order to gain control of the rich land that the Creeks had given to Lucien Bouchard. When Luke, then a young man, discovered the connection between Villiers and Pierre Lourat, a gambler and slave dealer whose secret backers were the Cournier brothers, he sent him packing. After Union troops burned Windhaven Plantation and forced the Bouchards to seek a new life, Luke and his first wife, Lucy, had gone to New Orleans with the other members of the Bouchard family. From there they proceeded to Texas, where they founded Windhaven Range.

In New Orleans, Luke Bouchard met John Brunton, who had taken over the bank previously owned by Jules Ronsart, the banker with whom old Lucien had first done business when arriving in America. Brunton, named head of the bank by Ronsart's aging successor, Antoine Rigalle, had become engaged to the lovely Laure Prindeville. One afternoon, Laure had tempted Luke beyond the point of self-control, and they shared a stolen hour of passion.

Soon after Lucy's death during a bandit attack on Windhaven Range, Laure wrote to Luke, telling him that John Brunton had died and that she had given birth to a blue-eyed, fair-haired little boy whom they had agreed to name Lucien in honor of Luke's grandfather. Luke, knowing the child to be his, returned to New Orleans to woo and finally win Laure, in the meantime operating Brunton's bank under her name. Armand Cournier appeared as a speculator, trying to buy shares of stock to gain control of the bank, slandering Laure and, finally, accusing Luke of being one of the detested Bouchards who had dishonored his grand-father's name. Luke was forced into a duel with pistols, and Armand Cournier fired before the order had been given. Luke's second shot Armand Cournier down and Luke, to save his second's life, was obliged to kill Cournier's second.

But now on this sunny morning, all the spectres of the shadowy past seemed interred forever. Luke Bouchard tightened his hold around little Lucien and smiled down at his fair-haired son. He looked around the table at his step-mother, Sybella Bouchard Forsden, now sixty-seven, whom he had always venerated as if she had been his very own mother. (After the death of Luke's father, Henry, Sybella had married her overseer, Matthew Forsden.) Beside her sat his son Lucien Edmond, who at just thirty-one years of age was titular head of Windhaven Range, and his wife, Maxine, not yet thirty. Luke's daughter, Mara, just thirty-two, and her husband, Ramón Hernandez, sat nearby. They were expecting their second child in December. For all of these family members, now close by him, Luke Bouchard said a silent prayer of thanks to God.

Luke turned to Maybelle Belcher, who was his dead wife Lucy's younger sister and who had married his half-brother, Mark Bouchard. Mark had abandoned her soon after the birth in 1837 of their only child, Laurette. He had been dissolute and as wild as Luke's own father, Henry, and he came to a violent end. But now at last Maybelle knew happiness, as the wife of Henry Belcher, a widower,

3

and she loved his children—sixteen-year-old Timmy and fourteen-year-old Connie—as much as if they had been her very own flesh and blood.

Now in his middle years, Luke Bouchard could look back with relish at what he had accomplished. He had tried always to put into effect the lessons he had learned from his grandfather, old Lucien, and his life had been nearly as eventful, especially in recent years. After the tragedy of the Civil War, he had begun anew by leading the family safely to Texas. He made peace with the warlike Comanche leader Sangrodo, by coming unarmed to the chief's stronghold and restoring to him his lost son, Kitante. (The boy had been found on the plains suffering fever from a snake-bite, and had been restored to health.) Thus was peace secured for all time between the Comanches and the people of Windhaven Range.

Luke also had defeated the ruthless attacks of bandits and bushwhackers on the cattle range, though it cost him the life of his wife Lucy. After her death, he turned his prospering ranch over to Lucien Edmond, went back to New Orleans to marry Laure, and ultimately returned to Alabama, to restore Windhaven Plantation to the glory of its earliest days. And now he would take back little Lucien, his and Laure's first child, safe after his harrowing abduction.

Yet even in this moment of rejoicing, Luke's thoughts traveled to Dr. Ben Wilson, whose wife, Fleurette, Sybella Bouchard Forsden's younger daughter, had died from diphtheria this very year, in Pittsburgh, at the tragically early age of thirty-seven. After her death, Ben took his little son and baby daughter and, leaving them at Windhaven Range, went to live among the Creeks on their reservation in Indian Territory, so that he might nurse the sick of this once-proud Indian tribe and thus assuage his grief. Meanwhile his four-year-old boy, Thomas and one-year-old daughter, Sybella, were here at Windhaven Range, being cared for by their grandmother while the bereaved young doctor was trying to begin a new life.

And Luke thought of Laurette, Maybelle's only child, who lived in Chicago with her enterprising young husband, Charles Douglas, the owner of a thriving department store. She had presented her husband with twins, Arthur and Kenneth, now four, and Howard, now one.

4

One Bouchard was missing from this happy reunion: the flirtatious Arabella, Luke's half-sister, who lived in Galveston with her husband, James Hunter, a cotton factor. She was now the mother of Melinda, seventeen and Andrew, fifteen; soon, at the age of forty-five, she would give birth to a third child whom they hoped would be a girl, whom they would call Joy. Luke considered his brother-in-law a sedate and quiet fellow, but in fact James had managed to tame Arabella once and for all, by spanking her with a hairbrush after she had upbraided him for helping a young widow—when she herself had been guilty of a flirtation with the debonair land swindler, Durwood McCambridge.

Luke made a mental note to himself to urge Arabella and James to come with the children to visit in the next few months. He had noticed that Sybella Bouchard Forsden was looking unusually drawn and pale this morning. Well, she had had a long, exciting, and rewarding life, and she was of sturdy stock, he knew; all the same, Arabella really should pay her a visit soon.

Luke bent down to kiss little Lucien on the forehead and then suddenly exclaimed, "Good Lord, in all the excitement of finding Lucien here when I rode in yesterday and then thanking God in the new chapel that Friar Bartoloméo so kindly dedicated, I'd forgotten all about relieving poor Laure's mind about our son—"

"I've already attended to that, Father," Lucien Edmond spoke up. "Just a few hours before you rode in, I sent Joe Duvray to Austin, to send a telegraph message to her. It was directed to Montgomery, and I'm sure a courier will take it directly to Lowndesboro."

"That was very thoughtful of you, Lucien Edmond. God bless you. I guess I'd best be thinking about going back to Windhaven Plantation with little Lucien. It's a long journey, and I know how anxious Laure must be about him. But the boy has been through a harrowing ordeal. He should have at least another day or two of rest before we make that long journey."

The tall Comanche chief, Sangrodo, who sat with his wife Catayuna at the long table, now spoke. "Let me ride with you, *Taiboo Nimiahkana*. I would see you and your little son safely to Corpus Christi, and there is much I would say to you." Then, turning to his beautiful young

Mexican wife, he added with a smile, "It will do you good to rest here, Catayuna, as it will for Inokanti, our first-born."

"If my husband wishes, it shall be so," Catayuna responded, glancing at him quickly with deep affection.

"Inokanti," Luke Bouchard repeated. "It is Comanche for He-Who-Is-Loved, is it not, Sangrodo?"

"That is true, *Taiboo Nimiahkana*," Sangrodo replied. "The Great Spirit has been good to us. When Catayuna killed the *bandido* Carlos Macaras, it cost her the life of He-Who-Walks-In-His-Father's-Footsteps. But in return we have been blessed with a fine, strong son."

"There is much we have in common, Sangrodo. I, too, am blessed to have known so loyal and generous a friend as you. It would please me greatly if you would ride with Lucien and me to Corpus Christi. Let us say, then, in two days we start the journey."

"That is good."

"We'd be delighted to have Catayuna and the little boy stay as our guests for as long as they both like," Sybella Bouchard Forsden eagerly spoke up. "And maybe Catayuna will show me some of her newest weavings. I see she's made a little jacket for the baby with pictographs woven in."

Catayuna blushed and, lowering her eyes, softly responded, "It was Sangrodo who asked me to make this jacket and to tell the story of how it was I lost our first born only to be blessed with Inokanti."

"It was my wish that all of our tribe should know how truly you are Comanche, woman," Sangrodo smilingly explained. "She has the spirit of our people, the courage, the honor, and the truthfulness we value."

CHAPTER ONE

"Yes, Lucien, you will ride with Daddy. We're going to have a long journey, but we'll be home to Mother soon," the tall, graying, bearded man assured his son as he carefully lifted him in his arms and mounted his horse. The mare had once been a restive mount, but Luke Bouchard's firm yet considerate handling had soothed her considerably. She nickered softly as she felt her rider's weight. One-armed Andy Haskins, at Luke's order, had gone into the storeroom of the bunkhouse and returned with two Spencer repeating rifles, ammunition, and saddle-sheaths. As the Comanche chief Sangrodo mounted a superb gray gelding, clutching the feathered lance which was a symbol of his leadership of his tribe, Luke turned to him.

"This rifle and the sheath are yours to keep, my blood brother," Luke Bouchard said, as Andy Haskins expertly (despite his handicap) attached the saddle-sheath to the gelding and thrust the rifle into it, then moved to Luke's mare and repeated the procedure.

"It is a generous gift, *Taiboo Nimiahkana*, and it is more than that because it is the gift of one who is my friend as he is my blood brother." Sangrodo extended his hand in friendship.

"I'll tie the pack horse's reins to your saddle horn, Mr. Bouchard," Andy Haskins volunteered. "Kate Strallis packed flour for biscuits and a jar of wild honey—the little tyke'll like that for sure—and there's a good supply of jerky. Just before dawn this morning, I slaughtered a calf and cut up enough so that you and Sangrodo and your boy can have a good taste of fresh meat as well. It's wrapped in a tarp and salted down so it'll keep a few days."

"Thanks, Andy. And thank Kate for me, too. By the way, when is her wedding to Pablo Casares?"

"Next Sunday, Mr. Bouchard. Oh, here's Friar Bartoloméo Alicante. He said he wanted to be sure to see you off and say a prayer for your safe journey."

Luke turned to see the portly, nearly bald Franciscan friar approach them, beaming with satisfaction. "It was kind of you to think of me, Friar Bartoloméo," he said. "I mean to keep the vow of which I told you when I knelt to thank God for His great mercy in giving me back my lost son. I wish you might come to Windhaven Plantation to dedicate the chapel I shall build for my family and for all my workers."

"That is an invitation I would gladly accept, Mr. Bouchard, if it were not that I must go where I am most sorely needed. It is a kind of penance I have set myself— you understand it."

"Yes, Friar Bartoloméo. You truly follow the teachings of St. Francis of Assisi through your humility, joyful poverty, and devotion to all men. I have never met any priest who better exemplified the truest meaning of this faith, and you have set an example for me which I shall cherish the rest of my days."

"My son, you give me too much credit. I am only the simple servant of Him who watches over all of us. But now on this beautiful morning let me pray with you for the swift return of you and your son to your beloved wife. I pray, too, that He will watch over the great chief of the Comanches who has taught his people how to live in peace and whose way of life shows once again that all of us are brothers." Friar Bartoloméo then knelt down, clasped his hands, and looked up at the sky. "Oh merciful God our Father, bless Luke Bouchard and Sangrodo and the little son of Luke Bouchard, and watch over them on their journey. Let Luke Bouchard and his son be happily reunited with his wife, and let Sangrodo return to his wife and child and thence to his people whom he guides so ably. Observe, dearest Lord, the lasting friendship between these two men of good will, and may their example induce others who are fearful to accept a brotherhood and a friendship which is based on Thy laws of goodness and justice and mercy unto all men. Amen."

Luke Bouchard echoed that last word as he crossed himself, and Sangrodo, his alert, strong face taut with concentration as he strove to understand the friar's every word, nodded and turned to smile at Luke.

8

"Thank you and God bless you, Friar Bartoloméo," Luke softly said. "Where will you go from here?"

"After I marry Kate Strallis to her warmhearted vaquero, Mr. Bouchard, I shall go into the Panhandle and try to serve some of the Indian tribes there. It may be I shall return to the Creek reservation after my wanderings, if only to see again how magnificently Dr. Wilson devotes himself to those rejected people. In his selflessness he recalls to me my own dedicated vows which cost me my post in Santa Fe. And it's good for a man to be reminded of his purpose in life, Mr. Bouchard. Go with God, all of you." Again he made the sign of the cross.

"May He watch over you also, Friar Bartoloméo," Luke said as he repeated the sign. Then, turning to Andy Haskins, he said in a low voice, "You'll do me a great service, Andy, if you'll tell Lucien Edmond and Maxine to look after Mother Sybella. She looks very peaked. She works as hard as a man, and at her age that's not the best thing for her."

"I take your meaning, Mr. Bouchard. I'll mention it to Mr. Lucien Edmond directly. Well then, sir, good luck to you, and I hope you come back to see us real soon."

"I'd like nothing better, Andy. And give my best to Joe Duvray when he comes back from Austin. You both can take a great deal of credit for the success of this range."

Andy Haskins flushed and kicked at the ground. "Shucks, Mr. Bouchard, Joe and I just did our jobs. We're the ones who are grateful to you, sir, for giving us a chance here. Anyway, we'll both take care of Mr. Lucien Edmond and everybody else here, you can depend on it."

Luke Bouchard reached down to grip Andy Haskins's hand and then, with a nod to Sangrodo, kicked his heels against the mare's belly. The journey back home had begun.

Lucien proved surprisingly durable during the first day of the journey. To be sure, Luke Bouchard did not gallop his mare and made frequent stops to let the little boy down so that he could walk about. Andy Haskins had, thoughtfully enough, included a leather flask of milk taken that very morning from a cow that had just calved, and the little boy drank thirstily and made a good lunch of nearly two biscuits and a small portion of jerky. San-

9

grodo's eyes glowed with approval as he watched Lucien, the meal over, hold out his arms to his father and saw Luke lift him up and then mount the mare. "There is much strength in the *niño*," he remarked. "And in some ways it is good that he has already endured hardship—this is what the Comanche boy is taught as early as he can walk, to understand that life is not easy and that survival must be earned. From what the Penateka brave told me when he rode into the stronghold with your little son, the man and woman who brought him in that wagon must have come by a dangerous route. Yet he seems unmarked by that—it is a very good sign."

"Yes, thank God, Sangrodo." Luke smiled down at his blond son, who sleepily hugged him and smiled up at him. Then Lucien closed his bright blue eyes and drowsed. "He said very little about what happened to him. I know only that he did not like the man who took him away from New Orleans and that he said the poor lady who looked after him was afraid of the man and that he was bad to her." A shadow crossed his face, and then he smiled. "But it's all over now, it can be forgotten. It was good of you to come with me, Sangrodo. When I went back before, after my wife Lucy's death, I had a strange feeling that I would return again to Windhaven Range and that I would go back joyously after sorrow."

"I, too, have had glimpses at times into what is to come, and it is as if I had expected these things to happen," the Comanche chief vouchsafed. "Before the raid on the village from which I took the *esposo* of Catayuna, I had a dream in which the Great Spirit showed me that out of death would come life and out of hatred, love. And it was so. I did not believe that Catayuna would ever take me as her man, and yet now it is as if I had not lived until she entered my life."

"In some ways, Sangrodo, I have the same feelings about my young wife Laure, the girl I met in New Orleans when I was on my way with the family to Windhaven Range. I am older than you, and yet I have begun a new life with the greatest joy and hope for the future. Even though I am nearly twice my young wife's age, there is no difference between us in spirit."

"Yes, that is good. Yet if you had told me years ago, when I sought to make war on all my enemies, that I would

10

be content to live in Mexico and to think of this fine gift which you have given"—he reached down to pat the Spencer in its saddle-sheath—"to bring meat to our camp-fires instead of using it against the white-eyes who wish to drive us from our land, I would have called you mad from having eaten the loco weed."

They fell silent as they rode past the tall, yellowish reeds, as high as a man's head, which marked the winding pathway of the Nueces River, and entered the rolling prairie with its clumps of pecan, elm, and oak trees, and the massive clumps of mesquite whose green hanging pods were as long as a man's hand.

They made camp just before sunset. Sangrodo cooked part of the freshly slaughtered calf and, to Luke's amusement, even made biscuits, proclaiming the honey spread upon them a great delicacy. Lucien, animated and keenly observant of the sights around him, plied his father with repeated questions about when they would see Mother again, and Luke soothed him and promised that when they got back home, he would teach Lucien to ride his very own pony. The little boy excitedly clapped his hands and hugged his father, and soon fell asleep as Luke drew a blanket over him. Then they moved away from the sleeping child. Sangrodo took out his calumet and tamped coarse tobacco into it, and with his tinderbox struck a light and lit it, puffing at it and then passing it to Luke Bouchard.

"You have told me, *Taiboo Nimiahkana*," he began in a low voice, "how your grandfather came many years ago to live with the Creeks and how he killed a she-bear and took its claws to the chief of the stronghold to prove his courage as a hunter. I would know more about you and your family, that I may understand what brought you to this lonely land near the Rio Grande. Were you and your family not afraid of the Comanche, the Kiowa Apache, and the others who looked upon the white-eyes as ene-mies because they came where the buffalo dwelt and tried to drive us away from our hunting grounds?"

"No, Sangrodo, I was not afraid. No more than my grandfather Lucien was afraid when, many years ago, he journeyed by pack horse from the port of Mobile up to the village of Econchate. When old Lucien presented him-self there, before the leader of the Creeks, and asked for

11

a chance to work on the land and to share his life with them, he believed, as I do, that all men are equal before God, whom you call the Great Spirit and whom the Creeks call Ibofanaga, the Giver of Breath."

"There are few white-eyes who would believe this, and I think in the years ahead there will be still fewer," Sangrodo sadly observed as he took the calumet from Luke Bouchard and meditatively puffed upon it before returning it.

"I wish I could say you were wrong, Sangrodo, but in my heart I know that what you say is true. And it is not only that the white-eyes seek to rob the Indian of his land, but even among my own people brother tries to rob brother. You know that we have had a great war lasting four years and that the people of the North hated those of the South because the Southerners upheld slavery. Now the blacks have been set free—yet my grandfather and I never kept slaves. You see, Sangrodo, the white-eyes had laws that slaves could not be free unless they were taken across the borders of one state to another, and even if they were, slave traders often captured them and sold them again into even worse slavery. So my grandfather and I told our black workers that they were free and that they were never to call us master. And in our account books we kept records of the wages they had earned, so that they might have them when they needed them—though even that was against the law of the South at that time."

Sangrodo shook his head. "We Comanches have taken slaves often, as you know—Catayuna was to be my slave, but when I saw how proud and brave she was, I knew that she would soon win her freedom. And when we did take slaves, we let them learn our ways and see if they did not wish to become what we were, and when they did, they earned their freedom. It is hard for me to understand how the white-eyes, who are so many and so powerful, could make war on their brothers over slaves."

"But even though four years have passed since the peace treaty was signed between the North and the South, Sangrodo, there is still war among the white-eyes. It is not war with guns, but war that a conqueror inflicts upon the defeated. Now the selfish, greedy leaders of the North wish to punish the South for having broken away from the Union. They have sent not only hateful and thieving white-eyes to hold office throughout the South, but they also have appointed blacks to act as if they were superior to the white-eyes of the South. It is not a good thing."

"And yet you would go back there and not stay on the ranch?" Sangrodo wonderingly demanded.

"It is hard to explain, Sangrodo. Perhaps it is because it was my grandfather's dream to build a great house on the land that the Creeks gave him, a house like the one he was born in, across the seas. As a boy I helped him build that house, and I walked with him in the fields and saw how he treated white and black workers alike, and how he loved the Creeks because they were wise and honorable men. Perhaps it is fitting that as I come to the twilight of my years, Sangrodo, I should continue to uphold his beliefs that men are brothers and can work together in harmony and peace. Yes, I believe that my workers and I can till our soil, and that one day there will be peace again and we shall be a united nation under God."

Sangrodo tapped out the ashes from the calumet, filled it again with tobacco, and lit it. He rose, staring at the sky in which a quarter moon hung like a silver scimitar. Now in his forty-ninth year, he stood nearly six feet tall, taller than all of his braves. His black hair was parted in the center and the part painted a deep carmine. The hair was in braids on either side of his head, with a scalp lock falling from the top. His side braids were wrapped with strips of buffalo hide, and he wore a red feather thrust through the scalp lock. His ears were pierced, and in the left ear there was a ring made of white shells cast up on the bank of the Nueces River, and through the right ear there was a ring of silver. He wore beaded buckskin and moccasins, and as he walked forward as if to ponder over what Luke Bouchard had just told him, he was lithe and catlike in his movements, silent yet vibrant with an energy that a man half his age would have envied him.

Finally he turned back, lifted the calumet, puffed at it to get it going, and then handed it to Luke as he seated himself again. "It is a strange thing, yet I feel I know your grandfather. Will you not tell me what his life was like, in the old days? And there is something else, too. You do not speak of your own father, but only of your grand-

13

father. I do not wish to offend you, but I wish to know you better than I do now, for there is so much between us and you are my good and trusted friend."

"You do not offend me, Sangrodo. I will tell you. You see, my grandfather worked on the land that the chief of the Creeks gave him, and when he was wounded by the she-bear, it was the chief's daughter, Dimarte, whom they called the beloved woman, who cared for him. He fell in love with her, and he won the right to marry her. She bore him a little son, but she and that son were killed by the bite of a snake."

"What sorrow it must have been for him to lose such a woman."

"He mourned her all his life, and he talked with her spirit. He buried her and her child at the top of a high bluff on the river beside the great house that he finally built toward the end of his life. He would go to the topmost tower and his thoughts would be with her and their little son. And he would hear the hooting of an owl and know that she was with him."

"It is so with us also. We hear our ancestors in the voices of the wind, in the murmuring of the river, in the songs of the birds, and even in the animals we hunt," Sangrodo murmured.

"Then, not long after, a family came from another state where once the Creeks also had ruled. But they were in the pay of a man who wished to destroy the Creeks and to kill the chief, who was Dimarte's father. This family had brought with them a white slave girl, whom we called an indentured bond servant—she had been sentenced to death in her country, called England, but instead of being put to death, she was made a slave to this treacherous family who moved near my grandfather. One day, when the chief of the Creeks and old Lucien came to visit this family, the father of the household, a violent blackguard, shot and killed the chief. There was a battle, and all the family was killed save one son, who escaped, and the white-eyes girl, their slave. The angry Creeks sentenced this girl to die, but my grandfather begged for her life and took her as his squaw. A year later, she gave him a son. But then the boy of that evil family, the one who had escaped, returned and fired a musket at Lucien. This brave girl stood in front of him and gave her life for him. Later,

14

my grandfather suffered even more tragedy when his son also died, of the river fever."

"Your grandfather indeed must have had great courage to endure such sorrow. But then he must have taken another squaw, to have had your father?"

"Yes. He was told that an English girl and her brother, who surveyed the land and made maps, had been captured by another Indian tribe. They had killed her brother and put her to the torture stake. My grandfather dueled with the chief with knives and won her freedom. Then he married her, but she died in giving him the son Henry, who was my father, Sangrodo."

"I understand. Was your father like you and your grandfather, *Taiboo Nimiahkana*?"

"No, alas, he was very different indeed. He believed in slavery, and he was greedy for land. The white-haired woman whom you know as Sybella was his wife—but I am not her son. There was a man from the same state from which the family who had killed the Creek chief had come. He brought his young daughter with him, and they sought to buy my grandfather's land. My father killed the man and forced his daughter to marry him—and after I was born, she drowned herself in the river."

"Yet you are indeed like your grandfather, and there is nothing of your father in you. It was the will of the Great Spirit. The goodness of a man's heart is not made by his father and mother only; it is what that child learns as he comes to manhood. I respect you, *Taiboo Nimiahkana*." Sangrodo turned to Luke Bouchard and pressed his palm upon Luke's forehead and then on Luke's heart and finally on Luke's lips and inclined his head. "The Great Spirit destined you, as He did your grandfather, to take only good from what evil surrounded you, and He gave you both great courage to withstand such evil. I remember what our old shaman Mingride said of you when I had him cast the bones. I knew then that you were a man who would never speak with a forked tongue and that you would respect all those whom you met whose ways were different from yours, *Taiboo Nimiahkana*. I am glad that it was destined that our paths should cross. I think, even though I grow restless at times in my new life on the land, that I have learned from you how to begin again. I thank you, *Taiboo Nimiahkana*, for having opened your

15

heart to me as you have this night. I will ask only one more question—why was it that your grandfather gave up his great house and came across the ocean to live with the Creeks?"

"Perhaps because he was in love and found that the object of his love betrayed him, Sangrodo. In the country of France, my grandfather's father was a nobleman, which means that he was ranked above the common people. My grandfather had an older brother who, by the laws of the land, would have inherited that title before my grandfather could. The girl my grandfather loved told him that she wished to marry his older brother to obtain that title. She proposed that she be my father's sweetheart after she had given his older brother a son. In honor he refused, and he saw also that the common people were about to revolt against the noblemen. He urged his father and mother to leave and take safety in England or some other nation where there would be peace, but they would not. So he came to this country, a young country, where there would be land and where he could begin his life over again. That was how it was meant to be for him."

"I see that the Great Spirit has put many trials in the way of you and your grandfather, *Taiboo Nimiahkana*. And yet you have overcome them and you are the stronger for having done so, as your grandfather was."

"Yes, Sangrodo, through the grace of God. That is why I can go back to the war-torn land where once my grandfather knew great happiness and be at peace within myself and know assuredly that I can withstand whatever trials are yet in store for me."

After two weeks, they had come to the outskirts of Corpus Christi. Little Lucien had thrived despite the rigors of the journey, and Sangrodo had fashioned him a flute made out of reeds and shown him how to play upon it. The Comanche chief also had made a bird out of the yellow reeds for Lucien to play with.

"My heart is heavy to think that we must part now, *Taiboo Nimiahkana*," Sangrodo said as he reined in his gelding and stared down at the dusty streets and the row of false-fronted stores which bordered the muddy shallows of the port.

"We can keep our friendship by letters, Sangrodo. I can

16

write to you in the Spanish tongue and send the letters to Windhaven Range, and when you and Catayuna visit again, they will be there waiting for you."

"Ho, that is very good!" Sangrodo chuckled. Then, proudly, "It was wise that Catayuna taught me how to read and write in Spanish."

"I read Spanish well, and I will take joy in having a letter from you. They will tell you at the ranch how to send it to me. But do not go back yet—there is one more gift I would give you. It is in return for the flute and the bird you have made for Lucien. Will you wait here until I return?"

"Gladly. Though I know how eager your little son is to be back in his mother's arms, I would have wished our journey could have taken longer, *Taiboo Nimiahkana*."

"Perhaps one day we may ride together on a hunt or as old friends talking of the past and the future as we have done on this journey, Sangrodo."

"Let us hope the Great Spirit grants us that before our years are at an end, my blood brother."

Luke Bouchard smiled and nodded, then wheeled his mare toward the town. As he reached the dock, he uttered a cry of joy, for the steamer *William Wallace* was moored at anchor there. How appropriate and symbolic it was that the testy old Scottish captain who had brought him and his family to Windhaven Range and then taken him back on his journey to New Orleans, where he had courted and won Laure, should be here again to return him to Windhaven Plantation!

Dismounting from his horse, with little Lucien putting his arms around his neck, he walked toward the dock and hailed one of the stevedores: "Is Captain Jamie McMurtrie aboard?"

"He's in the saloon whetting his whistle, Mister."

"Thanks. When do you sail for Galveston?"

"In two hours."

"That's all the time I'll need. Thank you." Luke Bouchard strode toward the saloon. Inside, he found the bearded captain standing talking to three cronies, lifting a whiskey glass to toast them.

"Can you take another passenger, Captain McMurtrie?" Luke called.

The steamboat captain whirled and uttered a cry of joyous recognition. "It's Luke Bouchard—man, you have a habit of turning up at the most unexpected times! That your boy with you?"

"Yes, Captain McMurtrie. He was kidnapped from Windhaven Plantation. Thank God he was found by friendly Indians who recognized him from his pendant of turquoise that you see around his neck. It's good to see you again, Captain McMurtrie. I have a quick errand to do, and then I'd like to board your steamboat."

"We'll wait as long as you like. Not much cargo this time, Mr. Bouchard. It'll be my pleasure to have you aboard, sir."

"Thank you. My errand won't take too long, and I'll not delay your sailing. I'll see you aboard, Captain."

Luke emerged from the tavern and walked down the street. In one of the store windows he saw a display of guns and knives, and he entered. The clerk, a bald little man with a waxed mustache, came out from behind the counter, smiling. "How may I serve you, mister? Cute boy you've got there with you. You're not about to want a gun or a knife for him, though, I'll be bound."

"Hardly," Luke Bouchard chuckled. "I was wondering if you had one of those fine bowie knives, and a leather sheath for it, perhaps a sheath-belt."

"Indeed I do, sir. Here you are!" The clerk moved behind the counter, opened the back of the case, and drew out a glistening nine-inch curved blade, made to the specifications of the hero of the Alamo. With it was a glossy black leather sheath-belt.

"That's perfect. I'll take it—how much do I owe you?" Luke Bouchard delightedly asked.

"It's a fine specimen, isn't it? And about the only one I've got left. That's why I have to ask you forty dollars for the knife and five more for the sheath-belt."

"That's a fair price. Here you are." Luke Bouchard laid down several gold coins.

"Here's your change, mister. Thanks and come in again, any time."

"I may, the next time I'm back." Luke smiled as he turned and left the store.

Mounting his mare, he rode back to where Sangrodo waited. "This is my gift to you, my blood brother," he said, as he handed the bowie knife in its sheath-belt to

18

the Comanche chief. "It has a meaning that you will understand. You remember how Catayuna killed the *bandido* with her skinning knife? It will remind you always of her courage and of my admiration for her and for you."

Sangrodo strapped the belt around him and touched the handle of the knife almost reverently. He compressed his lips as his harsh features sought to show no emotion. At last he said, "She will be pleased that you think of her so, *Taiboo Nimiahkana.* You do me honor in your respect for her who is the mother of my son. She, like your grandfather's Dimarte, is the beloved woman of our tribe. May the Great Spirit watch over you till your return to her who is your living, faithful squaw. May He let our paths cross again so that we may never forget our friendship and our brotherhood."

Then, lifting his feathered lance in salute, Sangrodo wheeled his gelding toward the west and rode off at a gallop.

CHAPTER TWO

There were only three other passengers beside Luke Bouchard who had boarded at Corpus Christi; hence, Captain Jamie McMurtrie had ample time to renew his acquaintanceship with the tall, buckskin-garbed man. He had brought Luke from this very port two years ago when after his wife Lucy's death in the bandit raid, Luke had returned to New Orleans to court and marry Laure Prindeville Brunton.

For the three-year-old boy, this trip aboard the packet was an exciting adventure, one which happily served to erase the memories of the dreadful trek from New Orleans across the lonely wilderness with Cournier's henchman, Roger Benson and his unwilling wife, Amy. Luke told the genial Scotsman about Henri Cournier's dastardly plot, and the latter marveled, "For sure, Mr. Bouchard, it was the hand of God that made everything turn out all right. That's a fine little boy you've got, and he's bright and cheerful and chipper as you please. Maybe it was a good thing he was so young; he's bound not to have any bad memories of it, especially now that you're on your way home to your missus."

"That's true, Captain McMurtrie. And I'll have a chance to visit with others in my family while you lay anchor in Galveston—you say that'll be for two days?"

"That's right, Mr. Bouchard. Well, sir, I can't tell you what a pleasure it is for me to have you aboard this time, under such happy circumstances. I'll have one of my men bring some refreshment to your cabin shortly."

"You're very kind, Captain McMurtrie. I hope we'll have a chance to meet again, because my wife and I intend to visit my oldest son and his family in Texas from time to time. We Bouchards believe that we must be of help to one another in times of stress and tragedy, no matter how great the distance between us, and it strengthens us all to care for one another the way we do."

The bearded old Scotsman sighed and nodded, his eyes narrowing with reminiscence. "I think that's what I've missed most of my life, Mr. Bouchard. I was married to a fine Creole gal when I was a young buck in my early twenties—but she took sick with yellow fever and died just a year after we stood before the priest. Never had a child, and my own kinfolk are long since dead back in Scotland, but this life on the sea and on the Gulf is what I guess I was born to. Well now, that's enough of me, I'm thinking. Will you share a draught of good Scotch whisky with me? I've been saving a bottle for an occasion, and I think this is it indeed."

"With the greatest of pleasure, Captain McMurtrie," Luke Bouchard smiled. "And it was kind of you to let Lucien put his hands on the steering wheel. He felt himself to be very much a man even though I held him up to it."

"Bless you, Mr. Bouchard," the old sea captain chuckled, "he had a true steerman's grip, he did for a fact! Who knows, maybe when he grows up he'll want a life like this."

"Very possibly, Captain McMurtrie. I think the wisest thing is to give a child plenty of love and advice and respect and then let him discover what he's best suited for in later life. I'd never try to dictate what profession my children should be drawn to."

"Amen to that, Mr. Bouchard. And here's your whiskey —many good long years to you and your lovely missus, and a happy life to little Lucien!"

"A toast I'll drink gladly, Captain McMurtrie!" Luke Bouchard clinked his glass with the captain's.

The *William Wallace* docked in Galveston on the afternoon of November 6, 1869. Lucien had fallen asleep, and his father held him carefully as he boarded a carriage which would drive him to James Hunter's sturdy two-story frame house. The stevedores aboard the steamer had befriended the little boy, and many of them had given him presents like bright pennies, whistles, oranges, and even a pet lizard in an ingenious little wooden cage. Luke Bouchard had been intensely grateful to these kindhearted men,

21

realizing that their affection for his son would do much toward restoring the boy's cheerful spirits after his arduous ordeal.

Shifting the sleeping little boy to his left arm, Luke reached for the knocker and rapped three times. The door was opened by Melinda, now seventeen and taller than her mother. With a joyous cry, she exclaimed, "Uncle Luke! My goodness, it's wonderful to see you again—and that's your little boy! Whatever are both of you doing out here and where is your wife?"

"Who is it, Melinda?" Arabella Hunter called from the salon, where she was resting on a *chaise longue*. She was in the final month of her pregnancy.

"It's Uncle Luke, Mama!" Melinda excitedly explained. Then to Luke, almost conspiratorily, she whispered, "Mama's going to have a baby, and it's getting awfully close to the time. Come right in, she's in the salon. I just know she'll be ever so glad to see you."

"Thank you, my favorite niece. Tell me, where's your brother Andrew?"

"He's still in school, but he ought to be home in a few minutes. Mrs. Ponson's Seminary for Young Ladies was closed today because she's down with the chills, so we all had a holiday, that's why I'm home right now," Melinda explained as she led Luke into the salon.

"Oh my goodness! Dear Luke, what a wonderful surprise—and that must be Lucien—" Arabella exclaimed, sitting up, not without an effort, and flushing as she self-consciously drew the flaps of her peignoir together.

"This is really wonderful, Bella," Luke chuckled as he drew up a footstool and sat down beside her, shifting sleeping Lucien in his arms so as not to waken him. "I should say, my dearest sister, that your life is now serene and happy—and the proof I can see for myself."

"Oh Luke!" Arabella Hunter's blushes furiously deepened. "My scamp of a daughter, who thinks herself quite a young lady now at seventeen, has been spreading the news all around the neighborhood. I've half a notion to take a hairbrush to her."

"Oh, Mama," Melinda petulantly complained, "I'm much too old for that. You know, Uncle Luke, I even have a fellow now. Mama chaperones us, of course."

"Well, young lady," Arabella tartly observed, "don't forget that I could always change my mind if you don't behave yourself. But now, Luke dear, tell me all about yourself. What in the world brought you out here this time of year?"

"It's a long story, Bella, and not a pleasant one, except for the happy ending. You may remember the duel I had with Armand Cournier. It seems that he had a brother, Henri, who wanted revenge." Luke quickly described Henri Cournier's machinations and the kidnapping and rescue of little Lucien. "I'm on my way back to Windhaven Plantation now," he concluded, "and I'll stop over briefly in New Orleans."

"How terrible it must have been for you and poor Laure," Arabella exclaimed. "Melinda, go fetch your uncle a nice cool glass of mint tea and some of that syllabub."

"Just the tea, Melinda dear," Luke amended with a winning smile at the charming, black-haired girl, who curtseyed and hurried off. Then, his face grave, Luke leaned forward and said, "I wanted to see you, Bella, to urge you to visit Mother Sybella."

"James and I have been planning to do that, Luke, but one thing and another—and now with the baby coming in about three weeks—but certainly, once I've rested, we'd like very much to go there," Arabella declared.

"I don't want to alarm you, but when I left two weeks ago, she seemed to have lost some of her energy, and I didn't like her color at all. She's had such an active, adventurous life, as you know. And I'm sure she'd love to see you, and Melinda and Andrew too."

"I promise faithfully we'll make the trip as soon as I'm able, dear Luke. Thank you for telling me. What I can do is write Mother a letter, and I'll do that this very evening, I promise."

"That's good of you, Bella. You know about Fleurette, I imagine?"

Arabella Hunter's face, to which her late pregnancy had added a serene glow, was suddenly shadowed. "Yes, Luke. How dreadful, she was so young, such a wonderful, sweet girl! What is poor Ben doing now?"

"He left the two children at the ranch, and he went to the Creek reservation in Indian Territory to be of service

23

to the sick and the old. He's a wonderfully dedicated man, and I think he understood that by caring for others he could help assuage his own grief."

"I feel so badly about it all, Luke. I didn't write to Fleurette as much as I ought to have, and now I blame myself constantly. But I'm going to write a letter to Ben—I suppose I can send it to the ranch and someone will forward it to him?"

"One of the vaqueros, of course, dear Bella. That would be a very good thing for you to do. I know that Ben would appreciate it very much."

Arabella sighed. "It seems only yesterday that Fleurette and I were back in that red-brick chateau, and I remember how she loved to see the little birds outside the window. My poor sister—she was so happy with Ben, it's just dreadful that she wasn't allowed to have more years. I've been very lucky with James."

"So I can see," he teased her. "Thank you, Melinda. I'll drink to your health, my lovely niece, and one of these days, I shouldn't be surprised that you'll make some very worthy young man the most wonderful wife, as your mother has done for your father."

Luke Bouchard led Lucien into the Brunton and Barntry Bank on Greenley Street. It had formerly been known as Brunton and Associate, but was renamed in recognition of Jason Barntry's loyal direction of the bank's affairs. Jason Barntry himself sprang up from the desk in his office and hurried out to meet Luke. Lucien was occupied with eating a praline which Luke had bought for him at a street stand, but forgot his absorption in it long enough to look up at the tall, gray-haired bank manager who shook his father's hand.

"How good it is to see you, Mr. Bouchard, sir! And this is your little son Lucien, I'd guess?"

"You're unerring as always, Jason," Luke chuckled as Jason Barntry led the way to his office. "I'm staying only a day in New Orleans, but I wanted to learn from you first-hand how the bank is doing. I'll report to Laure when I reach Windhaven Plantation."

"May I say first," Jason Barntry spoke in a low voice so that the little boy might not overhear every word, "that all of us here said prayers of thanksgiving when we learned

24

that your wounds from that duel with that vicious scoundrel were not serious. Thank God you found the child— if I may ask, where did you find him?"

Luke told him the story of Lucien's discovery by Comanches, who recognized the turquoise around the boy's neck and took him to Sangrodo. "I owe an old conjure woman back at Windhaven Plantation a very generous gift for having told me to mark my little sons with a sign," Luke concluded.

"Thank God for that!" Jason Barntry solemnly observed. "Thank God, too, that we have nothing more to fear from the Cournier family. And now, to give you a quick appraisal of the situation of this bank, you of course know that in September, because of the 'Black Friday' panic on Wall Street, gold dropped from one sixty-two to one thirty-five. Fortunately, I had been able to foresee that Jay Gould and James Fisk were attempting to corner the gold market and that there would be a great deal of potential loss to investors as a result of their unsavory scheme. I was able to buy some land and a few buildings— one of them will interest you considerably. It's the Union House."

"Yes, that's where John Brunton set up headquarters after General Ben Butler thought he had New Orleans in his pocket," Luke put in.

"Exactly. And I sold it just last month at a very nice profit to a wealthy Easterner. He's married and has five children, and his wife has a sister here in New Orleans and always wanted to live here."

"I think that's a most appropriate ending to the story of the Union House. Legitimized bliss to replace illicit," Luke chuckled. "Has the bank been able to make any profit at all this past year?"

"A small one, Mr. Bouchard, which can't entirely be realized until I'm able to sell some of the land we acquired prior to the Wall Street panic. But I think that by next October, at the end of our fiscal year, I'll have very satisfactory news for you and Mrs. Bouchard."

"That's welcome news, Jason. Your stewardship of this bank couldn't be surpassed. And how's your dear wife?"

Jason Barntry's homely face lit up with a smile. "Her health has greatly improved, Mr. Bouchard. And that, sir, I owe mostly to you and Mrs. Bouchard. We had bad

25

times during the war, when I had to work as a green-grocer's clerk, and Martha was ailing a good deal of the time. But now that she sees that I'm comfortably settled and with a fine job here, it's done her a world of good. I'll never be able to thank you enough, you and your wife."

"You've already done more than that in the way you've handled the affairs of this bank, Jason. Now I think Lucien and I will go back to the hotel for a nap before some lunch. We'll go sightseeing this afternoon and take the steamer to Mobile in the morning. Do keep in touch, Jason. And if there's anything happening around Lowndes-boro I think you ought to know about, I'll get off a letter to you."

"I'll continue sending you and Mrs. Bouchard my usual monthly report, sir. And please give her my very warmest regards, and my wife's as well."

Little Lucien, seated on his father's lap, had still a sizable piece of praline left. With a winning smile, he turned to Jason Barntry and held out his hand. "You're a nice man. Daddy likes you. Would you like candy?"

"No thanks, Lucien, but it's very good of you to offer it to me." Jason Barntry reached out to stroke the boy's head and then kissed him on the forehead. Rising, he shook hands with Luke Bouchard. "That's something I envy you, Mr. Bouchard. Martha could never have any children."

"Don't reproach either her or yourself, Jason. You have each other, and you've contributed so very much to all the Bouchards by the way you've handled our affairs at this bank. It is only fitting that the bank now includes your name in its title. That reminds me, I want you to give yourself a substantial raise, at least two thousand dollars a year. And that's an order—in which I know Laure will concur."

"Thank you, Mr. Bouchard." Jason Barntry was deeply moved, had to turn away for a moment and blow his nose. "God bless you both, and little Lucien here." Then, squatting down, he put his hands on the boy's shoulders and said earnestly, "I promise you, the next time you come in, I'll accept that offer of candy from you. Now you have a good trip and look after your daddy."

CHAPTER THREE

Old Captain Horace Tenby uttered a surprised gasp, then turned to shake his head as the stevedore in charge of the *Alabama Belle*'s whistle was about to sound the signal for departure. "You just hold your horses, Ernie," he admonished the lanky worker, "till that passenger with the little boy in his arms gets safe aboard, you hear me?" And then, with a great show of virtuous indignation, he made his way down from the steerman's deck to the gangplank that Luke Bouchard was ascending slowly, gently holding little Lucien in his arms.

"By all that's holy, Mr. Bouchard, it's mighty good to set eyes on you and the little fella again!" he exclaimed. In his haste to welcome Luke Bouchard aboard, he almost jostled two ornately dressed middle-aged women, who sniffed and drew back with annoyance. Wheeling, he doffed his gold-braided blue cap apologetically and hurriedly declared, " 'Scuse me, ladies, my eyesight's not what it used to be." Then, turning back, he urged, "Let me hold him for you, Mr. Bouchard, sir. This is a mighty fine day for me to welcome you back and to take you upriver to Windhaven Plantation."

"You're much too kind, Captain Tenby. He's almost asleep. He's had a trying time of it."

"Poor fella! I'll take him right to my cabin. Do join me, sir. We'll get under way presently, but they don't need me at the wheel these days, thank the Lord. I've earned that much as captain of the *Alabama Belle*, I reckon." He permitted himself a pleased chuckle. "Come to think of it, I've got a packet of horehound candy in one of my drawers in my cabin and a bottle of mighty fine Madeira which I'd like to open to drink a toast to your both being back with us safe and sound. Besides, I've been plum worried ever since I heard what those scoundrels had done at

27

your place. Kidnapping's a blackhearted thing if ever there was one, sir! There now, little fella, don't you worry none, Captain Tenby'll make you right comfy in a jiffy!" His homely face aglow, the steamboat captain led the way to his cabin, and Luke Bouchard, as he had done so many times on his journey back home from Windhaven Range, found his eyes misting with tears at the genuine kindness and sympathy of the people he had known and who had learned of his misfortune.

First instructing his little son only to suck and not to swallow the bit of candy which the captain handed him, Luke Bouchard clinked his glass of Madeira to his host's and wished him many more years navigating the Alabama River. After some small talk, Captain Tenby energetically avowed, "You know, Mr. Bouchard sir, us folks around here were mighty glad to learn what happened to the blackguards that Creole enemy of yours in New Orleans hired to invade your house and steal away this fine little boy here. And I read in the *Times-Picayune* that you fought that Creole in a duel and, even though he did wound you some, you gave him his just desserts. Good riddance, I say, along with that man who dared to harm your wife! You'll be happy to know, Mr. Bouchard, that the judge in Montgomery gave Jack Stallman twenty years at hard labor in the state penitentiary. For sure he won't last that long, not the way they'll work the fat off his ornery hide!"

"I'm grateful it's all over, Captain Tenby. And I'm going to do my best to try to forget it—I only pray my wife will be able to as well. But now, since I've been away from Lowndesboro these few months, perhaps you can fill me in on what's been happening in this part of the country."

Captain Tenby squinted, tugged at his white beard, then scowled. "You remember I told you once before how the Klan and the carpetbaggers and the scalawags were hurting Alabama mighty bad. They're still doing that, Mr. Bouchard. I don't like what I see at all, nor what I hear."

"But I've had no trouble with the Klan since I drove them off after they'd taken my foreman Marius Thornton and threatened to kill him. I thought I'd seen the last of them," Luke anxiously countered.

Captain Tenby shook his head. "Not likely, Mr. Bouchard. Maybe they're not around your parts, but they're all through the state. They just don't want to see any Republicans elected, that's what, and this Governor Smith we've got, with all due respect, he's a damned scalawag. A funny thing, about twelve years ago he was a registered Democrat, and now he's a Republican governor and siding with the North. Why, he hasn't once asked for Federal troops to put down the Klan. Even when the legislature authorized him to organize a militia, he said he was afraid that putting a militia to work would make enemies with the Alabama whites. And a militia raised in Alabama would be just about all black because we don't have a large white Republican community in this state, as you well know, sir. Now they do in Tennessee, that's a fact, but don't forget that Governor Smith is the first Republican governor we've ever had." He shook his head dolefully. "I don't see how he's going to be reelected next year, and there's going to be lots of bloodshed when the Klan gets busy discouraging Republicans from going to the polls."

"Thank you for telling me this. But can't we get the ear of the president to ensure more moderate treatment of the decent citizens who live in Alabama, Captain Tenby?"

"Well, sir, we do have Senator George E. Spencer who seems to be on pretty good terms with old U.S. Grant in Washington. But don't forget, Mr. Bouchard, Spencer came here from New York and organized a regiment of Federal cavalry among north Alabama Union sympathizers. What else can you call him but a carpetbagger, in all honesty? He'll line his pockets with whatever he can get, sir, and that's my honest opinion. No, when we have those elections next year, there's bound to be trouble in Alabama, and you don't have far to look for it."

"That's hardly a cheerful prospect, Captain Tenby. But, to give me news closer to home, have you carried any cargo from my dock to Mobile while I was away?"

"Now that I have, Mr. Bouchard," Captain Tenby beamed. "Your foreman, a mighty fine man—I'm not a racist, Mr. Bouchard, but I'll say that if all blacks were like Marius Thornton, we wouldn't have any of the trouble we're seeing now—well, sir, he's been downriver twice with a fine load of fruits and vegetables and, the last time, a dozen calves down to Mobile. Well, Mr. Bouchard, you'll soon be home with your loved ones, and I know you'll be happy to have this fine boy back where he belongs."

As the *Alabama Belle*'s huge paddlewheels slackened their chugging pace, Luke Bouchard felt the stir of excitement of returning home perhaps more powerfully than at any time before. Standing at the rail, holding Lucien in his arms, he drank in the sights of a narrowing bend in the river, watching the foamy little waves recede in the distance. Then with a gasp of joy, he saw the towering red bluff come slowly into view, at whose top his grandfather and the beloved woman and their tiny son slept in their eternal peace and unity. And then the sight of the red-brick chateau, glistening under the warm November sun that had emerged after two hours of incessant rain. The rain had given a glossy patina to the red bricks of the sturdy foundation with its twin towers, so that the chateau looked as if it had been built only a few weeks ago and was now ready to receive him for the first time, for a new life with Laure and Lucien and Paul, and with the loyal men who had come to work side by side with him.

Captain Tenby turned to the stevedore at the steam whistle and energetically nodded. "Now, Ernie!" he bawled. At once, the mournful whistle emitted three short blasts and then a prolonged one, the perennial signal that the steamboat would drop anchor at the dock of Windhaven Plantation. Luke Bouchard kissed his son and murmured, "Now we'll see Mama, and your little brother too! It's all over now, Lucien, and we'll all make it up to you, you'll see!" Then, almost impatiently starting toward the gangplank, which four burly stevedores were beginning to lay down, he said to the captain, "Thanks for a most pleasant trip and for the kindness you've shown my son, Captain Tenby."

"It's been my pleasure, Mr. Bouchard. That's a wonderful little boy you've got there. You'd never know what he's been through the last few months by looking at him now. God bless you and your family, Mr. Bouchard, and I'll look forward to having you again on the *Alabama Belle* in happy times."

"Amen to that, Captain Tenby. Good-bye." Luke Bouchard descended the gangplank and smiled to see that Marius Thornton, Dan Munroe, and Hannah Atbury were already waiting there. Just then, the door of the red-brick chateau opened, and Mitzi Vourlay, accompanied by golden-haired Laure with little Paul in her arms, hurried out to join the welcoming group at the dock.

"Thank God you're back home safe with the little fellow, Mr. Bouchard!" Marius Thornton exclaimed as he hurried up to extend his hand, his handsome face glowing with delight.

"Thank you, Marius. Everything well with you and Clemmie?"

"Better than that, Mr. Bouchard—she had a little girl two weeks ago, and we named her Sheba."

"That's good news indeed, Marius. I want to talk to you later today about our crops and our prospects for next year. Come into the study in a couple of hours, please."

"I'll be glad to. I've got the reports all ready for you."

"Thank you again, Marius. And you, Hannah, how are you and how's Phineas?"

The mature black woman's face grew solemn and she shook her head. "Not well at all, Mr. Bouchard, sir. I don't want to trouble you any, but he's never been quite right after those awful men hit him when—you know." Then, brightening, "But thank the good Lord He brought you and Lucien back home safe and sound—there's Miz Laure, every time she heard the steamboat whistle, she come running out to the dock just hoping it would be you and the boy, Mr. Bouchard!"

"I'm deeply grateful for your concern, Hannah. And I'll see poor old Phineas just as soon as I can. You don't know how good it is to be back home again." There was a suspicious moisture in Luke Bouchard's eyes as he nodded to Dan and extended his hand to shake the wiry black's. And then Laure stood before him, tears running down her cheeks, holding out her arms to Lucien, who cried out, "Mama! Oh, Mama, I'm glad I'm back with you and Daddy!"

"You sweet angel! Luke, let me have him—oh you darling, you sweet darling! God has surely answered my prayers!" Laure sobbed as she cradled the blue-eyed little boy in her arms and kissed him ardently. Lucien, his arms clinging around his mother's neck, returned her kisses eagerly, and Luke felt his own tears falling unchecked as he watched his young wife's joy in being reunited with her kidnapped son.

Mitzi Vourlay, standing beside her beautiful young mis-

31

tress, had taken black-haired Paul, who was a month away from his first birthday, so that Laure might hold Lucien. The little blond boy suddenly began to cry softly as he hugged her tightly. "I missed you, Mama, I missed you lots!" he tearfully confided.

"Oh my darling, you don't know how much I missed you too!" Laure's voice was husky with tears as she bent to him and kissed his eyes. Then, fixing Luke with an intense look, she murmured, "Come, my darling, I want to be alone with you and to learn everything that happened. I went down on my knees and thanked God when I had the telegraph that you'd dueled that horrible man Henri Cournier and were recovering from our wounds. I was in such agony of spirit, not knowing where poor little Lucien might be and yet not able to be with you at your bedside to nurse you back to health. Oh Luke, come with me now!"

Luke squeezed her wrist and nodded, then turned to the eager workers who stood at a respectful distance, not wishing to intrude on their employers' intimacy. "If you'll forgive me now, I'll be with you in an hour or so. I want to talk over the affairs of Windhaven Plantation. But first please let Laure and me be alone together."

"Of course, Mr. Bouchard, sir," Hannah Atbury eagerly responded. "If you wouldn't mind, I'd like to fix you both some sandwiches and a nice cold drink. Miz Laure, begging your pardon, Mr. Bouchard, she hasn't been eating the way she should, not since that poor little fellow was taken from her."

"That's very thoughtful of you, Hannah. I think we'd like that, but don't go to any special trouble, please. Come, my dearest." With a grateful nod at Hannah, Luke, his arm around Laure's waist, and with Mitzi following behind with little Paul in her arms, walked through the doorway of the red-brick chateau which had been his grandfather's dream nearly a century ago.

Understandingly, petite Mitzi offered to take both Paul and Lucien into the nursery, a room opposite Laure's bedroom, so that the two of them might be alone. Luke assented, and as Laure put Lucien down, Luke bent to him and said, "Now you're going to be a fine little man and let your daddy and mama have a talk for just a little while. I promise we'll both be in to see you and your brother. And if you're very good, I'll have Hannah bring you one of her wonderful oatmeal cookies—would you like that?"

"Oh yes, Daddy! Please, can I have two if I'm very good?" Lucien eagerly petitioned.

Laure looked at Luke and both burst out laughing, their fingers entwining, a laughter close to tears, coming as blessed relief after the harrowing ordeal they had endured.

Once inside her bedroom with the door closed behind them, Luke took his golden-haired wife into his arms and kissed her tenderly on each cheek and then gently on the lips. "Our prayers have been answered, my dearest Laure. And in the strangest way. You remember how old Ellen, with her gift for seeing into the future, told me that I should mark each of our children so that they could be recognized in case of trouble? And you remember the necklaces made with bits of that great turquoise which the Comanche chief Sangrodo gave me back at Windhaven Range?"

"Yes, my darling. Come sit beside me on the couch. You look worn and drawn—did that vile man wound you very badly, my darling?"

"Not really, Laure. And there will be no more Courniers to cast a shadow over our future. I pitied him and his brother, but most I pitied their unfortunate grandfather, Auguste Cournier, who was so treacherously betrayed by the girl my own grandfather once thought he loved. All of it, all of that hatred over the generations, came because of that heartless, inconstant woman. But so much for that. When I was dueling Henri Cournier, there was a girl in his office who apparently had been the companion of one of the men the Creole had engaged for this filthy work of his. When I was recovering in the hospital, she came to see me to tell me that he'd said something about having Lucien taken to a new father and mother in the West."

"Oh, God, that could have been anywhere, we might never have found him!" In her anxiety, Laure dug her fingernails into the back of his hand.

"All I could think of, Laure, was going on to the ranch and asking Lucien Edmond to help me look for him. But when I got there, it was a miracle—you see, the man and the woman whom Henri Cournier had commissioned to

33

take our little boy to the West had been attacked and killed by a raiding party of Penateka Comanches. The leader of the hunting party recognized the chip of turquoise in Lucien's necklace as part of the great talisman of the tribe. He sent one of his braves with our boy to Sangrodo's camp, in Mexico. Sangrodo, in turn, with his lovely wife Catayuna, brought Lucien back to Windhaven Range. Thus when I came there, sick at heart, I found our son awaiting me."

"Oh my dearest, God surely watches over us!" Laure could speak no more, but bowed her head against his chest and burst into racking sobs. Gently he comforted her and then frowned at the discreet knock at the door. "Forgive me a moment, my dearest," he whispered, and went to admit Hannah Atbury with a tray of sandwiches, a sliced melon, and two tall glasses of lemonade. "Thank you so much, dear Hannah. I'll be with you all shortly," he murmured as he took the tray and went back to his wife. "This will refresh you, dear. Hannah's famous for her lemonade. And you must eat now that I'm back."

"Oh I will, Luke! I want to thank God in my own way for bringing you and our little boy home safely to me!" Laure exclaimed.

"I met a wonderful Catholic friar, Bartoloméo Alicante. I had met him before in Santa Fe on that first drive, but he had been banished from there because his rich parishoners wrote to the Bishop of Madrid complaining that he neglected them in favor of the poor and the Indians. And he wrote back that the poor and the Indians are equally the children of God and that they needed him the more. He had come to our ranch and then gone with Ben Wilson to the Creek reservation in Indian Territory. He was there again when I came to find Lucien, and I made a vow in the chapel there that I would build a chapel here for all of us on Windhaven Plantation so that we may daily give thanks to our dear Lord."

"That's a beautiful vow, Luke, and I myself want to help build it, if I may."

"Yes, my dearest, just as I helped old Grandfather build this beautiful house of ours," he said tenderly. "Now drink your lemonade and try one of those thick pork sandwiches. Hannah's going to spoil us both, I can see that. That's a good girl. You've lost weight, Laure." Then, his face darkening with the terrible memory of what had taken place at the time of the abduction of Lucien, he tactfully added, "Has Dr. Medbury been to see you?"

"Oh yes. Just last week." Laure laughed softly after swallowing a bite of the thick sandwich, then blushed vividly. "I have good news, too, about myself. There will be no consequences from what that man did to me, my darling. None whatsoever. Yes, God indeed has blessed us. That's why I want to do what little I can to help build that chapel, because I owe Him my fervent thanks as you do for our happiness."

"Of course, dearest. Well now," he said in a bantering, cheerful tone, "I hear that Marius is a father again."

"Oh yes! Such an adorable little girl. Though I don't know why they named her Sheba, because you remember in the Bible Sheba was a black queen, and their baby is ever so light—that's because Clemmie's light herself and so is Marius. But she's adorable. Such a good baby too, she coos and laughs all day long and doesn't give a bit of trouble."

"And little Paul?"

"Well, dearest, I finished weaning him just about the time—you know—he's fine and strong, and Dr. Medbury's very pleased with him."

"Wonderful! Now I'll just have a sip of this lemonade and a quick kiss, and then I want to go talk to all our faithful friends here. And you must rest, dear Laure."

"But Luke," she said, half laughingly, "I'm not so fragile, and I only lost a little weight because I missed you and Lucien. And now that you're back—you see how much I've already eaten of this great big sandwich—why, it'll be no time at all you'll be scolding me for being too fat."

"Never that, never in a thousand years," he chuckled, then drew her close to him. And this time, as he kissed her on the mouth, her fingers entwined in his long hair as she pressed ardently to him, her eyes closed, surrendering herself completely, in the ecstasy of reunion.

After leaving Laure's bedroom, Luke went across the fields to Ellen's little cottage. The old conjure woman, though frail as ever, seemed considerably improved in health: As he approached, he saw that she was busy weeding her garden and preparing to plant some sweet potato cuttings. He watched appreciatively for a few moments and then softly called, "Ellen, I'm back, and I have a gift for you."

"Lawsa mercy—why, Mr. Bouchard, sir!" She dropped her hoe and turned, startled, then her wrinkled face was lighted with a radiant smile. "Sure good to see you again, Mr. Bouchard, sir—"

"Thank you, Ellen. You know, in a way, I owe getting my little boy back almost entirely to you."

"Moses Turner done told me when they got the telegraph at the house, Mr. Bouchard, sir! 'Bout yer boy Lucien being found an all—I'm mighty glad I said my prayers for him when he was took, Mr. Bouchard, 'deed I did!"

"I know, Ellen. I'm very grateful to you. You see, if you hadn't had that vision and told me to mark my sons, I might never have put the necklaces on them—and it was through those necklaces that some Indians found Lucien and brought him back to my oldest son's ranch, where I found him. Thanks to you, dear Ellen."

"I'm real glad, Mr. Bouchard, sir, if I could be of any help to a fine gentleman like you. You've treated old Ellen mighty fine. Nobody ever treated her any better in all this world, that's a fact."

"I got this for you in New Orleans, Ellen. It's a charm bracelet, with garnets and tourmalines, and there's a little cross." He took a jeweler's case out of the pocket of his buckskin jacket, opened it, and handed it to her."

"Lawsa mercy—that for me? Oh no, sir, that's too fine for a poor old nigger woman like me, Mr. Bouchard, sir!" she protested.

"No, it's not at all, it's just a small way of saying thank you so much and God bless you, dear Ellen. Please, I want you to wear it. Put it on for my sake. That cross, you see, is the sign of the dear God to whom all of us pray when we're in need of help. I know He'll bless you for what you've done to help my family and me, Ellen."

Her lips trembled, and she fought the tears as she hesitantly slipped the bracelet on. "Sakes alive, Mr. Bouchard, it fits real good—just like you must have taken my measurements—if that don't beat all"—then, the smile fading, she clasped his hand in both of hers and tears shone in her eyes as she murmured brokenly, "You're a good man, Mr.

36

Bouchard, and God knows what good men are and He blesses them. I'm only happy I could be of some help—this whole thing tore my heart to pieces. You're bound to have mighty fine years from now on, both you and your missus and little boys, I just know it, Mr. Bouchard."

"I pray God you're right, dear Ellen. Now, I ordered some other things in New Orleans for the folks here, and there's a brand new calico dress coming up on the steamboat in a few days, and it's got your name on it. And Hannah tells me you like coffee a lot."

" 'Deed I do, only it costs so much and they ain't much good coffee 'round these parts nowadays, I do without."

"Well, I got some wonderful Creole coffee in New Orleans too, and that's got your name on it as well. I'll see you again, Ellen, and when these things come for you, I'll bring them to you. Thank you again, from the very bottom of my heart, and my wife is grateful to you just as I am." He took her hand and brought it to his lips and kissed the bracelet, and Ellen burst into sobs, overwhelmed by her emotion.

Finally, pulling up her apron and blowing her nose on it with a great show of annoyance at herself, she stoutly declared, "Land sakes alive, Mr. Bouchard sir, it ain't right for a fine white gentleman like you to treat this here poor old nigger woman like I was special. You got me so fussed I can't rightly remember where I left off weeding."

He chuckled and patted her shoulder. "You are something special, Ellen. And here"—he moved over to the row of plants which she had weeded and pointed—"is where you left off. Now don't you work too late this afternoon, and I'll have Hannah bring you out some nice gumbo and corn pone for supper. Getting chilly these November evenings, you know. I want you to take real good care of yourself." He stooped, retrieved her hoe, and handed it to her. Ellen had thrust the jeweler's case into the pocket of her worn cotton dress, and she sniffled again as she accepted the hoe, bowed her head, and then, to hide her feelings, went back to weeding more energetically than ever. He watched her for a moment, and then went back to the chateau.

Although Hannah Atbury had often told Luke that she and her ailing husband should be quartered in a cottage out in the fields rather than in the chateau itself, old

Lucien's grandson had insisted that the two of them live in the chateau. In his opinion, they had both earned that right because of their courageous stewardship of Windhaven Plantation when John Brunton had appointed them as factors to acquire the property so that one day it might be returned to the original owners, the Bouchards. Remembering how both Hannah and old Phineas had suffered at the hands of the Ku Klux Klan led by Hurley Parmenter, Luke had resolved that the Atburys should continue to live comfortably in the chateau. After having left Ellen, he went directly to the spacious, cheerfully furnished room that Hannah and Phineas shared, to call on Phineas and inquire after the old man's health.

Before Luke had left the *Alabama Belle,* he had asked the old captain, once he reached Montgomery, to have one of the stevedores take a note to Dr. Jonas Medbury, asking him to call at Windhaven Plantation at his earliest opportunity. Now, seeing Phineas lying propped up on two thick pillows, his face drawn, breathing heavily, Luke frowned with deepest concern. "I'm back, Phineas, and I've got the little boy with me," he said gently.

Phineas Atbury slowly opened his eyes and slowly turned his head to stare at the tall, bearded man who stood at his bedside. Then, recognizing his employer, he forced a weary smile and murmured, "Good to see you, Mr. Bouchard. You got your little boy back safe and sound, for certain?"

Luke nodded. "Yes, Phineas. He's with my wife now. Everything's fine. Now there's only one thing troubling me, and that's your lying abed before it's really bedtime. I'm going to have the doctor in to see you in the next day or two, and he's going to prescribe a tonic or something that'll make you feel strong again."

Phineas Atbury slowly shook his head, heaving a long sigh. "Mr. Bouchard, I'm an old man, I seen lots of trouble, and I'm weary, real weary. There ain't no tonic that I knows of that'll make me young again—sure wish there was, though. Anyhow, I been restin' lots, and my good sweet Hannah, she been lookin' after me real good. I'm as good as I can be, my time of life, Mr. Bouchard. That's the truth."

"Just the same, you're going to take Dr. Medbury's advice and get well real soon, as a favor to me, Phineas.

38

I shan't ever forget how badly you were hurt, because you tried to protect my wife and son. As long as you live, Phineas, you'll be just like family to me here, and so will your wife, Hannah. So you just rest. Is there anything I can do for you now?"

"No thank you, suh. I'm just real weary, like I said. Maybe if it was spring or summer and nice 'n warm, I'd have more of a spark of life, but it's gittin' cold and rainy, and I never did like that kind of weather no how."

"It'll be spring before you know it, Phineas, and you'll be sound as a gold dollar, you watch and see. Now I'll go and make sure Hannah has something good for you to eat when you wake up."

"Thank you, Mr. Bouchard. That makes me feel real good 'n strong, just hearin' you talk like that to an old darkie like me."

"I've never thought of you that way, Phineas. I think only of good men and bad men, and you're one of the good ones, believe me. Now you get some sleep." He reached out to squeeze Phineas Atbury's hand, then drew the coverlet up a little higher on the old man's chest and left the room. Hannah was standing outside in the hallway, her face grave. "He's going to get some sleep now, Hannah. I told him you'd cook him something real nice when he woke up."

"God bless you, Mr. Bouchard. I never saw a man that took the trouble with folks that you do. It was a lucky day for us both when you got that letter of mine and came out here to see what was troubling us so much. I'm beholden to you, and so is Phineas."

"No, Hannah, you owe me nothing, and neither does Phineas. On the contrary, I'm the one who's in your debt, because it was you who lived here and kept this property from going to the carpetbaggers and the profiteers. I'm only sorry you had to pay the price you did to keep it for my family. I know my grandfather would be just as grateful as I am. By the way, I left a message which Dr. Medbury will get by tomorrow, and I asked that he come out here as soon as he could. I want him to examine Phineas thoroughly. He's lost weight, and I'm not happy about that at all."

"I'm not either, Mr. Bouchard. I cook him lots of nice fancy things he always used to like, but he doesn't seem to have much appetite. When the little boy was taken away that awful day, he sort of started pining away, as if he felt it was his fault."

"You just have to talk to him and get that idea out of his mind once and for all, Hannah," Luke Bouchard firmly averred. "I have the feeling that even if I'd had armed guards posted all around the chateau, the cunning scoundrel behind that kidnapping would have found a way to carry out his vengeful act all the same. Thank you, Hannah, and the only order I have to give you until Phineas gets well is to spend all your time looking after him. He's a wonderful man, and I want him to get better."

"I'm sure trying, Mr. Bouchard, God knows that." Hannah sniffled and turned her face to one side. Understandingly, he nodded and went to his study where Marius Thornton awaited him.

The young foreman sprang to his feet as Luke entered, his right hand gripping a tightly folded piece of foolscap. "Sit down, Marius, no need to be so ceremonious," Luke chuckled as he seated himself at the escritoire and leaned back in the chair. "Judging from the way you're holding that sheet of paper, I'd say you've been working up a very elaborate report for me."

"I have, Mr. Bouchard. And I think you'll like what it shows. You remember, you told me to break it down into percentages and dollar shares for each of the workers."

"That's the only sensible, fair way, Marius. You'll remember that when I came back here, I suggested that we all pool our efforts and work together. But every worker is entitled to a fair share of profits, like wages. And in addition, if the profit statement is good enough, I intend to give incentive wages. I can do this because I can count on the loyalty of all of you at Windhaven Plantation. That's a plus we have and something that's lacking in the rest of this state, I'm afraid." His face grew serious as he suddenly leaned forward. "Marius, what I've tried to put into effect here is an extension of my grandfather's ideas. They weren't popular then because we were in the toils of oppressive slavery, and he had to keep his distaste for the institution secret from the neighboring plantation owners. Now, with freedom, the profit system is the only practical way to operate any sort of large land holding such as we have here. Unfortunately, because of the North's policy of vindictive Reconstruction, we still have to keep our methods to ourselves. They'd hardly be popular in many of the adjoining counties."

"That's true, Mr. Bouchard. But now you take Buford Phelps. You remember how he came here from the Freedman's Bureau, dead set in his mind that you were just another old-time plantation owner who was going to take advantage of the blacks now that they were free and didn't have any leadership to tell them how to work or whom to work for. He's turned out to be one of our best producers, Mr. Bouchard."

"That's heartening news indeed, Marius. Now, as you very well know, we're in a very fortunate position because with Emancipation, the blacks were given fifty acres of land and a mule. Accordingly, much of the land of Windhaven Plantation which my grandfather owned was passed over to them, all except the original fifty which included this house and which my late friend John Brunton was able to arrange for Hannah and Phineas Atbury to purchase as factors. As a consequence, we needn't dread the annual taxes, as so many unfortunate and patriotic Confederates have had to do ever since the end of the war. And all of our workers agreed that they would ultimately sell the land back to me, when the time is right for it, and I'll see to it that they have a handsome profit. Meanwhile, they'll get their share of the profits and incentive wages out of my own pocket. Happily, I still have a good deal left of my grandfather's legacy in gold from the Bank of Liverpool, even after the purchase of land in Texas for the rest of my family. So we can look to the future with greater optimism than most of our neighbors, God be praised."

"I'll admit, Mr. Bouchard, that your system has made it a lot easier for me as your foreman," Marius Thornton boyishly grinned. Folding the sheet of foolscap, he cleared his throat and then explained, "We didn't plant too much cotton this year, just as you told me. Cotton didn't bring a very good price, anyway, only about thirteen cents a pound."

"That's because the English mills have found other sources and because, during those four years of war, they found they couldn't rely on Southern cotton any longer. How much did we plant, Marius?"

41

"We shipped five thousand bales, at five hundred pounds to a bale, down to Mobile just about ten days after you took off to find your boy, Mr. Bouchard. That earned us $3250, and after paying the factor down at Mobile and the shipping, we had about $2900 left."

"That's not too bad," Luke mused, touching his pointed beard and then the back of his head. "Good Lord, in all this time I'm afraid I haven't kept up proper grooming. I certainly have to have my hair cut and trim this beard before much longer. Well now, are the cotton gins still in good working order?"

"Oh yes, Mr. Bouchard. No trouble there at all. We might have to lay out a little money next spring for some minor repairs, but it won't be much more than two or three hundred dollars at the worst."

"Take it out of that profit and put it in the reserve fund, as I've shown you before, Marius. Then you'll take out a commission of ten percent, since I provide the dock and arrange for the transportation and the sale in Mobile. The rest is to be divided equally among those of our workers who produced and picked and ginned the cotton."

"I've already done that, Mr. Bouchard," Marius Thornton grinned again. "Next, we made about six hundred dollars in marketing our cattle, mostly calves and a few cows, about half to Mobile and the rest to Montgomery. And Mary Turner's selling milk and cream up in Montgomery added about two hundred dollars to our take, sir."

"I'll take the usual ten percent commission there again, acting as a factor for the men," Luke Bouchard directed. "Just make an equitable division of the rest of it as you know how to do. But just take five percent out of Mary's earnings, and see she gets credit for almost all the rest."

"Yes, sir. Produce and vegetables brought us a really good profit this year, Mr. Bouchard. Even old Ellen's little garden got us a hundred dollars."

"I want all of that money to be credited to her, and I'd like it if you'd go tell her tomorrow. See if she wants to have the hard cash; or, if she wants to have just a little now to buy supplies, show her how we can open an account for her in her own name so that she can have the rest whenever she's a mind to."

"I'll do that, Mr. Bouchard. Now as to the rest of it, Hughie Mendicott and Moses Turner grew most of the produce and fruits, and between the two of them they earned $1150—you know, sir, a good part of that was bought by that one-armed fellow who took over Hurley Parmenter's store in Lowndesboro."

Luke chuckled at this. "I shouldn't be surprised that Mitzi Vourlay indirectly had something to do with Mr. Sattersfield's interest in our wares, Marius."

"I think you're right, Mr. Bouchard," the foreman grinned again. "You know, though I shouldn't be telling tales out of school, while you were away, she's been going at least once a week to buy supplies for the house."

"You're not telling tales out of school because I already predicted that Mr. Sattersfield and she are going to get married one of these days, Marius. And she couldn't find a more decent, honorable man if she went hunting with a shotgun for him."

"I agree with that, Mr. Bouchard. He's a very courteous man, his prices are fair, and he's decent to everybody, black and white."

"That's usually the sign of a real gentleman, Marius. I think that's what I'd like as my own epitaph—but let's hope that's a long time off. Well, you know how to allocate those produce profits. I assume that the taxes for our black workers were much lower than the bill for my own fifty acres and the house?"

"Oh yes, Mr. Bouchard. Yours was about four times what theirs is. I sent a check soon after you left for New Orleans."

"Good. I'm glad I had my lawyer, Jedidiah Danforth, draw up a power of attorney, so you could take care of such things in my absence. Well, I'd say that considering my own commission, there's household money enough for a few months, and I'm quite satisfied with your steward-ship, Marius. In the next several years, I don't anticipate that we'll make huge profits. But we can keep our heads above water, and most important of all, the people who work on Windhaven Plantation won't have to worry about jobs or food or incentive. I'm not interested in being rich, I'm interested in a good, useful, purposeful life. And so far I've been very greatly blessed. Well, you give my best to Clemmie and little Sheba."

"I'll be glad to do that, Mr. Bouchard." Marius sprang to his feet, folding the sheet of foolscap and tucking it away in his lapel pocket. "Maybe in a few weeks you and I could sit down and plan what we're going to do on the land next spring, Mr. Bouchard."

"Yes, I'd like that, Marius. I'd like to do more with cattle if we can. We've got very good grass here—better in some ways than on Windhaven Range. We might even expand with planting rice. Heaven knows there's enough rain to sustain it, and we always have irrigation from the good old Alabama River. That crop should do very well in Mobile and New Orleans especially."

"Yes, you're right, Mr. Bouchard. Well, I wish you a good evening then."

"Thanks, Marius. You've relieved me of many of my burdens, and as a matter of fact, I want you to take twenty-five dollars out of my commissions and buy little Sheba and Clemmie something they'll like, and that's an order."

"That's very kind of you, Mr. Bouchard."

"Not at all. There's one more thing, Marius." Luke's voice was solemn now. "When I found my son in Texas, I promised Friar Bartoloméo that I'd build a chapel here on Windhaven Plantation to thank God for returning little Lucien to me. My wife, Laure, wants to have a part in that building herself, as do I. It would be good if we could find a place near the bluff on the downriver side, Marius."

"Yes, indeed, Mr. Bouchard. I'll tell the men about it first thing tomorrow."

"A very simple chapel, with an altar. I'm told that Moses Turner's good wife is a fine seamstress. Perhaps she'd like to make the altar cloth. I'm sure she'll find inspiration in the Bible for an appropriate decoration. And now, if you'll excuse me, I'm going to take a scissors and a razor to myself, have a bite of supper, and then go see the children."

CHAPTER FOUR

Luke had trimmed his beard and cut away the shaggy locks which had grown during his long journey. He had eaten a frugal supper and then bathed, and at about ten o'clock had gone to Laure's room to chat with her and tell her what he had arranged for the workers in the building of the chapel.

Little Paul and Lucien had been entrusted to Mitzi's safekeeping, and Luke sat beside his wife's bed, her hand in his, as he explained the details of his conference with Marius Thornton.

"It was very good of you to remember Ellen, darling. You've a very good heart. It took me a while to discover that," she said with a smile. "Remember now, I want to help build that chapel, even if it's only driving a single nail into a piece of wood."

"I promise you and I will both work together in building it, my dearest."

"I'm so happy now, Luke. It's all over, all this hatefulness that's been lurking in our lives ever since I came here, isn't it? You know, for a time I thought that perhaps I'd brought you bad luck."

"How can you say that? You've given me a new life, you've given me two wonderful sons. I am privileged beyond most men."

"I'm glad you feel that way about me. Do you know, I've never once thought about the difference in our ages." Again she sent him that provocative smile which had so kindled his desire when he had first met her in New Orleans. "Maybe it's because you look a little more civilized now with your beard and your hair trimmed. And much younger and very distinguished in that nice white linen suit—though I do confess you look very manly in Indian buckskin. I'll never forget how Mitzi came shrieking to me that there was a *sauvage rouge* outside Union House when you first came to call on me after I'd sent you that letter about John and the birth of our son."

"I remember that too," he laughed, then lifted her hand to his lips and kissed it. "But you know, darling, the Indians aren't really savages. The Creeks my grandfather knew certainly weren't, and neither are Sangrodo and the braves of his tribe. Out there in Texas, what I'm very much afraid of is that the white settlers will keep thinking that the Indians are bloodthirsty animals who ought to be exterminated. And in the northwest territories, I've heard of public sentiments against the Indians. I only wish people who talk like that could have met men like Sangrodo and Tunkamara and Nanakota and that marvelous chief of the Kiowas, Setangya. Yes, and Emataba on the Creek reservation too, for that matter."

"I agree, dearest Luke."

"Did Hannah bring you some supper?"

"My goodness, after that melon and that sandwich and the lemonade, do you suppose I could eat very much? Besides, my heart's too full of happiness today."

"I'm very glad. I wish it could have been sooner so as to spare you all that terrible time."

"Yes, it was frightening, because when you left, even though I knew you were going after the man who brought about all this, I couldn't be sure that you'd find Lucien. And I was so worried about him. But you know, darling, Mitzi helped me to forget my worries so much—do you know, she is very seriously in love for the first time. It's not just a flirtation, such as she wanted to have with you the first time you came to the Union House."

"I know. It's Dalbert Sattersfield. Even Marius Thornton knows about that," Luke chuckled.

"Mitzi has stars in her eyes whenever she talks about him. He's so gallant, so gracious, and so much a gentleman. She's very impressed, but she's also in love. Besides, it's high time," Laure laughed softly.

"I hope we shan't lose our wonderful nurse."

"No, I don't think it's going to happen in the next week or two, but I'm afraid that once she sets her cap for him, she's going to move in with him, and then we'll really have to find a replacement."

"Well, in the meantime, we'll think about giving her

a wonderful wedding present and arranging everything to make her wedding day something she and her husband-to-be won't ever forget," Luke proposed.

"You're very sweet, my darling. And most considerate of other people's feelings."

"You've made my life complete, Laure. You're sure you've no regrets?"

"None." She shook her head till her golden curls danced on the pillow. Then, her face serious, she softly asked, "Do you ever think of her—I mean, Lucy? Do you ever try to compare us in your mind?"

"Never. There'll always be a place in my heart for Lucy, but this is a new life, in which sometimes I hardly recognize myself. Being with you seems as natural as breathing itself. Then, too, the fact that you're so young and beautiful makes me determined not to grow old too quickly—and I think a man needs that, especially a widower as I was. No, Laure, you'll never have any reason for jealousy or thinking that I withhold anything of myself from you. Why, don't you see, coming to New Orleans as I did, finding that you wouldn't marry me at once, trying to court you by learning an entirely new business in running that bank of yours—it was exactly as if I were reborn and starting afresh."

"I'm so glad you feel that way. I hope you always will, my dearest."

He rose and leaned over to kiss her gently on the cheek and the lips. "I want you to rest tonight, my dearest. It's been a strenuous time for you, and the excitement of having Lucien back—I'll see you at breakfast. Goodnight, my love."

He kissed her on the lips again and then left the bedroom to go to his.

In the foyer of the chateau, the old grandfather clock had just chimed the last stroke of midnight. Outside, there was a full moon, hazy with the foretelling of imminent rain, and the sound of the waters of the river flowing more swiftly than usual hinted at a coming storm. But inside the house all was still, and no candles or kerosene lamps illumined the dark silence.

Luke Bouchard slept, but fitfully. Fragmentary images surged through his mind like the kaleidoscopic patterns of intermingled dreams, with swift and illogical transition. He saw himself at the foot of the stairway in the Union House as John Brunton came down to welcome him to New Orleans. He saw Laure Prindeville for the first time, coquettishly appearing indifferent to him. Then he was riding out with Lucien Edmond to discover Sangrodo's little son Kitante sick from the bite of a rattlesnake. Then his first meeting with the tall, heroic Comanche chief. Once again he relived the duel with Armand Cournier, and then that scene merged into the savage rapier duel with Armand's older brother, Henri. It was so real that he could almost feel the prick of the rapier's point against his flesh for, out of weariness, he had flung himself down naked on his bed and fallen asleep at once.

The duel seemed to continue—once again he felt Henri Cournier's rapier touch his skin, and he uttered a stifled cry and woke—

Woke to find a woman wearing a black domino and black velvet cloak standing above him and felt her sharp fingernails score his shoulders as she bent to him and fused her mouth with his.

"Who—what—the domino—" In his still sleep-drugged mind, the symbol returned to him, the black domino Laure herself had worn when she had paid a surprise nocturnal visit to his bachelor quarters in New Orleans.

"Laure—Laure," he gasped, incredulous.

"Yes, my dear one. What else could a neglected wife do but come to her husband's bedroom if he leaves her pining for him?" she teased in a husky whisper as she seated herself on the edge of his bed. He reached up to embrace her, but with a soft little laugh she slipped out of his embrace. "Not yet, my darling. Do you know, I thought you were going back to your old sobersides habits when you kissed me ever so finally and walked out before I could tell you that I wanted you to stay?"

"But my darling, you need rest, after all you've gone through—"

"Shh!" She put a finger to his lips and shook her head. "You're so very gallant, aren't you? You thought that because I was raped by Arnie Grimes, I wouldn't want to think about having my own husband make love to me, didn't you? But you forget, dearest, that before I met John Brunton, I had to choose a Union corporal or his entire platoon to submit to. But I managed to overcome those terrible memories."

"All the same—" He tried to speak, but again her finger touched his lips.

"All the same, you know what Dr. Medbury said—that there wouldn't be any consequences from what happened. Don't you think I'd want my own dearest husband to prove that he still loves me after all this time he's been away? And more than that, Luke"—now she bent to him and whispered into his ear—"I want another child—a child who'll keep up all the wonderful traditions of Windhaven that you have taught me."

"Oh Laure, Laure, I want that too—"

She straightened, and with a single gesture swept the black velvet cloak to the floor and was naked in sandals and the domino. "Let's pretend once more, *mon amour*," she whispered as she stood, her hands stroking her flanks and thighs, proud in her splendid nakedness, "that I'm that forward hussy who teased you so unmercifully at the Union House. After all, that's what really created Lucien. This time, maybe we'll have a girl—wouldn't you like a girl, Luke?"

"As beautiful, as good, as loving as you, yes, my dearest one!" He flung away the sheet that covered him and reached out for her. With a gasp, Laure came swiftly to him and sinuously clambered beside him, turning to him, her nails gouging his shoulders as her mouth merged to his.

Then, in the rapt darkness, the silence of the night knew the music of their sighs of total and fulfilling passion, a passion that was at once joyous thanksgiving for reunion and the fervent desire wrought out of understanding and deepest need and hunger.

CHAPTER FIVE

It was the late afternoon of December 18, 1869. That morning, there had been a cold wind and driving rain, but now the sky was a serene blue with hardly a cloud visible in its limitless sweep. The wind had died away, and there was a stillness to the air, even a grudging warmth. Not far from the gradual ascent to the tall bluff atop which old Lucien Bouchard, his beloved Dimarte, and their tiny son Edmond lay in eternal rest, Luke Bouchard, Laure, and Mitzi Vourlay stood beside the loyal workers of Windhaven Plantation as Dan Munroe clambered down from the ladder and declared, "There now, Mr. Bouchard, everything's in place. I made extra sure the cross on top of the chapel would stand firm in its base, even if we have a real storm."

"I'm grateful to you, Dan, and to all of you who took part in building this house of God where all of us may come when we wish to praise Him, each in his own way," Luke Bouchard replied. He held Lucien in his arms, while Laure cradled Paul in hers. "I wish we might have had that wonderful Franciscan friar I met in Texas and about whom I told you so much," he went on. "Yet I think by rights it is Hannah who should be first to pray and to help dedicate this chapel."

Hannah Atbury was dressed in black, and her eyes were swollen with weeping. Two nights ago, old Phineas had died quietly in his sleep. The complications resulting from the concussion dealt him by the men who had come to kidnap little Lucien Bouchard, following his cruel flogging by the hooded terrorists of Hurley Parmenter's klavern, had weakened his frail constitution beyond endurance or convalescence.

The chapel was made of a durable red clay, the same kind of clay which had been shaped into bricks nearly forty years ago when old Lucien had undertaken to recreate here the beautiful chateau in which he had been born in Normandy. The red clay, hardened in the kiln, was supplemented by sturdy pine wood and oak beams. The chapel had been painted white, and Laure herself had taken great delight in wielding a paint brush. There was a small door, and inside there were five pew benches, with a narrow aisle between them, leading to the altar. Moses Turner's wife, Mary, whose health had greatly improved over the past several months, had sewn the altar cloth. During his brief stay in New Orleans, Luke had purchased a large piece of pure white silk as well as many spools of colored thread. Using these threads, Mary had depicted on the altar cloth Abraham's sacrifice of his child, the return of the prodigal son, and the infant Jesus in the Madonna's arms. Finally, at Luke's suggestion, she had sewn the figure of the tall Comanche chief Sangrodo holding little Lucien in his arms as Luke himself knelt down with hands clasped in fervent prayer of gratitude.

"You shall be first to open the door, Hannah," Luke gently prompted.

"God bless you, Mr. Bouchard!" she murmured in a choked voice as she came forward, turned the knob of the door and opened it.

"How wonderful it is, Luke," Laure murmured. "And best of all, Hannah will dedicate it on the very day of your grandfather's birth. If he were alive, how old would he have been today?"

"A hundred and seven years, my darling. Yet I know that he is with us now in spirit, as is Dimarte whom he loved so much. I think he would approve and agree that there was no blasphemy in it, of Mary's showing Sangrodo restoring my lost son to me."

"I'm sure he would have, Luke. He knew while he was alive how you shared his belief in the basic goodness in all men, everywhere."

"Yes, Laure. That's the meaning of this chapel, really."

Hannah hesitantly entered, walking down the narrow aisle until she reached the altar, and then she knelt down before it and clasped her hands. She bowed her head for a long moment before she spoke, and then she said, "Dear Lord, Jesus and Mother Mary, bless our chapel which all of us helped build in Your honor. Bless the soul of my

51

husband Phineas, who was a good man, and also Mr. Bouchard and his wife and their two little boys. We will come here many times to thank You for being so good to us and showing us the way. Amen."

She rose, turned to face them at the door, and then burst into tears, covering her face with her hands. It was Hughie Mendicott who hurried forward and soothed her, leading her out of the chapel while the others made way for her.

"Let the others go first, my darling," Luke murmured to Laure, who nodded in agreement. Then he said to his workers, "My good friends, you are as much a part of my family as my children. All of you have built this chapel, and it is only fitting that all of you should be first to enter it and to say what is in your hearts. My wife and I will enter alone afterward, for we have our own dedication and devotional to make."

Then he stood back while Marius Thornton and his Clementine entered, Marius carrying the little boy and Clementine carrying the baby Sheba, along with Moses and Mary Turner, Dan Munroe and his wife, Katie, and their two children Tom and Elsie, and then Hughie Mendicott with his sons, Davie and Louis. Buford Phelps, first with a word of respect to Luke and Laure, was next.

Luke Bouchard watched them kneel to pray. It was a chapel whose purpose was to bring together men and women of good will to unburden their souls to Him who guides the universe. It was not a chapel for any one faith or creed, for just as old Lucien Bouchard, though born into the Catholic faith, had never been narrowly confined by it, in his liberal outlook, so Luke believed as earnestly in the equality of all faiths before God.

When all of the workers and their children had filed out of the chapel, bidding a good evening to Luke and Laure, he and his wife and Mitzi and the little boys entered.

Side by side, Luke and his lovely wife knelt before the altar, his right hand holding her left, as they took this moment to reaffirm their pledge to each other. The solemnity of this simple ceremony so impressed Lucien and his younger brother Paul that Mitzi had no need to shush them during the time Luke and Laure knelt and prayed.

When at last Luke rose, he turned to Mitzi and said

softly, "Laure and I are going up to visit grandfather, *ma petite*. Would you be kind enough to take the children back to the house?"

"*Bien sûr,* m'sieu," Mitzi eagerly responded. Then, carrying little Paul and whispering to Lucien to follow her, she left the chapel.

"Here is where the path begins, dearest." Luke turned to Laure, clasping her hand. "Just a year ago today I came here alone—that was just a month before you and the little boys joined me to begin our life here on Windhaven Plantation."

Laure lifted her other hand to touch his forehead, her eyes softly luminous with the joy she felt at being part of her husband's destiny. "And here, my dear one," she murmured, "is where you moved aside the grass and the flowers which hid the path after all those years you'd been away from the man after whom John and I named my first-born."

He stared quizzically at her for a moment, and she shook her head almost reprovingly. "No, my love, my dear one. John never knew of that hour when I teased you so unmercifully—and when I married him, I swore I should never do anything to shake his faith in me. You know how he stood by me in those terrible days of the war after my father's suicide and my own shame. If God had willed it, I would have been a good wife to him until the end of my days."

"You could have been nothing else, Laure. As you are now to me, as we shall share our lives for what time He allows us," Luke replied as he drew her to him and kissed her.

"You say that you've begun your new life here, Luke—well, so have I. And you know that Lucien was surely yours—though sometimes I grieve that poor John couldn't have had children of his own to carry on his name—"

"But his name will always remain on the bank and will always stand for honest dealing and compassionate aid to those worthy in their endeavors," Luke consoled her.

"Yes," she sighed deeply and bowed her head for a moment. "What a shame he had no family at all. He'd told me about a younger brother who'd gone off to Ohio and been killed in one of the first battles of the war. His mother and father had died at least ten years before I met him—and that's the only kinfolk he ever told me about." She raised her eyes to the darkening sky and murmured wistfully, "I pray God that John's spirit somehow knows and understands and forgives."

"From what I knew of him in his life, I'm certain he understands now and has rancor for neither of us. And you know, Laure, I've often prayed—as I did just now back in the chapel—for his spirit to be blessed, because he was perhaps the most loyal friend my family and I ever had. If I were to die childless, I could ask for no better epitaph than that. Now come, it's chilly, and I don't want you catching cold. Take my hand and let us go up the path."

Hand in hand, they went up the pathway on the eastern slope of the tall red bluff, pausing now and again to look down at the stretch of fields below. They saw the cottages of the workers, and they saw the white chapel. They looked at each other, their eyes silently pledging love and faith and remembrance.

Three-quarters of the way from the top of the bluff, the path suddenly narrowed, took a winding turn, and grew steeper. Rains during the previous spring had washed out this section of the path. Luke paused, dug out a secure foothold with the toe of his boot, and, planting himself firmly, grasped Laure by both hands. He drew her to him, holding her securely so that she could not slip, until at last the path became easier. They reached the summit and the clearing in front of two huge hickory trees. A year ago, after his return from Texas and New Orleans, Luke had found the clearing covered with waist-high plantain grass. He had torn it away by handfuls till at last he had revealed the rich red earth to which the Creeks had given the distinctive name of "Econchate"—red ground. Now, as he stared at the moist earth on which only a sparse growth of thick-bladed grass had grown since his last visit, he thought of what old Lucien had once said to him: "I left a rich soil in Normandy, but when I came to Econchate, I found a virgin land of a richness that surpassed it. But most of all, I found friends and I found love, and these made the tilling of the soil the more heartening and rewarding."

Laure stood beside him now, looking down at the earth

54

which showed no sign of those two graves. Luke turned to Laure and kissed her tenderly, and then knelt down and placed his left palm over where he knew old Lucien's grave would be. In a whisper, he said to Laure, "And hers is just beyond, to the south, my dearest. She guards their little one who was taken so tragically, and she joined him in death by the same way. How often my grandfather spoke of her, the beloved woman, so that in his heart she never died, nor their child either."

Laure had knelt down beside him now. "Perhaps he knew, somehow, all through those years, that you would truly be the son he dreamed of but never had."

"Without disloyalty to my father, Laure, I should say that even as a boy I felt a strong kinship with my idealistic grandfather. My father was impatient with me, thinking me a dreamer, a fool who was content to work on the land without profiteering or taking advantage of it by selling it. Perhaps by that alienation which my father imposed upon me—because I did not meet his own standards—he made me turn to Grandfather. And do you know, Laure, that never once was I conscious of Grandfather's age or the difference in generations between us. His ideas were so young. He believed so fervently in loyalty and decency and the unity of the family. Yet he was not just a dreamer. He was practical, and he worked hard all his life, with his hands as well as with his mind. He dealt fairly with all his neighbors, and he did not distinguish men by the color of their skin or their religious beliefs. He knew well enough that none of us is perfect, but he himself sought in his own endeavors the utmost good for his family, friends, and neighbors."

"He truly would have been proud of you if he had lived to watch you in the years which followed his death, my dear one," Laure whispered. "I am proud and honored to be a Bouchard, to have given you two sons and—yes, my darling—I hope very soon to tell you that I shall be with child again. It will be another proof of the love I have for you."

He reached for her hand and squeezed it, his face filled with emotion, and for a long moment was silent. Then he spoke. "Once again, Grandfather, I come, this time with my beloved wife Laure, to bring you tribute on your birthday; and to your beloved woman Dimarte, we humbly come to show that we are mindful of the lesson of love that she gave you, my grandfather."

In the tall trees beyond this clearing, there was the faint chittering of the night birds, slowly wakening as the shadows began to engulf all of the bluff. Now a kind of mist, as if from the river, had risen into the air, and it grew darker still.

"Grandfather," he resumed after a pause, "today we have dedicated a chapel where all of our family and our workers may come to pray as each is moved to do. In that chapel, we shall always venerate your soul and those of your beloved woman and your tiny son who was not destined to know the heritage of the Bouchard name—a name to which you brought such honor that, everywhere in our growing nation where a Bouchard dwells, he or she is respected and admired. All this was your doing. You knew how to make friends with those who dwelt first upon this land. And their descendants, even though they have been cruelly set down in a desolate place, far from this rich red earth where once they roamed free and proud, remember your name also. My son Lucien Edmond and I learned that when we visited the *mico* Emataba. Yes, even the powerful and feared Comanches, who could not have known the Creeks, learned that the name of Bouchard stands for truth and honesty and courage. It was Sangrodo, their mighty chief, who gave me that talisman which I entrusted to you to keep, as his own tribute to you. And thanks to it, from those tiny pieces I took back from it, your great-grandson and namesake, Lucien, has been safely returned to me. Thus today, your birthday, Grandfather, is more meaningful perhaps than it has ever been before to Laure and me. God keep your soul through all eternity until we meet again."

"Amen," Laure softly echoed, as the tears coursed slowly down her cheeks.

He rose now and moved to the other grave. Kneeling down, he touched the earth, then he reached for Laure's hand as she knelt down beside him. "Beautiful Dimarte, may your spirit forever watch over us and all of the Bouchards. And because you were of Creek blood, I ask of you this special blessing—let your spirit touch the heart of Emataba, *mico* of your own people. Let him guide Ben Wilson, my sister Fleurette's husband. Let him be consoled

56

by helping the descendants of your tribe, so that in turn he may find a rich purpose to his life and—if God wills it—a companion who will lighten his grief and ready him for a new life of dedication and joy."

"Amen," Laure again echoed.

Then she too touched the ground with her left palm and silently murmured her own prayer.

They rose at last. Darkness was all around them, and now the birds were still. They went back down along the path, and as they did so, the rays of the moon suddenly emerged from behind a thick cloud to illuminate their way.

After they had passed that winding, steep turn and came upon the easier and broader descent down that gentle slope, they halted a moment and looked at each other in wonder as, far above them, there sounded thrice the soft call of an owl.

CHAPTER SIX

Three days before Christmas, the *Alabama Belle* docked at the wharf of Windhaven Plantation, and the stevedores unloaded several boxes of supplies and gifts which Luke Bouchard had ordered from New Orleans. That same afternoon, Mitzi Vourlay asked Dan Munroe if he would drive her to the Lowndesboro general store so that she might purchase some necessary staples for a gala Christmas dinner. Luke Bouchard had invited all of his workers to dine with Laure and him and his two little sons. Since he suspected that Mitzi was enamored of Dalbert Sattersfield, the new owner of the store, he had casually remarked to her that it might be an excellent idea to make sure that the kitchen larder was furnished with all the necessary supplies for a sumptuous feast. Mitzi could not hide her blushes, but, in as nonchalant a tone as she could muster, blithely replied that it would be her pleasure to run the errand.

So, on this chilly Thursday afternoon, she descended from the wagon and entered the store. The tall storeowner came out of the back room, and, recognizing Mitzi, he gave her a courtly bow and a smile as he greeted her. *"C'est un grand plaisir pour moi de vous accueillir,* Mademoiselle Vourlay."

"Merci bien, Monsieur Sattersfield. *Moi aussi, je suis très heureuse de vous voir encore."*

By this time, her blushes were uncontrollable, and she fumbled in her reticule for the brief list she had made up. If truth be told, there were very few items needed for Hannah's well-stocked pantry. Nevertheless, Luke Bouchard had known very well that Mitzi would welcome this opportunity to visit the storeowner and would doubtless invite him to partake of Bouchard hospitality. As he had told Laure, "I'm afraid I would have embarrassed her dreadfully if I had come out and asked her to invite Mr. Sattersfield to our Christmas dinner. This way, she'll be able to feel that she thought of it all by herself."

"It is my pleasure to serve you, Mademoiselle Vourlay," Dalbert Sattersfield said, waiting until Mitzi at last located the crumpled piece of paper. "I may tell you that last week I received a shipment of excellent Creole coffee, and while the price is a bit high, it's certainly better than it was during the war. Two dollars a pound—but because Mr. Bouchard has given me such good business all this year, I should like to express my appreciation by offering it to him at just a few pennies over my own cost—a dollar eighty cents a pound."

"That's very kind of you, Monsieur Sattersfield. Yes, indeed, we do need some coffee. Ten pounds, if you can spare it."

"Certainly, mademoiselle." He turned to one of the shelves and, despite his handicap, deftly lifted a ten-pound cloth sack of coffee onto the scale. "There, you see, exactly ten pounds, Mademoiselle Vourlay."

"*Merci milles fois.* Let me see now"—again Mitzi consulted her list—"I shall need some flour—oh, yes, and some spices too. Hannah is going to bake a cake, a very special cake, for our Christmas dinner, Monsieur Sattersfield."

"I have a fair assortment of spices, Mademoiselle Vourlay. And the quality of flour is quite good this month, I'm happy to say."

Mitzi hesitated, glanced toward the door to make sure that Dan Munroe was sitting outside in the wagon, then stammered, "I—I wished to ask you, M'sieu Sattersfield, whether you are engaged on the night of Christmas."

"I do not understand your meaning, Mademoiselle Vourlay," he replied with a pleasant smile. "I have no social engagements, if that is what you mean. I shall prepare my own dinner as I customarily do—"

"That is what I meant, m'sieu," Mitzi impulsively broke in. "I—that is, M'sieu Bouchard, would like it very much if you would come to dinner at Windhaven."

"Why, that's most kind of you and Monsieur Bouchard." Again he gave her a courtly bow.

Mitzi felt her heart beating faster. "I mean, you are so

lonely here, and we are all—I myself, too—so grateful for the way you have dealt with us this year. Could you come about six o'clock, if that is convenient?"

To her bemused delight, he reached for her hand, brought it to his lips, and kissed it as a gallant at court might have done. She felt compelled to stammer, "I—I must apologize, M'sieu Sattersfield—you know, months ago, I said that I would ask my mistress to invite you to supper some evening—and I meant to—but then you know how *distraits* we all were when the *pauvre petit garçon* was taken from us—"

He had straightened, but not yet relinquished her hand, and Mitzi's fingers trembled in his grasp. Her face was scarlet now, and she had never been so bewitching as at this moment. "I heard of it, mam'selle, and I said prayers that the child would be returned. Thank God they were answered. All is well now, Mam'selle Vourlay?"

"Oh yes—*tout va bien, très bien*—so then it is arranged, *n'est-ce pas?* You will come?"

"With the greatest of pleasure—provided I may sit beside you, *ma charmante demoiselle.*"

"You—you do me too much honor, m'sieu—" she stammered.

"Would you think me too bold if I permitted myself to call you Mam'selle Mitzi?" he asked.

"Oh no! I should love that—I mean, it would be very nice—and you—may I call you Dalbert, if it does not offend you?"

"On the contrary, the way you pronounce my name makes it sound better than I ever heard it before, except when my darling Odile used it."

"Oh, M'sieu D-Dalbert!" By now, Mitzi was completely flustered. She glanced at him and then very reluctantly withdrew her hand from his grasp. "And now, since—since that is arranged, there are just a few more things I shall need."

"Of course, *ma chère* Mitzi. I am completely at your service."

Dalbert Sattersfield himself carried the supplies out to the wagon, helped Mitzi into it, and promised that he would be prompt at the Christmas dinner. Her face was so radiant that Dan Munroe could not hide a knowing smile as he picked up the reins and clucked to start the horses up on the return journey to the chateau.

Over a generation ago, the huge dining-room table at Windhaven Plantation had seated members of the Bouchard family and friends and neighbors, and old Lucien had presided at the head of the table to give thanks for the bounteous provender and the ties of family and friendship which made Christmas so memorable. Now, many members of the Bouchard clan were absent, and it was old Lucien's grandson Luke who sat at the head of the table with Laure at the other end and her two little sons beside her. The other guests were the loyal black workers of Windhaven Plantation and their children, including Buford Phelps, who had once been the most carping of Luke's critics and was now one of his most loyal supporters.

Hannah Atbury, aided by Mary Turner, had prepared a lavish dinner of baked ham, sweet yams, salad, vegetables, cakes and puddings, and even homemade candy for the children. Luke had commissioned Jason Barntry to ship several cases of excellent French wine and brandy to complement this holiday menu. After dinner, toasts were drunk. Then Luke and Laure presented Christmas gifts to everyone. Even old Ellen, the conjure woman, beaming and proud in her bright new calico dress, was an honored guest.

On one side of the table, at about the middle, Dalbert Sattersfield was seated next to Mitzi Vourlay, with Katie Munroe at her right and Hughie Mendicott at his left. Throughout the dinner, Mitzi had not been able to keep from glancing in his direction. He was elegantly dressed, with a fine new cravat, and his brown trousers were neatly pressed. As before, she had observed that the left sleeve of his cambric shirt had been rolled up and tied just below the shoulder. Although at first the widower had seemed somewhat ill at ease, Luke had made him feel completely at home.

When the ham was ready, Hannah proudly carried it in on a huge silver platter and set it down at the head of the table. There, Luke Bouchard carved slices, and the plates were passed along the table until each one had a generous portion. Impulsive as she was, Mitzi observed that Dalbert

61

Sattersfield had begun to cut the ham with his fork, and so she whispered, "Please, M'sieu Dalbert, *permettez-moi de vous aider.*"

She reached over with knife and fork and deftly cut the huge slice into convenient pieces. Both Luke and Laure observed this, exchanging a knowing look, and others did as well; Mitzi, suddenly abashed, turned red and hastily began to manage her own portion. But she was more than rewarded for her thoughtfulness when the former Confederate officer leaned over to whisper. "I'm in your debt, *ma belle.* And later, if we can be alone together for a moment, I should like to tell you something that is in my heart."

After dinner and the giving of presents (there was a lovely cameo brooch for Mitzi, and Luke and Laure had presented Dalbert Sattersfield with a meerschaum pipe and a leather pouch filled with imported West Indian tobacco), Dan Munroe's children, Tom and Elsie, and Hughie Mendicott's boys, Davie and Louis, thanked their hosts and said goodnight. They were bidden to fill their pockets from the plates of nuts and raisins and candies placed on a sideboard near the door to the dining room.

Seeing that Luke was busy chatting with Marius Thornton and his wife Clementine, Mitzi caught her mistress's eye and whispered, "Would you mind, madame, if I took M'sieu Sattersfield on a tour of the chateau?"

"I should be disappointed in you if you didn't, you forward minx," was Laure's teasing whispered reply. "He's mad about you, it's very obvious to all of us. Now don't you let him get away from you."

"*Mon Dieu*—I—oh yes, *c'est vrai,* I want him so very much—I am in love with him, I confess it, Madame Laure."

"And there's another very good reason why I am happy to see you ready to settle down with that gentleman," Laure bantered. "Once you're married, I shan't have to worry about you making eyes any longer at my husband—I can remember how you used to ogle him at the Union House!"

Mitzi uttered a gasp of confusion and then fled to the other end of the room to find Dalbert Sattersfield, the pouch tucked in his right armpit, trying somewhat awkwardly to dip the pipe into the tobacco.

"Oh, you must let me do that, please, M'sieu Dalbert!" she exclaimed.

"If you wish, *ma belle.*"

She took the pouch and dipped the pipe into it, packed the tobacco down with her thumb, handed the pipe to him, and went to the table to get one of the candles to light it. As she did so, a drop of wax narrowly missed his shoe, and she scolded herself: *"Comme je suis stupide!* Oh, that was thoughtless of me—"

"Not at all. Quite the contrary, *ma belle,* it shows what a wonderfully good heart you have."

"You—you are so kind—I don't deserve it. I—I wanted to ask you, perhaps you would like to see the chateau?"

Again Dalbert Sattersfield bowed. "I should like nothing better, especially if it assures me the privilege of being alone with you this evening." With this, he offered her his arm, and Mitzi linked her left around his as she led him down the corridor of the left wing of the chateau. To conceal her own excitement, she forced herself to play the role of a museum guide, explaining the arrangement of the various rooms, taking him through the kitchen and pointing out its many features, until at last, wanting with all her heart to take him at his word of wanting to be alone with her, she proposed, "I think you might enjoy the view from the tower, M'sieu Dalbert."

"That would please me very much, *ma pigeonne,*" he gravely responded.

At this intimate endearment, which she had surely not expected so soon, Mitzi turned a vivid scarlet. Yet at the same time, unconsciously, her arm tightened its hold on his as she led him toward the stairway of the right wing of the chateau, the stairway that old Lucien Bouchard had climbed so many nights to look out at the red bluff where Dimarte lay.

Once they had begun to ascend, she began to quiver with a feverish nervousness—for she was still a virgin despite having been a *soubrette* in the Union House in New Orleans. Several times she glanced behind her, as if to ascertain that no one was following them. When she turned, she saw his handsome face, his neatly trimmed black hair graying at the temples, his high-set cheekbones, and firm jaw and chin. She noted most of all the generous fullness of his mouth and the warm blue of his eyes. He wore neither mustache nor beard, and though she knew him to be in his late forties, he seemed fascinatingly young and virile to her.

After the two had been silent for a moment, Dalbert spoke. "I recall that you told me that your parents were born in Cannes, Mam'selle Mitzi."

"*C'est vrai*, M'sieu Dalbert!" she confirmed, delighted that he had thought enough of her to remember this fact which she had told him during their first meeting. Then, striving further to hide her feelings, she volunteered, "You know, of course, M'sieu Dalbert, that Lucien Bouchard, who was the first of the family here, came from the town of Yves-sur-lac, which is in Normandy. He lived with the Indians here who gave him this land, and it was his son Henry who arranged to have an architect come all the way from New Orleans to plan this chateau, so that it would be exactly like the one he had lived in back in *la belle France*."

"It is truly a magnificent chateau. I have heard that the Yankee troops set fire to it toward the last of the war."

"*Oui, vous avez raison*," Mitzi promptly agreed. "But M'sieu Luke, who is his grandson, as you know, restored it. It is so very beautiful now, it is as if that fire had never been. I am so glad for him and for my dear mistress, Madame Laure."

"That is what I like about you, *ma belle*. You are very loyal and very generous." They had reached the top of the tower and stood before the open casement window which looked out onto the distant red bluff. In the darkness of this Christmas night, it was scarcely visible. The river was still and hushed, and there was not even the call of the night birds to break the silence.

"Isn't it beautiful out there, M'sieu Dalbert?" Mitzi's voice was hushed as if she were afraid to break the silence. She stood beside him, her arm still linked around his, not seeing that his eyes were admiring her.

"It and you are very beautiful, *ma chérie*," he murmured.

She turned to look at him. "M'sieu Dalbert, you—you've said such sweet things to me all night long, you mustn't lead a girl on—" she stammered.

"I have no wish to lead you on, Mitzi." His smile was gentle. "I'm only a poor storekeeper, I haven't much to offer, and as you see, I've only one arm. But, if it does not

64

offend you, I should be proud if you would consider my proposal of marriage to you."

"Dalbert—" Mitzi's mouth gaped in her consternation at this sudden avowal. She had not dreamed that the tall widower could possibly have had the same interest in her that she had had in him since their very first meeting—not so soon, at least.

"I hope I have not offended you, *chérie.*" Now his tone was almost apologetic as he reached for her hand and held it. "Of course, I'm much older than you—I'm all of forty-seven. You're such a young and beautiful girl—I'm sure you must have other suitors who are more worthy of you—"

Her eyes were brimming with tears as she shook her head. "Oh, Dalbert, there's no one else—oh it's true—ever since I first walked into your store last summer, I—I've prayed, I've hoped you would like me just a little. I do like you—more than that, I—I love you, Dalbert. There aren't any other suitors, and—and I'll try to make you half as good a wife as your Odile."

He blinked his eyes quickly to hide his own emotions as he brought her hand to his lips and then murmured, "You need never try to compare yourself, *ma chérie.* Odile and I had a wonderful life together, and I mourned her when she died. But you are so different, and to have this happen to me after my loneliness and all the losses of the war, it is almost like the gift of a new life."

"Dalbert, oh *mon cher amour!*" she breathed, and then arched up on tiptoe to offer him her mouth. His right arm circled her shoulders as he drew her to him, and with a sigh, Mitzi Vourlay pledged herself to Dalbert Sattersfield.

Hannah Atbury had stayed in the kitchen to put things back into order long after the guests had finished dinner. She assured Katie and Mary—and even Clementine, who had volunteered to help her—that she could manage quite well by herself. And indeed, still mourning Phineas as she did, she found her domestic chores to be a merciful boon of solace and distraction.

Hughie Mendicott had watched his boys, Davie and Louis, stuff their pockets with raisins and nuts and candy and then whispered to them to go back to the cottage and wait for him, as he wanted to talk to someone. He made his way to the kitchen and stood for a moment watching Hannah vigorously scrub the dishes from the feast.

"I'd like mighty much to help you, Miz Hannah, ma'am."

Hannah Atbury turned and smiled. "That's mighty nice of you, Mr. Mendicott, but I reckon I can do this by myself. Work's good for the soul, you know."

"I know, Miz Hannah." He shifted nervously from foot to foot, coughed, looked around the kitchen, and then hesitantly spoke. "We all miss Phineas a lot—I know how much you must, Miz Hannah. I'm right sorry."

"That's kind of you, Mr. Mendicott."

"My goodness, I don't think I've been called that since I came to work here for Mr. Bouchard, Miz Hannah. I'd like it mighty fine if you could just call me Hughie, the way the rest of the folks do."

"Sure, Hughie. You know, you've got two fine boys there. They're hard workers and they never give anybody a mite of trouble.

His face brightened at this. "Good of you to say so, Miz Hannah, ma'am. I hope you won't take no offense at what I want to say, but when you mentioned about Davie and Louis, that sort of brought more to mind what I've been thinking for some time now—I mean, after poor old Phineas."

She turned to face him, frowning a little at his sudden seriousness. "Shucks, Hughie, a man like you doesn't give any offense. Just say what's on your mind."

"Well then," he took a deep breath, and stared intently at her, "what I've been thinking—well, you know that my Pearl passed 'bout nine years ago. I've had to bring the boys up by myself—"

"And you've done a fine job of it, too, I can tell you. And everybody else around here knows that, Hughie."

"Well now, I was thinking—I know it's much too soon for you to be thinking of such a thing—that's why I ask your pardon if what I'm going to say hurts you any—well, Miz Hannah, you'd make a wonderful mother for Davie and Louis. 'Deed you would, Miz Hannah. 'Sides which, if you want to know the truth, I've always liked you an awful lot. I think you're a wonderful woman, with lots of courage and savvy. Oh, Miz Hannah, don't just stand there looking at me that way, tell me I'm a fool and to mind my own business, and I won't ever bother you again."

The buxom, attractive widow bit her lip and turned for a moment to hide the tears that had sprung to her eyes. Then she said very gently, "That's about the nicest compliment you could pay me, Hughie. Yes, it is a mite too soon. Phineas was a wonderful man, not as strong as you are, but maybe that's just why I cared for him so much. Now I know you've a need too, and I like your boys a heap. Just give me a little time, Hughie, and maybe I'll see things your way."

"Oh, Miz Hannah, you don't know how happy you've made me by saying that! I won't bother you again about this, but when the time comes, I'll be mighty grateful if you'd let me know when we can plan things—you know, sort of . . ." His voice trailed off, and then, with a quickly stammered, "G—g—goodnight, Miz Hannah!" he hurried out of the kitchen to rejoin his sons.

Hannah Atbury bowed her head and wept silently for a moment. Then, taking a red cotton kerchief out of the pocket of her apron, she vigorously blew her nose and turned back to her dishes.

CHAPTER SEVEN

In this month of December, 1869, historians of the era saw the further extension of the North's inflexible Reconstruction policy toward the defeated South. Congress ordained that Georgia must ratify the Fifteenth Amendment and restore the expelled Negro members of her legislature if she wished restoration to statehood. Some two weeks before, a Negro convention had met in Washington, D.C. to create a national labor union—a publicized event which was anathema to the South. For the small Southern plantation owner, virtually reduced to sharecropping, it had become increasingly difficult to obtain the services of the emancipated blacks in most communities. As freedmen, they were enjoying the privilege of offering their services to the highest bidders.

There was also the widespread growth of the movement toward women's suffrage. During this year, the Wyoming Territory granted full suffrage to women. To some observers, this seemed yet another deplorable consequence of the Civil War.

But in the Indian Territory (out of which the Oklahoma Territory would later be created), none of these winds of change could be felt. Widely scattered Indian villages on the plains, out of touch with each other and with the United States, felt only the full force of winter during these grim, chilly days of December. One such village, consisting of little more than a few tepees and wigwams, was the Creek village, numbering some 275 men, women, and children, under the leadership of their *mico,* Ematába. They stood alone with no friends or neighbors to ease their lot.

Dr. Ben Wilson had come to live with these Creeks early in October of this year, after having left his son, Thomas, and his baby daughter in the care of his mother-in-law, Sybella, after whom his daughter had been named. Several of Lucien Edmond Bouchard's vaqueros had accompanied him on the more than six-hundred-mile journey from Windhaven Range, while he drove a wagon containing his own medical supplies, and food and blankets that Lucien Edmond had contributed. Ematuba gravely welcomed him and then remarked that he expected the white-eyes medicine man to stay only a short time. Greatly to the *mico's* surprise, Ben Wilson shook his head and said, "No, Ematuba, I want to stay with you through the winter. Lucien Edmond Bouchard has told me that many of your people are sick, that you do not have enough food, and that the agent doesn't always bring you the supplies agreed upon by our government."

"You would live with us, in this poor village?" Ematuba asked.

"I am a doctor, Ematuba. I took an oath that I would help the sick and the dying, that I would give all my strength and my skill to those who need me. I have lost my wife, and I shall mourn her for many years. But if I can be of help to your people, then perhaps I may forget my grief, and I shall be employed to the best of my abilities."

The tall Creek chieftain shook his head. "But we have no way to pay you for this work."

"Have I asked for pay?" Ben indignantly demanded, his fair skin flushing. "Yet, if that disturbs you, I would gladly take my pay, as you call it—if you would choose one of your braves who speaks English to teach me how to speak Creek. In that way, I could be of much more service to your people."

"It is a very good thing you do," Ematuba solemnly replied. "I will have young Sipanata instruct you in our tongue. He has seen four and twenty summers, and for two of them he was apprenticed to a white-eyes in Mobile, where he learned to speak as you do. But his longing to share our destiny, his loneliness among the white-eyes, and the cruelty of his master, made him come to find us in this lonely place. Yes, I think Sipanata will find this a good thing, too. He will teach you our words and our thoughts, and in doing this, he will know once again the pride of being a Creek."

Sipanata, a wiry young man who defiantly wore his hair in a long braid and with the traditional scalp lock, at first glowered at the gentle Quaker. But when Emataba angrily told him that this was a white-eyes friend of the Creeks and a relative of Lucien Edmond Bouchard, Sipanata glumly nodded. "I will do it because you are my *mico*," he responded. "But you cannot change the feelings in my heart that I have against the white-eyes. To me, this is but another one of those who helped drive all of you from your birthplace and who now let you starve while they grow fat from the money they were given to buy food for us."

At first, Dr. Wilson had found Sipanata a grudging, almost brusque teacher. Then, about two weeks after he had come to the impoverished reservation, a young mother tearfully hurried up to him, holding her two-year-old boy. The boy had gulped down his food and was choking on it. Swiftly, the doctor forced the child to regurgitate and soon had him breathing normally. The mother, who spoke no English, knelt before him and touched his feet in a sign of reverent thanksgiving, and Sipanata silently watched, his rugged features constricted with curiosity and wonder. After Ben had comforted her, using what few words of Creek he had already learned to assure her that what he had done was not magic and that it had been his joy to restore her son to health, the young brave approached him. "I have seen and heard how Leotake thanks you for your great medicine which saved her son. I have been wrong. You are not one of those white-eyes who drove my people away from their land. From this moment on, I will teach you with all the skill I have, and I will be your friend—if you will let me."

"I have always thought of you as a friend, Sipanata," Ben Wilson responded, holding out his hand. Sipanata's dour features softened, and he grasped his new friend's hand and energetically shook it.

When he had left Pittsburgh with his two little children, resolved to make a fresh start, Ben Wilson had closed his savings account and brought with him $3,000 in gold and a bank draft for $12,000. He had asked Lucien Edmond to deposit the bank draft in the family's San Antonio bank. He then brought most of the gold with him to the Creek reservation, for after hearing from Lucien Edmond how shabbily the Creeks had been treated by the Indian agent, he believed that he might be able to alleviate their suffering by purchasing the necessary food, clothing, and medicine.

Shortly thereafter, Emataba, who at the age of thirty-eight was three years older than Ben, showed the doctor an unusual mark of respect by inviting him to live in the tepee that the old Creek shaman Equitaba had occupied until his death last year. "It is fitting that you take his place in our village," he told the Quaker. "In our religion, the shaman helps us banish the spirits of evil and makes magic to summon the spirits of good for all of our people. And you, though you are a white-eyes, have learned how to do battle with the spirits of evil and drive them from us—thus in a sense you will become our new shaman."

So Ben Wilson adapted himself to the simple, monotonous life of this small village. He shared the Creeks' food, careful never to take more than his share and often less, when he began to see their supplies dwindle. The bull and three heifers which Lucien Edmond had brought to the village during the summer had been penned in a corral just outside the village, and the heifers would bear their calves next spring. Till then, of course, they could furnish no milk for the children. When he had first examined the children of the village, Ben found that several were suffering from malnutrition. Some of the young mothers, too, who had borne babies recently had been unable to nurse properly because they themselves had not had sufficient nourishment. The doctor devised a kind of gruel or pap, made out of water and a little flour, and when he indignantly demanded of Emataba when the government supplies were due, the *mico* shrugged and said, "The agent should visit us with the supplies next month, but we are given what he sees fit to give us, and it does no good to ask for more."

At the end of the first week in November, a wagon approached the Creek village from the northwest, flanked by an escort of six soldiers. Ben himself hurried out to open the rickety gate at the entrance of the village. The driver of the wagon, a corpulent man in his early fifties, nearly bald but with a bushy sand-colored beard speckled with gray, slowly descended and grimaced in distaste as he stared at the tepees and wigwams. "All right, you boys," he called, "come help me unload these goods. You know I can't lift nuttin', I got a bad ticker."

71

"Good afternoon. I take it you are the Indian agent?" Ben inquired.

The fat man grunted assent, his watery blue eyes squinting at the lanky Quaker. "That I be. Name's Matthias Stillman. Who might you me? Don't usually see any white men out in this Godforsaken place."

"I do not think that God has forsaken these people, Mr. Stillman. I should say rather it is shortsighted and greedy men."

"Now hold on there, mister!" Matthias Stillman drew himself up with a great show of righteous indignation. "Where do you come off at, saying a nasty thing like that? I'll have you know I take real good care of these dirty redskins. The government gives them so much a month, and I see they get it, understand?"

"I'm anxious to see exactly what bounty you've brought them today, Mr. Stillman," was Ben's answer.

The six soldiers had dismounted and, going to the back of the wagon, began to unload its contents. There were barrels of flour, two large tin containers of milk, a dozen frayed and almost threadbare blankets, a bag of salt, several sacks of dried beef and pork, and a few other staples.

Out of curiosity, Ben opened one of the barrels of flour and turned to the Indian agent. "Mr. Stillman, did you inspect this flour before you brought it here?"

" 'Course I did. Anyhow, what's it any of your business? Who are you, anyhow?"

"My name is Dr. Ben Wilson; I've come to live with these people and to help cure the sick. Some of that sickness is caused by not enough food, Mr. Stillman. Just look at this flour in this barrel, sir. Unless I'm much mistaken, those are weevils. The flour is old and stale and no doubt rancid, besides being buggy."

"Now you look here, Dr. Wilson or whatever your name may be," Matthias Stillman's face grew purple with anger, "we bought these supplies from settlers near the fort, you understand? And we paid them a good price. Do you expect to have fancy goods shipped in from maybe Chicago or New York to these dirty redskins?"

"They are hardly dirty, Mr. Stillman. And they're human beings. I wouldn't give prisoners in a jail flour like this. How fresh is that milk?"

"I don't have to answer your questions, Dr. Wilson.

72

And I'm not going to. I've come on my errand, I've done what I'm paid to do by the government, and that's all you have to know. You got any complaints, you write a letter to Congress or maybe even the president. All right, boys, let's get back to the fort." He turned back to glower at Dr. Ben Wilson. "Just you better not start any trouble here, Dr. Wilson, if you get my meaning. You go riling up these redskins, you'll get 'em on the warpath, and then you know what'll happen—you can take full responsibility for it, talking so high and mighty the way you do." With this, he clambered back into the wagon, took up the reins, and turned the horses out of the village. As he passed through the open gate, he hawked and spat at the doctor's feet.

After Ben had completed his inspection of the goods the Indian agent had delivered, he found that more than half of the flour was contaminated with weevils. "Has it always been this way, Emataba?" he asked the *mico*.

"Always, since we first came here. And perhaps what is worse than the bad food is the way in which it is given, just as one tosses a gnawed bone to a mangy cur who skulks nearby and begs food because it is starving," the tall Creek leader replied.

"Is there a fair-sized town near here where I might get decent food for your people, Emataba?"

"It is a long journey from here, and it is called Wichita. It would take perhaps six or seven suns to reach it and as many back—and you, who are not used to riding horseback, might find it an even longer journey."

"Give me one of your best horses, Emataba. I will ride to Wichita, and there I will buy a wagon and fill it with good food and clothes for your people."

"But why do you do this for us?"

"Because I can't stand to see human beings treated like animals, Emataba. That man, Matthias Stillman, should be imprisoned for what he is doing. I can guess that he pockets most of the money from the government."

"Alas, Dr. Wilson, my people long ago learned that that was the way of many of the white-eyes. That is why we have so little hope left, now that we are abandoned in a barren land."

"I want to start right away. Now you've seen me make that gruel for the little ones. Your squaws can do that. The dried meat the agent brought seems edible enough, so portion it out so that everyone has something, and try to make it last as long as you can. I'll see if I can't buy a cow that has already calved, so that it can give fresh milk for the children and the mothers."

"Ibofanaga will bless you for this, Dr. Wilson. And I, *mico* of the Creeks, say that my heart is too full for words to thank you."

It took Dr. Wilson six days to reach Wichita, and when at last he dismounted in front of the general store, he was bone-tired, having slept no more than four or five hours at night. As he entered the store, a jovial, thickly-bearded man wearing a black hat and frock coat greeted him from behind the counter. "Welcome, neighbor. You've ridden a long way, judging from the look of you."

"Yes, from the Creek reservation in Indian Territory. My name is Ben Wilson. I want to buy some supplies for these people. I am living with them and serving as their doctor."

"You are indeed a friend, then."

"A friend—are you perhaps of the Quaker inclination?" Dr. Wilson hazarded.

"It is truly my conviction. Are you also, friend?"

Dr. Wilson's homely face lit up as he strode forward and extended his hand, which the bearded storekeeper smilingly shook. "It's a joy and a comfort to know that I can find men of my own persuasion so far away from my former home," he confided.

"And where was that, good friend?"

"In Pittsburgh. I was a doctor at the hospital there. My wife died, and I brought our two little children to her mother's ranch in Texas, where they are being cared for. And, so that I am not useless and full of self-pity because of my grief, I have vowed to serve the needy—that is why I am the doctor of the reservation."

"God will bless you, Dr. Wilson, and your wife will know the joyous way in which you mourn her. But come, you must be exhausted. My good wife and I would be honored to have you as our guest for supper. There is even a bath with hot water. Perhaps you would like to enjoy it now—I will be closing the store in a minute. Then at supper, you can tell me your needs, and in the morning they will be ready for you. By the way, my name

74

is Jacob Hartmann, and I am pastor of our society here in Wichita."

"If God so wills, I shall come of a Sunday to hear your sermon, Pastor Hartmann." Ben Wilson sighed and nodded ruefully to himself. "I confess I am a bit tired. Your offer of a hot bath is like the promise of paradise."

The bath, a bounteous supper prepared by Jacob Hartmann's congenial wife, Tabitha, and the earnest exchange of homilies of the Quaker faith enormously heartened Ben Wilson. By noon of the next day, he was able to buy two dray horses and a wagon for his supplies, as well as two cows which had recently calved. He shook hands with Jacob Hartmann and Tabitha, promised to return as soon as he could, then took his seat in the wagon and urged the horses back toward the Creek reservation.

As he drove out upon the rolling stretch of plain, where already a few warning patches of light snow marked the coming of a bitter winter, Ben thought of Fleurette. He stared toward the southern horizon where he was headed, and he could almost see her lovely face before him and hear her gentle voice in the wind. He felt comforted as he had not been since leaving home.

He had estimated that the return journey would take at least two weeks, allowing for the slower pace of the milk cows. On the second evening out, he made camp near a little hill shielded from the wind by a clump of oak and birch trees. The wind had risen, and the dark clouds in the sky seemed to scurry along, blotting out the pale quarter-moon. From a distance came the mournful howling of a coyote. There was no human habitation to be seen for miles around, and despite himself, the Quaker doctor shivered at that sound which emphasized the desolation of this terrain. He carried no weapons: the Quaker faith prohibited that, and even when Lucien Edmond had offered him a carbine for protection when he had ridden to the Creek village in the fall, he had refused it. He had only a small claspknife which he used to cut off portions of jerky. This and some hardtack, which the friendly Wichita store owner had given him, constituted his supper, washed down with water from a leather canteen which he had filled from a creek.

After having made certain that the horses and cows were

75

securely tethered for the night, and having fed the horses from a sack of oats, he wrapped himself in his blankets and prepared to sleep.

As he drowsed, he was suddenly wakened by the sound of hoofbeats, and when he sat up, he saw that three men were looking down at him from their saddles, grinning and whispering to themselves.

"Where you bound, stranger?" a rangy, pockmarked man with a broad sombrero and two six-shooters holstered at his sides, drawled at him.

"I'm a doctor bound for the Creek reservation in Indian Territory," Ben replied.

"A doc, huh?" the pockmarked rider chuckled, then turned to his crony at his left, a short, heavy-set, black-bearded man with the purple scar of an old knife wound at the left side of his neck. "Fred, 'pears like to me this fella's plumb loco. Now why would a white man 'n a doctor to boot traipse hisself off to live with a bunch of mangy Injuns?"

"Mebbe he's got a yen for Injun tail," the rider at the right spoke up. He was a man in his early thirties with thick blond sideburns and a heavy mustache. "I hear those red-skin squaws really put out for a white man who treats 'em right."

"Say, you got a point there, Lance," the pockmarked rider grinned crookedly. Leaning forward in his saddle, his face hardening, he addressed the Quaker. "Now we're mighty peaceable men, savvy, Doc? You jist throw your six-shooter or your rifle or whatever else you got out here where we can see it; we might jist let you live. And then you can go back and poke those squaws all you've a mind to. All we want's the wagon, the cows, the horses. Seems to me that's a fair exchange for your life. What do you say about it, boys?"

His two cronies agreed as the doctor threw off his blankets and stood to face his tormentors. "I have no guns, gentlemen. I happen to be a Quaker."

"Hey, Dan," the younger man called Lance proffered, "I heard about them. They got a bunch of Quakers up in Wichita. Yeah, now I remember what I heard about 'em. Seems like you slap a Quaker on the cheek, he'll turn the other one around so you can slap that one too. Ain't that

76

a card, though!" He took off his sombrero and whacked it against his thigh as he burst into raucous laughter.

"Well," the pockmarked leader Dan chuckled dryly, "That makes it a helluva lot easier. So Doc here doesn't wear a gun. That's mighty fine for you, Doc. And seein' that you're a peaceable man, you won't mind if we jist help usselves, now will you?"

"I must ask you in all decency not to take these things— the food, the clothing, and the milk cows are for starving people who need them for this winter," Ben earnestly declared.

Dan scowled and put his hand to the butt of the six-shooter in his right-hand holster. "Don't press your luck, Doc," he sneered. "Fact is, them Injuns'd be a lot better off dead. Hell, Doc, if you want to heal folks, whyn't you pick yourself up and go live in a civilized town like mebbe Wichita? There's white folks need what you kin do fer 'em, not dirty, murderin' Injuns."

"These Indians haven't murdered anyone. They've been driven all the way from Alabama to live out here where there's no one to help them," Ben retorted.

Dan turned in the saddle to wink at Lance. "He's got it bad, Lance. Guess that Injun tail must be real appealin'."

"Sure looks like it, Dan," Lance guffawed agreement.

Dan drew his six-shooter and leveled it at the Quaker's chest. "Now fun's fun, but we've had enough palaver fer tonight, see, Doc? You jist stand steady there and don't try anything stupid, and we'll be away from here before you know it."

"If any of you men have a spark of humanity or decency in you, I beg you not to steal food from these starving people," Ben bravely protested. "Look—I've some gold on me. You can have that, if you'll let me keep the horses and the cows and the wagon. Surely gold will do you more good than what I've brought along here for the Creeks."

"Why, now, since yer so obligin', Doc," Dan jeered, "we'll jist take the gold along too. Makes it a real good haul, boys. Stand where you are, Doc. I don't want to kill you, but I will if you give me any more trouble, get me?"

Then, turning to Lance, he ordered, "You an Fred drive the wagon. I'll follow you directly once you've got a good distance on Doc here. I jist aim to keep him nice and peaceful."

The Quaker's face was twisted with anguish and help-lessness as he watched the two riders dismount, lead their horses by the reins to the back of the wagon, and tether them alongside the cows and the black gelding. Dan chuckled: "Don't look so downhearted, Doc. You're lucky tonight. Me, I feel peaceful too. See these six notches on this gun here?" He reversed the six-shooter in his hand to hold it by the barrel, showing the notches cut into the butt. "And there's three more on my other six-shooter. Only you're getting a lucky break. Now you can jist hand over that gold you were talking about a little while back—and be quick about it. Go on, take the wagon off, boys!" he raised his voice to call.

Suddenly there was the whirr of an arrow, and the pock-marked leader jerked back in his saddle, the six-shooter dropping from his nerveless hand as he slowly stared down at his belly, where the shaft of a feathered arrow protruded. Then, with a cry, he slipped from the saddle and sprawled on the ground.

His two companions had turned the wagon toward the west and were beginning to ride off when Lance, peering round the side to look back, uttered a startled cry: "Hold it, Fred—the Doc's killed Dan—the lyin' bastid said he didn't have a gun on him—"

He leaped down from the wagon, drawing his own six-shooter from its holster just as a Creek brave on a gray mustang rode out of the clump of trees and, drawing back a tomahawk, flung it with unerring aim. Lance screamed shrilly as the blade buried itself in his left cheek near the ear, then pitched forward and lay with his arms flung out ahead of him, kicked convulsively once or twice, and then lay still. Fred, with a savage oath, drew his six-shooter out of its holster and fired at the brave but missed. As he turned to follow the Creek and to level his gun again, another brave, who had ridden out of the trees, notched an arrow to his bow and sped it into the bushwhacker's back.

Dazed by this unforeseen salvation, Ben Wilson uttered a gasp and turned toward the clump of trees in time to see Sipanata ride toward him with a wide grin on his lean face.

"But how could you have known this would happen, Sipanata?" he wonderingly asked.

"Our *mico* told me to take two of our youngest warriors

78

and to follow you and guide you back safely. He said that since you are now our shaman, you are dear to us and needed by us." Then he called to his two companions: "Ho, Nimasike, Bentijo, do not forget to take the guns and the bullets from those dogs who would have harmed our shaman. It may be that when again evil men come to harm the Creeks, we shall be able to protect ourselves with their own weapons instead of these we were taught as children how to use—when there were no evil ones to rob us of our land and of our freedom."

CHAPTER EIGHT

It was not until the first week of December that Dr. Ben Wilson, accompanied by Sipanata and the two young braves who had saved him from the bushwhackers, returned to the isolated Creek village. Their journey had been delayed not only by the necessarily slower pace of the wagons and the milk cows tethered to it, but also by a heavy snow and blustering winds.

As they came within sight of the fence that enclosed the reservation, Emataba opened the gate and came out to welcome them, his face grave with anxiety. Beside him stood two of the older braves, who were concerned over the illness of their wives, for several of the children and the older women had come down with the croup as a result of the bitter cold and poor food. The Quaker doctor dismounted from the wagon and hurried to the tall *mico*. "I give thanks to Ibofanaga that you have safely returned," the Creek leader solemnly declared as he clasped Ben Wilson's hand.

"Without the help of your three braves, Emataba, as well as God's help, I might never have returned—or I might have come empty-handed. But I have brought a wagonload of supplies from Wichita, and I also was able to buy two fine milk cows. You can distribute everything as you see fit."

"I am grateful to you, my white brother. You truly have taken the place of Equitaba as our shaman." The *mico's* eyes saddened as he shook his head with an air of anxious preoccupation. "But a sickness has fallen upon some of the children and old squaws. They do not breathe well, and they have fever and are restless when they sleep. It is because of the cold, and also because the blankets and the food which the Indian agent gave us were not good."

80

"I will see to the sick at once, Emataba. Take me to them."

"It shall be done. Ho, Sipanata," Emataba called out, "drive the wagon in and let the other two braves begin to share what our shaman has brought us among the neediest of the village." Then he nodded to Ben Wilson and went toward one of the wigwams in the center of the little village. As he parted the flaps and entered, Ben saw a white-haired squaw, lying on a rude pallet of straw and rags with a threadbare blanket wrapped around her, her eyes filmed and bright with fever. She was gasping for breath. Quickly he knelt down beside her, murmuring what few Creek words he had already learned from Sipanata in an attempt to comfort her. Then he looked up at Emataba and said, "It is the croup. It is a very common disease which we whites often have in winter. Fortunately, I have what I need to help."

"What can I do to aid my white brother?"

"Do you have pots or pans or cooking vessels that hold water?"

"Yes, we have these in abundance," Emataba said with an ironic smile, "even if we do not have food enough to cook in them."

"To help the breathing and to relieve the congestion in the lungs, I will give her steam to breathe," Dr. Ben explained. "We will build a small fire here and put the vessel filled with water over it. Then I will take a large cloth and make steam, which is moist hot air. When the woman breathes it, it will ease her suffering."

"This I did not know. It is good that you think of this. What else is needed?"

"She must not lie like this, but be propped up with her head higher than her body. I wish I had thought to buy pillows," the doctor frowned in exasperation. "But no matter, we can improvise something. And she must drink plenty of clear liquids. I know what will be good—a beef broth. I will take jerky and cook it in water to make a broth or bouillon, as we sometimes call it."

"And drinking this will cure her? That is a wondrous thing," Emataba exclaimed, eyeing the doctor with deep respect.

"With luck, these things should certainly put an end to

the congestion in her lungs. I will watch her and all the other patients till the danger is over."

"And I will pray to Ibofanaga to be merciful to all those who are afflicted. But I have more hope now that you are back among us." The tall *mico* put his hand on Ben's shoulder, then touched his own heart and his forehead in the Creek sign of grateful tribute to an ally.

With Emataba interpreting his requests, Ben asked some of the younger braves to bring in pots filled with water and to build a small fire under them. Ben then took his clasp knife and cut some blankets into large cloths which would serve to direct the steam toward the sufferer's nostrils. Then he asked Sipanata to call some of the younger squaws who were still healthy, so that they could watch him as he worked on the gray-haired woman who was his first charge. "Sipanata," he explained, "I will visit every sick person myself. But if you can tell the healthy ones to watch what I do here, then they will know how to continue caring for the unwell through the night, for they will need constant attending."

"We will watch you and we will learn from you, shaman," Sipanata said.

A small fire of coals, buffalo chips and bits of firewood was now kindled under the water-filled pot near the old squaw's bed. Ben Wilson knelt down and, when the water began to boil, he covered the pot with a large piece of an old blanket. Sipanata, at Ben's direction, urged the patient to lean forward and breathe in deeply. One of the other young squaws knelt beside the patient to hold her gently by the shoulders while she inhaled the vapor.

Meanwhile, also at the doctor's order, other squaws began to prepare the beef broth. In his own case of medical supplies, Ben had brought several straining cloths and a crude metal strainer. The squaws watched as he gestured to them to lift up the pot in which the thick broth was cooking and then pour it through the cloth or strainer into an empty pot. They exclaimed as they saw the liquid become clear.

When he stepped outside the last wigwam, Emataba came to him and said, "There are two others who begin to show the same sickness. They were well enough yesterday, but now I have seen that they have the same fever and they cough."

82

It was nearly nightfall, and Ben was almost reeling with fatigue. The last fifteen miles of the return journey had begun at dawn this day, and he had spent three hours already nursing the victims of the croup. Yet unhesitatingly he replied, "I will go there at once. Now that your squaws know how to prepare this broth and how to make pillows for the sick, will you ask one of them to come with me and prepare this?"

"It shall be done at once, my shaman." Emataba beckoned to one of the young squaws, a buxom woman in her early thirties, and spoke to her rapidly in the Creek tongue. She nodded, made the sign of tribal recognition by respectfully inclining her head and holding out her hands with the palms turned upward, then hurried off to fetch the necessary articles.

Ben drew aside the flaps of this wigwam which stood near the very end of the rows of these impoverished villagers and entered. He saw a strikingly lovely girl, not much more than nineteen, with delicate features. Her black hair was drawn into a single thick braid, and she wore a thick doeskin petticoat and jacket. She coughed and turned fretfully, as she clutched to her a little girl perhaps ten months old. The doctor saw at once that the little girl was feverish and her eyes dilated.

At the sight of him, the girl tried to sit up, uttering a frightened cry as she twisted herself with her back to him, huddling over her ailing child.

Emataba had followed him into the wigwam and now, in the Kiowa dialect, Emataba reassured her. "Have no fear, Elone. His heart is good, he is now our shaman. He comes to help you and the child."

Then quickly, in a low voice, he explained to the puzzled doctor, "Last summer, many evil men attacked your friend Lucien Edmond Bouchard and his *vaqueros*. They were driven off with heavy losses, but the survivors raided a Kiowa camp in order to get horses and killed all there except this young squaw and her child. She is Aiyuta Sioux, and she had been taken in a raid on her father's village by the chief of that camp and forced to become his wife. I do not speak the Sioux tongue, and only a little Kiowa, but already she has begun to learn a few words of our language. She fears you because it was a white-eyes whom she saw kill her mate and all the others."

83

At this moment, the buxom young squaw entered with several pots of water which she set down on the dirt floor of the wigwam, then brought in buffalo chips, bits of wood, and some jagged pieces of black rock. Emataba again explained to the Quaker doctor, "Not far from our village, one of our braves came upon a ravine and stumbled over these black rocks. Having not ever seen them before, he brought some back to camp and, for a jest, tossed them into our cooking fire. They began to burn and they gave much heat. So we have gathered these to protect us against the snows and the biting winds that besiege our village out here on the plains."

At the sound of a soft cry from Elone, Ben turned back to her. "Tell her to try to sit up and I will fix something that she can lean back against, and rest more comfortably," he said to the *mico*.

Emataba nodded, then spoke to the buxom young squaw who left the wigwam. She returned with two thick blankets taken from the supply wagon which had just been driven into the village. Then, as Ben watched, the woman gently knelt beside the young Sioux girl, gesturing and urging her to sit up while Emataba transmitted the doctor's instructions.

Half fearfully, Elone feebly sat up, her dark eyes fixed on the earnest face of the white man who stood watching her, and she held her little daughter even more tightly than ever.

An improvised backrest was now formed when the squaw brought in a crudely made wooden chest which one of her neighbors had used for storing strips of doeskin and buckskin. Ben Wilson nodded his approval as she placed the box behind Elone and then covered it with the thick blankets. Then, gently taking the girl by the shoulders, she eased her back against this comfortable support. Next she proceeded to make a fire, for it was essential that steam be prepared as soon as possible.

"She is very good at this, Emataba," the doctor praised her.

"Her name is Simanora. Last winter her husband died from the same sickness and, too, from the bad food the Indian agent brought to us," the *mico* said. "She will do whatever you wish, to help you save Elone and her child."

"Thank you, Emataba. If you will have her bring me

a pot filled with water, I myself will administer the steam."

Emataba spoke to Simanora, and the squaw brought forward one of the larger pots, which Ben took from her and placed on the fire, which by now was burning briskly. After a few minutes, when the water was boiling, he took the pot from the fire and placed it as close to Elone and the child as he could. Then, kneeling down, he held the blanket over the water, lifting it now and then to show the lovely young Sioux girl how the vapor rose. Then he gestured to her to hold her little girl under the blanket, and he maneuvered it so that the steam rose plentifully. The girl coughed at first and cried fretfully for a few moments, but when he paused, her color seemed better and her breathing less arduous.

"Now it's your turn, Elone," he said gently as he beckoned to her. With a shy smile, she leaned forward and let him direct the vapor toward her nostrils. He pantomimed that she must breathe in deeply and continue it for as long as she could, and she nodded comprehension.

Simanora meanwhile had begun to cut and scrape pieces of jerky into another, smaller pot of water which she then placed on the fire. After the jerky had cooked long enough to make a broth, she placed the straining cloth over an empty pot and, protecting her fingers with two strips of doeskin, she carefully tilted the broth-filled pot into the waiting receptacle.

"I see Simanora has brought a small clay cup," the doctor observed. "It should be washed in hot water. That is because perhaps someone who is ill may have drunk from it, and the hot water will kill the sickness in it."

Again Emataba spoke to the squaw, who proceeded to fill the glazed clay cup with water and then put it on the fire until the water began to bubble. Dousing its contents on the ground, she looked inquiringly up at the doctor, who nodded and smiled. Then, removing the straining cloth, Simonora dipped the cup into the clear broth and held it to Elone's lips.

The young Sioux girl drank thirstily, uttering a sigh of pleasure. Then Simonora washed the cup, filled it again, and handed it to Elone who, her left arm around the little girl's shoulders, gently raised the cup to her lips.

"Her child is called Tisinqua, Little Fawn," Emataba whispered.

"The name is lovely. And Elone, what does that mean, Emataba?"

"It means Bright Star, my shaman," the *mico* replied.

"It's a name that suits her well, Emataba. Now, if you will be kind enough to tell Simanora that I would like to have her and her friends—those who have already watched me prepare the steam and the broth—continue to visit all those who suffer and, as often as they can, let them breathe this steam. It will help drive away the fever and all that is in their lungs which makes them cough. Also, let them have the broth at least three times a day. I will visit all of the sick as often as I can. But now, because this child is so young, I will stay here and continue to prepare and administer the steam. This first night may be very critical. Will you tell Elone what I mean to do, and how it will help her and the child?"

The tall leader of the Creeks nodded, then spoke slowly in his halting Kiowa to the young mother. She listened to him raptly, sometimes glancing at the strained but still smiling face of the Quaker doctor, and then she nodded and said something to him in the Kiowa tongue. Emataba turned to Ben and explained, "She understands that you wish to help her and Tisinqua. She will do as you wish, but she asks you to save the child most of all. She is used to hardship—that comes from her life with the Kiowa band. I know of the tribe of Sioux into which she was born: those people are kindly, they are farmers, and they were never warlike except when they defended their land against other tribes who sought to take it. But you, my shaman, must rest. I can see how the journey back to us and the work you do now for all of our sick people has taken the strength from your bones."

"It is my duty, Emataba. And doing it gives me back my strength. That is what I was taught."

The *mico* stared at Ben for a long moment, then smiled and put his right palm against the young Quaker's heart. "It was our good friend Lucien Edmond Bouchard who said once to us, in the presence of our dead shaman Equitaba, that our god and his may be one and the same. Now, with you among us, I begin to believe surely that his words are true. I will pray to Ibofanaga to keep you strong and well." Again his face hardened as he added bitterly, "I would rather die and so would my people than have the soldiers and that Indian agent laugh at us and say that we were sick dogs who would soon perish."

"Once, Emataba," Ben Wilson softly responded, "it was set down in the history of our faith that our God sent his only Son down to earth to live among us. He healed the sick and helped the needy and He forgave the sinners who repented. But there were those who were jealous of him, and they brought him before a judge who sentenced him to be nailed upon a cross along with two thieves."

"It was a terrible way to die," Emataba shook his head.

"Yet this Son of God whom we call Jesus wished to give up His life to save men, so He did not fear that cruel death. And when the soldiers who had nailed him to the cross mocked him and gave him bitter gall in a sponge to drink when He asked for water, and wounded him in the side with a spear, He raised his eyes to the heavens and said, 'Father, forgive them, for they know not what they do.' Thus it is with the soldiers and the Indian agent who treat you with contempt and mock you and do not know how proud and free you once were, Emataba. You must remember this story, for it will give you courage to stand against your oppressors."

"You have taught me much this night, my shaman. May your God and my Ibofanaga look down upon you and see the measure of your goodness. I leave you now to your work—with my thanks, and the thanks of all my people." With this, the *mico* left the wigwam. A few minutes later, Simanora brought in several large cooking pots filled with water and more fuel for the fire, as well as a blanket. She smiled and nodded, then inclined her head toward Ben and made the same sign with her palms that she had shown to her chief. In what little Creek he knew, he thanked her and bade her good night.

For over an hour, Ben Wilson worked tirelessly, despite his almost overwhelming fatigue, to keep the steam going, to light new fires under the other pots filled with water, and to move the blanket up and down until it seemed to him that his arms must drop from sheer weariness. When at last he uttered a sigh of exhaustion and sank back on his heels, he observed that both Elone and the child were breathing much more normally and that the dilation of their eyes had subsided.

Elone turned to look at Tisinqua, who was drowsing in her arms. Her smile was radiant, and she nodded to him and then toward the child.

"Let her sleep now," he said, summoning all that he had learned from Sipanata's teaching of the Creek tongue. "I will stay here so that if you and the child need me, I will be ready."

She sank back against the improvised backrest, uttering a sigh of contentment. Carefully she shifted the sleeping infant against her bosom, smiling tenderly down at it. Ben took one of the blankets, spread it out on the ground, and wrapped himself in it. He lay on his side, watching Elone. A sudden warm joy filled his heart, an inexplicable emotion. It seemed to him at this moment, in the darkness of the wigwam illumined only by the few faint embers of the last fire, that the sensitive, sweet face of Elone almost resembled his remembered image of his beloved wife, Fleurette. As he rolled onto his back and closed his eyes, he whispered Fleurette's name, and then tears stung his eyes and he wept silently. And as sleep claimed him, he felt somehow a greater peace than he had ever known since that tragic hour when Nurse Emma Persky had wakened him, anguished over the news that she had been forced to convey.

CHAPTER NINE

With Christmas scarcely a week away in this eventful year of 1869, Laurette Douglas was happily counting the blessings of her happy marriage and her three young sons, as well as her husband Charles's exceptional achievements as the head of his own department store. Never once had she regretted sharing her lot with him and leaving Alabama for the bustling new metropolis of Chicago. Last night, in the salon of their spacious new house on Dearborn near Division Street, she had listened admiringly as he praised the Windy City's opportunities to their next-door neighbors, Mr. and Mrs. Ezekiel Benderson. Benderson, a plump man with enormous sideburns and twinkling gray-blue eyes, was the city treasurer, and he, too, confirmed Charles's lavish praise.

"Why, Mr. Benderson," Laurette's husband declared, "it's hard to believe we've almost 300,000 people living in Chicago, nearly triple what we had at the beginning of the war and a good deal more than our rivals St. Louis and Cincinnati. Only New York, Boston, and Philadelphia are selling more goods. And you know yourself no other city is packing as much pork and beef or shipping more grain."

"That's quite right, Mr. Douglas," the plump city treasurer beamed. "I estimate our railroads alone will earn us nearly fifty million dollars when we start tabulating this year's profits, and I'm told our exports will hit close to a hundred eighty million."

Charles Douglas uttered a low whistle of surprise. "That much?" Then, turning to his wife, he chuckled, "You see, Laurette dear? We couldn't have found a better place to live in and to bring up our children. All a man has to do is give an honest day's work for an honest day's pay, sell top quality goods at a fair, competitive price, and he'll make out just fine in Chicago. It'll be a great future for our three boys, you watch and see."

"I'm sure it will, Charles dear," Laurette concurred with a knowing smile at gracious, gray-haired Doris Benderson as if to intimate that basically all men, no matter how successful, were always really children at heart.

"Of course," Charles frowned momentarily, "speaking of competition, there's Field, Leiter and Company right next to old Potter Palmer's new Palmer House. I tell you, that man Palmer is really enterprising. He built up three-fourths of a mile along State Street, and he's converted it into a new street of merchants. I don't mind telling you that I'd like to steal some of the Field, Leiter and Company customers."

"Competition is the life blood of any city, Mr. Douglas, that's very true." Ezekiel Benderson sententiously agreed as he tugged at his sideburns, coughed, and then settled himself back more comfortably in the overstuffed armchair. "And we've got fine transportation for our citizens. All three divisions of Chicago are being served by horse-car lines carrying thousands of passengers to the new shopping district. Our river is spanned by no fewer than twenty-seven bridges. Beyond McCormick's reaper works—which cost him all of $600,000, I'm told—we have a thriving industry of breweries around the waterworks. And west, along the north branch of our river, we've got distilleries, canneries, flour mills, and ironworks. On the south branch to the west, there are no fewer than 160 acres of iron and brass foundries and small manufacturing plants."

"Yes, we mustn't leave out the world's biggest stockyards, right here at Thirty-Ninth and Halsted, and all those packing plants surrounding them," Charles Douglas put in. Then, smiling at his wife, he added, "Well, Laurette dear, you can take a little pride in that, because that wonderful mother of yours and Lucien Edmond, on that big Texas ranch, are shipping thousands of head of cattle to the pens in our stockyards."

"Now, Charles, that's something of an exaggeration and you know it," Laurette laughed. "You know my mother doesn't have anything at all to do with the cattle. Ever since she married Henry Belcher, she's had too much to do being a stepmother to his children to pay attention to the herds. Lucien Edmond has done that well enough

90

for several years now. Which reminds me, I want to get a letter off to her before Christmas and tell her all the latest news."

"Give her my very best, Laurette dear," her husband interposed. "And ask her if she's received that box of gifts for her and her family. I had my shipping manager send them out to Corpus Christi a month ago, and he assured me that there was a hauler at that port which would make the trip to Windhaven Range."

"Why, Charles," Laurette gasped, "you never told me about that! Darling, that was ever so thoughtful of you, but good gracious, the hauling costs must be exorbitant!"

"Never you mind, Laurette," Charles grinned, "I've made enough this year not to worry about hauling costs from Corpus Christi." Then, turning back to his guests, he apologetically added, "Excuse us, Mr. and Mrs. Benderson, for holding a little family discussion."

"No interruption at all, my dear fellow," the city treasurer chuckled genially. "It does our hearts good to see how much consideration a man shows his family." He sighed and glanced at his wife. "Alas, Doris and I were never blessed with children, so perhaps that's why we take such pleasure from your three boys."

"Oh yes," Doris Benderson eagerly assented, "and your youngest, that adorable little Howard, is he over his fretfulness from cutting a tooth?"

"I'm happy to say he is," Laurette Douglas laughed softly. She turned to give her husband an ardent look. "My only problem is keeping Charles from spoiling him and showing him more attention than he does Arthur and Kenneth. But all three of them will be ready for the Christmas feast—and don't forget, Mr. and Mrs. Benderson, you're invited."

"That's very kind of you, Mrs. Douglas. Doris and I will be delighted to accept your invitation."

There was really only one thorn in the rose of Laurette Douglas's content with the new house, and it was her discovery that Carrie Melton lived in a house across the street. This opulently formed, chestnut-haired young woman of twenty-five, who had grown up in a Chicago tenement and survived by her wits, had gone to work in Charles's department store some two years ago and had brazenly invited him to take her as his mistress. When he spurned her offer, she stole an expensive bracelet from the jewelry department in order to supplement her declining funds. Charles summarily discharged her, and out of vindictiveness the opportunistic young woman went directly to the Chicago Commercial Bank, which handled the department-store account, and found a position there. Then, by using all her feminine ruses, she won the fatuous interest of sixty-three-year-old Dalton Haines, a prominent official of the bank. She brazenly aroused both his carnal and protective instincts by histrionically narrating how Charles Douglas had tried to seduce her and, failing that, had terminated her employment. This prompted old Dalton Haines to go to Charles's store and deliver him a lecture on his unscrupulousness. Charles merely smiled at this and told the banker that he had made no advances toward the woman; indeed, that he had been forced to dismiss her. Dalton Haines accepted this explanation, unwilling though he was to believe that Carrie could have deceived him.

After Charles Douglas had laughingly related the story of his encounter with the elderly and overly amorous banker, Laurette decided that retribution was certainly in order. She went to a livery stable, purchased a horse whip, paid a visit to the bank, called out Carrie Melton, and proceeded to thrash her until the sobbing young woman was forced to confess both to Laurette and to Dalton Haines that she had lied about Charles Douglas's treatment of her.

This past summer, when Laurette had gone to her favorite butcher shop in the new neighborhood, she had been greeted by that detestable young woman and had learned to her consternation that Carrie Melton was now Mrs. Dalton Haines and, worst of all, a much-too-near neighbor.

Until now, she had kept that knowledge from her husband—not because she was in the least jealous of Carrie Melton Haines or worried that Charles would possibly succumb to such an amoral young trollop, but quite simply because she had determined to pretend that the creature did not exist at all. And she did not trust her own fiery temper—quite in keeping with the color of her hair, indeed—to want to be party to another encounter between Carrie and her faithful, loving husband.

The morning after they had the Bendersons to dinner,

Laurette seated herself at the writing desk in the garishly furnished salon and began to write invitational notes for the Christmas party. The Bendersons already had been verbally invited and had accepted. There were also the Trentons, an amiable couple in their late thirties who lived in the fashionable new township of Hyde Park. This township had been founded by the enterprising twenty-nine-year-old Paul Cornell, a lawyer and businessman who in 1853 had purchased three hundred acres of farmland bounded by Fifty-first and Fifty-fifth Streets, sixty of which he had deeded to the Illinois Central Railroad in return for a promise eventually to establish a commuter station at Fifty-third Street. He had planned the perfect suburb which would be free from the noise and pollution of Chicago's already enormously expanding industry. Only two years ago, Frederick Law Olmsted's firm had been engaged to design the great South Park and Boulevard System, which ran from Fifty-fifth to the Midway.

Edward Trenton and his wife, Mabel, had become good customers at Charles's department store but, only last year, they had decided to build a house in distant Hyde Park. She frowned as she folded the note and slipped it into a monogrammed envelope. She would have to send Polly Behting, their twenty-six-year-old German-born nurse, to take the note to the Trentons' house, so that she would have an answer back in time and know how much she would have to buy at the butcher shop and the greengrocers.

Then there were the Von Emmerichs, a sedate couple in their early fifties whom she and Charles had met socially at the Eastman Skating Park last February. Hans von Emmerich was already making a name for himself as an importer of European fabrics and leather goods and, amusingly enough, he was a great devotee of the new American game of baseball. Laurette looked up from the note she had begun to write and giggled to herself, remembering how the paunchy, jovial German had insisted that it would be healthy for them all to put on skates and to play baseball. Then he had led them to a part of the park where there was actually a wide ice rink on which blue paint marked off the baseball diamond, and Laurette had watched to her amazement the dexterity and skill of the club players who demonstrated this exciting new game for the enthusiastic onlookers.

Another rage in Eastman Park was a demonstration of the great Parisian novelty, the velocipede, a kind of bicycle with two enormous wheels, the front one several feet taller than the rear, which, it was claimed, could attain the dazzling speed of fifteen miles an hour. Hans von Emmerich and his portly but athletic-minded wife, Minna, had taken them to Ellsworth Zouave Hall on the corner of Adams and State Streets to show them Chicago's first velocipede riding school and sales room. The tuition was fifteen dollars, which included the use of the velocipede, but only ten dollars for those who already had their vehicles. Spectators might watch for a mere twenty-five cents, and of course ladies could watch for free.

The Von Emmerichs had moved far north, near the grounds of the Chicago Sharpshooters' Association (which one day would become a part of Lincoln Park). Despite the difference in their ages and hers and Charles's, she felt very comfortable with them. Yes, decidedly they must come to the Christmas party. So poor Polly would have to ride on the horse-drawn car from one end of the city to the other.

When she finished the note to the Von Emmerichs, she rang the little handbell and Polly Behting hurried into the salon. In Laurette's opinion, Polly was an absolute treasure. Reasonably attractive, with flaxen hair, a round, smiling face, and bright blue eyes, she was neat, industrious, and absolutely devoted to the children. She lived with her widower father in the German community on North Avenue, and she was engaged to a self-effacing, hardworking butcher's apprentice a year older than herself, who had told her that he intended to marry only when he had his own shop and estimated that it would take another two years. Consequently, Laurette had no worries over Polly's potential allure for Charles, since Polly was a strict Lutheran like her father and believed that a girl should save herself for her rightful husband. Indeed, if Laurette had not needed a nurse so badly (now that they had moved into this spacious house which required so much of her attention), she would have urged Charles to employ Polly at his store as a model employee who could be depended upon to attend to her work without paying attention to distractions.

"Polly dear, would you mind very much taking these

notes and delivering them? It's so close to Christmas, I'm afraid that if I were to mail them, the Trentons and the Von Emmerichs wouldn't have time to let me know whether they can come to our Christmas party. Here, I'll give you the fare, and do please buy yourself a decent lunch."

"I'll be happy to take them for you, Mrs. Douglas. The twins are playing, and Howard is taking a nap, bless the little lamb!" the young German nurse informed her.

"Thank you so much, Polly. Charles and I are very happy with you, and you may be sure there'll be a little bonus for you on Christmas, just to thank you for the way you've helped with the children," Laurette smilingly assured her.

After the nurse had left the house on her errand, Laurette sighed to herself and then began a long letter to her mother, Maybelle. It would be wonderful if, maybe by next spring, Maybelle could come up to Chicago for a visit. Even though her mother had seen the wonders of New Orleans, Laurette was convinced that the Queen City couldn't hold a candle to Chicago. Of course, Charles—ambitious dreamer that he was—the darling!—had often talked about paying a visit to Windhaven Range and seeing whether some of the larger Texas cities like San Antonio might not be worthwhile locations for the future department stores he one day hoped to open. Laurette smiled again to herself. They were talking about Potter Palmer and Marshall Field as the merchant princes of Chicago; one day the name of Charles Douglas would surely rank with those two, she was sure.

Her pleasant reverie was suddenly interrupted by a loud knock on the front door. She rose quickly and went to open it. Her eyes widened with surprise to see a tall, lugubrious-featured man dressed in a black cutaway coat and trousers, holding his bowler hat in both hands. At first glance, she took him for an undertaker. Finally she managed a quizzical "Yes?"

"I believe you are Mrs. Charles Douglas, ma'am. I trust I haven't disturbed you?"

"Yes, I am Mrs. Charles Douglas and no, you haven't disturbed me."

"Thank you, Mrs. Douglas. Mrs. Haines asked me to convey her invitation to you and your husband and the children to have dinner with her and her husband tomorrow night, if it is convenient. My name is Elmore, Cecil Elmore—I am the Haines's butler, ma'am."

"Oh—ohh!" Laurette's startled gasp turned into one of indignation. The very idea of that presumptuous hussy, daring to invite her and Charles and the children! And once again to meet that fat old fool who had been taken in by that little adventuress, who had gone so far as to marry her and set her up in an elegant house—oh, if that wasn't the last word in gall! Drawing herself up coldly, Laurette primly declared, "You may tell Mrs. Haines that I am sorry that I am unable to accept—now or any other time. I think that is all I have to say. Good morning."

"I understand, Mrs. Douglas. My apologies for having disturbed you. I shall tell my mistress." Cecil Elmore respectfully inclined his head, adjusted the bowler atop it, and marched back across the street as Laurette Douglas slammed the door with more emphasis than was necessary. However, it considerably relieved her outraged feelings. Of all the unmitigated nerve! When Carrie Melton Haines had accosted her in the butcher shop last summer and proposed that they get together some evening, she had turned away without a word. Certainly from that and the fact that since then she had not had even an accidental contact with that presumptuous creature, Laurette believed that the fat old banker's wife would have had brains enough to infer that no future social contact was ever to take place between them. But now, not content with boldly inviting her and Charles and the boys to her house, that audacious hussy had tried to prove her own social superiority to the Douglases by sending a butler—of all outlandish things!—to run her errand for her. Oh, it was simply intolerable!

When the prim butler had returned and informed Carrie Haines of Laurette's rejection of her conciliatory invitation, the young chestnut-haired woman had nonchalantly shrugged and said, "Thanks anyhow, it's not really important." But, once alone in her room and with the doors closed, she had burst into sudden tears. Since her marriage to Dalton Haines, this attractive graduate of a Chicago slum had done a good deal of thinking about her past. From the viewpoint of financial security, she had at last

96

achieved what few girls of her background might ever hope to equal, much less surpass. For years she had scratched and clawed her way up on her own, making the most of her ample physical charms and using her special talent for playing the role of a helpless but alluringly feminine waif. She had had no difficulty in wrapping Dalton Haines around her little finger in this fashion. Her story that Charles had designs upon her had won the sympathy of the old banker. But even when Dalton Haines had been confronted with the fact that she had lied about Charles—during the infamous horse-whipping scene—the banker had been able to overlook her falseness. Though a womanizer, he was capable of true benevolence. He had married her soon afterward.

With the marriage, the proof that a man, however elderly and lecherous, could show unwavering concern for her welfare, Carrie began to lose some of the cynicism and the tendency toward amoral opportunism that had motivated her earlier life. She discovered with a degree of wonder and delight that her infatuated old husband took real pleasure in showering her with pretty clothes and moving her into an elegant house in one of Chicago's finest suburbs. She thereupon made a genuine effort to be a good and reasonably faithful wife to him. Though his conjugal demands upon her were infrequent, because of his growing impotence, she devotedly sought to gratify him and to cajole him into believing that he pleased her sexually more than any other man she had previously known. In catering to him she actually began to grow fond of him and to consider herself extremely fortunate, after all her earlier misadventures, in having become the respectable wife of a prominent executive whose growing fondness for her guaranteed that she would never have to worry about poverty again.

However, it was not only the spur of her newly-acquired conscience which prodded Carrie Haines into seeking a social relationship with the woman she had so mendaciously affronted. A week after her chance meeting with Laurette Douglas in the butcher shop, Dalton Haines startled her with a stammering and embarrassed request she would never have expected. As he lay beside her, stroking her plump thighs and trembling with his excitement at her voluptuous nudity, he suddenly muttered in a voice that

97

was both humble and halting, "Carrie, my—my dearest one—please don't be offended—but what would you think —er, what would you think if we had a baby? I mean, of course, if you want to—"

She sat up, staring at him with her mouth open and her eyes wide with astonishment. His face turned very red, and he gulped at the sight of her sumptuous breasts. "You really mean it, Dalton?" she had gasped.

"Oh my God, Carrie, oh yes, my dearest darling! You see, I—I'm the last of my line, and I never thought I'd marry at my age—and you're so young and beautiful and healthy—I mean, I'd give you anything you want—oh Carrie, if I've offended your modesty, do forgive me, please!"

She was so touched by his naive appeal that she exerted herself to give him more pleasure than he had ever had before with her. A few days later, she had made an appointment with his family doctor and asked for an examination.

Two years before she had gone to work for Charles Douglas, Carrie had taken a transient lover from the same slum where she had been born. He was a thief, and three months after their affair had begun, he was shot to death by a policeman when he failed to obey the latter's summons to halt after being seen climbing out of a window. Carrie had discovered that she was pregnant, and as she had little money, she had to cozen an abortionist into taking his pay in the carnal favors she promised to accord him once he rid her of the unwanted child.

At the end of the examination by Dr. Joshua Porterfield, her husband's private physician, her worst fears were irrevocably confirmed. The abortion had been clumsily done, and although it had not injured her health, it had prevented her from ever conceiving again. She implored Dr. Porterfield to keep her secret, to which he of course agreed. He gently pointed out that she could always adopt children and further added that, in his opinion, old Dalton Haines was certainly at an age where he should resign himself to being childless.

When she returned home from her visit to the doctor, Carrie locked herself in her room and wept. Her old husband's unexpected kindness and thoughtfulness had served to melt the defensive, hard veneer which she had worn like a suit of armor in order to survive in a world of male predators. Perhaps for the first time in her life she thought of someone besides herself.

What made her secret regret even more anguishing through the past summer and pleasant fall was to watch Polly Behting take the twins, Kenneth and Arthur, and little Howard for a walk in the huge perambulator which Charles Douglas had proudly brought home shortly after Howard's birth. Just beyond Division Street, there was a stretch of park, with trees and benches and a small garden, and on many an afternoon, without Laurette's being aware of it, Carrie Haines had left her own house and gone out for a walk which ended near the bench where Polly Behting sat with the three little boys. On several occasions, she had made small talk with the young nurse, praising the children, but she had always been careful never to give Polly Behting her name.

Thus, the more she envied Laurette Douglas for being fertile when she herself could never be, the more she yearned to obliterate that ugly episode in the bank and convince Laurette that she had changed for the better.

That was why, on the morning before Christmas, she dressed in her best and went across the street to the Douglas house. For a moment she stood irresolute and even afraid, and then finally, taking a deep breath, reached for the brass knocker and rapped it smartly. The German nurse, who was preparing to take the little boys for a stroll to the park, since the weather was unusually mild, opened the door. Recognizing Carrie from their several past conversations, she eagerly volunteered to call her mistress. Not without trepidation, Carrie crossed the threshold and stood beside the long Chesterfield couch in the salon not wanting to be audacious enough to seat herself until she had been bidden to do so.

Polly Behting had gone back to the kitchen, where Laurette was getting ready for the elaborate dinner she planned to serve the next day for the Trentons and the Von Emmerichs. When the German nurse told her that there was a young woman who wished to see her, she asked Polly, "Did she give her name?"

"No, Frau Douglas, she didn't say. But I've seen her lots of times in the park when I take the little boys, you know. She's very nice, very pretty—*sehr schön.*"

"Now I wonder who that could be," Laurette murmured to herself, glancing irritatedly back at the counter on which she had laid out the cooking utensils she would need. "Oh well, I'll see her then, Polly. Thank you."

She briskly walked into the living room and stopped dead in her tracks. Her mouth opened, but for once in her life Laurette Douglas was speechless. Then her cheeks turned red with anger and her eyes sparkled.

"Please, Mrs. Douglas," Carrie put out a petitioning hand almost in self-defense, "I—I just had to come. I want—well, it's Christmas tomorrow, so—well, can't we let bygones be bygones and be friends? Yes—I—I know I pulled a shabby trick on your husband—"

"Mrs. Haines," Laurette Douglas said, her eyes narrowed with anger, "I thought I had made myself perfectly clear when that butler of yours came over here with your invitation. I'm glad that you realize what you did to Charles, but I assure you I haven't the slightest intention of forgiving or forgetting. You'll do me a great favor if you don't call here again. It may be unchristian, Mrs. Haines, but I'm afraid we have nothing in common to discuss. I will, however, wish you and your husband a merry Christmas. I think that is all I have to say." With this, she turned her back and strode back to the kitchen, where, to relieve her smoldering anger at Carrie's effrontery, she made a great clatter with the array of pots and pans she had set out before her.

Polly Behting followed her into the kitchen, clasping her hands behind her back and twisting her fingers in obvious distress. "I'm sorry, Frau Douglas—I didn't know—I'm sorry I let her in, but I meant no harm—"

"That's all right, Polly dear. It wasn't your fault at all." Laurette turned, forcing a smile to her quivering lips. "By the way, didn't you say that you'd seen her in the park when you took the boys there?"

"Oh, ja, ja, Frau Douglas! Sometimes, she's given them candy. Stick candy, you know—sometimes Herr Douglas brings the same kind back from his store, you know—"

"Polly, please, and this is an order, under no circumstances are you ever—do you understand me—ever to allow that woman to give anything to the children. If she tries to, you'll tell her they're not allowed to accept it, and

100

if she forces it on them, you'll throw it away. Now do you understand me about this?"

"Please, *ja,* I will do as you say—I am so sorry—" Polly was almost in tears now.

"I'm sorry, dear, I didn't mean to upset you." Laurette patted the nurse's shoulder. "Only she upsets me so. She did a perfectly terrible thing to my husband, and no matter what she does in the future, I shan't ever forget it. Now, why don't you run along while the weather's so nice, and give the boys their outing?"

As soon as Polly had left, Laurette went to the salon and, her lips tight and her forehead furrowed with an angry frown, dashed off a letter to Carrie Haines. It comprised a single paragraph: she hoped it would not be necessary to state again that she would much prefer Mrs. Haines to stay away from her, her husband, and her children.

Then, hurrying after Polly who had just left the house with the perambulator, she called, "Please put this in the letter box, Polly dear. And I don't want you to think that I'm angry with you at all, for I'm not. You'll see tomorrow when you get your Christmas envelope."

CHAPTER TEN

The auspicious new year of 1870 marked the fifth year of peace after the devastating Civil War, yet there were few signs that the North was ready to welcome back its Southern brothers and to bring serenity to the Union once again. The old-time Southern aristocrats who had found themselves disenfranchised and impoverished by the victory of the men in blue were still without political power. Congress, meanwhile, had welcomed its first black members, Senator Hiram R. Revels from Mississippi and Representative J.H. Rainey of South Carolina. Virginia was readmitted to representation in Congress and promptly sent agents to Great Britain and Germany to encourage immigration into the state to counterbalance its large black population.

In Alabama, the new year heralded a bitter gubernatorial race. As in most of the other Southern states, many able and well-qualified leaders of their communities were prohibited from running for public office because they had refused to swallow their pride and apply for Congressional removal of their political disabilities. Even those who had personally opposed secession, despite their Southern birth and education, idealistically refused to curry favor with Reconstruction authorities, avoiding any behavior that would brand them as scalawags. Instead, they adhered to their own belief in the right of qualified Southerners to govern themselves.

The critical heart of the matter lay in the first of the Reconstruction Acts which a vengeful Congress had passed on March 2, 1867, against the objections of President Andrew Jackson. That act became the new framework within which Union sympathizers in Alabama—and in all other Southern states—had to operate. That and subsequent acts gave the franchise to the blacks, but disenfranchised many Unionists who had served in some minor position under

102

the Confederacy, very often a post to which they had been appointed or elected well before 1860. Under the terms of the Fourteenth Amendment, such men were barred from holding office because they had violated their original oath of loyalty to the Federal Constitution. Neither of the Reconstruction Acts nor the Fourteenth Amendment made any provision for the fact that a good many Unionists had held such positions to avoid conscription into the Confederate Army.

In those regions of Alabama where there had never been large plantations and whose owners had been more nearly sharecroppers themselves than slave owners, most of the whites had bitterly opposed Alabama's secession from the Union: now, five years after Appomattox, they thought they were still being unjustly punished for their unswerving devotion to the Union, while the opportunistic carpetbaggers and their own black workers were enjoying the rewards of that Union victory.

Several weeks after his return to Windhaven Plantation with Lucien, Luke Bouchard spent all of one late January afternoon conferring with his foreman Marius Thornton and the other black workers who not only worked with him but also proposed, when the time was right, to sell him back their land at a considerable profit for themselves. Luke's reason for wishing to acquire the land was decidedly not one of greed: it was, rather, part of his fervent vow to restore the red-brick chateau and the land to exactly the condition they had been in before the agony of war. Once again, the dreams of old Lucien Bouchard would be realized and perpetuated, almost a hundred years from the time when that young nobleman had left Normandy to find a new home and a new purpose for living. Moreover, even when Luke acquired the land, he proposed to retain all of his workers on it and pay them top wages as well as guarantee them and their families the peace and security that they had earned after their years of slavery—slavery that he and his grandfather had never endorsed or practiced.

In the year 1802, old Lucien Bouchard had journeyed with his six-year-old son Henry, Luke's father, to Fort St. Stephens and, under the new Land Act of that year, purchased 640 acres for $1280, using a draft to be charged against his account at the old trading post in Mobile. Today that land would be worth from twenty to thirty times that much, for the title was clear and would be respected by even the Federal courts. Luke remembered how much the broad sweep of that rich land fronted by the chateau had meant to his grandfather. Even on that tragic day in 1865, when the chateau was burning and Luke and his stepmother, Sybella, had rallied the family to go to Texas, Luke had envisioned that one day he would come back and restore Windhaven Plantation to its former glory. And beyond that, he meant to improve upon it, not only by offering an equality of respect and opportunity to those who would work the land with him, but also by cultivating other crops besides the eternal cotton which had ruined so much of the land throughout the South.

"With cotton bringing us only a little over our cost, when we figure time expended and wages, Marius," he declared this bright, chilly January afternoon, "we should give a great deal of thought to our enterprises for this spring and summer. A hundred acres devoted to cotton is quite sufficient, and this year we should plant on land which hasn't had cotton for some time, because obviously it will have more strength to nurture a good quality yield."

"I've already made a study of the land, Mr. Bouchard, and I think I know just where we should plant this year," Marius eagerly volunteered.

"That's fine. Buy the best seed you can. You'll see to the new parts for our gin, so we won't have any loss of weight once the cotton has been picked and we're getting ready for shipment."

"I was over to Montgomery yesterday, Mr. Bouchard," his young foreman answered, "and old Mr. Dudley says the parts we ordered from back East ought to be arriving by next week sure. He'll send his manager over to help me install them."

"That's excellent, Marius. Thank you again for your foresight. Now then, we did so well with our truck gardens, fruit, and vegetables, that I think it would be wise to increase that kind of planting this spring. Also, our sale of milk and cream for butter showed a very rewarding profit as against cost of labor and maintenance for our cows. I've arranged to buy a dozen good Hereford cows, and they're to be shipped from St. Louis late next month. That should about triple what we can expect from that part of our agricultural business this year, I'd say."

"Just about, Mr. Bouchard," Hughie Mendicott put in. He sat beside Hannah Atbury, and she glanced over at him now and gave him a fond smile. It was obvious to everyone that the likeable widower would soon be consoling Phineas's widow.

"I'd say we ought to devote about a hundred acres to corn this year. And I'd divide that about half and half between sweet corn for the table and fodder for the cattle—because we can sell a good deal of the fodder to some of our neighbors downriver," Luke Bouchard continued.

"That's a mighty fine idea, Mr. Bouchard, sir," Moses Turner spoke up. "My grandpappy always had a lotta fun raisin' corn. And as far as sweet corn goes, you know yourself there ain't nuttin' tastier than a nice big ear of corn with lots of butter 'n salt—'n maybe some nice sweet yams and a good baked ham, the way Miz Hannah fixes it."

"Go along with you, Moses," Hannah Atbury laughed softly. "If you had your choice, you'd be sitting at the table eating corn and my ham and not doing a lick of work."

"Now, Miz Hannah, you know that ain't true," the arthritic fifty-two-year-old black protested. "I still do a good day's work, even if my old bones get achy now and again."

"You do indeed, Moses," Luke Bouchard smilingly interposed, "and with you and your good wife Mary to encourage you, you'll do even better this year than you've ever done before, mark my words. That reminds me, Mary —what would you think of having a flock of chickens? We might make some good money there. Fried chicken is still one of the most popular dishes on the family table. I know that Mr. Judpath, who runs the butcher shop in Montgomery, was saying to Marius that he can't ever get all the chickens he'd like to have for sale. They'll bring a fair price, plus which we'll have plenty of chicken for all of our own dinners."

"I think it's a wonderful idea, Mr. Bouchard," Mary Turner spoke up. "But you know I'm sort of looking forward to working with those new cows you said you were bringing up here. Now maybe I wouldn't have the time for the chickens, not the way I ought to, to make real money for us all."

"I'd like to handle those, Mr. Bouchard, if you've no objection," sprightly Katie Munroe offered. "Besides which, my Tom and Elsie, they're old enough to take a little responsibility for working on the land. Among the three of us, I'll bet we could keep that Mr. Judpath supplied with all the chickens he could sell every week, yessir!"

Everyone laughed at her energetic declaration, and Luke nodded agreement. "Well then, Katie, Marius will put a new page for the chickens into our ledger, and your name will be at the very top. Every week he'll enter the sales and the cost figures of the chickens, so you'll have a pretty good idea just how well you're doing. Well now, that's a very good prospect for the year ahead. And you may be sure that I'll be out there with all of you doing my own full share of work. That's the way my grandfather did, and that's the way I like it."

"I have to say, Mr. Bouchard," Buford Phelps smilingly spoke up, "I never thought the day would come when I'd see a white plantation owner getting along with us niggers just as if he was one of us. It does my heart good, Mr. Bouchard, and I'm mightly glad you gave me the chance when I came around here last year checking up on you. And that's a fact!" He looked around almost defiantly at the others, as if daring them to challenge him.

"I'm glad you feel that way, Buford. The way I feel, all of us are in this together, and if we work together as a team, we can help one another and individually improve our lot. It's true—and I've always been frank with you about it—that I hope one day I'll be able to buy your acreage back from you, but that's because then Windhaven Plantation will be as it was when my grandfather founded it. It won't change anything at all, I'll assure you again. You'll all live on here as part of my family—because that's what you are and that's how I regard you." He drew a deep breath and turned his face in the direction of the towering red bluff. "Many Northerners have condemned the South and said that it was our lack of manufacturing and our obsession with cotton and tobacco which made us weak and dependent upon human slavery. Well, I've always felt that if my grandfather's beliefs in equality of opportunity for all those who want to work hard for their

106

living could have been practiced in every Southern state, there might never have been a war at all. I look upon Windhaven Plantation as a kind of model community in which we pool our efforts not only for the greater good of all of us, but for that of our neighbors as well. Now that's enough talk. Hannah, I think it's time for your little surprise."

As everyone turned to look at the comely, mature widow, Luke chuckled and added, "She's made some of her famous blackberry cobbler and pots of fresh coffee with good thick cream. I think after all this talk refreshments will be very welcome."

Soon after Christmas, Andy Haskins hesitantly approached Lucien Edmond Bouchard to ask a favor. The twenty-seven-year-old Tennesseean, who had lost his right arm at Chickamauga, had proved himself to be an invaluable aide to Luke's oldest son on Windhaven Range. Luke himself had engaged Andy—along with his friend Joe Duvray—in New Orleans almost four years before, when preparing for the trek to Taxas. Both young men had since shown unswerving loyalty and had helped defend the Bouchards against bandit and bushwhacker attacks. Despite his handicap, Andy could throw a knife or fire a six-shooter or carbine with deadly effect, when the safety of his friends and employers was endangered.

Today Andy Haskins stood nervously with his sombrero in hand, staring down at his feet as he spoke to Lucien Edmond. "Mr. Bouchard, I was wondering if you'd mind if I took a furlough—you know, sort of like the kind we Johnny Rebs got after a real hard battle."

"A furlough? I don't see why not, Andy," Lucien Edmond replied. "What did you have in mind?"

"To tell the truth, Mr. Bouchard," Andy Haskins laughed nervously and scuffed up the dirt with the toe of one booted foot, "I guess I'm just plumb restless these days." Then he added hurriedly, "Of course, you'll probably be needing me for the next drive in the spring, but I'm pretty certain I could be back by then."

"Don't fret so, Andy," Lucien Edmond gripped Andy's shoulder. "We're in very good shape with the men. Ramón has gone to Nuevo Laredo with Pablo Casares to round up about a dozen more top hands. We'll be needing more vaqueros to drive the herd, now that we're getting all this new stock from the cross-breeding with the Herefords and our own Texas longhorns. And the Brahma bulls we bought have studded a number of our cows, so by early summer we'll have fine calves to put us in good shape for next year. That'll really be prime stock, and nobody will have to worry about Texas fever from our herds when that time comes. No, Andy, I can't think of a single reason why you shouldn't have your furlough. You've certainly earned it. But where do you plan to go—not that it's any of my business."

"It sounds sort of funny, Mr. Bouchard, and I wouldn't rightly mind if you told me I was plumb loco. Neither Joe nor me's got any kinfolk left back home, but I just had a hankering to go back to Tennessee and see what was happening. Then I thought maybe I'd mosey over to Alabama and pay my respects to your father and the family out there."

"Now that's a wonderful idea, Andy!" Lucien Edmond enthusiastically averred. "I'd like you to tell him about the Brahmas and how well they're doing for us. And tell him that Pablo and Kate are the happiest couple I've ever seen —and that Kate's going to have a baby sometime this summer."

"I'd be glad to give them all the news, Mr. Bouchard, that's a fact."

"I'm sure my wife and my sister, Mara, will have more tidbits of news they'd like to pass along to my father. I'd be grateful if you'd have a chat with them before you leave. And don't forget to talk to Mrs. Forsden—she'll certainly want to send some word back to my father. You know, she always looked at him as if he'd been her own son, not a step-son. And he's always felt the same way about her. She's a fine woman."

"Yes, sir, I know." Andy Haskins kicked at an imaginary pebble on the ground. "You know, Mr. Bouchard, your daddy was a mite worried about her. Said she looked a mite peaked."

"I know," Lucien Edmond nodded. "But Celia and Maybelle are both looking after her, and they're sort of having a contest in the kitchen these days to see who can make the tastiest dishes to suit her fancy. You can tell Father

108

they're fattening her up and that everybody here is looking after her with extra-loving care."

"That I do believe, Mr. Bouchard. Well then, sir, I'll tell you what. I'll just draw my wages tomorrow that you've saved up for me—unless it's inconvenient for you, not having all that cash—"

"I can give you some gold, Andy, and the rest can be in a draft drawn on the Brunton and Barntry Bank in New Orleans. You'll have to go to New Orleans on your way back to Tennessee and Windhaven Plantation, that's for certain." He grinned. "I'd recommend at least a week in the Queen City, treating yourself to some of those great dinners at the best restaurants and maybe even finding yourself a pretty girl. Speaking of restaurants, I am reminded of what father told me about old Felix Brissart's place on Eglantine Street. One of the lovely girls whom my stepmother, Laure, knew in New Orleans went to work for Brissart and married him, and father wrote after he got back to Windhaven Plantation that he'd had dinner there and that it was the equal of any restaurant in New Orleans. You make a point of having yourself a good meal with wine there at my expense. Matter of fact, Andy, you've a little bonus coming anyway, and this seems like the ideal time to tell you about it. There'll be an extra hundred dollars in the money you can draw from me tomorrow."

"That's mighty kind of you, Mr. Bouchard," the lanky Tennesseean flushed hotly.

"Take one of the best geldings. And it wouldn't do any harm to have a Spencer carbine along. By the way, you might visit some of the gunsmiths in New Orleans and see if there are any efficient new rifles or carbines on the market. Yes, that's a capital idea! When you come back through New Orleans on your return to the ranch, you can stop over there and wire me about anything you've found. Then I can always wire Jason Barntry at the bank and have him give you what money you'll need to buy a supply of guns and ammunition to go with them."

"I certainly will do that for you, Mr. Bouchard, and thanks again for the bonus." Now it was Andy Haskins's turn to grin, almost sheepishly. "But I don't reckon I'll be spending much time in New Orleans looking for a girl.

The truth is, Mr. Bouchard, I've always been skittish as a wild mustang around girls."

"Oh, I think you'd make a fine husband for any nice girl, Andy. One of these days I'd like to see you with a wife and children settling down here. Then you could really forget about the war and the losses all of us had in it. A man needs roots, Andy. Father's idea to move to Texas after the Yankees burned his grandfather's house was just about the best thing that ever happened to this family. But you can't have roots without a wife and children, Andy. Just think about it."

"I'll do that, Mr. Bouchard. Only I'd say right off that with all the fellows that have got both their arms, a girl would have to be a mite teched to pick a one-armed fellow like me."

"Now that's foolish, Andy!" Lucien Edmond countered. "You've got strength and courage and brains, and you're a lot more resourceful with your one arm than most men are with both of theirs. Besides, the sort of girl who'd look askance at you wouldn't make a good wife anyway. No, you mark my words, Andy, the right girl is out there somewhere waiting for you. And I shouldn't be surprised if you found her by the time you came back to us."

CHAPTER ELEVEN

On the last day of January of this new year, a cold, bleak day on which the clouds seemed driven across the dull gray sky by an angry wind, Luke Bouchard was sitting at his escritoire writing a letter to Sybella Forsden, with enclosures for Lucien Edmond, Maxine, and Mara. Marius Thornton would be going upriver to Montgomery tomorrow and would post the letters for him. Also, at Luke's request, Marius would visit Jedidiah Danforth, who handled the legal affairs of Windhaven Plantation, to obtain a survey of the properties in the district which were being sold for taxes.

Luke had learned that many of the remaining white landowners, impoverished by the war, hampered by their inability to pay for workers on their fields, had either abandoned their land and gone off West, or else were in danger of losing their property because they could not meet the exorbitant taxes levied upon it.

Back in October, Laure had kept a copy of the Montgomery *Advertiser* which published a list of property owners who were in arrears. When Luke returned from Texas, she called this list to his attention. One of the items particularly caught his eye: the four hundred acres which had once been owned by Edward Williamson, the father of Luke's first wife, Lucy, had been divided up into eight sections of fifty acres each and sold at a nominal sum to freed blacks. But the newspaper declared that six of these had already given up their holdings and decided to find work at higher wages in the Mobile area. Luke was anxious to know who would purchase the land they had abandoned. He was certain that it would be awarded to some prosperous carpetbagger, and for a time he dabbled with the notion of buying it for himself and expanding Windhaven Plantation.

However, he decided against taking such a step. The first and most logical act—and it was not even time for that—would be to buy back the land his black factory-workers now legally owned, in accordance with the plan he had already explained to them and which they had eagerly accepted. Even if he were to try to buy the former Williamson acreage through a factor of his own, such as perhaps Marius Thornton, he would be certain to encounter grave difficulties. Carpetbaggers were everywhere in the state. They had prevailed in Republican Party politics for some years and were now also to be found in the Democratic Party, the traditional stronghold of native Southerners before the war. One such Democrat, Hiram Pulford from New Jersey, had already openly declared at a public meeting in Montgomery that he personally would see to it that no former "tyrannical Confederate slave owner and land-oppressor will ever get away with amassing large acreage and hope to go back to the benighted days of cruel slavery so long as I am county assessor." And in spite of the fact that he himself had taken the oath of amnesty and never furnished arms to the Confederacy or taken any belligerent action against the Union, Luke Bouchard understood only too well the intolerant and vindictive attitude which carpetbagger officials took toward any long-time Southerner, no matter what the latter's background was.

Pensively, he sealed the envelopes and placed them on the edge of the escritoire, as his mind went back to his first visit to the old Williamson plantation. He remembered how his father Henry had disparagingly urged him to come along to meet Williamson's overseer Amos Greer so that he could pick up some pointers on how to handle land. This had been after Sybella had urged his father to appoint Luke as overseer of Windhaven Plantation. How well he remembered what had precipitated valiant Sybella's decision to force his father into giving him this opportunity. Henry had bought young Celia as a slave from Pierre Lourat in New Orleans and brought her home secretively to the red-brick chateau with the intention of making her his concubine. Mark, then only fifteen, had crept across the hall from his own bedroom and possessed Celia before Henry Bouchard could come to her. In the ensuing row, following Henry's entry into the room to discover his own

112

son in bed with the lovely mulatto girl, Mark had knocked his father down the stairs and broken his leg. Then it was that Sybella, taking charge of her dissolute husband, had nursed him and lectured him until he had grudgingly agreed to appoint Luke as overseer.

There had been other small landowners near the Williamson estate in those early days, a generation before the Civil War. None of these was left. That was why he was eager to see Jedidiah Danforth's survey, because it would be up to date and correct some of the errors the *Advertiser*'s printed list had shown. If memory served him right, the fifty acres near Lowndesboro which had once been owned by James Cavendish had been acquired last year by an elderly Virginian whose wife had died during the war and who had come to Alabama with his widowed daughter. Marius Thornton had ridden over to their humble frame house to welcome them to the community and to offer any help his employer could offer.

Luke frowned and pressed the bridge of his nose with right thumb and forefinger, trying to remember what Marius had told him about the newcomers. He'd been so absorbed with avenging Laure's degradation and seeking his kidnapped son that he hadn't had any time to think about them until now. Let's see—their name was Bambach, yes, that was it. Horatio Bambach and his daughter Jessica. Now he remembered what Marius had told him about them. Horatio Bambach had mentioned to his foreman that Jessica had been a schoolteacher in a rural Virginia school near Roanoke. She had married a second cousin, also named Bambach, who was killed by a sniper at Gettysburg. She went back to live with her parents. Then Horatio Bambach's wife died of pneumonia in the last year of the war, and rioting free blacks burned their house, forcing father and daughter to flee for their lives.

Evidently, Luke thought to himself, the old man must have had some hard money hidden away, or he could never have been able to come to Alabama and buy fifty acres of good land along the river. And Marius had said that they had two young blacks working for them at what he considered to be rather high wages. There were a few acres planted in cotton and the rest was produce and fruit. Still, two workers wouldn't be enough to take care of that much land, and Marius had added that he thought

113

old Horatio Bambach was just about blind from the way he stared past him and didn't seem to notice when he moved or put his hand out to be shaken. The old man would certainly be in difficult straits this year, as would everyone ever connected with the Confederacy: like as not that malicious county assessor would levy an atrociously extortionate tax on those fifty acres this spring.

Abruptly, Luke rose from the escritoire and strode to the window. Twilight was coming, but it had been so gloomy all day long that there was hardly much difference. How dreary life must be for old Horatio Bambach and his widowed daughter, friendless and trying to begin life all over again. Perhaps it would do no harm to pay them a visit next week and have them to dinner here at the chateau. Then perhaps he could learn the old man's true economic situation and offer such assistance as would not be looked upon as offensive charity. Once his father, Henry Bouchard, had taken over that very land by guileful dealing; perhaps, if Luke could aid the Bambachs, the land could be turned into a profitable livelihood for that old man and his daughter.

As he walked out of the study, intending to visit Laure, who by now would have awakened from her nap, he heard the loud rap of the knocker on the front door of the chateau and hurried to open it. Three men stood there, elegantly dressed, in stovepipe hats and overcoats and shawls round their necks to protect them from the January wind. Irrelevantly, he noted that the shawls resembled the famous one which martyred Abraham Lincoln had been so fond of wearing. One of the men he recognized, William Blount, who owned an animal feed store in Montgomery.

"Mr. Luke Bouchard?" William Blount, a portly man in his mid-fifties, respectfully inquired.

"I plead guilty, Mr. Blount. This is an unexpected pleasure. How may I be of service to you and your companions? Do come in. I think, in view of the temperature, you might all enjoy a glass of brandy."

"That's mightly hospitable, Mr. Bouchard, and I'll just take you up on it. Come on in, Ebenezer, and you, Clarence."

"Step into the salon, gentlemen," Luke Bouchard invited. "The brandy is on the sideboard, also some Irish

114

whisky and Madeira. I'll do the honors if you'll state your preference."

"Brandy's fine with me, Mr. Bouchard," Ebenezer Tolman, a tall, bony-faced man of about the same age as William Blount, spoke up, and the third, Clarence Hartung, not quite fifty, short, bespectacled, and nearly bald, gestured that he would have the same.

Luke motioned the three men to the comfortable upholstered couch as he poured out three glasses of brandy and handed them to his guests.

"Here's to your health, and thanks for your hospitality, Mr. Bouchard," William Blount lifted his glass and then took a generous swig. "I want you to meet my friends Ebenezer Tolman and Clarence Hartung. Ebenezer's an undertaker and Clarence is an officer in the Montgomery Commercial Bank and Trust."

"I'm pleased to meet you gentlemen." Luke Bouchard gave them a respectful bow.

"I'll get right to the point, Mr. Bouchard." William Blount leaned forward from his seat on the couch, fixing his host with an intense stare. "We're Republicans, Mr. Bouchard, all three of us, diehard Republicans. I think you know what that means in this state."

"I'm afraid I do, Mr. Blount. You've a tough row to hoe."

"And it's going to be a great deal tougher this year, Mr. Bouchard, because we've got an election this fall and we're trying to re-elect Governor Smith. We're going to have a lot of trouble with the Ku Klux Klan, of course. And the Democrats—you know they're mostly carpetbaggers these days—are going to be egging the Klan on to do their worst. It's amazing, isn't it, how the Klan and the carpetbaggers join forces when there's mischief to be done. It'll take a brave man to come out openly on the Republican ticket."

"Yes, I'm sure it will. But I'm not quite sure why you're telling me all this, Mr. Blount."

"Again I'll be direct with you, sir. We're hoping that you might be willing to run for the state legislature for Montgomery County this fall. There's a seat open, and a black man is going to run as the Democratic candidate. That's kind of unusual, but he's backed by a couple of

115

wealthy Democrats out of Massachusetts, and I don't mind telling you that we've found out that if he gets in, he's going to see that his backers get hold of some good rich Alabama land without paying anything near what it's worth."

"I see." Luke seated himself in a chair opposite the couch, his face taut with concentration. "I'm flattered and honored, but I must ask you why you think that I could possibly defeat him, knowing as you do what powerful backing your opposition seems to have?"

"I'll tell you why, Mr. Bouchard," Ebenezer Tolman spoke up. "First of all, we're pretty sure that Montgomery County is going to go Republican, and it's going to re-elect Governor William H. Smith. We think we can muster enough Republican votes for a really strong candidate to beat this black man—don't get me wrong, Mr. Bouchard, I'm not a racist and I don't hold that because a man's black he doesn't have brains enough to run for office, as some of our old-time friends and neighbors have always claimed. What I do say is that you're acceptable to all sides because you're known to be an honest and fair man. You've taken the oath of amnesty; you never indulged in politics before the war; yet you never gave any comfort to the Union. That means you're a true-blue Southerner at heart, but at the same time you can't be challenged as an unacceptable candidate under those damned Reconstruction Acts."

"That's right, Mr. Bouchard," Clarence Hartung chimed in with an energetic nod, "they couldn't discredit you no matter how hard they tried, I'd stake my political reputation on it."

"But you see, Mr. Bouchard," William Blount earnestly interposed, "the real danger is that this damned carpetbagger senator we've got, George Spencer, who got elected two years ago for a four-year term and is a Republican too, by God, is really trying to manipulate the selection and the federal patronage of our state so he can get himself re-elected in 1872."

"You think he can do that?" Luke wonderingly asked.

"I'm sure of it, Mr. Bouchard. Now, you see, Spencer's Republican colleague is up for re-election this year, and that's Senator Willard Warner. Now Spencer figures that if Democrats can replace both Smith as governor and

116

Warner as Senator, then he himself, as a man who's very close to President Grant, would be the only one who would have a say-so about doling out federal patronage in Alabama. Then, you see, Spencer would be able to use the men for whom he got his appointments and the money they controlled to eliminate any Democratic competition in 1872."

"It's a dastardly plan, Mr. Bouchard, and we loyal Republicans have to do something about it," Ebenezer Tolman indignantly interposed. "You see what he's trying to do, Mr. Bouchard. Even though he's a Republican, Spencer wants to weaken Governor Smith so that he can have a Democratic governor and a Democratic legislature that will surely choose a Democratic United States Senator. And here he is, appearing in the Senate as one of us, pulling strings like that! A man like that isn't loyal either to his party or his colleagues, by God!"

"I suppose you've heard, too, Mr. Bouchard, that Spencer, just like a lot of the other carpetbaggers, wants to organize a militia and keep federal troops here in Alabama. He'd like to get more troops from Washington to aid his re-election two years from now. One of my friends in Washington just wrote me that he's heard Senator Spencer say that Republicans are holding Alabama by a slender thread because we're all hampered here by weak-kneed officials and that our entire state is in a deplorable condition politically and socially. That, sir, is dastardly and in my book, it's traitorous, as well!" Clarence Hartung declared.

Luke Bouchard clasped his hands behind his back and strode to the window, looking out toward the river. After a long moment, he replied, "I must tell you in advance, gentlemen, that I know nothing of politics—that is, not the administration of the legislature, surely. I have my beliefs, but I'm afraid they're idealistic. I, as much as you, deplore the dreadful manipulation by blacks and white newcomers—whom you call carpetbaggers—to divide us internally and to weaken us so that they can take land and power and money. That, to me, is part of the wrongful punishment which certain factions in the North want to continue permanently, so as to force us to our knees."

"That sort of talk, sir, will gain you many good Republican votes," William Blount declared.

"I don't say I couldn't spare the time if—though I don't think it would happen—I should be elected to serve in the state legislature, gentlemen. What concerns me is that I'd be such a novice, and I know nothing of political bargaining. Very often politicians have to make deals at the cost of the constituents they've been elected to serve."

"But it is precisely because we need at least one honest man in our legislature, sir, that we're urging you to run," said Clarence Hartung, rising from the couch. "Say at least that you'll consider our prosposal, Mr. Bouchard."

"I will indeed, gentlemen. It's most flattering that you should think of me and seek me out. I'd like to study the matter for a time, if you'll allow me that. Also, I'd like to discuss with you exactly what your platform would be and what your aims are in the legislature. If I represent you, understand that I will not be beholden to you and expect to grant you favors in return for your support. I may be idealistic, but my view is that a public official is the servant of the people. Yes, I am a Republican, if I may be said to have any politics at all, and by that I mean I wish to adhere to the principles of our late President Lincoln. He gave his life for the welfare of the nation, and he dreamed that the North and the South would be reunited in harmony after the war. That is what I hope for, too. Here on my plantation, all of us are working side by side, white and black, to produce for the community as well as for ourselves."

"We know something of the Bouchard history, sir," William Blount spoke up as he walked toward the sideboard "May I replenish my glass—"

"By all means, and you, Mr. Tolman and Mr. Hartung, please don't stand on ceremony," Luke said.

"Thank you, Mr. Bouchard." William Blount poured generously from the decanter and lifted his glass toward Luke Bouchard. "Let me drink a toast, then, to our new Republican candidate for the state legislature from Montgomery County."

"Now, now, Mr. Blount," Luke protested, "That's somewhat premature. I haven't accepted yet. But I promise you I'll think about it very seriously. If I can be of service to the people of this county, that would please me greatly."

"As I said, Mr. Bouchard, we know something about your family history. The name of Lucien Bouchard of

Windhaven Plantation is remembered by a lot of folks around here who haven't forgotten about honor and decency and hard work and getting along with one's neighbors."

"Thank you. That's a compliment I deeply appreciate," Luke replied.

"Tell you what, Mr. Bouchard," Clarence Hartung offered, "I know we didn't give you fair warning and didn't send you a letter to ask for an appointment. We made a stop in Lowndesboro and just decided we'd take a chance and come see you. Perhaps we might come back next week and sit down with you, at your time and convenience, sir, to tell you about the Republican party and the program on which we'd like to run you against the Democratic candidate."

"I'd welcome that, Mr. Hartung. I plan to be in Montgomery the week after next. Shall we meet then? You have my word, of course, that I'll give the matter my most serious consideration in the meantime."

Luke agreed with his visitors that he would meet them on the tenth of February. Shaking hands, he escorted them to the door and then went back to tell Laure, not without a wry smile, of this startling suggestion which might well make a further alteration in his new life.

CHAPTER TWELVE

On February 9th, Dalbert Sattersfield and Mitzi Vourlay boarded the *Alabama Belle* from Windhaven dock to go to Mobile. They would be married by a Catholic priest there and then spend a two-week honeymoon in New Orleans. Petite Mitzi was radiant and starry-eyed as she clung to her fiance's arm and stood with him at the rail to wave goodbye to Luke and Laure and to Marius and the other black workers who had come out to see the couple off.

"Well, darling," Laure said as she took Luke's arm and turned back toward the chateau, "now we really have to think about finding another nurse for Lucien and Paul. Unless I very much miss my guess, Mr. Sattersfield and she will want to start a family of their own. I know that because last night she burst out with the remark that she did so hope her husband liked children because she wanted a large family."

"I'm very happy for them both, Laure darling. As for the nurse, I'm going up to Montgomery tomorrow to talk with William Blount about this political race he and his two friends want me to enter, and I'll stop over at the *Advertiser* office to look over their situations wanted list. It's just possible I might be able to find a suitable young woman."

"That's a wonderful idea, Luke. Only," Laure turned to make a teasing face at him, "I'd much prefer it if you'd choose someone not quite so attractive as our adorable Mitzi. Not that I've any reason to be jealous of you, mind. But now that I'm a sedately married woman with two children and expecting a third, I'd like to be sure that my husband won't be offered any unexpected temptations."

"You'll never have to worry about that, I assure you, Laure dearest." He took her by the shoulders and kissed her on the mouth.

"Not when you answer me like that, my dear one," Laure tenderly whispered as, their fingers entwined, they walked back into the red-brick chateau.

Andy Haskins had ridden his gelding to Corpus Christi, boarded the *William Wallace,* and soon struck up a cordial friendship with Captain Jamie McMurtrie. The latter remembered the one-armed Tennessean from that time, nearly four years ago, when he and Joe Duvray had accompanied the Bouchards on their journey to Texas. Learning that Andy intended to stop over at New Orleans, make his way to his birthplace in southwestern Tennessee, and then go on to meet Luke Bouchard at Windhaven Plantation, Captain McMurtrie urged him to convey his best wishes to Luke and his family. He insisted that Andy share supper with him in his cabin and regaled him with the very finest Scotch whisky, as well as numerous anecdotes about his own adventurous life as a packetboat captain.

In New Orleans, Andy Haskins went to the Brunton and Barntry Bank and was taken to lunch by Jason Barntry. He wisely decided to bank most of the draft which Lucien Edmond had given him as the balance of his wages. He stayed a week, enjoying the cuisine of old Felix Brissart's restaurant on Eglantine Street, and observed that the lovely Aurelia Dubois was now married to the proprietor, yet continued to sing the songs of the Auvergne for the delighted customers.

Mindful of Lucien Edmond's suggestion, he visited a gunsmith on Rampart Street, where he was shown the remarkable center-fire cartridge with a solid, die-drawn case and integral primer anvil devised by Colonel Hiram Berdan, the former commander of the famous Civil War Sharpshooter Regiment. "You see, Mr. Haskins," the gunsmith explained, "three years ago, after Colonel Berdan had invented this cartridge, a British officer by the name of Edward Mounier Boxer also invented a center-fire cartridge, but one that uses a separate primer with a self-contained anvil. Now, the stronger, solid-head Berdan case can take heavier charges than rimfire cases, but the Boxer cases are a lot easier to reprime when you are hand loading. And I think that's a feature your outfit could use on the frontier where cartridges are at a premium and often hard to find."

"I'll tell you what, Mr. Dennery. I'm going to get in touch with my boss back in Texas, and he'll like as not send me back an order payable through the Brunton bank here for what I'll need. So when I come back, maybe next month, I'd really appreciate it if you'd have put away a good supply of those cartridges and those English cases for reloading them."

"I'll be glad to do that, Mr. Haskins."

"Is there anything new in rifles or pistols, Mr. Dennery?"

"Well, sir, as it happens, a real smart gunsmith by the name of Oliver Winchester, who took over the New Haven Arms Company about three years ago, has brought out a lever-action rifle. He calls it the 44 brass-framed M1866 rifle, and it's a dandy."

"It certainly is, Mr. Dennery," Andy Haskins said, after carefully examining the rifle which the gunsmith handed him. "I think we could probably use at least a dozen of those Winchesters."

"And we've got some excellent Colt cartridge revolvers with bored-through cylinders. They're certainly safer than the six-shooters a lot of cowboys our your way are using."

"Don't I know it," Andy ruefully admitted. "Some of those guns will burst right in a man's hand and they'll misfire more often than not. I think my boss would like about a dozen of those Colts and plenty of cartridges for them. Say now!" He clasped his hand to his forehead and grimaced. "I plumb forgot about that durned telegraph strike. Wait a minute—I'll go back to the bank and see the manager there. He knows my boss real well—maybe he'll take it on his own authority to advance you the money, Mr. Dennery. I'll be back later this afternoon."

"No hurry, Mr. Haskins. A pleasure to serve a customer like you, who knows guns. I'll just take the liberty of getting the order ready, and then when you've made the financial arrangements, I'll store it for you, and you can pick it up whenever you've a mind to."

"Thanks, Mr. Dennery, I appreciate it a lot. I'll see you later this afternoon," Andy Haskins promised.

He went back to the bank and, much to his gratification, Jason Barntry agreed to advance two thousand dollars for the purchase of the weapons and ammunition. "I don't

122

know that Mr. Bouchard had a hunch there might be a telegraph strike," he told Andy, "but in that letter you brought me from him, he told me that if you found any useful supplies for the ranch, I was to give you this sum without further authorization. I'll draw up a draft payable to this Mr. Dennery."

"It's really a good buy, Mr. Barntry," Andy avowed, "and Dennery's prices are fair as anything you'll find in this part of the country, to my way of thinking. Well, then, I'll take the draft back to him, and then when I get back from visiting Mr. Luke Bouchard, I'll stop over here and cart everything back to the ranch. Thanks a lot, Mr. Barntry."

Andy Haskins was heartened by having carried out this necessary errand, the more so since his gratitude for Lucien Edmond's granting him not only a furlough but also a bonus had intensified his wish to serve his employer, even while on a vacation. He took his gelding to the wharf and there embarked on the ferry for Mobile, and then, after having bought what food supplies he believed he would need, set out for Tennessee.

His homecoming was not particularly happy. The few long-time friends and neighbors whom he and his father had known before the war had almost all died or moved from the little town. And as he rode through the state, he grimly observed not only the ravages of the war but also the oppression of the carpetbagger regime. From what he gathered from conversations with storekeepers and friendly passers-by on his journey, he did not think that his good friend Joe Duvray would care to go back to Georgia to see what had happened to his own birthplace.

He rode back across the border into Alabama and southward to Anniston, where he boarded a riverboat which would take him down to Lowndesboro. He told himself that he hoped he would find a happier scene when he reached Windhaven Plantation. For sure, seeing Luke Bouchard again would cheer him up considerably.

Luke Bouchard scowled as he studied the survey which Jedidiah Danforth had sent him. The lawyer, with the meticulous care befitting his dignified sixty-two years, had not only provided a list of delinquent properties in the

123

county, but also had taken pains to add lengthy parenthetical comments on the background and circumstances of the present owners.

There could be no doubt—judging from Danforth's detailed notes on the Bambach property—that the old widower was certain to lose the fifty acres that had once been the property of Luke's own father, Henry. The taxes posted against that acreage were exorbitant, and Luke Bouchard had more than a suspicion that Assessor Hiram Pulford had levied them out of spite to punish Horatio Bambach for having been loyal to the Confederate cause. If these taxes were not paid before the first of June, the fifty acres would be turned over for public auction—and doubtless some influential carpetbagger and friend of the assessor would acquire them for nothing more than the taxes.

The rich potential yield of those acres would, if properly cultivated by sufficient labor, provide a livelihood for the old man and his widowed daughter, Luke was certain. But he himself could hardly go before the assessor and offer to buy Bambach's holdings. He was well aware that, in spite of his own record and the evidence of his having taken the oath of amnesty and being cleared of all military collaboration with the Confederacy, he would be summarily denied the right to buy that land by the vindictive county official. What he had first thought of doing, to be sure, was paying the taxes and acquiring the land, then deeding it back over to Bambach and his daughter, and perhaps lending them two of his workers to devote part of their time to the Bambach crops when they could spare it from their own work on Windhaven Plantation.

No, the only possibility was to obtain a factor who could represent him and yet not arouse the assessor's suspicions as to any kind of collusion, however benevolent it was intended to be. John Brunton had cleverly managed to regain Windhaven Plantation by engaging Phineas Atbury to bid for it: Phineas had been black and therefore preferred as a buyer by Unionist officials. And Phineas had been unconnected with Luke's household at the time, or so it had appeared. If Luke attempted to empower Moses Turner, Hughie Mendicott, Dan Munroe, or even Marius Thornton to bid for the Bambach property, the assessor would be sure to smell a rat, knowing that all four of these men were associated with him and Windhaven Plantation.

There had to be some way to keep that worthy old man and his daughter from being ousted from their land, after the suffering and privations they had known and the sacrifices they had made during the war. Marius had told him that, during a casual conversation with the old man, the latter had declared that back in Roanoke he had had a dozen slaves and had manumitted them well before the Emancipation Proclamation. That fact had struck a sympathetic chord in Luke's mind, for that was exactly what he and his beloved grandfather had done years ago.

He paced the floor of his study, pondering what could be done to help Horatio Bambach and his daughter, Jessica. There would have to be a factor acceptable to that bigoted assessor, one whose own association with the Bouchards could not be suspected. But who could that be? Even granting that the assessor would accept bids from Luke's own men, he would be sure to ask where they had got so much money after having purchased their own land and paid their taxes. Luke Bouchard had carefully seen to it that when each tax bill came due to his tenant owners (as he liked to call them), he had arranged to give them the money out of his own account and instructed them to go to Montgomery to pay the bill in person at the assessor's office. Thus far, there had been no difficulties.

Luke abruptly started as he heard a knock on the door of his study and called, "Come in!"

The door opened and Hannah Atbury hesitantly entered. Lately, Luke Bouchard had noticed that she was smiling again and cheerful, an excellent sign that she was getting over the loss of Phineas and that she might very well soon accept Hughie Mendicott's proposal of marriage. "Excuse me, Mr. Bouchard sir, but there's a man says he wants to see you. Says he comes all the way from Texas."

"From Texas! You don't mean it! By all means, I'll see him, Hannah!" Luke said exultantly. "No, you needn't show him in, I'll go to the door myself. Oh, he'll stay to supper of course. After all, I want him to tell the folks out in Texas that we've got the finest kitchen in all Alabama."

"Land sakes, Mr. Bouchard," Hannah almost giggled,

125

"you always say the nicest things. I'll fix a supper you can be proud of." Then she added, in almost a conspiratorial whisper, "Poor fellow, he's sure done a heap of traveling from the looks of him. And he's only got one arm—"

"Why, it must be Andy Haskins!" Luke Bouchard exclaimed as he strode toward the front door of the chateau. It was indeed Andy Haskins, and he was standing, sombrero in hand, in the spacious foyer which fronted the winding stairway.

"By God, it's good to see you, Andy!" Luke Bouchard strode forward and offered the young Tennesseean his hand. Putting his sombrero back on his head, Andy Haskins shook hands and grinned from ear to ear, "Mighty good to see you again, Mr. Bouchard!"

"This is certainly a wonderful surprise! Whatever brings you to Windhaven Plantation? I thought you and Joe Duvray would be getting ready for the spring roundup, Andy. Come in, come into my study. Oh, Hannah, maybe a nice hot cup of coffee would be a good idea before Andy has supper with us—you're staying you know, whether you want to or not."

"You've always been my boss, you were the one that first hired Joe 'n me, so I certainly won't say no," Andy Haskins chuckled. "Matter of fact, I could stand a good strong cup of coffee. I've been doing a lot of traveling since I left the ranch right after Christmas, Mr. Bouchard, and that's no lie."

"I'll bring it right away, sir," Hannah smiled, then hurried off to the kitchen.

Luke led the way into the study, gestured Andy to a comfortable chair, and then turned the chair of his escritoire so that he could face his visitor. "Now then, start at the beginning and tell me all about it, Andy," he prompted.

"Well, Mr. Bouchard, I don't know why, maybe I was feeling sort of homesick, but I thought I could stand a furlough. And Mr. Lucien Edmond was very nice about it, he told me to take all the time I wanted. You see, Ramón and Pablo Casares—he married that young widow from Abilene after you left, you know—well, the two of them went down to Nuevo Laredo to hire some more vaqueros for the next drive. That was what made me think maybe they could get along without me on this drive."

"Well, you certainly deserve a vacation if anyone does, Andy. You and Joe too."

"Thank you for saying that, Mr. Bouchard. I'll never forget what you did for the both of us, and Joe won't either. That reminds me, I've got a letter from Mr. Lucien Edmond for you." Andy Haskins put his hand into the pocket of the heavy coat he had purchased in New Orleans as protection against the winter dampness. "Here it is, Mr. Bouchard. Oh yes, and Mr. Barntry at that bank gave me a letter for you too—said he wanted you and Miz Laure to have a copy of the latest account of how the bank was doing."

"Thanks a lot, Andy. Ah, here's your coffee now. I see Hannah thoughtfully brought two cups—I'll be glad to join you. It is damp and cold, just like Texas in the winter."

"It sure is, Mr. Bouchard. Thank you, m'am," Andy Haskins acknowledged Hannah's thoughtfulness in having set the cup and saucer on a little tray to which she had added a plate of her own molasses cookies. "Gosh, this is just like coming back home." He took a cookie, bit into it, and grinned. "Just as good as mama ever made, and that's no lie, ma'am."

"That's awfully nice of you, and you're quite welcome. Will that be all, Mr. Bouchard?" Hannah asked, with a fond look at the one-armed Tennesseean who was deftly sipping his coffee and giving not the least sign in the world that he missed his right arm.

"Yes, thank you, Hannah. Andy, if you think her cookies are wonderful, wait till supper," Luke chuckled.

After Hannah had left the study, Luke took a sip of his coffee and then resumed, "Did you spend much time in New Orleans, Andy?"

"Just about a week, Mr. Bouchard. I found some real good pistols and rifles and ammunition in a gun shop, and Mr. Barntry advanced me the money to pay for them. On my way back, I'll pick them up and take them back to Mr. Lucien Edmond."

"That's fine."

"Well, after that, I traipsed off to Tennessee. You know, that's where I came from." Andy's face grew somber. "I sort of wish I hadn't. Mr. Bouchard, it's like the war was still going on, in a way. Lots of carpetbaggers everywhere,

127

browbeating all the folks that have lived there all their lives, as if they were just slaves."

"I know, Andy. That's because a few powerful and misguided men on the Northern side don't want to let us forget that we lost the war. Men like that Thaddeus Stevens, as chairman of the Reconstruction Committee, who said he felt that all the seceding Southern states were guilty of treason. And there are others like him now in power today. That's the real tragedy of this war: they won't let hatred be forgotten."

"You're right about that. And after what I heard from folks I met there about what was going on in Georgia, I don't think Joe Duvray would want to go back either. Anyhow," Andy's face brightened, "if you want to know the truth, my main reason in wanting that furlough was to come see you and, well, just see how you and Miz Laure were making out."

"That's very thoughtful of you, Andy. And you'll meet Laure tonight at supper. Now, did you bring along baggage?"

"I didn't rightly figure I'd be staying too long, so I just have my carbine and the gelding Mr. Lucien Edmond let me take. I guess maybe I've got a few shirts and an extra pair of breeches in my saddlebag, but I travel light."

"Where's your horse now, Andy?"

"I came down from Anniston on the steamer and brought it along, Mr. Bouchard. It's outside tied to the rail."

"I'll have it put in the stable."

"Thanks, Mr. Bouchard. That's a good horse there. He covers lots of ground and he doesn't complain." Andy uttered an ironic little chuckle. "And one thing, he sure is friendlier than a carpetbagger."

Andy Haskins uttered a sigh, put down his napkin, and leaned back in his chair. "I have to apologize, Miz Laure," he said, "I really ate like a pig. But it was so darned good I couldn't help myself."

Laure laughed delightedly and glanced approvingly at Luke. The young Tennessean had thoroughly endeared himself to her by engaging both Lucien and Paul in conversation such as he might hold with an adult, telling them jokes and making them laugh. Also, he had brought along two Brahma bulls whittled out of wood by one of the vaqueros, as presents for the little boys.

"There's no need to apologize, Mr. Haskins," Laure said. "You've certainly found the way to Hannah's heart with the way you cleaned your plate. Now it's time for me to take the boys to bed, so I'll say goodnight until tomorrow and leave you to talk business with Luke."

Andy quickly rose from his chair and inclined his head respectfully toward Laure as, lifting both little boys up in her arms, she came over to kiss her husband goodnight and then left the dining room.

"What would you say to some brandy and a Havana cigar, Andy?" Luke asked.

"You're going to spoil me, Mr. Bouchard, so I won't be fit to go back and do my work at the ranch. But just for tonight, I'll say yes," Andy grinned.

"Let's go into the study. The brandy's on the sideboard, and the box of cigars is right next to it."

Once the two men had settled themselves, Luke leaned forward, his face grave. "You know, Andy, you can do me a favor. Not only that, you can earn some money for yourself, and you'll be doing a good deed into the bargain."

"I'm your man, Mr. Bouchard. You know what I said, you were the one who first hired me, so I figure I'm beholden to you. Only thing is, I didn't rightly tell Mr. Lucien Edmond how long I was going to stay away. I hope he won't get worried too much and try to replace me."

"I don't think my son would do that. But, to ease your mind, and since this telegraph strike is still going on, I'll get off a letter tomorrow and let him know that I'm planning to retain you here for a few weeks until this job's done."

"Well, that's fine with me. Now how can I help you, Mr. Bouchard?"

"It's not so much helping me, Andy, as it is a deserving old man and his widowed daughter downriver. They came here after the war, after they'd lost just about everything back in Virginia. The man is nearly blind, from what Marius Thornton tells me, and his daughter lost her husband fighting on the Confederate side. They've got just two free blacks whose wages are much too high for the sort of income they've been able to earn, and now I see that their property is listed for delinquent taxes. The taxes amount to $438—that's hard cash, and I'm sure they haven't anything like that saved up after buying that land and paying the taxes up until now."

"That's a darn shame, Mr. Bouchard. And I s'pose, because they're Johnny Rebs, the carpetbagger folks who set those taxes are just dying to have them give up the land and clear out."

"That about sums it up, Andy. And that's why I'm wondering if you could do me a great favor and help those people."

"I'd sure like to, Mr. Bouchard, if you think I can."

Luke Bouchard pondered a moment, turning to stare out of the window behind the escritoire, his hand touching his short, pointed beard as he strove to think of a plan. Then he turned back to Andy Haskins. "I'm pretty sure that if my lawyer Jedidiah Danforth were to pay the taxes and buy the land, the assessor would accept his bid. He was never involved in the war, and the fact is that he didn't believe that Alabama or the other Southern states ought to have seceded in the first place. A lawyer, Andy, likes to arbitrate and come to a peaceful decision. He wasn't very popular in Montgomery when the war was going on because of his views, but I've always respected him for holding onto them. And now his reputation isn't the least bit harmed for what he thought about the war. Yes, I think he could pay the taxes. Then what I'm thinking is that he could appoint you as foreman for that property. Of course, the Bambachs wouldn't lose the land at all; after a year or two, when this vindictive carpetbagging is over, Danforth would simply draw up a deed and turn it back over to them. And from what I know about this assessor, he wouldn't at all be adverse to a little bribe."

"I get your drift, Mr. Bouchard. You mean you'd want me to work there on the land and help the Bambachs."

"That's exactly what I mean, Andy. That's why I say I'll write my son that with his permission I've employed you on a very important undertaking. Besides, you've always loved to work with animals and the soil, and you'd be in your natural element."

"I'd like that, Mr. Bouchard," Andy Haskins leaned forward, an earnest look on his pleasant young face.

"Good! Help yourself to more brandy there and another

cigar. There's a steamer due at our dock tomorrow just before noon. I'll go up and visit old Jedidiah and arrange things. Meanwhile, you might like to ride downriver to call on the Bambachs and tell them what I've got in mind."

"That'd be fine, Mr. Bouchard. Anyhow, I like the idea of helping you this way—I owe you a lot, and it would ease my mind a good deal if I could do you a favor in return."

CHAPTER THIRTEEN

On the afternoon of the next day, Andy Haskins saddled his gelding and followed the trail downriver toward the old Cavendish land, little more than an hour's journey away. The weather was mild, though the skies were ominously gray. Andy drank in the magnificent landscape along the Alabama River—the stretches of fertile farmland and here and there the cottages of free black workers who had obtained their land during Reconstruction. In many ways, he was reminded of the place where he had been born, near a winding, shallow river where the soil had been bountiful and where, before the war, there had been an easygoing life. His own father had owned only a few slaves, but had never treated them as such. Before his death, and well before the Emancipation Proclamation, Caleb Haskins had manumitted those slaves, told them that he had kept an accurate account of their wages in his ledgers, and that they could buy whatever they needed at the general store and charge it back to him against those sums.

Andy's face was somber for a moment as he thought back to those days before the war. His mother had died from river fever when he was only ten, so his father and an elderly retired schoolteacher aunt had reared him. Aunt Cassie had taught him the three R's, and she had done a mighty good job of it, too. She had passed away just a year before the First Battle of Bull Run. When Tennessee seceded from the Union in June 1861, Andy enlisted in the Confederate Army. He had about two furloughs between then and the Battle of Chickamauga in September 1863, where he lost his arm. During that battle, he would have bled to death if Joe Duvray hadn't found him lying unconscious in a ditch. A shell had severed Andy's right arm just below the shoulder. Joe dragged him to shelter and

132

put on a tourniquet to stop the bleeding until they could get him to a field hospital.

Before he lost his arm, Andy had seen plenty of fighting. There had been the Seven Days Battle in Virginia in June in 1862, when General Lee forced General McClellan to withdraw from the peninsula to the protection of Union gunboats on the James River. He smiled grimly at the remembrance of that: the Confederate troops had lost twice as many in dead and wounded as the Union forces, yet Lee had really won that battle for the South. He'd fought in the Battle of Antietam in September, coming out of it without a scratch. Then, just before Chickamauga, there was the Battle of Chancellorsville in which old "Stonewall" Jackson had been mortally wounded when his own troops, not recognizing him, had fired on him in the savage melee. Again Lee had won against superior forces.

After Chickamauga, Andy spent about five months in a hospital far behind the battle lines, recovering from the loss of his right arm. But because he wanted to help the South, he begged the chief of the medical staff to assign him to clerical work if nothing else, so that he could do his part. He was later present at Appomattox where he saw Lee surrender like the gentleman he was and ask for consideration for all his men. Only then did Andy go back home, to find his house burned and his father dead from a combination of little food and lung fever—he had to learn that from a well-meaning neighbor.

So he headed for New Orleans, thinking that he could find work there and build up a stake, maybe head out to California and start all over again. His mustering-out pay hadn't gone very far: Confederate greenbacks were worthless. He survived by working down at the dock, helping the black stevedores load and unload, catching the fancy of a steamboat captain who took a liking to the way he could give a good account of himself and not shirk the toughest jobs. And then, like a kind of miracle, he saw Joe Duvray on the wharf, doing exactly what he was doing. They teamed up. Luke Bouchard and his family came along a week later, and now here he was with a good job and money in the bank. So the least he could do was to help Mr. Luke Bouchard, no matter how long it took.

He chuckled to himself now, remembering what Lucien

Edmond Bouchard had said to him about finding a nice girl, somebody who wouldn't turn up her nose because the right sleeve of his coat was empty. The fact was, he really didn't know much about girls. His mother had had a baby girl just before him, but it had died after only three months of life. Then, when Andy was about seven or eight, he came right out and asked his father why he didn't have any brothers or sisters. Caleb Haskins gently told him that such things were up to God.

Later on, when he was getting his booklearning, he really didn't have the chance to get to know any girls. Oh sure, when he was fifteen, there was a sassy red-haired filly who'd come to live on a neighboring farm. She was a flirtatious piece right enough, and she wasn't much older than he was at the time, but she preferred older fellows with pocket money to spend. When he became a soldier, there wasn't any time to think about girls. Long marches from town to town, digging in when those fellows in blue came at you with the bayonets, huddling down when you heard the whine of minié balls, trying to get a little sleep after a hard day's fight. . . . No, about the only time he'd been around girls was back on Windhaven Range, with Felicidad, Mr. Lucien Edmond's wife, Maxine, and his spunky sister, Mara, who'd married Ramón Hernandez. Maybe it was just as well there weren't any unmarried girls at the ranch, because that way he wouldn't have to think of how lonely he sometimes got and how it would be nice to have a pretty girl to share his life and to give him a reason for working hard.

He came in sight of a rickety frame house, originally painted white but now badly peeling. It was set about a hundred yards back from the trail. Thick grass and desultory weeds grew where once there had been a neatly cropped lawn. They were so abundant that the dirt pathway leading from the trail to the steps of a shallow porch was hardly visible. Here, directly to his left, stood a cotton gin barn, also badly in need of paint as well as restoration for some of the sagging timbers. Beyond the house and to the right extended the acreage in which he could see two blacks chopping weeds with hoes and preparing the ground for the spring planting of vegetables and cotton. On each side of the little house was the outline of a small truck garden. Andy Haskins shook his head at the look of poverty and desolation that emanated from the property. Dismounting, he tethered his gelding's reins to the low branch of a heavy live oak tree near the gin shed and walked slowly toward the house.

Just then, the front door opened and a young woman came out. She wore a cotton dress, a light cape, and the heavy work shoes of a man, and she carried a hoe. She was willowy, about five feet eight inches in height, her dark brown hair gathered in a thick Psyche knot above her nape. Her face was a sensitive oval, with high-set cheekbones, a delicately aquiline nose with thin, widely flaring nostrils, a determined chin, and a full mouth. Seeing Andy, she started in surprise with a little gasp of "Oh!"

"I didn't mean to frighten you, ma'am," Andy apologized as he doffed his sombrero and came slowly forward toward her. "My name's Andy Haskins. Mr. Luke Bouchard asked me to call on you and Mr. Bambach."

"Oh, I—I see. That's very neighborly of you, Mr. Haskins. My father's taking a nap now. Is there anything you wanted?"

Her voice was clear and sweet, her manner direct, and Andy irrelevantly noticed that her eyes were very large and gray-green with golden flecks at the iris. He floundered, not sure how to begin to explain his mission. Finally, he blurted, "I hear tell you and your daddy came from Virginia."

"Yes, that's true, Mr. Haskins. We came here at the end of sixty-five, and my father bought this land and the gin from the man who owned them."

"I understand, ma'am. Did he happen to be a Johnny Reb—no offense, ma'am, I'm one myself. Lost this arm at Chickamauga."

The young woman's face softened. "I'm so sorry, Mr. Haskins. I guess we both lost a lot in the war. My husband died at Gettysburg. He was in the First Virginia Volunteers."

Andy managed a feeble smile. "I was in the First Tennessee myself. I guess I was lucky. I didn't mean to cause you grief, ma'am."

"No, no, Mr. Haskins, you didn't. My name's Jessica Bambach. But to answer your question, no, the man who had the land here had come from Vermont just before the war to be near his brother. He married a local girl, from

135

what I understand, but after the war she wanted to go to California, so they sold this property to my father."

"I understand, Miss Jessica." Andy Haskins frowned, considered his sombrero which he had again begun to twist about, then hesitantly added, "It appears to me like you and your daddy were lucky to get hold of this place, seeing as how folks would put you down as seceshers, just like me."

Jessica's face shadowed and she bit her lips. "I'm afraid, Mr. Haskins, that's what's happening now. I guess whoever's in charge of land titles decided that we're still rebels and wants to get us off the land. We've got a terribly big tax bill, and I don't know how we're going to pay it, I truly don't."

"I'm not asking for myself, Miss Jessica. Mr. Luke Bouchard wanted me to come down here and meet you and your daddy and see if he could help you any. You see, ma'am, a long time ago this land belonged to his own daddy, Mr. Henry Bouchard. You might say he's got an interest in seeing that the land is kept by people who ought to be on it, and he thinks that's what you are."

"That's very kind of him. I've been told about the Bouchards, Mr. Haskins. I don't know why it is, but my father and I don't really get much chance to be sociable, not with all this work." She looked around. "When we first came here, we were able to hire ten hardworking blacks, but now it's down to two, and they're asking for more money than we can afford to pay. I truly don't see how we're going to manage this spring."

"Well, Miss Jessica, Mr. Bouchard found out about that tax bill the county assessor came down on you with, and he has an idea that'll ease your troubles—that is, if you and your daddy are agreeable."

Jessica laughed nervously. "Right now, Mr. Haskins, I'm so worried about my father—he's been ill recently— that I'd do just about anything if we didn't have that terrible worry about the money. You see, he had some gold saved up before the war, and he managed to keep it safe when we lost everything back in Virginia. That's what he used to buy this place, and the rest of it kept us going up until about last year. I—I taught rural school before I got married, and I've tried to teach here, but I have only two or three pupils. Their parents are poor and can't afford to

136

pay very much. And I don't see how we can produce cotton with just two men to plant and harvest it and gin it—"

"That would be quite a chore, Miss Jessica. And I'm sorry to hear that your father's ailing. I'd like to talk to him, but I wouldn't want to disturb him now that he's napping."

"Perhaps you'd care to stay to supper, Mr. Haskins. He should be up in about another hour. I'll have to apologize in advance, it won't be anything fancy, but we've potatoes and vegetables from my own garden, and there's just a little salt pork left."

"It sounds like a feast, ma'am. I'd like that—if you're sure I'm not putting you out."

"Oh no. I—I think Father would be happy to see a neighbor—and it's very thoughtful of Mr. Bouchard to send you." She turned away for a moment, but not before Andy had seen the suspicious hint of tears in her eyes.

"You know, ma'am," he spoke up cheerfully, "I haven't had much exercise lately, been traveling a lot to get here. Last couple of years, I've been in Texas, on a ranch working for Mr. Luke's son Lucien Edmond. Seeing as how you've invited me for supper, I'd like to get up an appetite for it. Why don't you let me take that hoe and clear away some of the weeds and grass here so you can walk out to the river when the weather's nice and admire the view?"

"Why, Mr. Haskins—good heavens, what must you think of my hospitality? You don't have to work for your supper—" she stammered, blushing.

Andy felt himself blushing too, not only at his own temerity, but also because of his awareness that Jessica Bambach was an exceptionally attractive young woman. "No, I mean it, Miss Jessica," he urged. "A man gets rusty if he doesn't exercise every now and again. Here, I'll show you. Let me have that hoe, please, ma'am."

"Why, all right—I don't know what to say—" she stammered as she relinquished the hoe.

The one-armed Tennesseean grinned, put his sombrero back on his head, and then began to attack the tall grass and weeds with a furious energy. Jessica's eyes widened with amazement to see how little his handicap hampered him. In ten minutes, he was able to cut a broad swathe through the tangled growth on one side of the dirt pathway.

"There," he chuckled, out of breath but grinning like a

137

schoolboy. "That did me a lot of good, ma'am. You know, I was raised on a farm in Tennessee, and I did chores from sunup to sundown. On the ranch, I could keep in trim. But I'm getting lazy these days, so I like nothing better than to get a good hoe or a spade or a shovel in my hand again and set to work. There's a powerful lot of satisfaction working in good soil, and that's a fact, Miss Jessica."

"You—you're really an amazing man, Mr. Haskins," Jessica confided. Then, as she turned away to conceal her blushes, she added, "You've done me a world of good just coming here today. I've been so worried about Father, I've just about lost hope. But you made me feel there might still be a chance for us to live here—"

"That's exactly what I aim to tell your daddy, Miss Jessica. Now why don't we stroll out to the fields and see how those two workers of yours are doing?"

Horatio Bambach was a tall man in his early sixties, with white hair that tumbled over the left side of his forehead. Andy Haskins sat with him at the table in the tiny dining room off the kitchen. The young Tennesseean had been touched to find that when his plate had been set before him, Jessica had been thoughtful enough to cut the pieces of salt pork so that he could readily manage them with his fork and not have to try to cut them. When she sat down at the table, he shot her a grateful look, and she lowered her eyes and blushed again.

"That's the long and the short of it, Mr. Bambach," he said as he reached for the cup that Jessica had just filled with strong chicory. "I have to compliment you on your daughter's vittles. One of the best meals I've had since I left Texas, and that's no lie."

"Oh, Mr. Haskins, you're just being kind. I wish we could have had real coffee, but—" Her voice lamely trailed off as she stared disconsolately down at her plate.

Andy hastened to make the pause less painful for her by addressing her father. "Now you see, sir, the way Mr. Luke Bouchard figures it, his lawyer will bid for your land, pay up the taxes, and then in a year or so, when these carpetbaggers go back north where they belong, he'll deed it over to you. Also, Mr. Bouchard thought you could hire me as your foreman—I don't mean for wages, because he's going to pay me—but you know, just put me in charge.

I've had plenty of experience on the land, as I told Miss Jessica. Then, too, I know good workers when I see them, and I might be able to round up a passel of them to help you plant cotton and the gardens and make you a little money come fall."

"I don't know what to say, sir," Horatio's voice quavered with emotion, and he cleared his throat and strove to steady his voice. "We've always paid our way, Mr. Haskins, and it hurts a man's pride when he can't do everything for his family that he wants. But I don't mind admitting to you that if we lost this place, we'd have nowhere else to go. And I want Jessica to have her chance. If things get better, she's bound to get more pupils—she's a wonderful teacher, dedicated, with a fine mind, and she loves children so."

"Now, Father, please," Jessica spoke up, blushing again.

"But it's true, Mr. Haskins. There are only the two of us left. You can see that I'm just about useless when it comes to running a farm. And Jessica's alone—you know about her husband—"

"Yes, sir, I'm deeply sorry."

"You understand, if I accept Mr. Bouchard's generous offer, we'll try to put away some of the money we might earn this year and pay that lawyer some of his interest on his capital. I wouldn't have it any other way, sir."

"I understand. I'll tell Mr. Bouchard. If you're agreeable, he'd like to come visit you, to seal the bargain."

"I'd like to meet him very much. He's a true gentleman, with a wonderful heart. I'm very grateful to you, Mr. Haskins. God bless you both."

CHAPTER FOURTEEN

It was mid-February by the time Ramón Hernandez and Pablo Casares returned from Nuevo Laredo with a dozen experienced vaqueros, some of whom would remain at the ranch to guard it while the others were away on the spring cattle drive to Abilene. Two days before the newcomers returned with Ramón and Pablo, the tall Ashanti, Carl, whom Luke Bouchard had made foreman over the Williamson acreage after discharging the brutal overseer Amos Greer, died in his sleep. He had served the Bouchards loyally and eagerly followed them to Texas after the old chateau had been set aflame by Union troops. He was sixty-one, but up until the day of his unexpected death, he had worked energetically in the corral and the bunkhouse. During the bandit raids by the brothers Macaras, he had valiantly defended his employers. Old Harry, three years older, had died six months before, so that now only Djamba and his wife, Celia, remained from the original contingent of those blacks who had once been Henry Bouchard's slaves and, freed by Luke, had followed the latter to Carrizo Springs.

This year, unlike last, Lucien Edmond Bouchard received by courier a circular from the tireless Joseph McCoy of Abilene, urging him to be sure to bring his herd to market. On the circular, McCoy had scribbled a note hinting that the prices offered by Midwestern and Eastern buyers were certain to be even higher than last year's.

Lucien Edmond intended to start the drive early in March, in order to avoid the withering heat of late July and August on the plains. Not only did such weather exhaust the cattle as well as the vaqueros, but there was constant danger of dust storms and sheet lightning which would stampede the herd. However, he was more than concerned over the news that he had a new neighbor on the land the Engelhardts had originally bought.

The Engelhardts had been murdered the year before by Durwood McCambridge, who was part of a gang involved in cheating honest settlers out of their land—a swindle they accomplished with fake Spanish land grants. After the murder, Norman Cantrell had sold the property to a Scotsman, Andrew Moultrie, and his beautiful Spanish wife, Anna. Moultrie had brought a flock of sheep to this land and almost precipitated a range war against Lucien Edmond Bouchard. When Lucien Edmond and Joe Duvray, at the anxious summons of Anna's old retainer Ramón Guitterez, rode over to the Moultrie house to intervene against Moultrie's brutal flogging of his wife, the Scotsman had tried to kill Lucien Edmond, who was forced to kill him to save his own life.

The sons of the Engelhardts, who regained the property after they had complained to the land office in Austin, decided to go to California and make a fresh start, saddened by the brutal murder of their mother and father. Accordingly, they put the land up for sale in Austin, and now there was a new owner.

Since the land adjacent to his own had changed hands so frequently in the past few years—and with such unfortunate consequences for Windhaven Range—Lucien Edmond was more than a little apprehensive about his new neighbors. He hoped, first of all, that they had not been duped into an illegal purchase by some swindler of Durwood McCambridge's ilk, so that their claim to the land would be tenuous at best. What the land really needed was a solid, reliable, and knowledgeable owner, who could gain clear title to the land in the proper way and then hold onto it for an indefinite period, developing it and making it prosper. Lucien Edmond resolved in any case to keep a close watch on his new neighbors.

There appeared to be a good deal of activity on the land adjacent to Windhaven Range. Joe Duvray and some of the vaqueros reported seeing about twenty Mexicans building a bunkhouse near the new corral, while another five strengthened the frame house where the Moultries and the Engelhardts had lived. These men were also applying a coat of fresh brown paint to the weatherbeaten structure. And

141

just last week, Joe Duvray had reported that several heavily laden wagons had been driven toward a large shed erected west of the frame house and at least a dozen vaqueros had unloaded bundles of wood and other bundles which, from a distance, vaguely resembled silver coils. As to what the new owner intended to raise, it was already evident to Joe Duvray that it would be cattle and not sheep, since he had seen some of the Mexicans drive wild longhorns out of the huge clumps of brush which lay well to the west of the frame house. That, at least, was a relief: after his encounter with Andrew Moultrie over the matter of sheep, Lucien Edmond sincerely hoped he would never have to face a similar situation again. Still, the situation gave Lucien Edmond cause for anxiety, and this was heightened by the fact that whoever the new owner of the land to the west was, he was clearly in no hurry to honor the customs of the range by paying a sociable call on his new neighbors at Windhaven Range.

As soon as Ramón Hernandez had ridden back to the ranch with Pablo and the dozen vaquero recruits, he closeted himself with Lucien Edmond to plan the details for the Abilene drive. "We may have to wait until the middle or perhaps even the end of March, Ramón," Lucien Edmond declared. "At least since we've made this trip several times now, we'll be able to take shortcuts and avoid troublesome sections of our original trail. Very likely we might succeed in cutting off a week of driving the herd if we're lucky, and then we'll be arriving in Abilene just about when we originally planned to get there. But until I know something more about that new outfit, Ramón, I'll feel a bit uneasy about leaving with most of our outfit just in case there's any trouble ahead."

"I think that's a very wise idea, Lucien Edmond," the handsome Mexican agreed. *"Con su permiso,* I'd like to introduce the new vaqueros to you when we've finished our chat. Just as last year, we should take about thirty men all told, all well armed. And with these new men, that would leave about twenty to guard the ranch while we're gone."

"That really should be enough," Lucien Edmond mused. Then he chuckled reminiscently. "Don't forget that Henry Belcher with his Whitworth was more than a match for those two bandit attacks we suffered. So he's certainly worth counting as two good defenders, and he's as good a marksman as any of our vaqueros, no matter how old that rifle of his is."

"*Es verdad*, Lucien Edmond," Ramón affably concurred. "Djamba and Lucas will accompany us, of course, though I do not think that our charming Felicidad will be very happy about that—you know, of course, that she is going to have a child."

"That's wonderful!" Lucien Edmond exclaimed. "They're such a perfectly matched couple, and it's very obvious they love each other dearly. But I must confess I wasn't aware of what you just told me."

"My wife, Mara, being a woman, would of course have Felicidad's confidence more than you or I would, Lucien Edmond," Ramón grinned. "Mara says that Felicidad first knew this in December. So it appears that she will have her child toward the end of the summer. But of course by then Lucas will be back from the drive. Felicidad loves him so much that she certainly would not want him to stay behind and not do his job. She is a very strong, brave *mujer*, that one."

"Indeed she is," Lucien Edmond nodded. He was remembering how, last year, when he and Ramón had started the drive for Abilene, two Kansas buffalo hunters had invaded the ranchhouse intent on the theft of gold and horses and the rape of the defenseless women there. Felicidad had hastened out to the shed, where she kept Coraje, a falcon she had nursed to health and trained. She brought Coraje to the house on one wrist, took a Spencer carbine out of the hallway closet, and concealed the carbine behind her back. As she entered the living room, she flung the falcon into the face of one of the desperados, then tossed the carbine to Lucien Edmond's wife, Maxine, who killed them both. Without Felicidad's bravery and quickness of thought, there might well have been tragedy awaiting Lucien Edmond's return from the drive last year.

"There's just one thing, Lucien Edmond," Ramón proposed. "We might have to think of getting a new cook for the outfit this year. Now that Pablo's married, with a house and land of his own—and that was very generous of you, Lucien Edmond—I think he ought to be promoted to riding one of the points this time."

"I agree," Lucien Edmond smilingly answered. "However, I don't think Pablo will look back and regret having had to take over the chuckwagon last year. If it hadn't been for that, he might never have met Kate Strallis." He was referring to the previous spring, when the vaquero had volunteered to take Felicidad's place as cook on the drive to Abilene, after she had been laid up by a rattlesnake bite. Along the way, Pablo lost his best friend in an attack by bushwhackers and for weeks was in despair. His duties as cook gave him responsibility as well for attending to the chuck wagon horses and others designated for special care. Accordingly, in Abilene, he took the horses to the only stable in town, and there by providence he met Kate Strallis, whose husband had just been gunned down by desperados. Out of deep sympathy for her plight, he interceded with Lucien Edmond, asking him to take Kate and her two little boys back to Windhaven Range and give her temporary employment. On the way back, Pablo saved her life in a battle with bushwhackers, then saved her young son from a scorpion. The Franciscan friar, Friar Bartoloméo, married Pablo and Kate in the chapel last fall, and as a wedding present Lucien Edmond Bouchard gave them fifty acres of his own land and helped the vaqueros build a little house for them..

Ramón nodded assent. "Certainly, Pablo's temporary duty at the chuck wagon rewarded him well. I for one am happy that *el Señor Dios* made it up to him after his *amigo* Vittorio was killed on the way to Abilene." Then, briskly, he added, "But one of the new vaqueros Pablo and I brought back from Nuevo Laredo is a fine cook. He used to work for a *patrón* who raised sheep in Durango. When I asked him if he thought he could handle our chuck wagon this spring, he took Pablo and me to a *parilla* which his cousin owns in Nuevo Laredo and made us the best *carne asada* we've ever eaten."

"I'd say that man has excellent credentials. Let's meet him, then, Ramón, and the others you've selected to work on Windhaven Range," Lucien Edmond rose from his chair and put his arm around his brother-in-law's shoulders as they went out to the bunkhouse.

There they found the newcomers waiting, having already been introduced by Pablo Casares to the other vaqueros. As Ramón and Lucien Edmond entered the bunkhouse, Pablo came forward with a broad grin. The once morose and taciturn middle-aged Mexican was now an almost unrecognizably outgoing, radiantly happy man. *"Buenos días, patrón,* and you also, Ramón, *mi amigo,"* he affably exclaimed. "I am sure the *patrón* will agree that we have found the very best men in Nuevo Laredo to come work with our other fine vaqueros."

"I'm sure, Pablo, that if you and Ramón approve of these men, I'll have no argument with you," Lucien Edmond responded.

"Tiburcio," Ramón beckoned to a stocky man in his mid-thirties who, at the sight of Lucien Edmond, had stiffened to attention, *"vengase aquí* and meet the *patrón,* Lucien Edmond Bouchard." Then, turning to his brother-in-law, he declared, "This is Tiburcio Caltran, the one who made such wonderful *carne asada."*

Self-consciously lowering his head, Tiburcio Caltran came forward with a nervous look on his mustachioed face. "It is a great honor, *patrón,"* he said respectfully.

"From what Ramón and Pablo tell me about your cooking, Tiburcio, you should hold your head very high here." Lucien Edmond extended his hand. "Perhaps they've already told you that we're going to drive our cattle to Abilene, Kansas, this spring. I should like it very much if you would run our chuck wagon so you can feed all these hungry vaqueros. Do you think you can manage all that work? I warn you, Tiburcio, Pablo spoiled them last year, so you will have to do better than he did." At this, there was a ripple of laughter from the other vaqueros, who were pleased with their employer's down-to-earth greeting to a recruit.

"I can only try, *patrón,"* Tiburcio Caltran stammered, glancing back at his fellows and then grinning again, more nervous than ever.

"Well, Tiburcio, the angels could do no more, so I'm sure you'll handle the job very well indeed. Pablo and Ramón have told you the wages we pay, *amigo?* They are satisfactory to you?"

"Oh yes, *patrón,* very generous!"

"Then it's settled. Pablo will find a place for you to put your gear and clothes, and in a little while there'll be a fine meal for you and your *compadres."*

Ramón then introduced the eleven other new vaqueros to Lucien Edmond. The youngest, Ignacio Valdez, tall and clean-shaven, was twenty-four and an expert with a lariat. He had worked on his father's little ranch since his boyhood and had spent time amusing himself roping yearling bulls—for his secret ambition, as he ingenuously confided to the amused Lucien Edmond, was one day to become a famous matador. Hearing this, Pablo Casares broke in, "¡Caramba! Ignacio, once you come along with us on a drive and there's a stampede, we'll see if you have skill enough to avoid the horns of the steers. If you come through unscratched, amigo, you will be ready for the bull ring, and I myself will certify it!"

At this sally, Lucien Edmond looked over at Ramón and winked. Decidedly, Pablo Casares's marriage had given this vaquero a gregariousness which was certain to win him a host of friends.

The oldest of the recruits was Santiago Miraflores, forty-two, a squat, nearly bald native of Guadalupe who had come to Nuevo Laredo not only to find work as a vaquero, but also to leave his personal grief behind him. His wife and two sons had been stricken with spotted fever and died within a week. The rico who owned the land on which Santiago lived told the latter that one of his friends was interested in buying the land, but that he would allow his present tenant to have first purchase rights. Poor Santiago Miraflores was already paying an extortionate rent for his use of the land, and the little savings he had had were exhausted in buying medicine and paying for a doctor for his wife and sons. He was forced to give up farming and become a vaquero.

Despite his mature age and short stature, Santiago had an exceptional talent for breaking in wild horses, which Ramón himself had observed one afternoon while visiting a stable in Nuevo Laredo. Ramón had promised Santiago that he would be kept busy breaking in wild mustangs and adapting them to mounts for the remuda. Moreover, the wages Ramón offered, twenty-five dollars a month, together with the promise of a good bonus after the cattle had been sold in Abilene, heartened the grief-stricken vaquero, and he seemed almost pathetically eager to please his new patrón, then and there offering to show Lucien Edmond how well he could break in the most skittish horse on the ranch.

The other nine men were between twenty-five and thirty-six, and three of these had already shown Pablo and

Ramón that they knew how to handle pistols and rifles. They would be assigned, Lucien Edmond decided, to the defense of the ranch when the main body of vaqueros left with the cattle for Abilene. As before, they would take thirty men to drive the cattle, and this would leave about twenty behind to do the necessary work in the corral and bunkhouse, to ride out to inspect the markers of Windhaven Range, and also, as Lucien Edmond himself suggested, to learn what they could about the new neighbor to the west—though he was quick to add that he did not wish them to be too obvious, lest the neighbor think he had sent them to spy on him.

Joe Duvray's remark that he had seen bundles of cut timber and what looked like silver coils gave Lucien Edmond some cause for concern. Could it be that his neighbor was planning to engage in something other than ranching? It seemed hardly possible that he intended to till the soil; the climate was too dry for that. As Lucien Edmond weighed various other possibilities, he remembered the land swindle involving the Engelhardts and decided that anything could happen. His own land, Windhaven Range, was particularly vulnerable and indeed attractive to any kind of scheming landgrabber, or even a ranching neighbor who was none too precise about boundary lines. Indeed, had Lucien Edmond known the true identity of his neighbor, he would have been all the more apprehensive.

CHAPTER FIFTEEN

"It's good to have you back here with me, Margaret dear." Robert Caldemare patted his fleshy mouth with his napkin, folded it neatly, and put it on his lap, then beamed at the young, light-brown-haired woman who sat across from him, her large hazel eyes demurely fixed on her own plate.

"Thank you, Father. It's so good to be back again with you—and it makes me happy to know that I can be with you now when you're all alone out here on this big ranch in the middle of nowhere."

He laughed indulgently as he meticulously cut a piece of roast pork with an ivory-handled knife, deftly skewered it with a matching fork, and brought it to his mouth. He smacked his lips as he tasted it, for he took a sensual pleasure in good food and drink. When he had swallowed the morsel, he replied, "It's really not so bad as that, Margaret dear. Texas is bound to expand. I could, of course, have gone farther north, and there would have been plenty of neighbors around—though hardly the kind I'd want you to associate with. You see, my dear, when the Southerners were defeated, a good many of them headed for Texas and California. The ones who settled here in Texas used to be plantation owners with many slaves. They find it hard to stomach the fact that their former slaves are now free and, supposedly—at least in theory—their equals. So they've banded together a good ways north from here, and they're still fighting the war and longing for the good old days. No, I've no interest whatsoever in cultivating such people, particularly for your sake, Margaret."

"I understand, Father," Margaret Caldemare softly replied. Then, self-consciously, her fair skin coloring, she added: "I was so happy, Father, when you wrote me at the school and told me that you wanted me to come live with you. You know—well, I've seen so very little of you all these years."

"That's exactly why I want you with me now, now that you've finished your schooling. You're a young lady, beautiful and well educated. Once we make our fortune here, there are places like San Francisco where I can take you, places where you'll find the proper kind of husband. You see, Margaret, I plan to be here at most a year. I've hired a fine outfit of men, devoted to me and very loyal. They know everything about cattle, and the market is improving both in demand and price. I didn't pay too much for the land, so I'll turn a very handsome profit by the time the drive is over at the end of the summer. Then we'll think about where to find you the sort of setting you deserve."

"Yes, Father," Margaret meekly responded.

"Let's drink a toast to your future, my dear." He reached for a silver handbell beside him, imperiously rang it, and a stocky, middle-aged Mexican promptly entered the dining room.

"¿Sí, patrón?"

"Más vino, Miguel!" he ordered. The Mexican nodded, left the room, and returned with a bottle of Bordeaux which he deftly uncorked with a flourish. Margaret hesitantly remarked, "I've never drunk wine, Father."

"Then it's high time you did, at least this once for my toast, my dear daughter," her father jovially countered, then nodded to the servant. "Leave the bottle here, Miguel. That will be all now, gracias."

"De nada, patrón."

Caldemare raised his glass. "How good it is to be with you and, God willing this time, for a very long time. Next year we shall go to San Francisco. Or perhaps even the City of the Angels, Los Angeles. It's still very Spanish there, the Old World niceties are preserved, and the caballeros will certainly appreciate someone of your beauty and wit, my dear. To us, Margaret!" He raised his glass again, then drank heartily from it. Margaret put the glass to her lips and tasted only a sip of wine before setting it back down before her. There was almost a wistful look on her face as she studied her father.

Robert Caldemare was fifty-one, robust, and slightly more than medium height, his black hair closely cropped

149

and without sideburns. It was slightly gray around the temples, at the sides, and at the back, which gave him an even more distinguished look; his head was leonine, with a high, arching forehead, thick brows, alert and appraising blue eyes set close together between the bridge of a broad Roman nose. He was fleshy but not paunchy, and he exuded an enormous vitality. He had a quick, deep smile, as he showed now in drinking to his daughter's future. But those who had known him back East most often saw him when his eyes were cold and narrowed and his lips compressed with an angry determination. Perhaps, too, they might not have recognized him because he wore neither beard nor mustache, both of which he had displayed with not a little vanity in the past.

Caldemare was Parisian by birth, the son of a wealthy vintner who grew his grapes in the Loire region, maintained a luxurious spring and summer home there and an elegant apartment in Paris. As his only heir, Robert had been educated in the lore of winemaking, but he had absolutely no interest in wine except for drinking it. Consequently, after Robert's mother died when the youth was eighteen, he had frequent quarrels with his father, not only on the subject of not following in his father's footsteps, but also as a result of his precocious debaucheries.

For Robert Caldemare was an unscrupulous and amoral voluptuary. Not content with seducing his father's own mistress and leaving her with child (the opportunistic young woman had been clever enough at the time to convince the older man that the child was really his), Caldemare spent a good deal of his time in Paris. Since he had plenty of pocket money and his father's elegant apartment to which to bring his lady friends, he brought a procession of women from every social class to the ornately furnished bedroom. Being a sensualist, he soon added huge mirrors to the walls so that he could whet his erotic capabilities by observing himself and his amorous partner.

Not only *midinettes* and attractive art students disported themselves with him before these mirrors, but also married women, and some of these from the most aristocratic stratum of Parisian society. By the time he was twenty-two, he had already fought two duels with enraged husbands, wounding the first and killing the second. When he was twenty-four, he seduced the previously highly moral wife

150

of a count who was a close friend of François Guizot, the great statesman and cabinet leader under the monarchy of Louis Philippe. Guizot himself forbade the count to seek the revenge of a public duel, but instead sent a courier to Caldemare's aging and ailing father to inform him that his son was *persona non grata* in France.

His father came to Paris and confronted his profligate heir. The latter was intelligent enough to understand that to remain in Paris might well lead to his incarceration by a *lettre de cachet,* which was a way that kings had of ridding themselves of unpopular citizens. He could be cast into a prison, no record kept, and die there before anyone was the wiser. So he bargained with his father, who grudgingly agreed to give him a third of his patrimony with the stipulation that he would leave for the United States and never return. When he tried to haggle to obtain a more generous settlement, his father, livid with rage, hissed, "At last I have found out what a viper I have nursed in my own house. Louise finally confessed just before I came here that the child was yours, not mine. You have denied me that joy, you dared to cuckold your own father. I want nothing more to do with you, and if you do not take the money and get out of my sight forever, I will turn my back on you and let them put you in some dungeon where you can starve to death, for all I care."

It was, after all, a handsome settlement, all things considered. It amounted to about forty-five thousand dollars in gold, surely enough for an enterprising young man to start a new life in a young country, where there were still frontiers to be pushed back and scheming to be done to increase one's capital. So Caldemare sailed to New York and, since he had learned English in school, quickly adapted himself to his new environment.

Through speculation and investment, he doubled his patrimony within three years. He found that land speculation offered exceptional possibilities and sold tracts of land in upper New York to wealthy immigrants. The fact that he did not have clear title to all the land he sold in no way disturbed him. But some of his victims complained to the authorities, and Caldemare decided it was time to move elsewhere; his choice was Boston. There, for a few years, he contented himself with buying and selling commodities, possibly the most honest period of his entire life. And there, also, six months after his thirtieth birthday, he met Margaret's mother, Marguerite Delmar, the shy, lovely, only daughter of a Boston financier who had married a French girl during his vacation as a young man in Paris.

Margaret was born some eighteen months later, and her mother, who had a very difficult delivery, was so weakened by the ordeal that she died after three months. Robert Caldemare had named his daughter Margaret, the Anglicized version of his wife's name. So far as he could love anyone, he had loved his wife and deeply mourned her. However, being involved in business affairs, he found it expedient to engage a nurse and, later, an English governess for the child. Also, since his sensual nature could not keep him a continent widower, he took on a succession of mistresses, but maintained the little girl and her governess in a separate apartment so that neither of them would be aware of his erotic pursuits.

His mistresses were expensive, and he sustained several severe losses in his commodity business, which made him decide to turn back to land speculation to recoup his dwindling fortune. A year before the Civil War broke out, he arranged to put Margaret, by then eleven, into an exclusive young ladies' school in Boston and explained to her that he had lost nearly all of his money but that she would be well provided for. He would go on, he said, lonely as he was and still mourning her mother, inspired by his love for her, and one day they would be together again. Margaret wept and clung to him, avowing that she didn't care if they were poor so long as she could be with her father. Doubtless, had Caldemare thought of going upon the stage, he could have scored many a histrionic triumph: he was able to console the little girl and to impress her with his dedication to give her every opportunity in life, even if it meant a long separation.

After a six-month flurry of land speculation in Ohio, Caldemare decided that the Civil War provided an ideal time to profiteer without much danger of legal censure. Although his political sympathies veered more to the South than to the North, he was convinced from the very outset that the South could not victoriously sustain a long-drawn war. Accordingly, he would deal with Union quartermasters, and the most obvious merchandise on which to turn a handsome profit would be food and especially meat.

Caldemare moved his base of operations to Indianapolis and, having astutely wined and dined a large slaughterer in that area, proposed to go into partnership with him. His partner was as venal as Caldemare himself, since he maintained a young, expensive mistress in a separate establishment from that which housed his wife and five children. He was therefore easily approachable on the subject of high prices for mediocre merchandise.

Inspection of meat was not yet uniformly required by law in every state and would not be until long after the Civil War and the opening of the Chicago Stockyard. Except for hasty inspections of herds by purchasing agents acting for the major packing houses, there were few attempts made to judge the health of animals to be slaughtered or the safety of meat. Hence, Caldemare and his partner had little difficulty in selling a large tonnage of meat, a good part of which was taken from scrawny and even diseased cattle. The slaughterer, William Osmund, encouraged the farmers of the area to "bring me everything you've got, so long as it can walk on four feet, and I'll give you top price for it."

Within a year, the quartermaster with whom Robert Caldemare dealt informed him that there had been various complaints on the quality of his meat. Moreover, he declared that he intended to seek a new source for his supplies for the troops. Caldemare understood that it was time to turn to a new venture. Near Richmond, Indiana, he found the owner of a tannery who had received a small contract for belts for the soldiers and entered into partnership with him for eighteen months. The tannery owner was also interested in quick profits for shoddy merchandise, and Caldemare, by dint of handsomely entertaining a colonel in the quartermaster's office, was able to wangle a sizeable contract. Most of the leather rotted, and within eight months that door, too, was definitely closed to Caldemare.

By now he might have amassed a considerable fortune, had his expenses not been almost on a par with his earnings. Though he had never intended to remarry, he had also never remained continent for any long period of time.

After leaving his tannery partner in Richmond to face growing complaints from the irate colonel, Robert Caldemare made a trip to Chicago and settled there for a year, maintaining a young, red-haired doxy as his mistress. She in turn was replaced by a young woman from one of Chicago's best families who had shocked her parents by being a violent nonconformist and insisting on living her own life without interference. It amused Caldemare to enjoy her intellectual companionship and then to savour her uninhibited ardors, which in their imaginativeness and boldness surpassed even the doxy's talents.

All this while, he continued to correspond with Margaret. He saw to it that she had plenty of spending money and that her tuition was always paid promptly, and his letters were filled with glowing accounts of his unrelenting efforts to find a suitable home for the two of them and a business that would assure their material comfort. When he paid the tuition, he wrote to the principal of the school to request regular reports on Margaret's progress. These indicated that his daughter was gentle, reticent, and extremely intelligent but without ostentatious show of it, and also (which pleased him greatly) that she revered him.

In one letter, the principal glowingly detailed a conversation she had had with Margaret:

> I know, Mr. Caldemare, that it must please you to learn that your daughter is doing so well. I do not think it remiss of my obligation to you to report what the dear girl said to me only the other day when your name was mentioned and I told her that I had a letter from you. She sighed and exclaimed, "Father is such a wonderful man, you know, Miss Emmons. He has never gotten over mother's death; she died when I was born, and the reason he doesn't come to see me is because he must work so hard to provide for both of us."
>
> It is obvious, Mr. Caldemare, that Margaret worships you. I myself am sorry that your many business affairs have prevented your visiting our school, for I am sure you would approve of it. Rest assured, however, that your daughter receives every care and attention as is due so charming and intelligent a young lady. She is indeed a great credit to you.

For the next several years, which saw Appomattox and an end to the war, Robert Caldemare was content to play the role of investor on the exchange. Because his business judgment was usually sound, he made more than he lost —though by no means as much as he sought. He did see Margaret on the rare occasions when he traveled to Boston. On these visits he took her out to dinner and the theater and was flattered by her almost idolatrous admiration of him. In New York, he had several expensive mistresses and tired of all of them after a few months. He had kept a bank account in Chicago with about $40,000, but the rest of his holdings had been transferred to a New York bank so that he could have ready cash for his broker.

His hope of a real coup was bitterly dashed on September 24, 1869, with the famous "Black Friday" panic on Wall Street brought about by Jay Gould's and James Fisk's attempt to corner the gold market. Caldemare found himself wiped out overnight except for his Chicago holdings.

He went back to Chicago, morose and embittered. Now that the war was over, there could be no more overnight profiteering; the stock market, too, offered little hope for the future. Then he began to think that the real hope of immediate money was through the raising of cattle and a number of quick sales to an ever-increasing market. Now that the nation was at peace, now that railroads were being built to connect the most distant parts of the country, there would be an increasing demand for meat. Even the poor man could afford it for his table and, after the privations of the war, would enjoy it as often as he could.

The logical start was at the very source where cattle were being raised most abundantly, and that meant most particularly the Southwest. He had read in the New York and Chicago newspapers of the Texans' difficulties in getting their cattle to Sedalia, Missouri, because the irate citizens were terrified by the threat of Spanish fever, which might be carried by ticks on the longhorns' bodies, and which would infect their own sound herds. Then he read that Joseph McCoy had opened the Abilene market and was welcoming Texans, and his agile mind began to weigh the possibilities. What he wanted was a few quick profitable deals, enough to bolster his savings so that he and Margaret could live at their ease in a city like San Francisco.

155

There he could find a new, exciting mistress for himself and a husband for his adoring daughter.

He went first to Baxter Springs in Kansas, for there, too, cattlemen had fought with townspeople over the right to bring in Texas cattle, and the town was filled with gunslingers and other riffraff. Here he found a desperado, Jackson Brundiger, who was as eager for money made the easy way as he himself was.

Jackson Brundiger was tall, lean, with weather-beaten features, a hawklike beak of a nose, thin, cruel lips, and cold gray eyes. He was thirty-two years old, and when he was fifteen had shot down a man who had made a disparaging remark about his sister. At twenty, he joined a gang of bushwhackers who robbed cattlemen of their cattle and often raided isolated little hamlets. When he was twenty-five, he married the daughter of a Kansas farmer. Her father angrily opposed the marriage, but the infatuated girl eloped with Brundiger and they were married in a little Missouri town.

For a time, because he was in love with her after his own fashion, Brundiger settled down as a foreman of a Missouri ranch, but the old restlessness for a free and easy life was still in his blood. When his young wife died in giving premature birth to a sickly girl who followed her mother to the grave three days later, Brundiger turned back to what he knew best: bushwhacking and rustling. He made few friends, but he was able to draw desperados and *pistoleros* to him like a magnet because he had a reputation for dealing fairly with his partners in crime. He wore two guns holstered at his sides, and when Caldemare saw him lounging back in his chair at a table in the Baxter Springs saloon, he knew that he had found the man who could help him bring about quickly what all his scheming over the past decade had failed to do.

CHAPTER SIXTEEN

When supper was over, Robert Caldemare rose from the table and, adopting his most affectionately paternal tone, suggested, "It would be a good idea, Margaret, if you got a good night's sleep. I know what a long, exhausting trip it was all the way from Boston, and you have been here just a week, hardly time to accustom yourself to this change."

"I'll be fine, Father, really I will," the young woman said. "And really, even if there aren't many people around, there's so much that's lovely about this country—it's so big, so new." She came to him, linked her arms around his neck, and kissed him on the cheek. "I'm so glad to be home with you, Father, you don't know how much. I made friends at school, but all the girls would go home on their vacations to be with their parents, and all I had was letters."

"I know, my dear," he commiserated as he patted her shoulder and stroked her fine-spun, silky hair. "But that's all over and done with now. All these years I had to work alone to build security for the two of us. Now it's come down to this place and this year, Margaret. You see, I'm going to raise cattle. There's a big demand for meat in the Midwest and the East. What I need is a big herd and I'll be rich again. Then we'll go to San Francisco, or if you don't like that, we'll find a place that'll be worthy of you. And I'll be there to watch over you. You know, you're at the age when you should think of finding a good man to marry and raise a family with."

"I've never really thought about that, Father." She blushed, averting her eyes. "First of all, I think mostly I want to feel I belong—now that I'm here with you, I'm beginning to feel that way. I never could enjoy being with the governess, and I hated being cooped up in that school all winter, even though everyone was nice to me."

"I know, kitten." Again he gently patted her shoulder. "But at least you won't be cooped up during the winter out here. This is about the coldest it gets, and it's really quite bearable when you think of the snows and blizzards back in Boston."

"Oh yes—and I'd like to have my own garden, could I, Father?" She turned to him eagerly.

"Of course you can, dear," he chuckled. "Why, you can put in tomato plants, even little strawberries. I'm told that it won't be long before the bluebonnet and the orange blossoms will be blooming. Now perhaps it's time for you to think about getting some rest. I have some business to talk over with my foreman."

"Of course, Father. Good night, then." She hesitated a moment on the threshold of the dining-room door and then impulsively came to him, again embraced him, and kissed him on the cheek. "Oh, Father. You've worked so hard all these years, do please take care of yourself. You're all I've got, you know." Then, crimsoning is if afraid she had said too much, she turned and hurried off to her room.

Robert Caldemare finished his wine. Then, his amiable expression altering into one of taut decisiveness, he lifted the little silver handbell and vigorously shook it. When the young Mexican servant entered, he snapped, "Get Jackson Brundiger, *pronto,* hombre!"

"Al punto, patrón," Miguel inclined his head, turned quickly, and left the dining room. A few minutes later, Jackson Brundiger entered, walked swaggeringly over to Margaret's chair, turned it, and seated himself astride it, eyeing his employer with a cynically amused look. "What's on your mind, Caldemare?"

"It's time we made our plans, Brundiger. I bought these three thousand acres at Austin on your say-so because you told me that this was the best spot in which to accumulate the cattle we'll need for a swift sale at Abilene this summer."

"Sure I did, and I know what I'm talking about. You remember back in Baxter Springs I told you I had ways of getting my hands on cattle."

"Yes, yes," Caldemare said impatiently. "And I got things done in a hurry so we'd have a base of operations, didn't I? I've moved onto the land—thank goodness there was already a house here for my daughter, Margaret, and myself—and I've ordered the fence wire and the posts. Now, what about the cattle? Of course, I suppose the vaqueros could round up longhorns out of the bushes, the way that fellow Bouchard's doing over on the ranch next to me. But that's too slow a process. You yourself said that."

"That's right, and I meant it." Brundiger gave him a crooked grin, gripped the back of the chair, and tilted it a little, mockingly appraising his employer's reactions. Don't be in such a sweat, Caldemare. By tomorrow, the boys I sent across the border will be back with at least five hundred head. Then we change the brands on them and include them in our herd for Abilene."

"That's a fair start," Caldemare grudgingly admitted. "But hardly the size herd I had in mind. And just how do the wire and fence posts come into this?"

"Caldemare, you've got to trust me if you want me to make money for you my way. And don't forget, we agreed on a fifty-fifty deal."

"I know that, man," Caldemare exploded. "Don't forget, I'm paying the expenses of the men you had me hire. And you've got no expenses at all."

Brundiger let the back legs of his chair settle on the floor and leaned forward, an ugly look on his face. "Now I wouldn't get too techy on that point if I was you, Caldemare. And I don't much go for your treating me like I was one of your hands, either. Fact is, we're more partners than boss and foreman, even if that's the monicker I'm supposed to have around here if any of the Bouchard riders start asking questions of my men and me. Understand that?"

"Very well! Get to the point, Brundiger."

Brundiger gave him a crooked grin again and leaned back, staring at the ceiling as he reminisced, talking as if no one else were in the room except himself. "You see, Caldemare, when you come out to a wild country and you meet a stranger, you take him on trust. You don't know a goddamned thing about him, but you like the look of him or the way he handles his guns, whatever. Well, the minute you sat down at my table in that Baxter Springs saloon, I sized you up all right. You're just as much a crook as I am. Only difference between us, you never dirtied your hands with killin' when it had to be done. You just wanted to get rich quick, but you didn't care how. Well, I'm the same way. There's no law out here, Caldemare. Meaning that a galoot who knows how to use guns and who thinks one step ahead of the next fellow, he's top dog."

"I understand all that, Brundiger. But you're wandering from the main issue. You told me that you know how to grab a good-sized herd without any real danger and sell it quick. Now what is your plan of action for doing this in the immediate future?"

"I was getting to that. First of all, you can see that this country is ideal for our purposes: a few big ranchers, no neighbors around them, and no law to bother you. But that's not the real reason I brought you down here. So I'll level with you, partner." Brundiger chuckled maliciously as he saw the older man wince. "Hard for you to think of me that way, isn't it, Caldemare? Well, I don't much mind if you leave the dirty work to me and my boys. We're used to it. So I'll get right to it. I had a good pal in Kansas, some years back, name of Jethro Reedy. The fact is, the two of us had a helluva lot of fun until he decided to get his own gang and go bushwhacking. Well, this fellow Bouchard who's next to you, he drove his cattle to Abilene last year. Reedy and his boys tried to bushwhack him, but got wiped out instead. Only a few of them were left, and when they tried again on the way back, that was the end of the Reedy outfit, savvy?"

"Now I begin to understand you, Brundiger," Caldemare coldly retorted. "You're really after revenge on this Lucien Edmond Bouchard you've been telling me about."

"Sure. Only it works out good in more ways than one, Caldemare. I'll pay him back for what he did to my pal, Jethro, we take his cattle—he's got plenty, and they're getting them ready for roundup any day now—we'll drive them on to Abilene and split the money. Then, if you've a mind to, you can go your way and I and my boys will go mine. Fair enough?"

"So long as I get the money you promised on a deal like this, I don't care what the hell you do," Caldemare retorted as he rose from the table, strode to the sideboard, and poured himself a glass of brandy. Turning back to scowl at his callous, mocking associate, he added, "I just want one thing understood. My daughter got here last week. She's a decent girl, and I have plans for her. I

160

don't want any of your *pistoleros* or you either to so much as talk to her. She's not to know what we're involved in, and I trust you'll keep that part of the bargain."

"Sure. I can buy all the floozies I want once I've got hold of that Bouchard herd, Caldemare. Besides, your daughter's a fancy young lady, and me, I'd rather take a dance-hall girl. That's more my style, if you get my meaning."

"I think that's enough talk about my daughter."

"As you say, Caldemare. Well, are you satisfied, or have you still got some more questions for me?"

Caldemare shook his head and sipped his brandy. There was a grimace of distaste on his face as he turned away from the wiry desperado. There was a long silence. Finally he turned to Brundiger again. "I think I can envision your plan—now that I understand you better. You're going to set up your own markers at a wire fence. You'll encroach on the Bouchard land, and that'll bring their riders in to argue. You're thinking that when they finally go on the drive, they'll have to leave some of their riders here in case of trouble."

"Now you're getting smart, Caldemare. You're starting to think the way I do," Brundiger chuckled humourlessly. "That's it to a T. They usually take about thirty men. And they've got good guns, repeaters, Spencers. We'll go ahead of them, once we see them finishing the roundup and readying the herd for Abilene. We'll take them before they get to the Red River. It's always a tough place to cross, and it takes two to three days, even with a top outfit like Bouchard's. We'll take them by surprise and we'll wipe them out. Then we'll just take their cattle, change the brand from that WR to RC, and we'll ride nice and easy into Abilene with nobody the wiser. That'll pay them back for old Jethro, and you and I will split the cash once we get back from Abilene."

Caldemare finished his brandy, then glumly nodded. "I know that you can do what you set out to do, Brundiger. I'm content to be a silent partner. You can understand that I don't care for violence and I don't particularly want a range war, nothing that would endanger Margaret. Just do what you have to do, and I'll give you a fair division of the money when you sell the herd. But remember, if you try to get away without bringing me the money, I shall come after you. Much as I abhor violence, I'll see that you're tracked down and killed. I took the precautions of learning who your enemies are, before I picked you up that day in Baxter Springs."

"Well now, so you're showing a little spirit after all, eh? Maybe we're two of a kind. But don't you worry about a thing, Caldemare. I'll shake on our deal and that will be that. Tomorrow, my boys will start putting up the fences and the wire. That ought to draw some of Bouchard's vaqueros away from the ranch and keep them wondering what the hell we're trying to do. It won't do any harm, either, if just by accident, let's say, some of the cattle wander in to our land and get fenced in with our herd. Well, I'll say good night to you." He rose from the chair, walked over to Caldemare, and held out his hand. Grudgingly, the latter shook it. After the desperado had left the room, Caldemare shuddered, shook his head, then filled his glass with brandy again and gulped most of it down in a single draught.

CHAPTER SEVENTEEN

It was warm and sunny this first week of March in Carrizo Springs. On Lucien Edmond's ranch the Brahmas, Herefords, and longhorns were placidly grazing, quite unperturbed by the occasional watchful presence of the vaqueros, and still less concerned about what was taking place in the world beyond their grassy terrain: Congress had established the U.S. Weather Bureau; the Territory of Utah had granted full suffrage to women; Mississippi was at last readmitted to representation in Congress; and Secretary of State Hamilton Fish was about to proclaim that the Fifteenth Amendment to the Constitution had been ratified and would be vigorously enforced.

Nor did this first week of March bring Lucien Edmond Bouchard any easing of his concern over the puzzling activities of his neighbor to the west. Joe Duvray had reported that the last time he had ridden over to the nearby ranch to have a look, there seemed to be some four or five hundred head of cattle penned up in a wide enclosure of posts and wire and that several Mexican vaqueros were busy building an adjoining branding pen. The cattle were not Texas longhorns, so far as he could tell from the precautionary distance he had put between himself and Caldemare's property: they seemed to be shorter, somewhat humpbacked, and were most likely Mexican cattle. Also, there was a large bunkhouse being finished for the men of this neighboring outfit.

When Joe and his companion Santiago Miraflores rode back late in the afternoon and reported what they had seen to Lucien Edmond, the latter frowned and shook his head. "Well, there's no law that says a man can't fence in his own property. So long as he doesn't change my boundary markers, I've really no cause to take issue with him. Just the same, Joe, and you too, Santiago, keep an eye on those western markers just to make sure they aren't changed in our new neighbor's favor."

"You can depend on that, Mr. Bouchard," Joe nodded. "Just the same, I don't like the looks of those vaqueros he's got. They look more like *pistoleros* to me. I think Ramón and Pablo, if they had a close look at them, would agree with me. When they were down in Nuevo Laredo recruiting men for us, I wouldn't be surprised if they'd passed up quite a few hombres like the kind working for that ranch. They all wear six-shooters or old Belgian pistols, and they're none too friendly, I can tell you that. When Santiago called to one of them and wished him a good afternoon, the fellow patted his holster with one hand and made a sign with his other hand for us to skedaddle. I tell you, Mr. Bouchard, I've got a pretty bad hunch about what's going on out there. Here we are, and whoever owns that outfit still hasn't come over to shake hands and say 'Howdy' or tell you anything about what made him pick that land next to yours."

"Well, Joe," Lucien Edmond pleasantly countered, "buying that land doesn't necessarily stamp our unsociable neighbor as a criminal. When I was in Austin, shortly after Mrs. Moultrie went back to Taos, I was told that the Engelhardt sons had sold their claim back to the land office for about the original price their poor father had paid for it. So I guess it could be sold to just about anybody who wanted it. And it's good land, no two ways about that."

"That's all very true, Mr. Bouchard," Joe grudgingly agreed, "but it strikes me funny about those Mexican cattle. He's still got plenty of longhorns to be popped out of the brush all the way west, I judge at least a thousand head. But his men haven't rounded those up at all the way we do ours. And the cattle they have so far don't seem to have the weight or the build of our longhorns. I just can't figure it out."

"Well, you just keep your eyes open then, and see what you can find out from day to day, Joe. I'd really like to start for Abilene in about two weeks, so I can cut as much as possible of that ferociously hot summer off our drive. However, if you're worried that our neighbor might try to start something—which God forbid—we'll certainly be ready for him. We've got all those new rifles and ammunition that Andy Haskins so thoughtfully bought for us in New Orleans."

"You mean Andy found some weapons for us, Mr. Bouchard? I didn't know that."

"Well, you see, Joe, when Andy found he was going to stay on quite some time with my father, helping out a neighbor on his farm, Father wrote to Jason Barntry. Jason had the guns and ammunition Andy had picked out shipped down to Corpus Christi and brought out here by wagon. The shipment got here last week when you and Santiago were out on the range, and it's been stored away in that shed back of the bunkhouse. So, as I say, we'll have fire power both for our drive and for anything those *pistoleros* might stir up."

Joe Duvray dryly chuckled. "Well, I sure hope I'm wrong about what I think might be going on there, Mr. Bouchard. But knowing about that shipment does relieve my mind just a mite. All the same, I'm sure going to do a lot of riding over there as close as I can get and see what that galoot is up to."

By the first week of March, Dr. Ben Wilson was gratified to observe that the health of the Creek villagers had vastly improved. The croup epidemic had been halted, and the only fatality had been one old squaw whose heart had failed during her slow convalescence. Even more rewarding was the fact that the children were now better nourished, thanks to the milk given by the cows he had brought from Wichita. Very soon there would be calves from the bull and the heifers that Lucien Edmond Bouchard had given Emataba during last year's drive to Abilene. Then there would be still more milk, and there would be meat to give strength to the old men and women and the young children.

The Indian agent, Matthias Stillman, had come with the soldiers in January and then again in February, grudgingly distributing the food that the government provided. In January, Ben had again angrily upbraided the corpulent agent about the poor quality of flour and the tattered blankets and cast-off clothing. In February, perhaps chafing under this censure, Stillman had sarcastically invited Ben to examine the barrels of flour and the blankets and the clothing, and this time they had been satisfactory. He was due again tomorrow, the first Saturday of March, and the Quaker doctor hoped that from now on the Indian agent would show more honesty in his dealings. There was no

165

doubt that he pocketed a good deal of the money allocated to the Creeks and bought the poorest quality goods and foodstuffs with the rest.

By now Ben had become fluent in the Creek tongue, thanks to his many hours spent with Sipanata. The once dour and suspicious brave was now the Quaker doctor's most steadfast ally.

During their many conversations, in which Ben would speak in English and Sipanata at once translate into the Creek so that his pupil might repeat the Creek words until they came readily, the young brave questioned him about his past life. His growing concern and friendship for this white man whom he had at first viewed with suspicion had led him to remark only last night, "You mourn your squaw, white-eyes shaman, and that is good. It shows you cared for her and that her spirit is not dead to you. But now that you are with us, you are alone, and it would be good for you to take another squaw."

"I had not thought about that, Sipanata," Ben replied. "The work I do here keeps my thoughts busy. There is no time for a squaw. But you are kind to think of me. You see, I am not alone even though my wife is dead. I have a little boy and a little girl whom I left with my wife's mother at the ranch of the man who brought the bull and the heifers to Emataba last summer. I will see them now and again, and they will remind me of my dear wife. As they grow older and lead lives of their own, Sipanata, I will see her in them, for she was good and kind and she loved all people and had no hate in her heart."

"I have never known a white-eyes like you before, my shaman." Sipanata addressed Ben by the term by which everyone in the village now called him, a mark of affection as well as respect. "We have talked many times, and I have told you how we believe in Ibofanaga, the Giver of Breath. You have told me of your God who is kind and teaches you that you must not hate even your enemies. I find this strange, indeed. Perhaps it is because I saw how the white-eyes treated my father and mother. How the white-eyes I worked for in Mobile looked upon me as if I were a trained dog to do his bidding. And Emataba has told me how the old ones of the village were driven out of their homeland to this place. I was proud of my blood, and I hated the white-eyes for what they had done to all of us who were Creeks."

"But you see, Sipanata," Ben Wilson gently countered, "it does no good to hate. You cannot change a man who is your enemy by hating him. But perhaps, as we are taught, if you show that love and kindness are more important to you, he may at last begin to understand you." He uttered a deprecating little laugh. "I will admit that it's not always easy, Sipanata, especially if your enemy has weapons and you have none."

"Yes," the Creek brave nodded, "just as you were when those evil white-eyes tried to rob you. I saw how they threatened you, and I heard you ask them to take your gold but to leave the wagon with the food and the blankets. It was then I respected you, my shaman. I am glad Emataba chose me to be your teacher."

"I could not have asked for a better one, Sipanata. You are truly my friend."

"Then let me speak like one, my shaman. You have said that you grieve for your wife, and it is good that you do. But it is not good for a man to shut himself up and say that he will not take another squaw. I know one who would willingly share your life with you and make it easier for you here in our village, where there is so little joy."

"I cannot think of anyone."

"But there is Elone. You saved her life and that of the child. Have you not seen how sometimes when you walk through the village, she stands and looks after you and there is happiness in her face?"

"I—no, I have not noticed that, Sipanata."

"It is true. And I will tell you something more. Just as you study with me to learn our language, so she is learning the Creek tongue from old Sabanta. Sabanta has been here many years, even before I was born. Emataba once said to me that there were Kiowas hunting buffalo near this place, and one of them saw Sabanta and wished to make her his squaw. He taught her the language of the Kiowas, and he came to see her many times, but she was loyal to her people and would not go with him. Well, now she helps Elone speak Creek as well as you do. And even if Elone does not speak the tongue of the white-eyes, you and she can now talk together."

167

The Quaker doctor stared at his young teacher. Then he said softly, "But she is more nearly your age, Sipanata. And you have no squaw. Why do you not take a wife, you who have never had one?"

Sipanata looked at him and then smiled. "Ho, this is very good. Now you begin to think almost like a Creek, my shaman. I have taught you well and Emataba will be pleased. I will answer you without a forked tongue because I am your friend. I did speak with Elone, and I told her that I found her good to look upon and that her little child was pleasing to me. I asked if she would not wish to be my squaw so that I could protect her and the child. Do you know what she said, my shaman?"

The Quaker doctor wordlessly shook his head.

"She said that it honored her to hear me speak so, but that she could not take a husband until she had paid the debt."

"The debt?" Dr. Ben Wilson wonderingly echoed.

"Yes, my shaman. The debt of her life and that of Tisinqua. And this is not strange, for although she is Sioux by blood and Kiowa by capture, she speaks as would a Creek. Do you not know that we believe that if someone saves our life, we owe that life and it is a debt that must be paid in honor?"

"Yes, I can understand that. Sometimes, among my own people, I have heard of that belief. But I would bind no one to me only because I had saved her life, Sipanata. You call me your shaman, and you know that it is my work to make the sick well again." Again he gave a soft laugh. "Surely, then, all of your people whom I made well in this village would then owe me their lives as a debt—no, I do not expect that. I have a skill which my God has given me, but there is nothing owed to me in using that skill to help others."

"It may be as you say. But you cannot change what she feels in her heart, and it is that her life belongs to you, as does that of her child. Speak to her. You will see that I talk straight, my shaman."

Greatly troubled, Ben Wilson nodded and pressed Sipanata's hand. Leaving the brave's teepee, he walked along the rows of tepees and wigwams, greeting in the Creek tongue the children, old women, and men who came out to see him. Their smiling faces, the marks of obvious re-

168

spect which they paid him by inclining their heads, crossing their hands together over their chests, made him bite his lips as a sudden deep emotion seized him. How open and direct these people were, in contrast to men like Dr. Elmer Drawley and George Hardesty. . . . Remembering that latter name brought tears to his eyes as he thought of how both Hardesty and his beloved Fleurette had had diphtheria, how he had performed the same operation on them both, and yet Fleurette, young and vibrant and a true helpmate, had been taken. How strange it was that the will of God did not always seem just at first thought, and yet behind this the most awful mystery of all, there was a reason, however unknown to him. Then, in the same moment of remembered anguish, he felt the deepest contrition for having condemned George Hardesty. For Hardesty had insisted on making all the arrangements and paying for them to transport him and the two little children to Windhaven Range. And Hardesty's own corrupt life had changed for the better, too. Yes, perhaps in that appeared the true hand of our Lord.

He blinked his eyes to clear the tears and turned to see that he had come to the tepee which had been given to Elone and her child. She knelt, her back to him, before a small cooking fire over which a metal pot was suspended from a crudely improvised tripod. She was busy stirring a kind of porridge made of cornmeal and a little milk. From inside the tepee, he could hear the happy cries of Tisinqua, and in these a smattering of the child's first words, for she was now thirteen months old. As he watched, entranced, Elone turned her head to call gaily in her own Kiowa tongue a reassurance to the child. Ben slowly approached and said in Creek, "Let me do that for you, Elone."

She gasped and straightened, her eyes wide with surprise. Then a shy, quick smile curved her soft lips and before he could stop her, she bowed her head, crossing her wrists over her bosom, and meekly murmured, "It is not right that the shaman do woman's work."

Answering her in Creek, he responded, "But the child calls for you. And this is my work, Elone. Besides, I wish to see Tisinqua and make certain that the evil spirit has left her body."

"It has, shaman, and it was you who drove it from her

169

as you did from me. My life and that of Tisinqua belong
to you now. You do not have a squaw to cook for you or
to make the fire or see that your bed is warm with many
blankets. I beg of you to let me do this for you, mighty
shaman."

"Elone, this is my work for which I studied many years
as a young man. My duty is to heal those who have evil
spirits within their bodies and to drive them forth. In my
language, I am called not a shaman but a doctor." He pronounced the English word.

Elone regarded him, with a look of wonder in her face.
"Doc-tor?" she repeated with curiosity.

"Yes, Elone. That is what I am. Among my people, a
doctor is paid in gold or silver when he heals the sick. It
is not a question that the lives of those he heals belong to
him. So you see, you must not think that you owe me anything. Yet I will tell you that I am happy to see you and
the child so well. You have had much sorrow in your life,
and I hope that here among these kindly people you are
happier."

"Oh, yes, Doc-tor." Her lips hesitantly and exquisitely
formed the strange new word, and there was a sudden flush
to her soft, coppery-tinted cheeks. "The Creeks are good
to me, they treat me as one of them. They share what they
have, but I see that they have so little. I am told by all
of them how good you are. Sipanata has told me how you
almost gave up your life to help these people. But you did
not do this for gold or silver, surely?"

"No, Elone. I did it because I wanted to with all my
heart. I cannot bear to see good people starved and treated
like stray dogs, people who are good and honorable in
their dealings."

"The porridge is ready now for Tisinqua. Here is a bowl
for it, Doc-tor." Once again, he smiled with delight to
hear how she pronounced his medical title. It seemed to
him that never before had that word carried such a connotation of gratitude and respect, and once again he felt his
eyes blur with sudden tears.

"Let me feed her, Elone," he said in an unsteady voice
as he took the bowl and ladled the porridge into it with
a crude wooden spoon. As she stopped to go into the tepee,
she turned suddenly to flash him a look of tenderness.

170

He entered after her, squatted down, and began to blow on the porridge to cool it, stirring it with the spoon. The little girl was dressed in a doeskin jacket and petticoat which Elone herself had made and lay in a wooden cradle padded with a thick blanket. Elone knelt beside Ben, reached out to stroke the little girl's forehead, then said to him, "She grows strong now, since you drove away the evil spirit from her, Doc-tor. She is a very good baby. She does not cry, and she sleeps through the night without wakening."

"That is very good, Elone."

Elone reached down to lift Tisinqua out of the cradle, then seated herself on the rude pallet of her bed, crooning to the little girl, who stared with curious interest, her little black eyes very wide, as Ben Wilson squatted down with the bowl in one hand and the spoon in the other.

"It is not right for the shaman to feed the child," Elone anxiously interposed in her soft voice. Though the Kiowa tongue was harsher, with more consonants, even when he had first heard her speak he had been struck by the gentleness of her voice. Using the Creek as she now did, it seemed to him that it was almost as lovely a voice as that of his own Fleurette. Once again, without warning, he felt the sting of tears as he rejoined, "No, Elone, it is also the doctor's work. I have children of my own, and I know how to do it. It gives me pleasure. Please let me."

She nodded silently, watching as he dipped the spoon into the bowl and held it toward Tisinqua's mouth, smiling reassuringly. She whispered something to the little girl, who promptly opened her mouth and accepted the porridge.

"She is such a sweet child. Perhaps she would like a doll to play with. The next time I go to Wichita for supplies, I will bring one back for her."

He used the English word "doll" and Elone, not understanding it, tilted her head to one side and questioned, "What do you say she would play with, Doc-tor?"

As he held the spoon to the little girl's mouth and watched her accept it, he tried to explain, groping for the descriptive words of the Creek which would clarify for Elone: "It is like a small totem, or an image which is like a person. It will be that of a little girl, such as she is. She

171

will pretend that it is hers, and she can talk to it, put it to sleep, play with it, and pretend that she is grown up already."

"But that is a wonderful thing!" Elone beamed. "You are kind to think of it, Doc-tor."

"Do you and Tisinqua have enough blankets to keep warm?" he asked as again he presented the spoon to the little girl's mouth. Now she was eating with relish, leaning forward a little and making contented noises to show that she found the porridge tasty.

"Oh yes, I have enough. More than I had with the Kiowas." For an instant, her delicate face was shadowed by a look of unhappy remembrance. Then, brightening, she added, "But it is you, Doc-tor, who is the kindest of all."

"You must not say that. I am happy that you are both well."

At last, Tisinqua was finished, and Elone rose and walked around the tepee, gently cradling the little girl in her arms and whispering to her. Ben Wilson watched, entranced at the sight of the devotion of this young Indian mother. How it reminded him of his dear Fleurette with little Thomas and then the baby Sybella! It was almost more than he could bear. He turned away for a moment to hide his emotions, and, when he had mastered himself, he turned back to say to Elone, "I will see that Tisinqua has a doll to play with as soon as I can."

"You are kind and good to think of us, Doc-tor." She looked at him intently. She had heard the story of his family from Sipanata, and she now could guess his thoughts. "Indeed you must have loved her very much, and I know she loved you, too. It was a joy to her to give you children. I see from the way you are with Tisinqua that your heart is full of love. My child and I will never forget what you have done for us."

He could not trust himself to speak. Nodding to her, he went out of the tepee. He walked to the end of the village and let himself out by the rickety gate. He stood looking toward the east whence he had come—it seemed an eternity ago now. Then, with no one to watch or hear him, he covered his face with his hands and wept unashamedly.

172

CHAPTER EIGHTEEN

Andy Haskins had gone back to Luke Bouchard to report his meeting with blind Horatio Bambach and his daughter Jessica. He told Luke that only two freed black workers were left to work the fifty acres, and they were dissatisfied with their wages and ready to quit on a moment's notice. Having been authorized by Luke to take charge as foreman, Andy then returned to the Bambach's property and paid off the two workers in gold specie, which immediately quelled their discontented grumbling, for even Union script could not equal the purchasing power of gold—the first these former slaves had ever held in their hands. They wished the Bambachs well and sauntered off, arm in arm, bent on spending a good part of their wages on rum and women.

Andy then sat down with Horatio and told him that he planned to hire about five trustworthy men to work the fifty acres in cotton and produce. Some of them would be white, poor sharecroppers who had lost their own farms through the excessive taxes levied by the anti-Southern county assessor. The others would be blacks, older than the two who had previously accepted employment, because they would be realistic enough to accept the transition between slavery and a freed status where they would be competing in an open market for secure and lasting work.

Jessica then insisted upon preparing a meager but nourishing supper for her father and the enthusiastic Tennessean. Andy was embarrassed by her gratitude and attentiveness, but the warmth and the intimacy of discussing problems in a forthright way with both the old man and his daughter began to thaw his natural reserve. He insisted on following Jessica to the kitchen and doing the dishes himself, jocularly explaining that he felt left out if he were not allowed to do his share. As for Jessica, she regarded him with open admiration. He seemed so capable and so eminently trustworthy that it was as if she had known him for many years. Her father had readily accepted him and taken him into his confidence, a further indication to the lonely widow that here was someone who was extremely dependable, who had almost miraculously appeared on their doorstep to help them solve their problems.

"Now the way I see it, Mr. Bambach, Miss Jessica," he expostulated as he accepted a second cup of strong chicory, "the sort of workers you need for this small piece of land are older men, maybe even with families. Men who aren't flighty, or liable to take off tomorrow for somebody who'll pay them a dollar more a week. Mr. Luke Bouchard told me about some fellows his lawyer knows in Montgomery. I'm going to talk to them tomorrow, and maybe by the end of the week I'll come back with some really fine workers to plant your cotton and get you some fruit and vegetables started. Oh, that reminds me—this morning, when I saw Mr. Bouchard, he said his lawyer was going to pay your taxes. Now mind you, you don't have to worry about them at all, you're not under any obligation at all to Mr. Bouchard, just you remember that. There'll be time enough, once this land turns you a profit, to pay that off, but you'll still own this piece of property. He wanted me to be sure to tell you that so you wouldn't have any doubts about it, you see."

Old Horatio shook his head and put a handkerchief to his trembling lips. Then he coughed and said in an unsteady voice, "It's like manna from heaven, Mr. Haskins. I just can't believe any more that folks can be so kind and thoughtful. I thought this war had turned everybody into looking out for themselves first and the devil take the hindmost. I don't know how I can ever thank Mr. Bouchard, but I do want you to tell him how grateful I am, and so is Jessica."

"Oh yes!" the young widow broke in, her eyes shining, "and we want to meet Mr. Bouchard and tell him so. Won't you invite him out here some evening, if he can spare the time, Mr. Haskins?"

"Sure I will, ma'am. Now I'll be back here in about two or three days, so don't you fret any. When I come back, I'll have some men who'll know just what to do to grow your crops."

174

Then, patting his mouth with his napkin, he rose, suddenly flushing with self-consciousness as he saw Jessica's eyes fix on him. "Well, I'd best be getting back. Can I pick up any supplies for you in Lowndesboro? You know, there's a real fine man running that general store there, Mr. Dalbert Sattersfield. He's back from his honeymoon now—he married a real nice girl who came along with Miz Laure to look after their two little boys. He deals fair and square, and he's a real gentleman."

"Father, wouldn't it be wonderful if we could have some real coffee for a change?" Jessica asked.

"When I come back, I'll see you get a couple of pounds of real good coffee. You know, ma'am, I'd sure like to drink a cup with you and your father. Sort of reminds me of when I was a boy back in Tennessee, when my daddy and I had a cup of coffee after a good long day in the fields and talked things over. You know, you're sort of like a family to me now—if you'll forgive my saying so."

"Not at all, young man," Horatio put in. "You're a fine, decent fellow, Mr. Haskins. It's my privilege to know you, and you'll always be welcome in this house, be sure of that."

"Oh yes, Mr. Haskins, I agree with Father," Jessica added.

Andy coughed to hide his emotion, gripped the back of his chair with his hand, and stared at it, half reluctant to put an end to this pleasant encounter. Finally, he declared, "Well now, I'll sure tell Mr. Bouchard you'd like to have him over, and I know he'll want to see you. I'll be going now, Mr. Bambach, ma'am. Thanks again for this fine supper."

"I'll walk you to the door, Mr. Haskins," Jessica volunteered as she rose from the table. "I'll be right back, Father."

"All right, my daughter. Good night to you, Mr. Haskins."

"Good night, sir. You'll be seeing me soon."

Andy turned to look at the light-brown-haired young widow, who came toward him, her lips wreathed in a soft smile, and suddenly he wished he had the right to say what he really felt about her. He'd never been more comfortable with anyone, and he'd never thought that he'd feel that way about any woman. She was so gentle, so kind, and really young and good-looking into the bargain—what a shame she'd lost her husband in the war!

"It was good of you to talk the way you did to Father, you do him a world of good, Mr. Haskins," she whispered to him as she walked toward the entrance of the old frame house.

"I respect him a lot, Miss Jessica. I promise you I'm going to do all I can to get this land paying off in a hurry, and I'll work right alongside the men I bring, you can count on it."

"Mr. Haskins—" She put a hand to his wrist, then suddenly dropped it with a start at her own audacity. "Thank you—and—and—God bless you. I'm so grateful for what you've done for Father, I can't begin to tell you—"

"That's all right, ma'am. I'm only glad I could help. Well, I'll see you soon, then, won't I?"

"Yes. I—I hope so, very much, Mr. Haskins." Before he could suspect her intention, Jessica had suddenly put her hands to his shoulders and kissed him impulsively on the cheek, then drew back, blushing and aghast at her own temerity.

Two days later Luke Bouchard rode with Andy Haskins to make his first official call on the Bambachs, having delayed it until he could bring them the news that they need no longer worry about the exorbitant tax levy imposed on them. When Jessica opened the door to Andy's knock, Luke perceived the delighted look on her face at the sight of the Tennesseean, and he told himself that his choice of Andy Haskins as foreman for the Bambachs would not only help two deserving people, but also very likely would provide Andy Haskins with a new and rewarding relationship.

Jessica, flustered and self-conscious, apologized for not being more suitably groomed to welcome guests, then led them to her father, to whom she had just finished giving breakfast.

"Good morning, Mr. Bambach," Luke cheerily introduced himself. "I'm Luke Bouchard, and I came along with Andy Haskins to bring you some good news. I've wanted to visit before, but I purposely waited until I could clear up the problem I know has been bothering you. And so, sir, I've brought along a copy of a receipt from the county assessor. My attorney, Jedidiah Danforth, cleared

176

up all the delinquent taxes and obtained a formal title to this property. But, as I am sure Andy has explained to you, he's already prepared a quit-claim deed transferring it back to you so that, after a reasonable time, you'll own it free of any encumbrance."

"Oh Father, isn't that wonderful? Mr. Bouchard, God bless you! You don't know how worried I was for Father's sake," Jessica exclaimed. She took a handkerchief and, turning aside, wiped her eyes, then chided herself: "Oh, it's dreadful of me to forget my manners this way—do please excuse me, Mr. Bouchard, Mr. Haskins. May I offer you gentlemen some corn pone? I baked it early this morning."

"I'd enjoy that very much, Miss Bambach. And so would Andy. As a matter of fact, I believe Andy has something that might go well with it."

At this, Andy came forward and handed a package of coffee to Jessica. "Here's your coffee, ma'am, two pounds like I promised. I think it'd taste good with the corn pone."

"Oh, thank you, Mr. Haskins. I'm sure it would." Jessica, her eyes shining with tears, hurried off to the kitchen to prepare the refreshments, while Luke and Andy seated themselves at the table.

Horatio turned his sightless face in the direction of Luke's voice. "I—I don't rightly know how to thank you, Mr. Bouchard, sir. I've been worried about Jessica—it would be just about the last straw for my poor girl if we'd had to give up this place. When we lost what we had in Virginia and the news of her husband's death came to her, I felt it was more sorrow than a young woman should have to bear at one time. I thank God that I'd put away a little hard money so that we could try for a fresh start here— and then, as you know, it looked as if even that was going to be taken away from us. I don't know how I can ever repay you."

"There's no need for that. All I've really done is to make an investment in good land and fine people. Now, Andy's going to come by this afternoon with some new workers who'll stay with you through the spring and summer planting and the fall harvesting. They're good men—I know because he's picked them himself—and they live around here so they appreciate the land. But as for repaying me, Mr. Bambach, I'll be quite satisfied if you take a

177

small percentage of the profits of your crops at the end of the year and pay me gradually as time goes by. Rest assured, I shan't press you for payment, either."

Jessica returned with a pot of strong coffee and a plate piled with slices of hot corn pone which she set down on the table. "I'll bring back the cups and saucers in a jiffy," she apologized.

"I'd like to help you, Miss Jessica." Andy pushed back his chair.

"Really, Mr. Haskins, I can manage—well, it would be nice—I mean—oh dear!" Jessica hurried out of the dining room with Andy following her. The look on his face was one of rapt devotion, and Luke smiled to himself. There could be no doubt that Jessica Bambach and Andy Haskins were discovering that they had a great deal in common, and that, to his way of thinking, was the ideal foundation for a happy courtship. He had a feeling that before much longer, he was going to have to write Lucien Edmond to tell him that Andy was about to settle down at last.

The next afternoon, Andy returned to the Bambach house to bring with him five workers whom he had recruited. Luke had instructed him to make certain that Horatio Bambach did not learn that Luke would be paying their wages until at least the end of summer, by which time the potential profit from the crops on this fertile fifty acres could be determined. The other two freed blacks, whom Andy had paid on his second visit, had already left their huts at the far back of the fields by the time Andy arrived with the new workers.

Two of these, Matthew Rensler, thirty-four, with a rangy build and a jovial nature, and Burt Coleman, twenty-eight, tall, and ingratiating, were white Southerners who shared a common sorrow: their wives had died during the war in which both had fought; both had been slightly wounded but seen active duty till Appomattox. They had been brought up on farms in Southern Alabama, their parents were dead, and their few surviving kinfolk had long since left the state in quest of a better future in northern Texas or California.

The other three workers were former slaves. Two of them were brothers, Cassius and Daniel Ardmore, who had come to Windhaven Plantation only a week before. Marius

Thornton had talked to them, explaining that all the land was owned by freed blacks who worked with Luke Bouchard, the owner of the original fifty acres on which the chateau stood. There were, he told them, no jobs there, but he promised to do his best to find a place for them. The Ardmores had worked together on the same large plantation near Talledega before the war. Since then, they had drifted from county to county, seeking what odd jobs they could find to keep alive. What impressed Marius most was that they were experienced hands in the cotton fields and were familiar with the operation of the gin. He relayed this information to Andy Haskins, who sought them out where they were living in an abandoned shed not far from the little town of Lowndesboro, and they were eager to accept employment on the Bambach land.

The third black was Jasper Cooper. Thirty-one, stocky, and reticent, he had done a great deal of gardening for his old master, whose name he bore. He, like Cassius and Daniel, ruefully admitted that "bein' free ain't no better 'n slavery, not if a man can't earn himself enough to buy some sowbelly 'n corn pone."

Since there were only two huts for the workers on the Bambach property, Andy suggested that the five newcomers spend their first few days making a shelter for themselves and then showed them the acres which had had their first start in the planting of cotton and those others where melons, corn, beans, tomatoes, and yams should be planted. Andy had also gone to Dalbert Sattersfield's general store and brought back flour, molasses, beans, some bacon, and chicory so that the workers could have enough food for the first week. Jessica Bambach promised to cook for them, and her graciousness impressed the men, all of whom avowed that it would be good to have regular work and a place to stay and decent food again.

Andy watched as the men began to work with zest, swinging axes to cut wood and uniting their efforts to build the rude huts that would be their temporary homes. Then he bade Horatio Bambach a good evening and walked toward the old dilapidated rail to which he had tied his gelding. Jessica followed him, glancing quickly at the house to make sure that no one was watching. "I'm ever so grateful, Mr. Haskins—"

"Shucks, I'd like it a lot if you'd just call me Andy.

Like I said before, Miss Jessica, calling a man mister makes him feel a lot older than he is. And I sure don't feel old now, now that there's work to be done and I can see some real progress made here for the two of you."

She lowered her eyes and her cheeks crimsoned. Very softly she said, "Well then, I'll call you Andy if you'll call me Jessica. Is that fair enough?"

Andy grinned from ear to ear. "Couldn't be fairer, Jessica. I sure like your name a lot."

"And—and I like you a lot, too, Andy," she confessed. Then, looking at him intently, she added, "You know, Andy, I was so worried because Father was getting to the point where he honestly didn't care whether he lived or not. Now you've given him new life and hope, you and that wonderful Mr. Bouchard. I—I just don't know how I can ever thank you enough." Then, quickly, she leaned forward and kissed him on the cheek. But this time, before she could draw back and hurry into the house, Andy impulsively put his left arm round her shoulders, drew her to him, and kissed her heartily, though on the cheek as well. "I had to do that, Jessica," he blurted, getting very red in the face. "You can go ahead and slap my face if you've a mind to, but I just had to do it. I think you're the pluckiest and prettiest woman I've ever seen, and I mean it, I truly do."

Then, dropping his arm to his side, he meekly added, "I didn't mean to get fresh with you, Miss Jessica."

"Oh, Andy, you couldn't get fresh with anyone! You're a fine, wonderful man, and if you ask me, you're much too modest about what you can do. And now that we've kissed each other, don't you think it's time you stopped calling me miss from now on?" Her eyes danced with a soft, sweet mischief.

Andy uttered a delighted sigh. Then he put his arm around her shoulders again and this time kissed her very soundly and very enthusiastically on the mouth. Jessica closed her eyes and, with a gasp, clung to him until the kiss was over.

"My gosh, Jessica, my gosh!" he hoarsely gasped. "I'm just a low skunk, that's what. Here I went and forgot all about your being a widow and mourning your husband—I ought to have had more sense, but my old daddy said I was the sort who acted first and thought about things later. I owe you an apology—"

"Do you know, Andy Haskins," Jessica put her hands on her hips and looked severely at him, "your trouble is you have to go and spoil everything nice by apologizing for it. If I hadn't wanted you to kiss me like that, I wouldn't have let you. Now you just think that over."

"Oh my gosh, Jessica—do you mean—oh glory be!" Andy let out an exultant whoop and tossed his sombrero high into the air. Jessica tilted back her head and burst into delighted laughter. "That's more like it," she admonished him as she turned to go back into the house. "I hope you'll be coming out to make sure the men do their work properly and don't take too long between visits. Good night now."

As she went into the house, Andy picked up his sombrero, clapped it on his head, and began to whistle as he untethered his gelding. Mounting it, he said aloud to himself, "Glory be, looks like I might not get back to Texas and Mr. Lucien Edmond for a mighty long spell, that's surely the way it looks!"

CHAPTER NINETEEN

Luke Bouchard, that same afternoon, had ridden to Montgomery to meet with William Blount, Ebenezer Tolman, and Clarence Hartung at the back of Tolman's funeral parlor. It was his third such meeting with these three courageous Republican politicians since they first called on him at Windhaven Plantation to urge him to run for the open seat representing Montgomery County in the state legislature.

He had satisfied himself that the cause was just. As a pragmatic idealist, just as his grandfather had been, Luke despised bigotry and, still more, the terrorism by which bigots sought to keep decent citizens away from the polling places. He understood that by agreeing to publicize his candidacy, he might call down upon himself the vitriolic fury of the Ku Klux Klan. He talked with Laure about this possible danger, concerned for her safety after the harrowing ordeal to which she had been subjected at the vengeful hands of Henri Cournier's henchmen.

Laure smiled and reassured him. "I feel just as you do, darling. If nobody stands up to the Klan and the carpetbaggers, you and I and our children will never enjoy the blessings of peace. To me, it's very much as if the war were being continued, except that instead of guns our enemies are infecting the minds of the people. So I say, fight them, expose their wickedness—but please, for my sake, darling, be very careful."

"I certainly intend to, my darling. I wouldn't accept this challenge Mr. Blount and his friends have offered me if I hadn't taken precautions. Blount assures me that there is no known klavern in this area. Every since Hurley Parmenter brought his group of abominable cowards around and caused so much grief, we haven't seen much of the klan. I'll never forget the way Hurley Parmenter and his men abducted Marius and threatened to burn him alive if I didn't join their hate-mongering group. But Parmenter's men seem to have dispersed, maybe even out of the county. Blount is reasonably sure of it."

"I'm glad of that," Laure replied. "I've read in the *Advertiser* about demonstrations by the Klan in Bullock and Macon Counties, mostly against freed blacks. How dreadful all that is! When Lincoln set the slaves free, he never envisioned how dearly they would have to pay for that freedom after his death. That's why, Luke dear, I'm proud of you for wanting to carry on the principles he lived and died for."

"I'm a very fortunate man," Luke gravely replied as he held Laure close to him and kissed her. "I promise you I'll be careful, and our workers here are well armed."

William Blount was the first, this pleasant afternoon, to congratulate Luke Bouchard on his decision. "We'll have a hard fight on our hands, Mr. Bouchard," he said as he shook Luke's hand, "but your courage, sir, will lend us strength against these carpetbagger rascals. As I told you, you'll be running against a black Democrat, by the name of Cletus Adams. He's forty years old, was a slave up in Tallapoosa County till the war, then came to Montgomery to live with his freedman cousin who runs a blacksmith shop on the edge of town. So he's established residence in this county and thereby qualifies as a candidate. By and large, there's nothing disreputable about him, but of course there is about the people who back him and their plans for him if he should take office. That's what we want to block, Mr. Bouchard."

"In the poorer counties, Mr. Bouchard," Clarence Hartung spoke up, "we're pretty sure of a majority of Republican votes. As you must know, sir, well before the war those landholders barely made ends meet, and the blacks they had working for them were practically their equals. Also, most of those people never wanted to secede, and they were Unionists and Republicans right along. They haven't gone over to the Democratic ticket like so many scalawags in other parts of this state."

"You remember, gentlemen," Luke earnestly declared, "that when you first called on me with this proposition, I told you I would not be beholden to any preferred group. I hope that you still agree that if I run for the state legislature, I may express my own views."

"Of course, sir, we understand that and we're heartily in favor of it," William Blount avowed. "Do you know what Senator Spencer—*our* Senator, a Republican—is saying in the Senate? Why, sir, that to be a Republican is a 'heinous crime'! And one of his associates is attacking Governor Smith, blaming him for all the Ku Klux Klan outrages and charging him with, mind you sir, 'criminal negligence in law enforcement'—that's shameful!"

"And worse yet," Ebenezer Tolman stood up, holding a newspaper in his hand, "Senator Spencer is denouncing our governor, a man of his own party, for 'being criminally derelict and flagrantly wanting in the commonest essentials of his office'—and that's a direct quotation from his Senate speech which our *Advertiser* printed a few weeks ago. I hope you can see from all this, Mr. Bouchard, how very much we need a man of your forthrightness and decency. But, alas, I fear they'll resort to the vilest libels to try to gain their evil end."

"Well then, gentlemen," Luke proposed, "I'll write out a statement of my views and the platform on which I'm running, and you may print this in the *Advertiser* whenever you wish."

"Excellent, sir! You see what Spencer's doing," William Blount replied. "He's trying to alienate white Unionists and blacks from Governor Smith's constituency by letting them think that the governor has abandoned them to the outrages of the Klan. But I say that with a man like you on the ticket, Mr. Bouchard, our levelheaded citizens will be shown how to see through these deceptions and restore our good governor to office."

The week after Mitzi Vourlay had married Dalbert Sattersfield, Laure had interviewed two young women who had placed notices in the "Situations Wanted" section of the *Advertiser,* seeking domestic work as nurses or governesses. Luke had himself selected the names of these candidates when he had visited the newspaper office in person, on a visit to Montgomery. He thus had been able to get first-hand descriptions of the applicants from the elderly bespectacled clerk who had talked to them and written out their advertisements, One of them, Delphine Watson, had described herself as having been a rural schoolteacher for two years. She had attended a young ladies' finishing school in Tuscaloosa before the war, was twenty-nine years old, and at present resided with her older widower brother. The other, Moira O'Connor, a year older, had been orphaned by the war and forced to sell her parents' house for taxes. She moved in with an elderly, ailing aunt. Ever since the end of the war, she had served as a nurse in the homes of three different families. Her last job ended when the family decided to move to the Wyoming territory.

The elderly clerk told Luke that both women were "plain, decent ladies, Mr. Bouchard, and I myself knew their families so I can vouch for them. Fact is, I wouldn't have accepted their notices if I'd thought they weren't proper females to enter a respectable household, if you get my meaning, Mr. Bouchard."

Of the two, Laure had selected Moira O'Connor. This personable young woman, of Irish descent, was pleasant, almost homely of feature, neatly dressed, her black hair pinned up primly in a huge bun at the back of her neck. She had impressed Laure with her tenderness toward Lucien and Paul, and so Laure had engaged her on the spot. For there was no doubt that Mitzi Vourlay Sattersfield fully intended to become a mother as well as wife: a week after she had returned from her honeymoon in New Orleans, she had visited Laure and blushingly confided, "It's just like a dream, Madame Laure! We're so much in love it's as if we'd known each other for years. And dear Dalbert wants children as much as I do. Oh, I do so hope you find someone to take care of the two boys. But if ever you do need me, you know you've only to send for me—I owe so much to you!"

Thus far, Moira O'Connor appeared to be an acceptable replacement for the petite French brunette. Laure had no fault to find with her, for she diligently took over the nursery, saw that both of the boys were fed on time, had their naps and their bedtime on proper schedule, and were amused during their waking hours by her telling stories and playing simple games with them. One afternoon, Laure entered the nursery and smiled to see Moira engaged in showing Lucien how to hold yarn between his hands while she crocheted. Looking up, she greeted her employer

185

with a respectful nod and said that she was crocheting a little sweater for baby Paul. And Lucien piped up, "I help her make it, Mama!"

Luke Bouchard's statement on his candidacy appeared on a half-page of the Montgomery *Advertiser* on the first Monday in April. Laure came to his study to congratulate him. "I'm so proud of you, my darling," she told him as she kissed him gently. Then, straightening, and with that inimitable teasing smile of hers which he remembered from their first meeting at the Union House, she added, "However, sir, you needn't think that you're the only one in the house who has something important to announce."

"Oh?" He looked up with a wondering smile.

"I think that by the beginning of October, we might have an addition to our nursery," Laure airily announced. "That would come just before the election in November, wouldn't it? I do hope it won't distract you too much from winning, darling."

Luke laughed exuberantly as he rose from his chair and hugged her. "You know it'll spur me on to greater efforts than ever," he avowed. He kissed her neck and dainty ears, stroked her golden hair, and stepped back, pride and love shining in his eyes. "But this time, I'd really hope for a girl, my darling, a girl as beautiful as you. The women of our family have always been strong and have attracted the very finest type of man, to add even more strength to our lives."

"I'd like a girl, too. But this child hasn't even been born yet, and you already have her marrying!" Laure teased. "And there's a drawback with a girl: when she marries, she changes her last name—or has my able politician forgotten that?"

"Of course not," he chuckled. "Lucien and Paul in their time will continue the Bouchard name, well enough. But don't forget how Arabella strengthened her side of the family by marrying that quickwitted and capable James Hunter. And our dearly beloved Fleurette brought Dr. Ben Wilson into the family, just as Laurette had the good sense to marry Charles Douglas. You know, speaking of Charles, we may live to see a chain of department stores all over this country—it wouldn't surprise me in the least! And now, my darling, why don't we go out to the kitchen and see if Hannah can make us some nice hot biscuits with honey and a pot of good strong coffee so we can both celebrate the news we have for each other?"

Arm in arm, laughing and whispering like young lovers, Luke Bouchard and his golden-haired Laure walked toward the kitchen.

CHAPTER TWENTY

In the back room of the billiard parlor on Thomaston Street, a short, fat man with a gray beard and large, nearly bald cranium took a gold watch out of his vest pocket, noted the time, scowled, then replaced it with a muttered oath. He wore a swallow-tailed coat and plaid trousers, a flowery cravat with a diamond stickpin thrust through it, and monogrammed gold cuff links in his silk shirt. He had placed his new bowler hat on a stool beside his chair and now crossed his legs, waggling his right foot from side to side as he again consulted his watch and this time muttered aloud, "Goddam nigger, can't even keep an appointment on time!"

The back room was separated from the billiard parlor by a narrow entrance covered by a thick green baize curtain. Beyond it, he could hear the clicking of the billiard balls and the cues, the jocular repartee of half a dozen players engaged in this ancient game of skill. The convivial sounds, however, only made him grow more morose as he consulted his watch for the third time and then, uncrossing his legs, stamped his right foot and swore violently, "Where the hell is that damned nigger anyhow? If he wasn't a good Democrat and I didn't need the bastard, I'd have the Klan put the fear of God into his dimwitted brain!"

A moment later, the green baize curtain was pushed aside and a pleasant-featured black entered. "Sorry to be late, Mr. McMillan, sir," he apologized as he ambled forward. He was six feet tall, lanky, with high cheekbones and an angular chin. His smile was friendly and his voice deferentially soft. "Came as quick as I got your message, Mr. McMillan."

"All right, Cletus, no harm done so long as you're here.

Pour yourself a shot of whiskey, and there's a box of stogies right next to the bottle. Help yourself."

"Very kind of you, Mr. McMillan." Cletus Adams went over to the small table against the wall, opened the box and took out a cigar, picked up a lucifer from the little saucer beside the box, scratched it on the wall, and lit his stogy, puffing at it contentedly until it finally drew satisfactorily. All the while, Barnabas McMillan scowled at him, an almost contemptuous sneer on his fleshy mouth. He watched the black pour two fingers of whiskey into a dusty jelly glass, turn to him, hold it up, and nod his head before imbibing, as a mark of respect. He grunted acknowledgement of the tribute. "Well now, Cletus, time to get down to cases."

"Yes, sir. I'm your man, you just tell me what you want done, Mr. McMillan, I'll sure do it."

"Sit down over there. It's not much of a chair, but it'll have to do. I picked this place because I didn't want half the damned Republicans in this town to see us meet. Oh yes," Barnabas McMillan chuckled humorlessly, "they'll find out all about me in November once you've won that seat in the legislature, Cletus boy, but till then it's just as well they don't know I'm behind the scenes, if you take my meaning."

"Sure do, Mr. McMillan," Cletus Adams nodded as he seated himself facing his political mentor.

"Did you read the *Advertiser* last week, Cletus?"

"No, sir. Had a lot of work to do."

"Well, it just so happens I kept a copy for you. Here." The corpulent man reached into his coat pocket, took out a folded page from the newspaper, and tossed it to the black, who had to rise from his chair and stoop down to retrieve it. "Read it carefully, Cletus. You *can* read, can't you?"

"Yes, sir. I had schoolin', I really did, Mr. McMillan."

"Then read it and tell me what you think when you're done." Barnabas McMillan leaned back in his chair and glowered at the black.

Five minutes later, Cletus Adams looked up. "It sure sounds good, Mr. McMillan. This Mr. Bouchard, he's a mighty fine man. We all heard tell of him here in Montgomery, that's no lie."

"I'm sure you have, Cletus. But don't forget, that's the son of a bitch you're going to have to beat at the polls. Now, Montgomery County is likely to go Republican, but Senator Spencer doesn't want that, understand? We're going to have to make a good fight, and we might even have to bring the Klan in to scare some of these nigger Republicans into staying at home on election day—no offense meant, Cletus boy."

"That's all right, Mr. McMillan. I know what you're driving at, sir."

"You're pretty educated for a nigger yourself. Guess that's why I picked you. Don't forget, there are lots of other niggers in this town I could have found to run against Bouchard, but I'm backing you. That means you're beholden to me. Once you get into the legislature, you're going to do something about these land bills and the taxes."

"I'll do what I'm told, Mr. McMillan. I really 'preciates the honor." The lanky black shook his head and chuckled to himself. "My oh my, if my mammy could be alive today and see that her Cletus is bein' put on a ticket for folks to vote for, to represent all the folks of this county—wouldn't she be proud!"

"Well, she will be proud if you do what you're told by the time November rolls around, Cletus. Now listen carefully." Barnabas McMillan leaned forward, his hands on his knees, his eyes narrowed and intent. "I know about this fellow Bouchard, too. He's going to be a mighty tough opponent. What we've got going for us is that being a Republican these days isn't exactly healthy in Alabama— or anywhere else in the South, either. I've got a few friends who know where to get the Klan out when it comes time, say around October. We have to discourage folks from voting any way except Democrat. But don't worry, Cletus. The Klan visits white folks as well as niggers who don't mind what they're told."

"I understand, Mr. McMillan, sir."

"Thing is, it would be better if we could find something we can pin on this Bouchard, something that'll make the damned Unionists and niggers want to vote Democratic without having the Klan show them why it's healthy to vote that way, you follow me?"

" 'Deed I do, Mr. McMillan, sir." Again Cletus Adams

bobbed his head, his smile more ingratiating than ever as he puffed at his stogy to keep it going.

"He's taken the oath of loyalty, he didn't help the damned Rebs in the war, and he's even got niggers on the land he and his grandpappy used to own. That gives him a clean bill of health—but that's only on the surface, Cletus. What I've got to do—and you leave that to me, because that's what the boys back East are paying me for—is to dig up the skeletons he's got buried in his back yard. Don't you worry, I'll find out about them. Every man's got skeletons he wants to hide, Cletus."

"Yes, sir."

"That's a good nigger. You keep on doing as you're told, Cletus, you'll make a little money for yourself. And then, when you're into the legislature, when you're walking into that courthouse down on the main street here, and the folks are respecting you and taking off their hats and saying, 'There goes our representative for the county,' you're going to remember who your friends are, aren't you?"

"Oh yes, sir, I sure am, I sure am, Mr. McMillan!" Cletus Adams anxiously agreed with another vigorous bob of his head.

Barnabas McMillan closed his eyes and stroked his beard for a moment as he thought. At last he rose and walked over to the little table to whet his whistle. Uncorking the bottle, he tilted it to his lips and took a generous swig, then belched and set the bottle down. "That's a lot better. Now I was just thinking, Cletus, the best way to find out about a man's skeletons is to get into his house and live with him and find out what he says and what he does."

"How are you going to do that, sir?"

"I've got ways, Cletus. I don't mean I myself. I told you I was staying out of this. You know I'm from Massachusetts, and you know I made a lot of money selling provisions and knapsacks to the Union Army. Of course, these stupid, goddamned Johnny Rebs around here think I'm a carpetbagger—well, maybe I am. But if a clever Massachusetts boy can't outsmart a secesher, then we didn't deserve to win the war, isn't that right, Cletus?"

"Oh yes, Mr. McMillan, it sure is right, right as rain, sir!" the lanky black eagerly agreed.

"That's the way to talk, Cletus. Help yourself to more whiskey. You can take the bottle with you, matter of fact.

Now then, I'm going to let you in on a little secret. I arranged with old Hiram Pulford—he's a good Easterner himself and, what's more important, the county assessor—to pick up about four hundred acres of good Alabama land downriver. It's not too far from Bouchard's place, either. And I had a nice house built on it last year to be ready for my takeover in this county. So I'll be on hand close by to keep an eye on things. Something else, too, Cletus. I found out by asking questions around town here that Bouchard's married to a young filly, got himself two little boys by her, and just hired a nurse to look after the brats. Well now, maybe I could work it out so's that nurse took suddenly sick and had to leave town, and maybe her sister or cousin or someone like that could take her place right inside that big house Bouchard sets himself up so proud in. Now, if I was to be real friendly with that cousin or that sister, Cletus, wouldn't you think she'd have sense enough to tell me what she saw and heard going on inside that house, wouldn't you now?"

"I sure would, Mr. McMillan. Yes, sir, I sure would."

"Then that's what I think I'm going to have to work out, Cletus. Meanwhile, I've written out a little speech you're going to make on the steps of the courthouse next Monday. Here it is." He took a folded sheet out of the other pocket of his coat and handed it to the black. "Study it good, memorize it. And don't go adding any of your own notions to it. This is exactly what we Democrats want people with brains in this county to know about our platform and about you, Cletus. I'm having a copy printed in the *Advertiser* the day after you make your speech. So you just better not gum up the works by changing it around any, you hear me?"

"Yes, sir. I'll study it real good, you'll be proud of me, Mr. McMillan."

"I'd better be, Cletus. You know, I'd hate to have to repudiate you once you got elected. Accidents can happen before a man takes his seat in the legislature. You be a good boy, and you'll have money in the bank and a lot of respect from all these white folks that used to look down on you. Now you get out first, and I'll follow later out this back door. Go have yourself a round of billiards, if you've a mind to. I'll have a stogy and think about getting that nurse to come down real sick before much longer."

192

CHAPTER TWENTY-ONE

By the twentieth of March Lucien Edmond Bouchard had not yet begun his intended drive to Abilene. Ten days hence, Congress was to readmit the state of Texas to representation as having fulfilled the terms set down by the Reconstruction Acts. But the fact was—and one that considerably worried Lucien Edmond—that a singular kind of reconstruction was taking place on the neighboring ranch to the west.

Soon after lunch, young Eddie Gentry, the cowhand who had driven Dr. Ben Wilson and his two children from Corpus Christi and been offered a job on Windhaven Range, rode out with Joe Duvray. Both men had Spencer carbines sheathed at their saddles and ready for use, a precaution Lucien Edmond had urged them to take because of the singular goings-on much too close to his own wooden markers for his own peace of mind.

The lanky young Texan was riding a sturdy piebald gelding which Ramón Hernandez had picked for him out of the corral, his pleasant face wreathed in a grin of enjoyment. He hadn't forgotten how Ben Wilson had spoken on his behalf to Lucien Edmond Bouchard about giving him a job. Born in San Antonio and just turned twenty-six, Eddie Gentry had lost his parents when he was nine and been brought up by a well-meaning but inebriate uncle and left most of the time to shift for himself. For about five years, he had worked as a stable boy for a cantankerous old widower in San Antonio. There he had developed a love for horses and become an expert rider. He preferred the elemental directness of animals to the coarse brutality and sly chicanery of the many desperados, *pistoleros,* and adventurers who patronized his employer.

Eddie later went to work for a wealthy Mexican who had purchased some barren land near Corpus Christi from Norman Cantrell, during the time that Cantrell was running his brief but profitable land-swindle scheme, using forged Spanish land grants. When the Mexican discovered that the acreage he had bought was good neither for growing crops nor for grazing cattle, he angrily went back across the border and left Eddie without a job. Now the young Texan was enjoying the hard work of the well-organized cattle ranch. He looked forward to taking part in the roundup and drive to Abilene. Lucien Edmond Bouchard had assured him that he would be one of the riders and help Ramón with the remuda when the time came.

Eddie turned to Joe Duvray as he rode alongside and pointed toward the northwest. "Look over there, Joe. Isn't one of our markers down?"

"I think you're right. When I rode out this way last week with Ramón, I could have sworn I saw one of our boundary posts there. Now look at it. There's a stretch of that damned wire up—tarnation if that new neighbor of ours hasn't gone and swiped just a little of Mr. Bouchard's land for himself."

The two men galloped their horses toward the stretch of wire Eddie had pointed out. Dismounting, Joe squatted down and stared at the grassy strip of level land on his own side of the fence, then straightened and peered over it and swore under his breath. "Look there, Eddie—they've pulled up our boundary marker, all right, but they forgot to cover up the hole where it used to be—see there? It's about twenty-five feet from this section of fence they've put up. Oh, they're clever, all right, because they've left a lot of the land unfenced, and only this section here running about an eighth of a mile, I'd judge, has been stuck up here for us to notice."

"What do you think it means, Joe?"

"Unless I miss my guess, they're doing it little by little, Eddie. Now you see that marker of ours they took down. They just added a little land to their holdings and stole as much from Mr. Lucien Edmond. Now what they'll do, figuring we're getting ready for our drive, is put up a little more fencing every couple of days or so. I'll bet you every time they do it, a couple more of our markers will be pulled out so that our vaqueros, who of course can't be expected to remember where every marker was to start with, won't think anything about it."

194

"But fencing—that's the first time I've seen anything like this in Texas, and you know I'm a born Texan, Joe."

"I don't like it at all, Eddie." Joe dolefully shook his head and scowled. "I damned well don't. If it comes to the point that all the ranchers start fencing in their land, that'll cut down on the work for the cowhands and the vaqueros, you mark my words. There won't be any open range. And if somebody gets here first and fences in the land right near a creek or a river, he'll be taking water rights away from his neighbor and letting the neighbor's cattle die of thirst. No, I don't like it one little bit. And I still don't know who owns that place over there. He hasn't even bothered to come calling on Mr. Lucien Edmond. That's not neighborly where I come from in Georgia, Eddie."

"It's not neighborly for a Texan, either, Joe. Hey, somebody's riding up to us. Look out, he's reaching for his rifle—"

"And somebody else is riding up with him, with holstered guns. Looks real nasty from here—he's a real *pistolero*, take my word for it, Eddie," Joe growled under his breath as he pulled his Spencer carbine out of its sheath, cocked it, and let it lie across the saddle as he took the reins of his gelding in his left hand and slackened them to keep his gelding halted.

"No need to aim that rifle at us, *amigo!*" Eddie called as he saw a stocky Mexican riding up toward the wire fence, brandishing an old Belgian rifle. The man beside him, with guns holstered in his belt, was Jackson Brundiger. A black sombrero was pulled down over one side of his face, and his eyes were narrow and cold. He halted his gray stallion, which snorted and reared up in the air. With an oath and a vicious tug at the bit, Brundiger forced the stallion to halt, its front hooves pawing at the ground in thwarted revolt. "Something bothering you gents?" he asked in a cold, impersonal voice, without a flicker of emotion in his face.

"Why, yes, now that you mention it, mister," Joe Duvray drawled. "Eddie and I here were wondering why in the world a man would want to put up wire fencing when the range is free."

"It's really none of your goddamned business, now that you've said your piece," Brundiger contemptuously responded. "My boss owns this land, and he's given me the orders to mark it off so that your cattle won't do any grazing off his grass. Now why don't you and your friend there go on back and mind your business?"

"No offense, mister," Eddie broke in with an amiable grin. "We're all of the same mind, when it comes to that. We don't want your boss's cows meandering over on our land, either. But we were here first and our boss never told us to put any fencing. Happens we did put up boundary markers."

"And that's no lie," Joe added with a sly wink at the lanky young Texan to show that he had taken his nonchalant cue from the latter. "I thought I saw a hole in the ground, a little back of where your Mex friend with that old rifle is sitting his horse, where our boss put a marker a long time before your boss even moved in on this land."

Jackson Brundiger's lips tightened, and his right hand edged toward the butt of his holstered pistol. "I don't like what you're trying to say—or what I think you're trying to say, mister," he slowly answered. "Are you saying that my boss is stealing your outfit's land?"

"You're the one that said it, mister, not me," Joe shrugged. "I'm not looking for any trouble with you or your friend over there. I'm just wondering, that's all. I swear when I rode out this way a couple of weeks back, one of our markers was standing there bold as you please, and now there's just a hole in the ground. I don't see the marker, but I sure see the hole."

"Listen, you talk like a Johnny Reb—I can smell 'em a mile away." Brundiger bared his teeth as he vituperatively enunciated every word, his hands still near the butt of his pistol. "I say there wasn't any marker there. Now if you want to call me a liar, mister, we can settle this thing fair and square. Right now you've got the edge on me with that carbine. But if you've got guts enough, you can always come out here with a six-shooter or a Colt and see how good you are on the draw. I'll tell you this, I don't take kindly to a man who comes nosing around and starts off by making me out to be a liar. I can tell you it's lucky for you I feel in a good mood this afternoon, or I might just take a notion to cut me another notch on one of my pistols here. I've got a few of them, mister, so why don't you and your friend just go back where you came from?"

"I guess we'd better, Eddie. I don't want any trouble. Are you the top hand of the outfit?" Joe asked.

"Happens I am," Jackson Brundiger snapped.

"Then Eddie 'n me'd appreciate it a lot if you'd tell your boss that Mr. Lucien Edmond Bouchard would like to talk to him. Maybe he'd come over to the ranch house so the two of them could have a nice friendly talk and get acquainted."

"I'll tell him, mister, but I don't think he's going to give a damn one way or another what your boss thinks. He minds his own business, he's got affairs he's tending to, and I'm running the outfit for him. Now that's plain enough, isn't it?"

"Sure it is. All right, Eddie, let's ride back." He turned in his saddle to stare at the somber, wiry gunmen. "My name's Joe Duvray, mister. Mind giving me your monicker?"

"I'll tell you what, Duvray," Brundiger said with a mirthless, thin-lipped smile, "the next time you come over here and want to start trouble, you can just call me out like I told you you could. Then I'll tell you what my name is. And it'll be the last time you'll hear it." Then, turning to the Mexican with the rifle, he said, "Manuel! ¡Vamanos!" Wheeling his horse and turning back to give Joe a last malevolent glance, Jackson Brundiger galloped off with the Mexican rider.

"Whew!" Eddie took off his sombrero and mopped his brow with a red bandana. "I thought for sure we were going to have some gunplay there."

"We will one day, I'm afraid," Joe said slowly. "That range boss, he's a professional killer if I ever saw one. You can tell from the way he squints his eyes and never takes them off you, the way his hand kept sneaking toward his holster, and then that last bit about cutting a notch in the butt of his pistol—that's a killer, all right, Eddie. But he knew that at that short range our Spencers could cut him and his vaquero down before either of them could get off a shot."

"You think it means real trouble?"

"I'm sure it does, Eddie. But I don't know which way it's coming, and that's what is going to worry Mr. Lucien Edmond, too. I wonder if he's trying to slow down our drive, keeping us guessing about what he's going to do

197

next to bother us. Well, I'm not the boss of this outfit, that's for Mr. Lucien Edmond to figure out. Let's go tell him right now."

On the afternoon of the day following Joe Duvray's and Eddie Gentry's confrontation with Jackson Brundiger, Margaret Caldemare decided that the weather was sunny and warm enough for her to go horseback riding. Indeed, in her many letters to her father from the finishing school, she had written enthusiastically of having learned how to ride sidesaddle and even to make her horse perform graceful steps and flourishes. To be sure, these maneuvers were extremely staid, for Agatha Emmons, the decorous principal, looked askance at any feminine activity that could not be justified by the standard of gracefulness and harmonious behavior. Indeed, it was only because she felt sorry for Margaret's isolation at her school—with so few visitors and her own father's prolonged absence—that she permitted Margaret to ride at all.

Shortly after arriving in Texas, Margaret had shyly asked her father if she might not have a horse of her own —since there were so many available at the ranch. Caldemare, conscious that he had been neglecting her while he pursued his own profiteering schemes, offered no objection to her riding when the weather permitted, and he told Porfirio Costado, one of the *pistoleros* whom Jackson Brundiger had hired, to select a gentle mare for his daughter. Costado had been an inveterate horse thief, and he knew enough about horses to have been able to select them for a remuda if he had been inclined to the work of an honest vaquero. Margaret was enchanted with his selection and especially with the light star-like marking on the mare's forehead. Having been particularly proficient in French at Miss Emmons's school, she promptly named the mare *Belle Etoile* (Bright Star) and, using the lady's sidesaddle she had brought along with her luggage, she began to ride on a regular basis.

On this pleasant March afternoon, seeing that her father and Jackson Brundiger had gone off riding to the west and seemed intent on a private conversation, Margaret saddled Belle Etoile and let the mare take a leisurely gait in the direction of Windhaven Range. She observed with some curiosity the several stretches of wire fencing attached to solid posts, but there was enough open range to continue as she wished. Having seen in the distance the outlines of the Bouchard ranchhouse and bunkhouse encircled by the protective stockade, she suddenly had an impulse to pay a visit to this unknown neighbor. The country was beautiful, but so vast that she felt the same loneliness she had known back in school. It was evident that her father was planning something very important, something which, of course, she knew would make money so that he could keep his promise to her. Wistfully she thought to herself that she didn't really care about going to San Francisco or anywhere else, so long as she could stay here with her beloved father and get to know him after all these years. The brief reunions they had enjoyed ever since she had started in that Boston school had become more and more infrequent, until it was almost as if her father had become a stranger.

Lost in thought, Margaret hardly noticed that the mare was ambling toward the northeast and at an angle that would carry its rider well beyond the Bouchard ranch house. For about five hundred yards, this part of the terrain had little grass, but was profuse in mesquite bushes. As she turned in her saddle to glance back at her father's house and to observe with another twinge of loneliness how remote and isolated it seemed, there was a sudden rattling sound, and her mare whinnied in fright and shied to one side, nearly throwing her. A rattlesnake, coiled and sunning itself on a sloping rock, had drawn back its ugly head to strike, its rattles vibrating in sinister warning.

Margaret uttered a cry and jerked at the reins, almost slipping from her sidesaddle. But the mare, having seen the venomous reptile, tossed its head and frenziedly galloped away from the danger. "No, no, Belle Etoile! Stop, oh please do stop—please!" Margaret was really frightened now as she tugged at the reins and tried to maintain her precarious seat during the mare's pellmell, irrational run.

Joe Duvray had decided to inspect Lucien Edmond's markers again this afternoon and had made a wide circling tour of the grassy range toward the northwest which, he had slyly calculated, would bring him toward the as yet unknown neighbor's land. He had already noticed that another section of wire fencing had been put up since yesterday, and he scowled irritably. If things like this kept up, the drive to Abilene was going to be stalled until sometime in April, maybe even later. That would be tough on the cattle as well as on the men, for it would take them until about the end of August to reach Abilene and dispose of the herd, and they would cross the plains through the worst time of the year for scorching heat and dust storms.

Margaret's mare was racing headlong now, her eyes wild, her flanks wet with a sweaty lather, and there was foam at her mouth. Margaret employed a gentle bit, not the kind that would bruise or cut the horse's mouth, so that her frantic tuggings at the reins did not punish the frightened mare into an obedient halt. Now she cried out again, as a sudden veering by the mare made her nearly tumble from her saddle. She was jostled, almost breathless, and her face was pale with fright.

Joe heard her faint cry and, halting his gelding and posting in his saddle to look in the direction whence it came, saw the mare heading at full speed toward the northeast. Crouching over his gelding's neck, he urged it it into its utmost speed to overtake the runaway mare.

Almost hysterical now as she realized that she could not stop, fearing at any moment that she would be thrown bodily from the saddle, already bruised and aching from the furious jostling of her slender body by the frenzied mare, Margaret began to pray aloud as she closed her eyes and with despairing, weakening strength continued to tug at the reins.

Reaching back with his sombrero to smack his gelding's withers and urging it to greater speed, Joe watched the young woman as he began to close the gap between them. Now he was only a hundred yards away, but suddenly the mare veered again, this time directly west, nearly throwing its helpless rider, and again Margaret uttered a shriek of raw terror: "Oh my God, please, please, stop, Belle Etoile! Oh God, help me!"

"Come on, Brazos!" Joe shouted to his gelding as he whacked it again with his sombrero. The sturdy horse raced forward, and gradually Joe came up abreast of the fleeing mare. "I'm going to pull you off that mare, lady!" he shouted. "I'm going to count to three, understand?"

Margaret turned to look back at him, her face wet with

tears, then nodded, her knuckles white with the tension of holding onto the reins as her only security against being thrown. "When I call three, let go of the reins and just let me pull you off, understand? One—two—now, three!" he shouted.

Nervously, Margaret dropped the reins, her eyes tightly closed, shuddering as she heard the mare emit its shrill, frantic whinny of terror. At that instant, Joe, dropping his reins around the pummel of his saddle, reached out with both arms and seized Margaret by the waist, lifting her into the air and setting her down ahead of him. "Steady, lady— there now—whoa, Brazos, you ornery critter, whoa, I said!" he shouted as, holding her with his left arm, he grabbed at the reins and tugged, repeating his command to halt. The gelding slackened its pace while the mare, free of its burden, raced off toward the west.

"It would have been a lot safer if you'd ridden like a man, lady!" Joe panted, gritting his teeth against the spasm of muscular pain which surged through his left arm as he held Margaret Caldemare securely in place, half-turned away from him. "If you're going to ride a horse like that, you'd better put on some trousers, that's all I've got to say!"

For an answer, Margaret burst into hysterical tears and bowed her head as the gelding halted at last.

Joe slipped down from his saddle and lifted the weeping young woman down to the ground, then held her against him until her paroxysm of anguished sobs began to subside. "There now, it's all over, lady. I didn't mean to be rough with you, but I don't mind telling you I was scared as hell—begging your pardon, but I was."

At last, she was able to control the fitful tremors that shook her slim, graceful body. Almost convulsively, she clung to him now, burying her face against his chest as she exhaled her tearful relief at this unexpected salvation.

"That's right, go ahead and have a good cry. You were damned lucky I happened to be here, lady—sorry if I sound like I'm scolding you—guess it wasn't your fault—"

"It—it wasn't," Margaret at last managed as she fought to regain self-control. "I think Belle Etoile was scared by a rattlesnake—Father said there were quite a few of them out here and that I should be careful wherever I rode."

201

"That's for sure. But it's all right now. Your mare will run herself out and then she'll go back to the corral. Now, my name's Joe Duvray."

"Th-thank you, Mr. D-Duvray. I—I'm Margaret Caldemare. You—you saved my life. Thank God you were riding out there—I didn't know what to do—she's such a gentle horse and I've ridden her so often—"

"Never mind, Miss Caldemare. Happens to the best of riders when there's a rattler around. I don't know about Brazos, he's never been up against one yet, but there's always a first time," Joe grinned as he tried to cheer her. "Feel a little better now?"

"Y-yes, th-thanks to you, Mr. Duvray. Oh my, I didn't mean—I mean—I'm sorry—" Margaret Caldemare suddenly realized that she was clinging to him with both arms. Her cheeks flaming, she backed away, then buried her face in her hands and began to cry again.

He grinned and shook his head, then suddenly scowled. So that was the name of the galoot who owned the spread next to Mr. Bouchard's, was it? And she'd said "father," so she obviously wasn't his wife. A right pretty girl, too, Joe thought to himself as he detailed her with a quick glance. Slim, about five feet six, he judged, her light-brown hair drawn away from the sides of her head and fixed into a thick oval bun that left the back of her neck bare. That fancy riding habit with the hobble skirt—well, he could think of a better outfit for a lady to wear if she was going to ride out here in this wild country. With a skirt like that, no wonder she couldn't ride astride the way any sensible vaquero would do. Come to think of it (now he grinned to himself as he remembered his own Georgia background, back in the old days before the war), it *was* scandalous to hear of a girl wearing trousers and riding like a man. There'd just been one he'd remembered, little Marty Tompkins, but then she was a known tomboy.

As Margaret slowly dropped her hands at her sides and sniffled, trying to appear more presentable, Joe observed that she had lovely, large hazel eyes with tiny green flecks at the iris, that she had a dainty little turned-up nose, and a sweet, trembling mouth that made her look very helpless and certainly very feminine. He glanced down at her boots and grimaced again. Those were ladies' boots all right, and they certainly didn't have enough length or thickness of

202

leather to make it possible for her to grip the horse's belly and slow it or steer it the way she wanted the critter to go. His curiosity got the better of him. "I don't mean to get personal, Miss Caldemare, but you weren't born out in this part of the country, were you?"

"Oh no, Mr. Duvray!" She furtively rubbed her eyes with her handkerchief to clear them of the tears, sniffled again, then straightened and tried to force a pleasant smile to her lips. "I—I was born in Boston. My—my mother died soon after I was born, and I went to school in that city— I was there until Father sent for me a few weeks ago."

"I see. I didn't mean to get too nosy, Miss Caldemare. I work for Lucien Edmond Bouchard. He owns that spread next to your father's, and over there," gesturing broadly with his right arm, "you can see the ranch house and the bunkhouse."

"Yes, I do. It's a very large ranch, isn't it?"

"Fair size," Joe Duvray grinned. "Bigger than I ever saw in Georgia—that's where I came from. Went through the war and was real lucky, but there wasn't anything to come back to once we Rebs had to give in to old Ulysses Grant— funny that the general who beat us should run the country now, I guess you might say."

"How did you get out here, then, Mr. Duvray, if you were born in Georgia?" Margaret found it disconcertingly interesting to talk to this amiable young man. His black hair and blue eyes and frank, regular features were certainly pleasant to look at, more than the surly faces of most of the workers on her father's ranch, she told herself. Then, remembering Miss Emmons's advice that a gently bred young lady should never stare boldly at a strange young man, she lowered her eyes and blushed vividly.

"Well, you see, Miss Caldemare, when we Rebs lost the war, most of us came back to find we'd lost our homes and just about everything else. There wasn't any work back there in Georgia, or chance of it anyway, so Andy Haskins and me—too bad you can't meet him, Miss Caldemare, you'd really like him—well, we just drifted on down to New Orleans and picked up odd jobs wherever we could find them. Then Mr. Lucien Edmond Bouchard came along with his father, Mr. Luke, and Mr. Luke it was who hired Andy and me to work out here on the range. That was nearly five years ago. Been here ever since, Miss Caldemare, and I really like it. It's open country and a man can see something good come out of his work."

"Yes, I—I suppose so. Is Andy Haskins your best friend, Mr. Duvray?"

"Just about, Miss Caldemare. Andy and I went through the war together. He's from Tennessee. Guess he wouldn't really want to go back there and settle down any more than I'd care to pick up and set down in Georgia again. Anyway, a shell blew off his right arm and I sort of saved his life, so we've been through a lot together. But let me tell you, Miss Caldemare, even though he's only got one arm, old Andy can handle a gun or a knife or even a lariat with the best of them. When he gets back here, I'd sure like to introduce him to you."

"I—I'd like to meet him, Mr. Duvray. I—oh my, how am I ever going to get back to my father's house?" Margaret was suddenly flustered as she looked around and remembered that her mare had run off and by now was nowhere to be seen.

"No need to worry. I'll ride you back myself. But I'd like to ask you a couple of questions, if you don't mind. Maybe you can help my boss feel easier about what your father's doing over on his spread."

"I—I don't think I know what you mean, Mr. Duvray, but—but I'd be glad to answer any questions if I could that would help you. I certainly owe you that much and a great deal more. Oh my, I'm still a little shaky, I guess." The aftermath of her narrow escape from probable death had made Margaret suddenly tremble again, and she put her hand to her forehead and swayed unsteadily.

"That's all right, don't fight it. I'd get the jitters too after the narrow escape you just had, Miss Caldemare. Here, just lean your head against my shoulder till you feel better. That is, if you don't mind getting that nice jacket of yours dirtied a little. The cattle we brushpop sure kick up a lot of dust, and a man can't clean himself up till after sundown when the work's done." Seeing that she was still trembling, he gently took her by the shoulders and drew her toward him, letting her chin rest on his shoulder. "Maybe that'll help a little—I'm not trying to get fresh with you, Miss Caldemare."

"Oh no—I—I know that, Mr. Duvray. I don't know what's got into me, really I don't! You—you're very kind."

"You had a bad scare, that's what. No reason to blame yourself. Why," he tried to reassure her with a genial chuckle, "if Brazos here had seen that rattler, you might have been the one who'd had to ride after me and pull me off my horse."

"Oh my goodness, I don't think I ever could have done that—dear me, oh my—" Despite her exhausting ordeal, Margaret was able to giggle and then laugh uninhibitedly at the ludicrous thought which he had just proposed.

"Now that's a lot better. Shows you're not scared any more," he grinned.

"I—I think I'll be fine—but my mare—"

"When she's run herself out, I told you she'll come back to where she belongs. Any sensible piece of horseflesh does that, Miss Caldemare."

"I—I suppose so. Well, I'd best get back, or Father will be worried."

"I'll help you up on Brazos. There we go. He's nice and mild, used to my ways, so he won't shy any."

"Oh yes, thank you very much, Mr. Duvray."

Joe Duvray mounted into his saddle, took up the reins, and hesitantly circled her waist with his left arm. The delicate fragrance of the lilac scent she used came to his nostrils, and it was a new and unexpectedly exciting experience for him. At the same time, he flushed with embarrassment, trying to maneuver his left arm so that it would not embarrass her, yet at the same time wanting to make certain that she wouldn't slip off the gelding. "All set now? We'll go back at a nice slow pace."

"Thank you. I don't know what I would have done—it was very good of you, Mr. Duvray."

"If you really want to thank me, Miss Caldemare, you just call me Joe. Everybody else does on Windhaven Range."

"All right," she said glancing quickly back at him and then turning away as she found herself blushing. "But then you'll have to call me Margaret."

"That's a nice name. Margaret. Well, that's fine. Am I holding you too tight?"

"Oh no, it's—it's just fine."

Kicking his heels against the gelding's belly, Joe turned the horse back toward Robert Caldemare's property. As he did so, he observed a group of four vaqueros hammering

205

posts into the ground, while two others lifted sections of wire which had already been cut into calculated lengths and began to attach them to the new posts. Frowning, he said to her, "What I don't understand is why your father thinks he has to fence in his range. Nobody's going to steal it from him. Certainly not Mr. Lucien Edmond Bouchard. There isn't a more honest man in all the Union, and I'm here to vouch for it."

The attractive young woman gave him a quick, hostile look, her brows arching almost with anger. "Are you implying, Mr. Duvray, that my father's dishonest?"

"No, no, Margaret, don't get me wrong," Joe floundered, trying to extricate himself from her sudden and unexpected change of attitude. "It's just that—well, I've never known anyone in these parts to use wire. The range is open. And when you've got neighbors, if his cattle wander over on your land, you just send them back. You brand with your own brand, so the riders can easily make out what belongs to who. Leastways, that's what I've always believed, and so does Mr. Lucien Edmond."

"I won't have you say a single word against my father, Mr. Duvray!" Margaret flashed. "He's worked hard all his life, ever since my poor mother died, to give me the very best of everything. I was educated in one of the finest finishing schools, and that's where I learned to ride, I'll have you know. And Father was the one who sent money every month so that I could be fed and clothed and given a good education. He sacrificed a great deal for that, Mr. Duvray. So I don't take kindly to your innuendo."

"I don't follow you, Miss Caldemare." Joe understood that in view of her sudden change of mood, any use of her first name would hardly be welcome. "I didn't say your father was dishonest. It's just that Mr. Lucien Edmond would like to have him come over and saw howdy and make himself known, that's all. All we've seen the last few weeks is your father's men putting up these posts and that wire. And as it happens, yesterday some of those posts went over Mr. Lucien Edmond's own markers."

"Now you're accusing my father of stealing your employer's land, Mr. Duvray. Oh how I wish I had Belle Etoile back right now! I'll thank you to ride quickly so that I can be home and not have to listen to your slandering words against my father," she flared.

"Oh Lord, Miss Caldemare, don't say that—I didn't say any of those things, I just wanted—"

"I really don't care what you want, Mr. Duvray. Will you please take me home as fast as you can. Thank you very much." Her tone was icy, and she did not look back. Joe damned himself for all kinds of a fool and made Brazos begin to trot.

CHAPTER TWENTY-TWO

It was midnight on the first Thursday in April. The full moon had hidden behind a thick shield of cumulus, and the night was dark and still. The Alabama River, swollen two weeks before by a sudden downpour, had subsided into its usual placid, rippling murmur. Along its banks, frogs croaked and the occasional soft cries of night birds mingled with the sighing of the trees, stirred by a gentle, unseasonably warm wind. The town of Montgomery was dark and silent, hardly a kerosene lamp or candle showing through any of the curtained windows of the more elegant residences. On the outskirts of town, there were old, sedate frame houses badly in need of paint alongside the more rustic hovels of the freed blacks who sought to show their equality to their former white masters. Here, too, it was equally dark and silent. From a distance came the yapping of a mongrel dog in search of food. In the center of town, the Union flag at the top of the mast drooped, moved now and again by a sudden gust of night wind.

From the east, down a winding dirt road which led through a small forest of cedar and live oak trees, came half a dozen men on horseback. They wore white robes, and their hoods were peaked, with slits for the eyes and mouth. The man who rode ahead had a bullwhip coiled round the pummel of his saddle, and his mount was a jet-black stallion who snorted and whinnied and sometimes jerked his head this way and that to fight the imperious bit of his rider.

They came in single file, in a slow procession, silent among themselves and certain of their destination. At the crossroads, the leader halted his stallion and lifted his right hand, waved it toward the right, for the other path led toward Lowndesboro. As he turned his stallion, his companions followed without a word. In the dark silence, in the soft air of nightfall, the hooves of the horses could scarcely be heard, moving slowly as they did on the dirt path.

They came at last to an old frame house, set apart from other houses on this block. There were no lights showing through the thick chintz curtains of the wide front window. The leader drew his stallion to a halt, dismounted, and strode up the rickety steps to the porch. At least a decade ago, white paint had covered porch, steps, roof, and walls of this old house. Now the paint was peeling, and here and there one could see the boards of the porch and steps badly sagging.

The other five hooded men remained on horseback while the leader, looping the coiled bullwhip round his arm, carefully ascended the rickety steps, hammered on the door, and called out in a stentorian voice, "Esther Murtons, come out! The Ku Klux Klan summons you to appear before its august members to be judged and warned!"

From across the deserted street, a black freedman plucked aside a tattered curtain and peered out into the night, then hastily replaced the curtain and vanished. The sight of the white hoods the riders wore told its own story eloquently enough without his having to hear the dreaded summons.

There was silence for a moment, and then the leader of the robed sextet again hammered on the door and called out, "Esther Murtons, do not try to escape the justice of the Klan, or your fate will be dreadful! Come forth to judgment and warning!"

The five riders whispered among themselves, and one of them called out softly, "I see a light, guess the old bitch was sleeping hard!"

There was, indeed, the flicker of a kerosene lamp seen vaguely through the worn chintz curtain. Then there was the sound of a bolt being drawn back, and the door opened to reveal a frail, gray-haired woman clad only in her shift with a cotton robe hastily drawn over it. Her hand trembled as she lifted the lamp up, and then she uttered a stiffled cry of terror as she saw the leader's wraith-like disguise. "Oh God—I ain't done nothing, what do you folks come wanting to hurt a poor old woman for?"

"No, Esther Murtons, thus far you have done nothing to provoke the justice of the Klan," the leader replied, "but

209

we have summoned you tonight to harken to our warning. If you fail to heed it, you and your niece Moira O'Connor will face the grim justice of our righteous society—so be warned, Esther Murtons!"

"For God's sake, what—what do you mean, what do you want for me to do?" the old woman quavered.

"Your niece is employed as a nurse for the brats of a certain Luke Bouchard at Windhaven Plantation, is she not, old woman?" the leader demanded.

Trembling, stricken with fear, Esther Murtons could only nod.

"He is a damned, black-hearted Republican. Your niece must leave that disloyal house at once."

"But—but we are poor, and I'm sick and Moira pays for my medicine, there's no harm in that—" Esther Murtons quaveringly tried to propitiate the Klansman.

"If you do as you are told, Esther Murtons, you will receive money for your ailments. But in return, you must get her to leave that situation at once."

"Perhaps she needs a touch of the whip to make her think straight," one of the riders interposed with a sinister chuckle.

The leader moved closer to the trembling old woman and gestured to the coiled bullwhip round his arm. "I do not think you and your niece would enjoy thirty lashes of this bullwhip. Thirty apiece, old woman, tied to a tree out in the woods where no one can hear your screams. And then hot tar smeared on the marks of the lashes."

"Oh God, have mercy, I told you, I ain't done nothing! Please, what do you want me to do?" she wailed.

"Stop whining! Now listen carefully. Send her a note by messenger tomorrow, without fail, do you understand?"

Esther Murtons could only nod, biting her lips and trembling violently.

"You will tell her that you're very ill and that she must come stay with you at once. You will tell her also that her cousin Stacey Holbrook will replace her as the Bouchard nurse."

"But she doesn't have a cousin—"

"Silence, you stupid old bitch! I've just about lost my patience with you. You listen good, or you'll have a taste of this whip before the night's over!" he menaced.

"Oh I will—yes, yes, I'll do it—you say Moira's cousin—"

"Stacey Holbrook. You'll tell your niece that she's to recommend her cousin very earnestly, do you understand? She's to come back to town to see you as soon as she gets your note, and then she will send back her cousin. Don't say anything—the girl will be here tomorrow morning and will remain with you till your niece comes back from that den of vipers. Is that clear?"

"Why—why—yes, s-sir," Esther Murtons faintly stammered.

"And you, Esther Murtons, you're a good Democrat and that's the way you'll vote at the polls in November—is that clear?"

"Oh yes, yes, I mean to do it, just like you say, s-sir!"

"You'd better if you don't want to feel this whip, old woman. Now listen carefully. This cousin, Stacey Holbrook, comes from New Orleans. We know that Luke Bouchard's wife was born there. Your niece is to tell Mrs. Bouchard that that's one reason she thought Stacey would be accepted in her place. You're to say that in your note, and don't forget it."

"Maybe we ought to take her into the house right now and watch while she writes it." The man who had suggested a taste of the bullwhip spoke up.

"Oh no, I—I swear I'll do it—" Esther Murtons was nearly hysterical by now, swaying against the side of the door and nearly dropping the kerosene lamp.

"No, I think she knows what she has to do—don't you, you stupid old bitch?" the leader mockingly demanded. When the frightened old woman nodded again, her eyes huge and glazed with terror, he added, "We will send a messenger ourselves at ten tomorrow morning to this house, Esther Murtons, to deliver your note to your niece at Windhaven Plantation. It had best be finished by then and it had best say what we have told you to say, because the messenger will read it—you're not to seal it until he has, remember that well."

"Oh yes, yes, s-sir, I—I promise I will, I swear I will, s-sir—please don't hurt me—I'll do whatever you want—"

"That's showing sense. We will leave you now, Esther Murtons, and tomorrow we will see if you have heeded our warning—if not, our justice will be terrible for both you and your niece!"

With this, the leader turned and went back down the steps, mounted his horse and, flourishing the bullwhip in his right hand with a hollow laugh that drew another cry of fear from the gray-haired woman, rode off with his followers whence they had come.

CHAPTER TWENTY-THREE

Moira O'Connor was in tears as she faced Laure Bouchard in the nursery just before supper on the next day. "My poor old aunt's taken bad, Miz Bouchard, ma'am," she sniffled. "I feel just terrible about leaving you in the lurch like this, but she's been everything to me—when my folks passed, she took me in and shared what she had with me—"

"Of course, Moira, I understand. Don't cry, please," Laure gently interposed. "I'll confess that I'll miss you, and so will Lucien and Paul. They've already taken to you, and you've been a very good nurse to them. I'll certainly give you every recommendation when it's possible again for you to look for a situation. But of course," she frowned and tapped her cheek with a slim forefinger, "I do have to find a replacement for you as soon as possible."

"Well, Miz Bouchard, I have a cousin. Her name's Stacey Holbrook. She came up from New Orleans last week just to visit Aunt Esther and me for a spell, but she says she likes Montgomery and she wouldn't mind finding a situation for herself."

"Oh?" Laure responded. "Has she had any experience with small children, do you know, Moira?"

"Oh yes, Miz Bouchard! She worked for a fine family in New Orleans, that she did, she told me herself. She had to take care of a couple of babies there too—just like Lucien and Paul, I mean."

"You say she comes from New Orleans? Well, I was born there myself. Perhaps we'll have something in common, then. Can you get hold of her right away, Moira?"

"Oh yes, Miz Bouchard! Like I said, she's over at Aunt Esther's now. I could ride back and get her—if there was someone to take me and bring her back, I mean," the Irish woman eagerly responded.

"I think that can be arranged, Moira. I'll have Dan Munroe hitch up the wagon and drive you into town. Of course, your cousin might not want to come out so late this evening—but on the other hand, I really do need someone."

"Oh I'm sure she wouldn't mind coming, Miz Bouchard! Matter of fact, I—I wrote her before she came up here, when she was still in New Orleans, I mean, and I told her how nice you folks were and what lovely little boys Paul and Lucien are. And Aunt Esther wrote me in this note she sent by messenger this afternoon that Stacey was all-fired interested in taking my place, that is, if you'd like her."

"Well, then, Moira, I'll just have Dan Munroe take you to Montgomery as fast as he can, and it's certainly a relief to be able to find a suitable replacement for you on such short notice. If she's your cousin and she's had experience, I'm sure we'll get along famously. That reminds me—let me give you your wages for this week so far. There you are, my dear. I do hope your poor aunt will get well soon. Perhaps then, if this Cousin Stacey of yours doesn't find herself too happy here, you could always come back. I know Mr. Bouchard is quite pleased with your services."

"That's awfully nice of you to say, Miz Bouchard, ma'am." Moira O'Connor's face fell and she looked down at the floor. "Trouble is, Aunt Esther's getting awfully old, and she's weak, and I don't know how long it will be before she gets well—if she does at all, ma'am."

"I'm so sorry, Moira. There now, please don't cry any more. I'll go get Dan. You remember now, if things go well and you are able to come back—or, if you want to and this cousin of yours doesn't work out—I'll certainly be glad to hire you again," Laure reassured her.

Stacey Holbrook was twenty-nine, tall and willowy, her burnished chestnut hair piled in an imposing pompadour, her face pretty except for the hint of a sharpness of nose and chin. Her large, lustrous dark-brown eyes were fringed with very short lashes, which gave them an ingenuous look. Her voice was soft and husky, with a charming touch of Creole drawl, and the occasional *patois* into which she lapsed verified her New Orleans birth and background.

She had decided not to ride with Dan Munroe the same

evening that he had driven Moira O'Connor to Montgomery. She arrived instead the next afternoon, in a wagon driven by a freed black man who, as soon as she had descended with her two pieces of luggage, whipped up his spavined horse and headed back toward Montgomery.

Laure found her chatty and informative, pleasant of manner with a deference that belied her physical self-assurance and poise. To be sure, Laure was rather amused that this applicant for the post of nurse to Paul and Lucien should be so confident that she would bring her personal luggage to an interview. However, the imperative need for a replacement loomed ahead of all other considerations, and certainly Stacey Holbrook could speak—if perhaps a trifle glibly as if she had been coached on the theme—of her experience with very young children. So she was engaged to begin at once, and Laure herself found a room for her on the second floor of the chateau in the northern wing.

At breakfast the next day, Stacey made an excellent impression on Luke Bouchard by seeing to it that Paul and Lucien were fed and by taking charge with enthusiasm and skill. He chatted with her for a moment or two after he had finished breakfast, then kissed Laure and went back to his study, for William Blount had asked him to draw up a statement for the *Advertiser* on his own background and political views. Laure remained at the breakfast table with Stacey and followed her back to the nursery to watch the new nurse amuse the children for a time before she returned to her own pursuits.

"So you were born in New Orleans, were you, Stacey?" she casually asked.

"Oh yes, Mrs. Bouchard. On Bayou Road."

"Yes, I know where that is. I was born there, too." For a moment, Laure's exquisite face was shadowed by the remembrance of her father's suicide and her own desperate plight at the hands of the victorious Union soldiers. "But of course I willingly left there to marry Mr. Bouchard, and now that I'm here on Windhaven Plantation, I feel as if I've always been here."

"I see what you mean, Mrs. Bouchard. It *is* a lovely place. Such a big, beautiful house, almost like a castle."

"Yes, it's true. Luke's grandfather, after whom the older boy is named, always dreamed of having a replica of the

215

house of his own birth, and I'm so happy that he lived long enough to see it built and to enjoy it for a good many years."

"By the way, Mrs. Bouchard, where did you live in New Orleans?"

"Before I left," Laure replied, "I lived on Honoree Street."

"Oh? I think I remember that street—wasn't the famous Union House on it?"

"Of course. My first husband, who died of yellow fever, had his bank there—and of course if you know New Orleans history, Stacey, you must know that General Benjamin Butler took over all the New Orleans banks and put in his own men. So John—John Brunton was my first husband—very cleverly transferred his financial operations to that place so that Butler's officers wouldn't suspect that he was still continuing to serve worthy New Orleans citizens."

"My, it sounds almost like a story about spies, very daring and exciting," Stacey commented with a soft, slurred laugh.

"You might say that. Yes, it took a certain ingenuity. Of course, since Union officers visited the house, it was really well protected. They'd never think of looking for a bank there. Well, I'll leave you with the boys. My husband is very pleased with your work, Stacey, and so am I."

"I'm happy to know that, Mrs. Bouchard. I'll work real hard and do my best for them—they're such darling little ones!" Stacey gushed.

Laure gave her a smiling nod and left the room, closing the door behind her. Stacey stared after her, the lips of her somewhat sensual mouth curving in a crooked little smile.

"My, Barnabas will certainly be pleased with me," she said to herself with a low voice. "It's better than I thought. If she lived in the Union House, she had to be a whore, never mind what she said about her husband's bank. Oh, just wait till I get off a letter to him! He's sure to buy me that necklace I've wanted in old Mr. Johanson's jewelry store." Then, turning back to where the two little boys were playing, her smile deepened.

For the past two years she had been Barnabas McMillan's mistress. He had met her in New Orleans a year after the war, when he and several members of the House of Representatives had visited various areas of the conquered South to project plans of Reconstruction. Previously, Stacey Holbrook had been married twice. Her first marriage, to a callow young cadet with whom she had run away at sixteen, had been annulled. Her second marriage was to a wealthy Georgian who had made a fortune in smuggling contraband through the Union blockade, only to be killed in a squalid tavern brawl just before the end of the war.

McMillan had found her in one of New Orleans's most elegant houses of pleasure and became so enamoured of her erotic talents that he made her a lucrative offer to be his mistress. Now he held her to him by the promise of marriage and respectability, though she was by now heartily disgusted by his sadistic brutality and lecherous perversions. "You pull this off for me, Stacey girl," he had told her, "you get yourself into that fellow Bouchard's house and get me all the skeletons out of his closet, and you'll be Mrs. Barnabas McMillan with all the nice dresses and jewels you can ask for."

McMillan had cleverly arranged for the freed black who had driven Stacey to Windhaven Plantation to come by every evening at six, on the pretext of carrying a letter from the new nurse to her cousin and the latter's ailing aunt. Stacey could hardly wait for this evening, and her only concern was finding pen and paper and an envelope to write in detail what she had learned about Laure Bouchard's past. There couldn't be any doubt about it. Everybody knew during the war that the girls in the Union House on Honoree Street were down in the parlor for the Union officers to pick and take to bed. She thought to herself that Luke Bouchard must certainly be a stupid old fool to marry a girl who was just about half his age and who'd spread her legs for Union officers. Of course, she herself had had to do the same thing, but she'd never wanted to; she'd always been a true Southerner, by birth and inclination, but a girl had to live somehow. And a smart girl knew what side her bread was buttered on: after the South had been beaten to its knees, there wasn't any point in looking for romance and the smell of jasmine and a fine young Southern gentleman to woo and win her.

She went back to the two little boys and began to tell

217

them a story about a frog in a pond who puffed himself
up so much that he burst. As she did so, she was thinking
of Luke Bouchard, and her eyes glittered with malicious
mischief as she heard Lucien laugh when she finished the
story.

CHAPTER TWENTY-FOUR

A few days before Joe Duvray had saved Margaret Caldemare from being thrown by her frightened mare, Celia left Windhaven Range to journey to the little Mexican village of Maxtime, to visit her daughter Prissy. Prissy, the young, attractive daughter of Djamba and Celia, had become the squaw of the Comanche brave Jicinte, and they lived in the stronghold that the Comanche chief Sangrodo had established several miles from Maxtime.

At this time, Sangrodo and his people lived in peace and tilled the soil like farmers. Most of the men had taken Mexican women as their squaws. In earlier days, though, when Sangrodo and his people lived in Texas, there had been violence and warfare. Comanches were killed by whites for the bounty on their scalps, and to avenge this, Sangrodo abducted the *alcalde* of a small village and his wife, Catayuna Arvilas. During her captivity, Catayuna heroically resisted Sangrodo's determination to enslave her, and she won his grudging respect by her courage and honesty. Then the troopers of ruthless Captain George Munson rode into Texas and massacred the women of the Comanche village. Though herself seriously wounded, Catayuna rode to fetch Sangrodo and his men so that they might avenge the murder of the helpless.

Catayuna was now Sangrodo's joyously loving squaw. She had displayed the courage of a true Indian just two years ago when she killed the bandit Carlos Marcaras, during his raid on the Comanche stronghold in Mexico. Because she lost the child she was carrying as a result of that struggle, the child she bore later on, Inokanti, was all the more dear to her. Indeed, his name meant "He-Who-Is-Loved." Sangrodo idolized the child, and Catayuna was now known as the "beloved woman" of this Comanche stronghold—just as, a century before, Dimarte had been so named by the Creeks of Econchate.

News had come from one of Sangrodo's couriers that Prissy was with child again, and Celia, who had been aging noticeably and whose health was beginning to fail, determined to visit her daughter and be on hand for the delivery of the child. Kate Strallis and Maybelle Belcher volunteered to take over Celia's duties as cook for the ranch, even though lovely young Felicidad, now the pregnant wife of Djamba's son Lucas, insisted on working in the kitchen until such time as her condition would prevent such chores.

Djamba himself rode with Celia across the border, arriving at the stronghold on the morning of the sixth day. There Sangrodo and Catayuna eagerly welcomed them, and Prissy emerged from the lodge with steadfastly devoted Jicinte beside her.

After mother and daughter had had a tearfully happy reunion, Sangrodo beckoned to Djamba to enter his lodge and smoke the calumet of friendship. "There is one of our braves, Djamba, who has great gifts," he declared. "These will be wasted here. I should like to send word to the *Taiboo Nimiahkana*, for perhaps he can help Lopa-suta."

"Mr. Luke will be glad to help him if you think so much of him, Sangrodo, I'm sure of that," the Mandingo assured him.

"My squaw Catayuna has taught me to read and write in the Spanish tongue which she knew from birth," Sangrodo confided.

"I think Mr. Luke could understand it if you wrote a letter to him. And if he couldn't, he'd sure know how to get someone to turn it into English for him," Djamba said.

"I would like to do this," Sangrodo said. "Or better still, since you have learned enough Comanche to understand me and you speak the tongue of my blood brother, would you not listen to what I say and tell it to my blood brother's son, so that he can write to his father in their own tongue?"

"I'll be glad to do it, Sangrodo. Tell me what you want to say to Mr. Luke."

Sangrodo puffed at the calumet, then handed it to

220

Djamba, who as solemnly performed the ritual. Then, closing his eyes, choosing his words carefully, he spoke. "In our tongue, Lopasuta means He-Who-Is-Wise. He has known twenty-two summers. His mother and father died when that *gringo capitán* rode into our stronghold to kill those who had never harmed him. Catayuna says that he reads and writes in the tongue of my blood brother as well as in the Spanish." Here the Comanche chief permitted himself a wry smile. "He thirsts for knowledge. I have adopted him as a son, but he longs to help his people. Perhaps the *Taiboo Nimiahkana* could help give him greater knowledge, let him work in the fields to earn his keep in that far-off land, and speak one day for the Indian so that the white-eyes will understand that we are not a cruel, warlike people. We fight only for the land that was stolen from us. We were at war only with those who lied to us and made treaties that they never meant to keep."

"I'll carry this message back to Windhaven Range at once, Sangrodo. Then Luke's son will write to his father."

"That is good, Djamba. Lopasuta is wiser than many a man twice his age, yet he does not boast of his knowledge. Come, let us enjoy the evening air." Sangrodo rose with the nimbleness of a young man and walked out of the lodge as Djamba followed him. "See how peaceful we have become. We grow fruits and vegetables now, we even raise some cattle for our own needs, and sometimes we sell some of the meat to people in Maxtime and to others who have asked for it. There is nothing here for Lopasuta, except to take a squaw and have children who will have no more opportunity than he in such a life."

"I understand what you say, Sangrodo. I'll remember every word. When I get back to Windhaven Range, I'll speak to Mr. Lucien Edmond, and he will send a letter as fast as possible to Mr. Luke."

"You are a good friend, Djamba. Like me, you were a chief in your own village far across the seas long ago; the *Taiboo Nimiahkana* has told me of this. I respect you."

"And I respect you also, Sangrodo." The two men looked at each other and clasped hands to symbolize their understanding and friendship.

A few moments later, Sangrodo led Djamba to the lodge of Lopasuta, a small house made of adobe and resembling

221

the *jacal* of a peasant, strengthened with timbers which the brave himself had hewn from the scrubby trees around the stronghold. He was almost as tall as Sangrodo, wiry, with light coppery skin, high-set cheekbones, a high-arching forehead, and a sharply aquiline nose. But what impressed Djamba the most was the honest look of his dark eyes and the cordial smile on his lips. When Sangrodo introduced him to the Mandingo, Lopasuta offered his hand without hesitation and said, "My chief has told me much of your courage and your wisdom, Djamba. The family of the *Taiboo Nimiahkana* are fortunate to have you as their friend. I, too, wish to be your friend."

"You speak excellent English, Lopasuta. How did you learn it?" the Mandingo asked interestedly.

Lopasuta shrugged with a smile and modestly answered, "My mother was a young girl from a Mexican village not far from here. When the Comanches raided the village and took her, my father chose her as his squaw. But she was not a *peón*; she was the only daughter of a *rico*, who was the *alcalde* of that village. He had sent her to a school in Mexico City, where she learned to speak English very well. She came to my father in love, for her own father wished to marry her to a cruel landowner whom she hated. She saw at once the honesty of our people and how they respected bravery and truth above all other things."

"As did old Mr. Lucien Bouchard and his grandson Mr. Luke and Mr. Luke's oldest son Lucien Edmond," Djamba interposed. "Sangrodo tells me that you wish to learn more so that you can help your people."

"Yes, I wish that very much, Djamba," the young Comanche responded. "My father told me how the government agents treated the Comanches—or, 'the people,' as we call ourselves in our language. It seems to me that no Comanche has been able to speak for us so that the agents would not deceive us or make treaties they would not keep. I think that the Comanche has rights, just as does the white man and now, since you are black and free, your own people."

"Yes, that's true, Lopasuta."

"The Spanish I have, I came by also from my mother. Besides, we here speak Spanish all the time, since our braves have taken Mexican women to be their squaws. Now it is true that I have had no chance to read books, and I hunger for them. My mind is eager to learn all that I can so I can help the people."

"It is a good feeling, it is a good wish, it is from the heart," Sangrodo gravely broke in as he turned to Djamba. "Lopasuta is a strong young brave, we are proud of him. But he cannot do much besides tilling the field and helping to raise the few cattle we have. It is too dull a life, there are no great deeds to be done in it. I myself am growing old now, but I have a strong woman, Catayuna, beside me, and my little son Inokanti and the older boy Kitante who will one day be a strong leader of the people. Yes, Kitante will take my place, if the Great Spirit grants me years enough so that he will be of age to earn the respect of our people."

"I'm sure that Mr. Luke will think of some way to help Lopasuta," Djamba promised. When he returned to Windhaven Range, he talked to Lucien Edmond about his meeting with the young Comanche. Lucien Edmond that very afternoon sat down at his desk and wrote his father, Luke, a lengthy letter, urging that help be given this deserving brave.

On the very April evening when Lucien Edmond Bouchard had entrusted the letter to one of the new vaqueros, who would ride to Corpus Christi and see that it was posted via the *William Wallace,* Mary Turner left the kitchen of the red-brick chateau with a bowl of hot gumbo for old Ellen, the conjure woman. The latter had been confined to her bed for the past three days, and Luke Bouchard had solicitously sent Hughie Mendicott to fetch Dr. Medbury. After examining Ellen, the physician had taken Luke aside and said, "It's just age and a multitude of things creeping up on her all at once, Mr. Bouchard. The fact is, it's a miracle that she survived that brutal flogging by those cowardly Klansmen. There's not much you can do except let her rest, give her plenty of nourishment, and ease her mind as much as possible."

As Mary Turner entered the little hut, she gasped with alarm to see the frail, white-haired old woman struggling to rise on her pallet. "Oh no, Ellen, you mustn't tire yourself! You lie straight back down, you hear me? Now I brought you some nice hot gumbo, I'll spoon it for you so's you won't have to sit up none. My, you did give me a

223

turn, you sick and all, but trying to get up! What do you think Mr. Luke would say if he knows how ornery you're being?"

"Mr. L-Luke, yes, I wants to see him—hurry, tell him quick—I don't think I got much longer in this here old world—ask Mr. Luke if he can come see me quick!" Her wrinkled face was twisted in an expression of anxiety, and her thin, sere lips trembled from the exertion of trying to speak.

"All right, I'll go get him quick—but mind you, don't you dare try to sit up again, you hear me, Ellen?" Mary warned. "I'll just set down this gumbo, and when I come back with Mr. Luke, you'll eat it up every drop, won't you—you've got to promise me that or I won't git him!"

"Hurry, mercy, hurry, I'm gettin' so weak I can't hardly see no more!" The old woman struggled for breath, her eyes sunken in their sockets, yet glowing with a feverish intensity.

"I'm going, I'll be right back," Mary anxiously exclaimed. With a last glance at the old woman, who had begun to shiver and whose bony fingers dug into her palms, she hurried back to the chateau.

Luke Bouchard had just sat down to dinner with Laure and the two boys, and this time his young wife had told Stacey that she would feed them herself and carry them back to the nursery, wanting to be alone and have a private chat with her husband.

Mary Turner entered the dining room and gave Luke her agitated report. Luke rose from the table. "Ellen's taken a turn for the worse, my dear. I'll go see her at once."

"The poor soul!" Laure sighed. "Could I be of any help, dear? You know, I feel I owe her just as much as you do. If it hadn't been for her, God knows what might have happened to Lucien."

Luke, saying he would go alone, followed Mary out of the dining room. Then, as they went through the kitchen and out the door into the fields, he asked Mary in a low voice, "How serious is it, Mary?"

"Mighty bad, 'pears like to me, Mr. Luke, sir. Poor Ellen said she didn't think she had much time left."

"I was afraid of that, after what Dr. Medbury told me," he said, half to himself. "We'll try to ease her all we can, Mary."

Entering Ellen's hut, he came forward to her pallet, drew up a low wooden stool and, taking the bowl of gumbo, said gently, "Now I'm here, Ellen dear. Won't you try a little of this gumbo? Mary made it specially for you. It'll make you strong and help you get well again."

She had lain motionless as he had entered, staring at the roof of the hut, her lips moving silently. Hearing his voice, she slowly turned her head, blinked her eyes, and in a faltering, faint voice exclaimed, "Thank the good Lord you here 'fore my time is up, Mr. Luke."

He forced a smile to his anxious face. He was touched to see that she wore the charm bracelet around her right wrist and the little cross with its gold chain round her neck. The cross lifted spasmodically now with her labored breathing. "Just a spoonful, Ellen dear?" he softly urged.

"No sir, ain't got time to eat—gotta tell you what I saw in my head while I was lyin' here thinkin' how good you and Miz Laure been to me." Her voice grew weaker, and with an evident effort, she tried to turn herself onto her side so as to face him.

"You mustn't move about, just lie still and rest, dear Ellen," he anxiously exclaimed as he took her hands in his and leaned closer to her wrinkled face. "What do you want to tell me?"

For a moment, her eyes closed, her breath came more and more slowly. Then again with a visible effort, she opened her eyes and tried to bend her head toward him so that he might hear her. "I see a man—he comes from a long way off, Mr. Luke sir—he gonna try to badmouth your wife."

"Yes, Ellen dear." Luke shivered with a sudden terrible presentiment, such as he had had when the old conjure woman had urged him to mark both his sons. He did not lean to superstition, and yet the uncanny coincidence of what had happened to Lucien could hardly be explained by pure logic or cold reason. "Is that all you saw, dear Ellen?" he prompted.

"No sir—I saw lots more—oh God!" Her eyes rolled upward, and her breathing grew harsh and sporadic as she struggled to speak. "God, just a few minutes more 'fore You call me to You—gotta tell Mr. Luke what I saw!"

"I'm here, Ellen, I'm with you. Don't force yourself, try

225

to rest," Luke murmured. Behind him, Mary Turner stood, tears running down her cheeks.

Again the frail old conjure woman closed her eyes and seemed to lie back, then was silent for a long moment. Then again she regarded Luke, and he felt her fingernails dig into his hands as she forced herself to speak. "You gonna show that he be all wrong, you gonna punish him good, but Miz Laure is gonna suffer. . . ."

"Oh God—hasn't she suffered enough already?" Luke Bouchard looked up at the roof of the hut as if directing his remark to Providence. Then, leaning even closer to her, he urged, "You say Laure will suffer—tell me all you know, all you saw, dear Ellen!"

"She ain't gonna die—oh no sir—but she have to wait till next year for the good news you both wanted—oh, Mr. Luke, it's getting so dark—I still has to tell you what I saw —just a little more time, dear Lord, then I'll go! Oh, Mr. Luke!" Her head fell back, she closed her eyes, and Luke uttered a stifled cry, believing her dead. And yet, with incredible tenacity, the frail little woman clung to life. Her eyes slowly opened, glazed now and wandering, as if not seeing Luke's anxious face so near hers. At last, her voice nearly a whisper now, she gasped, "Yes sir, it all come out fine next year—and you gonna help someone—just like you helped me when the Klan whipped me. That man you gonna help gonna pay you back through one of your good friends. Yes sir, Mr. Luke, I saw it all plain as day. I saw it three nights in a row and—and—"

Suddenly she lifted herself from the rude pillow on the pallet, gripping his hands with an unbelievable strength, and then with a choking sigh her head slumped forward against his chest.

"Ellen—oh God, poor woman!" Luke groaned. He gently eased her down on the pallet, then felt for her heartbeat and then her pulse. Slowly, his eyes wet with tears, he rose and turned to Mary: "She's gone, Mary. Poor unhappy woman—I only hope she had some little peace and joy here."

"She sure did, Mr. Luke!" Mary valiantly exclaimed. "Lots of times, she said to me, she said she'd never forget how you and Miz Laure treated her like white folks. That's a fact, Mr. Luke. And she was so proud all the time of that bracelet 'n that cross you gave her—at least she didn't have any pain now, did she, Mr. Luke sir?"

"No, Mary. God was good to her. May He rest her soul in His eternal peace."

"Amen, Mr. Luke. Oh, Lord, amen!" Mary Turner sobbed.

CHAPTER TWENTY-FIVE

Lucien Edmond Bouchard had sent two of his vaqueros to San Antonio during the middle of March to bring back supplies and the mail, for he had been expecting a letter from Jason Barntry concerning an investment that the manager of the Brunton and Barntry Bank had made on his behalf. Lucien Edmond had sought to increase his capital so that he might buy more Brahmas and a few Herefords for breeding cattle with greater stamina and weight. With this in mind, he had invested five thousand dollars of his profits from the Abilene sale of last summer. Jason Barntry put that sum into the acquisition of a piece of property near Eglantine Street. Just before Christmas, he wrote to Lucien Edmond that he might expect to triple his investment, since a wealthy Connecticut banker who had decided to retire to the Queen City was greatly interested in building a fashionable hotel on the land.

When the vaqueros returned, by the end of March, they brought back the good news that the sale was going through and, as Jason Barntry wrote, Lucien Edmond would soon be receiving a bank draft in the amount of $14,500. He determined to allocate a portion of this sum to bonuses for the vaqueros, if only because they now faced the double risk of the long drive to Abilene and the trouble which was brewing on the ranch to the west. Besides the letter from Jason Barntry, Lucien Edmond received one from Arabella Hunter, ecstatically announcing the birth of a daughter whom she had named Joy. He was all the more happy because this birth had nearly coincided with that of Jaime, Mara's and Ramón's little boy. Both children had been born just before the turn of the year. There was more news from Arabella, too: her daughter Melinda, now eighteen, was engaged to Lawrence Davis, the twenty-one-year-old son of the Galveston city treasurer.

It was a union of which Arabella and her husband, James, thoroughly approved. As for their son, Andrew, now sixteen, he had begun to show a marked interest in his father's work as a factor for Cousin Jeremy's cotton mill and would spend this summer's vacation working as an apprentice clerk in the office.

Lucien Edmond smiled broadly when he read Arabella's comments on Melinda's engagement; it was very evident that Arabella was greatly relieved that her beautiful, flirtatious daughter would no longer be a rival. For Arabella doubtless saw herself reflected in Melinda's mercurial and impulsive nature, and she probably knew that Melinda, like herself, required a gentle but masterful husband to guide her.

Though delighted by all this good news, Lucien Edmond was vexed at having had to delay the roundup and drive to Abilene. He had set the vaqueros to work branding the yearlings and those Texas longhorns that his riders found in still plentiful numbers along the border of the Nueces River and in the brush. There had been several disconcerting incidents this last week of March, which made him reluctant to take most of his men away from the ranch house. By now, indeed, he had resolved to ride over to the neighboring ranch and confront the owner to learn the latter's intentions regarding the fencing operation, during which several of Lucien Edmond's own boundary markers had already been removed. The high-handed action which Robert Caldemare was taking mystified him: was the man actually so stupid as to try to steal his land outright? Surely he must know that such an attempt could only lead to violent reprisals, which Lucien Edmond preferred not to contemplate except as a final resort.

On the day that Celia and Djamba returned from the visit to Sangrodo's stronghold, Ignacio Valdez, the youngest of the new vaqueros engaged by Ramón Hernandez on his recent trip to Nuevo Laredo, rode out with two other men, lariats coiled around their saddlehorns, to round up any strays that might have wandered back into the bushes near the shallow, winding river. As they neared the southern edge of Windhaven Range, they saw three of Caldemare's Mexicans hammering posts into the ground, while a fourth stood by giving orders and a fifth walked toward the group with a coil of wire.

Eddie Gentry, who had been put in charge of the trio this morning, rose in his saddle and squinted suspiciously at the posts. Then, halting his gelding, he said to Santiago Miraflores, "Isn't that one of Mr. Lucien Edmond's markers lying over there near that post they're hammering in?"

"*Sí, amigo.* It is surely one of the *patrón*'s. Señor Duvray showed me how to recognize them," the squat, nearly bald vaquero asserted.

"Why, then, seems to me like those hombres are doing a little landgrabbing, wouldn't you say?" Eddie drawled. Spurring his gelding forward another twenty yards, he halted it and then gestured for his two companions to ride up beside him. "Look there—there's a hole in the ground. They pulled Mr. Lucien Edmond's marker out, and they're putting their own about ten feet closer into his land! And now they're starting to put up the wire."

"*¿Qué pasa, hombre?*" The swarthy Mexican who had been directing his four companions strode forward now, his right hand edging toward his gun belt and near the holster of his six-shooter. "This is *el Señor* Caldemare's land. We work here at his orders, *comprende usted?* It would be wise to stay on yours, *señores.*"

"Wait now, *amigo,*" Eddie placatingly grinned as he held us his hand. "All I want to know is why you pulled up our boss's marker and stuck your own inside his land. Now we're might peaceful *hombres* as a rule, but we're not going to stand for landgrabbing, sure as not in broad daylight."

"My name is Jaime Ruiz," the bearded Mexican arrogantly declared. "And I am the *jefe* of Señor Caldemare's vaqueros. He would not like to hear you say such a thing, *gringo.*" He pronounced the last word sarcastically, intimating that Eddie Gentry was an unwelcome English-speaking stranger.

"You know, *hombre,*" Eddie pretended he did not know the Mexican's name, in order to return the insult, "your boss and mine ought to get together and talk this over. Why don't you tell him to ride on over and have a chat with Mr. Lucien Edmond Bouchard?"

"It is very kind of you, *gringo,*" Ruiz sneered, "but I do not think the *patrón* has time to waste on yours. We have work to do. Now ride away on your own land and let us do it, or there will be trouble."

Young Ignacio Valdez, eager to prove his worth as a recruit, had dismounted and now, picking up the uprooted wooden marker on which the burned-in brand of WR could plainly be seen, held it aloft and vehemently exclaimed, "But this is not right, *compadre*! I see there the hole from which you took this, and now you put your own posts and your fence up to the east, not to the west where it belongs. It is not right, that is being a *ladrón*!"

"*Hijo de puta*, no one calls me a thief!" Jaime Ruiz snarled as his hand darted down to grip the butt of his six-shooter, level it, and trigger it. The young vaquero uttered a horrified cry as he saw the movement, and at the explosion staggered back, his eyes wide with agonized astonishment. He stood swaying an instant, then pitched forward and lay lifeless.

The other four men had drawn their guns so that Eddie Gentry and Santiago Miraflores, despite having Spencer carbines sheathed at their saddles, had no chance to avenge the murder of their young companion. Eddie swore under his breath, shook his head, and then said in a voice that shook with thwarted fury, "You got the draw on us, *hombre*, damned lucky for you you've got it—for now."

"*Sí*, I can see you have repeating carbines, *gringo*," Ruiz jeered. "But my *compadres* and I are *pistoleros*, and before you could reach them at the back of your saddles, they would shoot you down like the *gringo* dogs you are. Go back to your *patrón* and tell him that *el Señor* Caldemare wishes to be left alone. He has given me, the *jefe*, the order to fence in his land so that your *patrón* will not steal it nor let his *ganado* eat the good grass that my *patrón* owns. And now, *deja usted pronto!*" He had lowered his still smoking six-shooter toward the ground, but now raised it menacingly, a vicious grin twisting his sensual mouth.

"All right, we'll go. But we're taking our *compadre* back with us—and I swear, Ruiz, if you try to stop us, I'll take a chance I can trigger my carbine faster than you can kill me with that peashooter!" Eddie Gentry drawled. Courageously, he dismounted, walked over to the inert body of the young vaquero, lifted him, and carried his dead body over his shoulder back to his gelding. Then, laying the body over the rump of Ignacio's mount, he used his lasso to secure it, the muscles of his jaw convulsively working in his anger at this callous murder.

"Very well, *gringo*. Your *compadre* was a fool. I see you are wiser. And all of you vaqueros would be wiser to stay away from Señor Caldemare's property. Take that message back to your *patrón*," Ruiz mockingly called after him. Then, to his men, "Go on, *amigos*, there is much work to be done!"

Eddie Gentry sent the Mexican foreman an undisguised look of hatred, then wheeled his gelding back toward Windhaven Range, leading the dead young vaquero's horse behind his. Santiago Miraflores, crossing himself and mumbling prayers for the murdered young vaquero, followed him at a gallop.

CHAPTER TWENTY-SIX

On April 10, Luke Bouchard's declaration to the voters of Montgomery County was printed in the *Advertiser*. It was brave and forthright, and it went far beyond party politics in seeking to define broadly the scope of his own views on what peace should be after such internecine conflict. It was the second of his political declarations, and although William Blount had mildly objected to the phraseology in several of the paragraphs, Luke had remained determined to let his fellow citizens know exactly what he thought and where he stood.

This statement went at once to the crux of the problem which Luke sensed he would face before the ballots were cast in November:

In declaring myself as a candidate on the Republican ticket for the seat in the State Legislature, I am well aware that I shall be called a scalawag—and doubtless many other things as well. But let us examine this singular new word which has come into frequent use in Alabama. It designates a Southern white Republican who has been born in the South or who lived in the South before the Civil War. Most people consider it a term of political opprobrium.

If the word *scalawag* implied only what is suggested by the general definition, men of principle and good conscience would have nothing to fear from it. But there are baser connotations to the word which give offense, and these have wide circulation. For to most of us, a scalawag is anyone who wants to toady up to the Union and most particularly to the Reconstruction Acts which the victorious North has seen fit to impose upon the defeated South.

I do not and shall never subscribe to the principle

of vindictiveness. Where Reconstruction is imposed upon us to punish us, first for having seceded from the Union and second for having lost the war, I stand against it. My Republican views have been based rather on the standards which the martyred Abraham Lincoln adopted in his wise understanding that a house divided against itself cannot stand. Had he lived, he would have brought about a peace with dignity and honor, a peace in which the spiritual wounds of this unfortunate struggle could be gradually healed.

I was born on Windhaven Plantation near Lowndesboro. Except for a brief period when I accompanied my oldest son to Texas to help him establish a cattle ranch, I have lived here all of my life and intend to die here. Hence I may call myself a native Southerner. As such, I firmly believe that our progress in this state and in this county can come about only through a sensible, rational outlook, free of hatred. Work, both agricultural and industrial, is what must be done now.

As a native Southerner, therefore, it is my unwavering conviction that your representatives in public office who speak for you as free citizens should be chosen on the basis not only of merit but also of a broad comprehension of the problems indigenous to me. Therefore, if you call me a scalawag, remember that, in one sense at least, that is an asset. It means that I was born here, and I consider that an advantage I hold over any Johnny-come-lately opportunist (whom we call carpetbagger) who was sent to us from distant states of the North for the purpose of exploiting our weaknesses and our impoverishment.

I know that many of you will say that by declaring myself a Republican, I ally myself with our President, Ulysses S. Grant, whom most Southerners remember only as the victorious Union general who exacted surrender from General Lee at Appomattox. Yes, that is true. But in the same breath, I tell you that I do not subscribe to all of his governmental policies, nor do I endorse all of the men who constitute his cabinet—any more than I do those who come here in his name bent on lining their own pockets and ignoring the needs of our citizens.

In offering myself as a candidate, I say that it is

time to forget the prejudices and the hatreds born out of the war and to work in unison toward a better economy for this state and particularly for the county that I have the honor to seek to represent. I myself, like my grandfather Lucien Bouchard before me, never owned slaves, for we manumitted them long before President Lincoln signed the Emancipation Act. The then existing laws of Alabama did not recognize our manumissions, but our black workers knew that they were free so long as they worked with us on the land of Windhaven Plantation. Today, I am a simple farmer, raising produce, cotton, even cattle. I am your neighbor and your friend, and I seek your vote precisely because of these attributes: I shall be available at all times to hear your grievances and your desires, and I shall seek with the utmost vigor to carry out the wishes of my constituents.

This, then, is my platform: fairness and justice, equal representation for the humblest as for the wealthiest, and vigorous opposition to whatever impedes the progress of Montgomery County. You have but to examine my record to learn that I never gave aid to the Union cause during the war, and equally that I did not take up arms for the Confederacy, because I earnestly believed that tilling the soil and providing food was my first duty. I ask for your support, and I shall try to earn it to the best of my intentions, ability, and strength, so help me God.

Luke Bouchard.

The public reaction to Luke's candid declaration was mixed, but generally favorable. His chief critics raised the issue that his statement of not having owned slaves was specious and that its purpose was to win the black vote. Two days later, in the *Advertiser*, a man signing himself "A Loyal Confederate" countered on the editorial page:

We suspect that Mr. Luke Bouchard's pure and noble motives, when reduced to their lowest common denominator, mean only that he considers the *nigra* eminently fit for a voter, but not to hold office: that is reserved for a scalawag like himself. For all his attempt to show that he is not a scalawag, he inescapably is one and will be damned for it at the polls come November.

On the day this malicious rejoinder was published, Luke Bouchard had ridden into Montgomery to confer with Jedidiah Danforth to assure himself that the latter had arranged for the formal legal purchase of those fifty acres on which the Bambachs were living. The tall, white-haired lawyer left his desk as he saw Luke enter the office and came to shake his hand energetically, declaring, "By God, Mr. Bouchard, you're a man with plenty of intestinal fortitude, and I only hope the citizens of this county have brains enough to realize that!"

"That's kind of you to say, Mr. Danforth. Now, about that Bambach deal you and I arranged—" Luke began.

Jedidiah Danforth held up his hand, then chuckled dryly. "All taken care of. And at a reasonable time, say by the middle of next year, God willing as well as the damned carpetbaggers, we'll just transfer the land back to Mr. Bambach and his daughter."

"I've a still better idea, Mr. Danforth," Luke smilingly countered. "You remember I wrote you about Andy Haskins, that young fellow from Tennessee who helped us get to Windhaven Range? Well, he came up here on a furlough, and I asked him if he'd mind doing me the favor of hiring some good men to work Bambach's land for him. He's fallen in love with Jessica Bambach, and unless I miss my guess, there'll be a wedding for those two one of these days. I'd like to make him a present of that land, so just hold up the transfer back to Bambach till I give you the latest news."

"That'll be even better, Mr. Bouchard. Andy Haskins is a much better prospect to turn that land into a profitable venture and to be able to pay the yearly taxes than poor old Horatio Bambach ever will be. Well, sir, so much for that. By the way, I've a letter for you. Seems as how Captain Tenby had some passengers who didn't want to delay their journey to Montgomery and, since he only had this letter for Windhaven Plantation, he had one of his stevedores bring it to my office for you."

"Thank you, Mr. Danforth." Luke opened the letter, cursorily scanned it, and then turned to the lawyer. "It's

236

from my son Lucien Edmond. A most unusual piece of information which just might concern you."

"How's that, sir?"

"I've told you about the Comanche chief Sangrodo. Well, it appears that one of his young braves is extraordinarily gifted, speaks Spanish and English fluently, and has a tremendous desire for a formal education so that he can help his people. From what Lucien Edmond writes me, he had a Mexican mother who came from a wealthy family and who herself was quite well educated. That gave him the foundation for his enthusiasm for learning."

"A young man like that, Mr. Bouchard, would certainly help stop all this talk about the only good Indian being a dead Indian." The lawyer snorted with distaste. "I remember my father's telling me that the Creeks here in Alabama were more civilized and better educated than most of the white settlers who prided themselves on being upright, honorable men. But I don't quite see what you've got in mind, Mr. Bouchard, as to how I can help this young Comanche."

"You know what I was thinking, Mr. Danforth? Why couldn't he stay with me at Windhaven Plantation? I could legally adopt him—since his parents are both dead. Then he might study law with you. Lucien Edmond writes that Lopasuta—that's his name—is eager to learn how we whites govern our people so that he can better understand these laws which oppress his."

"That's a mighty ambitious project, Mr. Bouchard." The white-haired lawyer's keen blue eyes twinkled. "No reason why he couldn't be admitted into the bar if he were your legally adopted son—by God, sir, here is another of your bold undertakings that I'd be proud to have a part in! All right then, you send for him, bring him here to my office, and we'll have a good long talk. You know, Mr. Bouchard, I'm not getting any younger, and I'll admit I could use an efficient, industrious clerk who doesn't look at the clock all the time. Had to discharge the last one I had, some pampered son of an Eastern carpetbagger who thought all he had to do to be admitted to the bar was come to my office in his fine new clothes and lollygag around with the young ladies in the public square during lunchtime. Yes sir, I think it might be very interesting to have an Indian

237

boy in this office. I'll say this for you, Mr. Bouchard, the work you give your lawyer can't ever be classified as dull!"

"Then I'll send off a letter to Lucien Edmond at once to arrange for Lopasuta's coming to stay with me at Windhaven Plantation, Mr. Danforth. I'm grateful to you for your interest. For my own part, I owe Sangrodo a debt that can hardly be repaid, and I'd like very much to sponsor the education of this unusual boy. Well now, you'll be hearing from me soon. Good day, sir." The two men shook hands, and Jedidiah Danforth clapped Luke on the back and called after him, "If you get that young fellow up here in time for me to draw up the legal adoption papers and have them put through court, Mr. Bouchard, he might just be able to cast a vote for you this November!"

Then, clapping a hand to his forehead and grimacing with annoyance at himself, he called, "Mr. Bouchard, damned if I didn't forget to give you a mighty important piece of news. I tell you, sir, reading that campaign statement of yours and then this news about the Indian boy drove it out of my mind—that's just another sign I'm getting old and need help here in my office."

Luke Bouchard turned and walked back to the lawyer's desk. "What news is that, Mr. Danforth?"

"Why, sir, it appears that the four hundred acres which your late father-in-law owned long ago have just been acquired by a certain Barnabas McMillan. He's a downright carpetbagger and, from what I've heard about him, something of a scoundrel to boot. Rumor has it that he's supporting your opponent in the November election, Cletus Adams, on the Democratic ticket."

"So he's going to be a distant neighbor of mine, is he? Well, Mr. Danforth, it can't be helped." Luke sighed nostalgically. "I remember that land very well, as if it were only yesterday. How many times I visited sweet, gentle Lucy Williamson before I asked her to marry me. And her poor father, tricked into feverish gambling beyond his means by that double-dealer Pierre Lourat. Williamson allowed himself to be hoodwinked by that vicious animal Amos Greer whom he'd hired as overseer." Luke closed his eyes for a moment, remembering the past. "I was the one to discharge him, I remember, and I had to thrash him into the bargain. Then he got himself killed by one of the two sisters he'd viciously brutalized. Well, I can only hope that this Mr. McMillan uses the land to better purpose than ever Amos Greer did."

Hannah Atbury was in a happy mood this afternoon. She had decided that she and Hughie Mendicott would jump over the broom, and she would become mother to his fine boys. She got along just fine with Davie and Louis, and it would really make it up to her not having ever had children by poor old Phineas. God rest his dear kind soul, she thought to herself as she opened the front door of the red-brick chateau to take a stroll out by the river and enjoy the warm spring air before starting supper.

There was something nailed to the door right below the knocker, a piece of paper or such—frowning, Hannah turned back to stare at it and then clapped her hand over her mouth, her eyes wide with indignant anger.

It was a crudely printed handbill, the ink still smeared on it to indicate how recently it had been printed. It read:

A VOTE FOR LUKE BOUCHARD
IS A VOTE FOR HIS WHORE!
BOUCHARD'S WIFE LAURE
RAN THE INFAMOUS
UNION HOUSE IN NEW ORLEANS—
SHE WAS A FANCY GAL FOR
UNION OFFICERS FOR MONEY!
WE WANT A DECENT
FAMILY MAN FOR
MONTGOMERY COUNTY THIS
NOVEMBER—
VOTE FOR CLETUS ADAMS
ON THE DEMOCRATIC TICKET,
NOT FOR A SCALAWAG
MARRIED TO A WHORE!

Hannah Atbury tore the offending handbill off the door and crumpled it in her hand, shaking her head: "I never in all my life—poor Miz Laure, to go and say such a wicked, sinful thing about a fine good woman like her— just wait till Mr. Luke comes home and sees this—he's going to be powerful angry! Who done this, anyhow?"

She went back to the kitchen, to find Mary Turner heating a pot of coffee. "Mary, I believe I'll have some of that coffee right this-here minute. Land sakes, I had me a turn just now!"

"Why, whatever is the matter, Hannah?"

"Matter enough," Hannah angrily averred as she unfolded the crumpled handbill and showed it to her. "Just have a look for yourself, Mary. That's the wickedest thing I ever saw, saying a thing like that about sweet Miz Laure with her two darling boys—I don't know how anyone could have the nerve to print such an awful lie!"

"Oh, that's awful, Hannah!" Mary commiserated. "Who knew she came from New Orleans, anyhow? You and I knows that, but it's none of our business. And for sure I'd swear on the Bible a sweet lady like that wouldn't have no truck with no fancy house, not ever!"

Hannah Atbury regarded the handbill again and then, reflectively frowning, said slowly, "You know, Mary, I've just been thinking. Sort of funny about this here new nurse Miz Laure's got herself. That nice Miss O'Connor had to leave real sudden-like, didn't she?"

"Sure, Hannah. She said her aunt was awful sick and needed her bad. And she said her cousin would be glad to help out till things got better at home," Mary proffered. "Here, coffee just come to a boil, good 'n strong. Here's your cup, Hannah. Me, I need it more than ever after seeing that nasty thing!"

Hannah gratefully accepted the cup of steaming coffee from her friend, took a sip, and smacked her lips. "Real coffee. It's a joy, it sure is, to have it when we didn't know what it tasted like during that awful war. Wait now, I'm starting to remember something."

"What is it, Hannah?"

"As soon as that new nurse got here, Mary, there used to be an old nigger driving up with a wagon round about this time of evening. Sure, now I recollect! Couple of weeks back, this Miss Stacey was hurrying out the front door when I was in the hall mopping up just a little, and she said she had to send a letter to her cousin and her aunt."

"Can't be no harm in that," Mary doubtfully replied.

"No, maybe not, but now I recollect Miss Stacey told Miz Laure she came from New Orleans, too."

"Hannah Atbury! Are you saying what you're makin' me

240

think?" Mary Turner gasped as she put down her coffee cup and stared at the handsome widow.

"Uh huh. Don't you think it's mighty funny Miss O'Connor taking off so quick without hardly any warning, then her cousin coming here and being from New Orleans just like Miz Laure, then going out to meet that nigger in the wagon and giving him letters? Maybe she had something to do with all this dirty talk about poor Miz Laure," Hannah declared.

Just at that moment, Laure entered the kitchen, and the two black women fell silent, glancing guiltily at each other.

"Why, Mary, you've made fresh coffee! I thought I could smell it from down the hall," Laure brightly declared. "Is there enough for a cup for me?"

"Oh sure, Miss Laure! When do you think Mr. Luke will be home for supper?" Mary hastened to divert any possible suspicions by making small talk.

"Pretty soon now, I'd say. He went into Montgomery this afternoon, and he said he'd be back in time for supper." Laure sipped from her cup. "My, that's wonderful! I declare, you and Hannah are the best cooks around here for miles and miles."

"Real nice of you to say so, Miz Laure," Mary nervously giggled, sending a covert glance at Hannah.

Laure intercepted it and, glancing at Hannah herself, observed that the widow still held the handbill crumpled in her left hand. "What's that you're holding, Hannah?" she innocently asked.

"Oh, nothing, Miz Laure, nothing at all!" Hannah gulped, putting her left hand behind her back to hide the telltale handbill.

"Hannah, we've been friends so long, we shouldn't have any secrets. What is it? Come, give it to me."

"Please, Miz Laure, don't make me do it," Hannah begged. "I don't want to cross you none, you know that, but please don't ask me."

"But what could it possibly be to make you carry on so, Hannah dear?" Laure pursued. "Now you've aroused my curiosity, and you should know that a woman's curiosity is a very powerful thing. Come on, I promise I'll take the consequences even if it's something I shouldn't see, as you think."

"Oh, Lord!" Mary Turner groaned. This only served to heighten Laure's puzzled wonder, and as Hannah reluctantly drew her hand from behind her back, Laure reached out and took the crumpled handbill from her, then unfolded it.

She caught her breath, then turned crimson. "It's despicable! To attack Luke by slandering me—filthy, despicable, cowardly!" she said in a low, shaking voice. "Where did you find this, Hannah?"

"It—it was nailed to the door, Miz Laure. I'm mighty sorry—I didn't want you to see it—please, that's why I didn't want to give it to you, Miz Laure," Hannah tearfully pleaded.

"Never mind. I'm glad I did see it. I'll have to show it to Luke. He's the best man in the county, and he deserves to win. But enough fools might believe a slander like this and vote against him, that's the real danger. How in the world could anyone have gone so far as to print this up and distribute it—just to strike at Luke?"

She folded the handbill neatly, her fingers trembling as she did so. Then, seeing Hannah and Mary both huddled together, weeping, she said in a voice that throbbed with anger, "I'll tell you the truth, Hannah and Mary. Yes, I lived in the Union House, and yes, it was a house for fancy girls, and I was the manager."

"We don't want you to tell us nothing you don't want to, Miz Laure, and we don't believe it anyhow," Hannah Atbury loyally spoke up.

"No, listen to me, please. It's important. My father ran a bank in New Orleans where I was born, but when the Yankees and General Benjamin Butler took over New Orleans, his men walked into my father's bank, discharged all his help, and replaced it with men of their own kind. Then a corporal who led a platoon of eight soldiers came in and told me that if I didn't submit to him, the whole platoon would have me."

"Lord God save us all," Mary Turner sobbed, shaking her head and covering her face with her hands.

"So I gave myself to the corporal rather than having to submit to all those animals," Laure went on, her head high, her voice unwavering. "Later, when it was all over, my father killed himself because of my shame and the terrible loss of all he'd worked for all his life. Then John Brunton, who was Luke Bouchard's banker, rescued me and, because his bank had been taken over by the Yankees, too, thought up the idea of opening a fancy house for the Union officers. He put me in charge of it, and it was a front so that he could go on handling Mr. Luke's affairs just as he'd always done. But I swear to you both and I'll do it on the Bible, that never once did I take a customer into a room for money, and I had no man until—"

Before she could finish, Hannah tearfully burst out, "Please, Miz Laure dear, don't say no more; we knew all the time you couldn't be anything like that, we knew it and that's why we didn't want to show you this awful piece of paper!"

"It's true, Miz Laure," Mary added.

"But I got me an idea—I oughtn't to say, it's only guesswork, but maybe, just maybe, it might help point out who did this dreadful thing to you, Miz Laure," Hannah continued.

"Tell me, then."

"Well, I was saying to Mary just now before you came in, Miz Laure, we thought it mighty funny that Miss O'Connor had to take off all of a sudden and send her cousin, that Miss Stacey, here to be the nurse for the boys. And then, one evening, couple of weeks back, Miss Stacey she rushed out the front door to meet an old nigger in a wagon and she told me she had a letter he was going to take to her cousin. And she's from New Orleans, too, isn't she, Miz Laure?"

Laure stiffened, her eyes narrowing, and then she said softly to herself, "My God, that must have been it! That was why she made such a point about finding out what street I lived on and knowing about the Union House being there—oh God, could she possibly have been a spy for Luke's opponent in this election?" Then she turned to the two black women and said, "Thank you for telling me all this. It's best to know who your enemies are. Luke will see this handbill when he comes home, but right now I'm going to have a word with Stacey Holbrook."

Stacey, having seen Laure go off to the kitchen and learning that her employer's wife intended to have a cup of coffee while awaiting her husband's return home, had hurried off to Luke's study and, seating herself, hastily opened a drawer and drew out a sheet of paper and a stubby pencil. She had begun to write a letter to Barnabas McMillan, in which she said, "I've told you all that I've found out so far, Barnabas dear. But I'll stay around a little longer, just like you want, and maybe I can find out something else. Don't forget what you promised, darling."

Laure, meanwhile, had gone to the nursery and, finding to her surprise that Stacey was not there with the boys, walked back down the hallway toward the other wing of the chateau. She saw the door of the study open and directed her footsteps there. Then she gasped as she saw Stacey bent over the escritoire, hastily scribbling her letter.

"May I ask what you're doing, Stacey? Don't you think it's a little unusual for a nurse to leave two small boys all by themselves while you're off writing personal letters on your employer's time?" she coldly demanded.

Stacey uttered a startled cry, dropped the pencil, and then began to crumple the sheet of paper.

"Not so fast! I want to see that letter!" Laure exclaimed as she came forward.

"Get away from me, Mrs. Bouchard! It's personal business, nothing to do with you!" Stacey's eyes narrowed, glowing with malice. "You've got no right to look at my letter."

"I think I do. And you know what else I think, Stacey? That it's not the first letter you've been sending out of this house."

"So what if I have?" The chestnut-haired young woman mockingly defied her. "I've got a perfect right, I have, if I want to send a letter to Moira and her aunt."

"I won't argue the point. But just perhaps one of those letters referred to the Union House where I used to live— but where I never worked, Stacey." Laure unfolded the handbill and held it toward the now frightened nurse. "It's a very odd coincidence, Stacey, that you should have been so interested in knowing about that place. And it's very likely you wrote to someone about it, and that's where that person got the idea for this contemptible filth."

"Oh you think so, do you, Mrs. Bouchard?" Stacey Holbrook jeered. "Fact is, Mrs. Bouchard, you're no better than I am. You're such a fancy lady here in this great big house and all these fancy trimmings, you forget where you started at, I'll be bound. Just like I did, too. Only

244

difference between us, Mrs. Bouchard, I'm not ashamed to admit it."

"Then it *was* you who's responsible for this handbill!" Laure hissed. "Give me that letter. I want to see to whom you're writing. My husband will want to know, too, and you can be sure he'll take proper action."

"Try and get it, you bitch!" Stacey hissed as, catlike, she moved away from the desk, trying to edge toward the door which Laure blocked. "Get out of my way. I'm leaving you and your brats here and I don't care what the hell happens to all of you, you understand?"

"No you won't, not till I have that letter," Laure retorted. Suddenly she lunged at Stacey, gripping the latter's left wrist with her right hand and twisting it behind the woman's back. With a cry of pain, Stacey struck at her, trying to break free, but Laure tenaciously held on to her wrist till at last Stacey's fingers opened and the crumpled sheet dropped to the floor. "Now then, we'll just see," Laure began as she stooped quickly to retrieve the fallen letter.

But Stacey Holbrook suddenly kicked out her right foot, catching Laure in the belly. Luke's wife uttered a scream of agony, clasping her middle and then sinking down on one knee, as she slowly slumped forward and rolled onto her side, writhing in unspeakable pain.

Terrified now at what she had done, Stacey forgot the discarded letter and ran out of the study down the hall, let herself out the front door, and began to run down the road that led to Montgomery.

Mary Turner and Hannah Atbury, who had heard Laure's agonized scream, came running from the kitchen. "Oh, God Jesus save us," Mary ejaculated. "She's bleedin' powerful bad, Hannah! We gotta carry her over to that couch. Poor thing, it's the baby! Oh, that wicked girl who done this—and Mr. Luke not home! Help me, Hannah!"

The two black women tenderly lifted Laure's writhing body and carried it to the couch near the window. "Get some hot water and some towels, fast, Mary," Hannah commanded. Then, stroking Laure's forehead, she murmured soothingly, "Poor child, I'll take care of you, Miz Laure honey! It gonna be all right, you'll see." Then, aside, "Oh, if I could only get my hands on that white trash that done this to sweet Miz Laure!"

Luke Bouchard let himself into the red-brick chateau half an hour later. When he did not find his wife in her room or in the nursery, he went toward the kitchen, just as Mary Turner emerged from the study, calling to him: "Mr. Luke, Mr. Luke sir, come right away, come quick, please, sir!"

When he hurried into the study, he found Laure on the couch with Hannah tending her. Hannah looked up, her eyes blind with tears. "She going to be all right, Mr. Luke. Only thing is, she lost the baby. Mary and I did what we could. The bleeding's stopped, Mr. Luke. It was that Miss Stacey, that new nurse, that done this."

"I'll ride back to Montgomery and get Dr. Medbury," Luke said, pale and trembling with anger.

"No, sir, you already rode there and back and you're done in," Mary boldly contradicted him. "I'll get Dan Munroe, he'll be there in a jiffy. And anyhow, Mr. Bouchard, Miz Laure wanted to tell you about this here piece of paper. Hannah and I, we think that Miss Stacey had a lot to do with it."

"What's this?" Luke said, noticing the discarded letter on the floor. Picking it up, he unfolded it and read it quickly. " 'Dear Barnabas, it begins—my God, Barnabas McMillan, the man Jedidiah Danforth told me about this afternoon!" Then, nodding, he said to Mary, "All right. I'd be grateful if you'd ask Dan to ride to Montgomery and fetch Dr. Medbury as quickly as he can. God bless you both for what you've done for my wife."

"And here's that piece of paper that made Miz Laure so mad," Hannah added, as she straightened from the couch and came toward him with the handbill.

He ground his teeth with fury as soon as he had scanned it. "I think," he said grimly, "I shall have something to say to Mr. Barnabas McMillan."

CHAPTER TWENTY-SEVEN

Although his first impulse was to confront Barnabas Mc-Millan at once with the damning evidence of that scrap of Stacey Holbrook's unfinished letter, Luke Bouchard's concern for his young wife kept him by her side for nearly three hours until Dan Munroe arrived with Dr. Jonas Medbury. Even though both Hannah and Mary had assured him that Laure was out of danger despite the miscarriage, he paced the floor restlessly outside the study, pausing only for a sandwich and a cup of coffee which Clementine almost imploringly urged him to take. Marius Thornton kept Luke company during the latter's vigil. "Look, Mr. Bouchard," he fervently declared, "I know just how you feel, believe me I do. And I'm going with you when you pay that call to this Mr. McMillan. Now don't you look at me like that, Mr. Bouchard. You saved my life from the Klan, and I'm not about to forget it ever, not ever. You can't go barging alone into that man's house without somebody else along to see that you don't get hurt by one of his servants or friends. No sir, I'm going to go with you just as soon as you're ready, and this time I won't take an order from you."

"You're a loyal friend, Marius. Perhaps you're right, too. The way I feel, I'd like to smash his face bloody for what he's done to Laure. In my rage, I might even have gone so far as to kill him—I, who all my life have tried to stand against needless violence and blind hatred. But this touches the most primitive core of my feelings—my beautiful young wife, robbed of the child we longed for by a spying little baggage who obviously was in the pay of this treacherous carpetbagger. Now that I remember what Lawyer Danforth told me about who's behind Cletus Adams, whom I'm running against in November, everything seems to fall into place. It's a damnable conspiracy, but the only one who has suffered from it is poor Laure. That man and his female accomplice are morally responsible for the murder of our child."

Haggard and unshaven, he at last slumped down onto a chair beside the escritoire, staring at Laure who lay on the couch to which Mary and Hannah had carried her. She was barely conscious now after her ordeal, and she slowly turned her head to look at him, her soft lips tremblingly forming his name in so faint a whisper that he could scarcely hear it.

As he sprang to his feet and came toward her, Dan Munroe and Dr. Medbury entered.

"Thank God you've come, Doctor!" Luke exclaimed. "My wife's had a miscarriage. Mary and Hannah have tended her, and they tell me that she's all right, but I had to send for you. I'm sorry to have brought you out this time of night on such a long ride—"

"Now, Mr. Bouchard, you don't have to say a thing like that to me. Poor Mrs. Bouchard, first she's mistreated and her boy spirited away, and now your man tells me she's lost her baby. I'm just as concerned as you; I happen to be very fond of her. Now go sit down and rest, man, you look as if you're ready to drop. I'll quickly see what's to be done."

Dan nodded to Luke and went out of the study, closing the door behind him. Then, shaking his head and saying a prayer for Laure's recovery, he went back to his cottage where he told his wife Katie what had happened. And she in turn knelt down to pray for Laure Bouchard's swift convalescence.

Half an hour later, Dr. Medbury turned to Luke and said softly, "I've given her something to make her sleep. Hannah and Mary did a remarkable job, they truly did, sir. She's going to be all right. They stopped the bleeding, which was the real danger, and they removed the fetus without impairing her. You've nothing to worry about, Mr. Bouchard. After a few months' rest, there's no reason why she shouldn't think of having another child if she wants it. She's a strong, healthy young woman."

"Thank God, Dr. Medbury!" Luke hoarsely exclaimed. He walked over to the couch, bent down, and kissed Laure's forehead and then her eyelids. Then, straightening, his face relentlessly grim, he said, "If you've no other calls, Dr.

248

Medbury, I'd appreciate your being my guest tonight. Hannah and Mary will fix you a bite to eat, and I have some good whiskey—or brandy or wine, if you prefer."

"That's very gracious of you, Mr. Bouchard. But I really hadn't planned on staying here overnight," the doctor dubiously responded.

"I'd take it as a personal favor if you would. You look just as exhausted as I do. Now I'm going to have to leave you for a bit."

"And where, may I ask, do you think you're going this time of night, Mr. Bouchard?" Dr. Medbury testily demanded.

"I have a little business to settle, and it can't wait any longer. Hannah, Mary, you make Dr. Medbury just as comfortable as you can. See that he gets something to eat and whatever he wants to drink. Then show him to one of the guest rooms in this wing. Hopefully, I'll be back before midnight."

"Well I never!" Dr. Medbury wonderingly shook his head, then shrugged as if to suggest that even Luke Bouchard could be unpredictable at times.

Marius Thornton was waiting for Luke outside the study. "I've already saddled two horses, Mr. Bouchard," he said quietly. "I'm taking along a pistol just in case we run into trouble. Do you have yours?"

"I've no intention of taking any weapon, Marius. I'm afraid the way I feel right now it would be too deadly a temptation. No, I'm going to settle this the most primitive way of all, and perhaps the most satisfying—with my fists, unless he's a total coward. Considering that he would send a spy here, to pose as the cousin of the nurse we had, and to do his filthy work for him, I think he may be exactly that. All right, Marius, we're going downriver to the old Williamson plantation. It's only about half an hour's ride from here."

Distraught and raging though he was, Luke Bouchard felt memories tug at him as he rode the familiar trail to the plantation where he had once courted gentle Lucy Williamson. The land itself, the trees, the shrubbery, and the flowers, did not seem to have changed since that far-off time in his youth. He remembered, too, with a sigh of bitterness, the first time he had ridden over there with his father, Henry. Henry Bouchard had told him, "Maybe you

249

could get some pointers from Williamson's man Greer. You could look around the place and keep your eyes open and maybe learn something useful."

How well Luke remembered those days with Lucy. They had met for the first time in December, 1834, when Luke was just eighteen and Lucy a year younger. Already idealistic in his adolescence, Luke saw in this self-effacing, quiet, yet highly intelligent girl the promise of a lifelong companion who could share his dreams. Their love was not the fiery passion of adolescence: young though they were at that time, both he and Lucy seemed to have come together in a kind of mature communication. After their marriage, even their lovemaking had a tenderness to it, a sensitivity which had no place for mere raw desires and which underscored the spiritual side of marriage.

Suddenly, Luke Bouchard halted his horse, and Marius Thornton called back softly, "Something wrong, Mr. Luke?" Luke uttered an ironic laugh, shook his head. "No, Marius, I just remembered something, that's all. We'll go on in a moment. I came this way many years ago, and it's brought back memories."

For Luke had just remembered with a sudden start that today was his fifty-fourth birthday. He remembered, too, his mother, poor Dora, niece of the Georgia land speculator Carl Trask. Trask and his niece had visited Henry Bouchard's land in an attempt to buy it from Luke's father. The Georgia speculator, angered by what he had considered the insolence of Ben, a tall Ashanti, one of old Lucien's workers, shot the Ashanti in cold blood. Thomas, Ben's strong young son, avenged his father by pulling Carl Trask down from his horse and beating him to death with his cudgel. Then Henry Bouchard forced Dora Trask to yield to him and undergo a Creek marriage in the village of Econchate, which was later legalized by a church wedding in Mobile.

Luke closed his eyes and bowed his head as he said a prayer now for his tragic young mother's unhappy soul. A week after she had given birth to him, she threw herself into the river to escape his father's cruelty. It was a heritage that his beloved grandfather old Lucien mentioned only a single time, reassuring him in the same breath, "You must not hold it against your father, Luke. Each of us in his lifetime is driven by ungovernable passions, and circum-

250

stances and background and emotions often lead a man to do what he will later repent and regret. Look forward to the future, you have health and a keen young mind, and your life lies ahead of you to do with it as you think best."

How wise his old grandfather had been! Surely destiny had willed it that what Luke had achieved in these fifty-four years of life had been inspired by his grandfather, not at all by his own sire. He turned back an instant to look up-river in the direction of that towering bluff where old Lucien lay at rest. Then, his face hardening, he turned and nodded to Marius, "I'm all right now, Marius. Let's go see this Barnabas McMillan."

"Right with you, Mr. Luke."

Back in 1834, the Williamson house had been one story high, built of wood and brick, with a small portico over the heavy oaken door. The windows had been made of wood, opening like doors inward, and in bad weather they had been closed and bolted, their ugliness concealed by curtains. Now, the house of Barnabas McMillan was two stories high. The windows were made of glass, and the house itself was of new red brick and solid timbers. As both men dismounted and tethered the reins of their horses to a post near the cotton gin shed, Luke could see the light of a candle lamp from one of the upper windows. "At least he's awake, Marius. I'd hate to wake him out of a sound sleep. I want him fully conscious of what he's done," Luke said, as the two men walked toward the heavy front door of the house. Marius thrust his right hand into his trousers pocket to grip the butt of the pistol he had brought with him, as a precaution, and placed himself to Luke's left and slightly behind him, his expression wary.

Luke reached for the brass knocker, lifted it, and struck it three times vigorously as Marius tightened his hold on the butt of his pistol. From upstairs, suddenly, there came a man's boisterous guffaw, followed by a young woman's tipsy laughter. Marius glanced at Luke and shrugged as he glanced upward. Now there was the sound of footsteps, and a female voice irritatedly inquired, "Who dat?"

"I want to see Mr. Barnabas McMillan. This is Luke Bouchard," Luke called.

"He gone upstairs to bed. He ain't gonna see nobody this time of night. You best come around tomorra, mister," the voice rejoined.

But Luke was not to be denied. Again he rapped three times, and this time the female voice was peevish: "You awful dumb, mister. Didn't you just hear me say that Mr. McMillan, he ain't gonna see nobody nohow, not this late?"

"I think you'd better let me in. Otherwise I'll have the law out here," Luke called back, his features tautened with an intense resolution. Marius, closely watching his employer, shook his head slightly and took a firmer grip of his pistol.

Having heard no response, Luke banged the knocker against the door, and called out angrily, "I demand that you let me in. Otherwise, we'll fetch the law from Montgomery!"

"Awright, mister, I let you in. Only please, mister, don't you go tell Mr. Barnabas that Verna did it, you hear?"

"I won't tell him anything, I just want to see him. Now open this door at once!" Luke impatiently ordered.

"All right, all right, but don't you blame me none if Mr. Barnabas get real mad at you for this!" the female voice protested as the door swung open.

Luke Bouchard shouldered his way into an elaborately furnished foyer, with Marius beside him. A pretty mulatto girl of about nineteen stood before them, wearing high-heeled slippers with rhinestone buckles and a black silk dress whose bodice had been cut daringly low. She shrank back at the sight of the two men, a hand at her mouth. "Don't hurt me, mister, I didn't do nothin'!" she gasped, catching sight of the butt of Marius's pistol.

"Where's Mr. McMillan?" Luke tersely demanded.

The girl jerked a trembling thumb toward the stairway. "He up in the bedroom with ol' Cletus and two of my cousins, they's Lucille 'n Ednamae," she said.

At that moment, Barnabas McMillan himself appeared at the top of the stairway, a red silk dressing gown loosely belted over his underdrawers. He was scowling and his face was flushed. "What the hell's going on, Verna?" he irately asked. Then, staring at Luke Bouchard who had advanced toward the foot of the stairway, he sniggered, "Why, Mr. Bouchard, sir, I hardly expected to have a fine Southern gentleman like you come calling this time of night. Or maybe you heard about Verna and her cousins and wanted to come have a nice sociable high-yeller girl all to yourself, eh?"

252

"I came for a reason I think you know very well, Mr. McMillan," was Luke Bouchard's cold answer. "There's the matter of a filthy, slanderous handbill which was nailed to the door of my house. Besides that, there's a girl named Stacey Holbrook whom I'm sure you sent to my house to replace Moira O'Connor so that you could spy on my household."

"I don't know what you're talking about," McMillan growled, his unshaven jowls quivering with anger. "You must be crazy, disturbing me this time of night with a cock and bull story like that. I wonder that your backers chose an unbalanced man like you to run against Cletus Adams." Then he descended the stairway to the first landing and, with a sweeping gesture of his arm, he bawled, "I think you'd better get out of my house before I have the law on you, Mr. Bouchard!"

"Not so fast. there, Mr. McMillan," Marius Thornton coolly spoke up as he let the Eastern carpetbagger see the butt of the pistol he carried, drawing it out just a little farther so that there could be no mistake about his being armed. "You're going to listen to what Mr. Bouchard says, and then we'll see who calls the law."

"A fine thing!" McMillan sneered. "You catch a man ready for bed and you make him listen to a pack of lies at the point of a gun. Not only that, Mr. Bouchard, you bring along a nigger to do your dirty work for you!"

"I marvel at your choice of words, Mr. McMillan," Luke riposted. "From what I'm given to understand, you're the principal backer of my opponent, Cletus Adams, who is, I am told, a black man. I wonder if you call him a nigger, too. And as for someone doing my dirty work, Marius is here with a pistol only to see that the encounter between the two of us is fair and square."

"I don't catch your meaning, Mr. Bouchard. But I'm really very tired, and as I think I already mentioned," this with a wink and a bawdy snigger, "I've some attractive wenches upstairs I'm anxious to get back to. If you've nothing more to say to me, I'll thank you to close the door on your way out."

"I've a good deal more to say to you, Mr. McMillan. After my wife read this villainous handbill, which I'm sure was an inspiration of yours—"

"Now just a minute—"

"Let him have his say, Mr. McMillan," Marius nonchalantly put in, lifting the pistol completely out of his trousers pocket and leveling it above Barnabas McMillan's head. The carpetbagger gripped the rail of the stairway, with a choking cry of fear, his eyes bulging, then hastily nodded. "Go ahead, go ahead, say what you want, but I'm unarmed, as you can see. Do you mean to murder me, Mr. Bouchard?"

"Don't tempt me, Mr. McMillan," Luke tersely responded. "Now, to finish what I started to say. My wife read the handbill and then remembered that Stacey Holbrook bragged about having been born in New Orleans and was most anxious to know where my wife had lived. She went looking for her, found her in my study in the act of writing a letter addressed to you, sir."

"That's a lie, you can't prove anything!" the carpetbagger blustered. Then, in a whining voice, "For God's sake, Mr. Bouchard, tell that nigger of yours to put his pistol away. I'm listening, I'm hearing you out, what more do you want of me?"

"The truth, sir, then an admission of your guilt, and then I intend to thrash you within an inch of your contemptible life," was Luke Bouchard's vengeful answer. "Your Miss Holbrook didn't finish her letter, but she left the sheet on which she was writing when my wife demanded to see it. I have it here with me. It's addressed to 'Dear Barnabas which I think any court of law will accept as reasonable evidence that it refers to you, sir."

"Well, very possibly, but all the same . . ."

"A moment more, Mr. McMillan." Luke's blue eyes were narrowed and cold, his voice incisive: "When my wife demanded that Miss Holbrook give her the letter, this creature of yours kicked her in the belly. As a result, my wife lost her child, and it's fortunate for you that her own life was, thank God, mercifully spared. Otherwise, I very much fear I might have come here with pistol in hand myself and shot you down. Your tactics are beneath contempt. If, sir, you find any blemish on my record which makes you believe that your candidate is the better man for the state legislature, say it to my face. But to attack my wife as a loose woman is unconscionable. No decent man would resort to such an infamous lie."

Barnabas McMillan looked frantically back up the stairway as if hoping that someone would come to his aid, then stammered, "I didn't tell her to do that. I mean—look, Mr. Bouchard . . ."

"That's another admission of guilt. I intend to have my lawyer Jedidiah Danforth bring that wretched girl to justice. But it's you, sir, who placed her in my house—by what means I as yet don't know, but I surely intend to find out—and so I hold you as the one mainly responsible for my wife's suffering and the irreparable loss of her unborn child."

"Jesus, Mr. Bouchard—I swear I didn't know she was pregnant—I didn't tell Stacey to do anything like that—look, I'll make it up to you, I'll pay the doctor and I'll . . ."

"Spoken like a true carpetbagger," Luke angrily interrupted, clenching his fists only by a supreme effort of will. "Do you think you can come here and spread corruption and lies among our people and then buy your way out of a situation like this with money? Pay the doctor bill indeed! You're a cowardly swine, and you're going to retract the slander against my wife by making a statement in the *Advertiser* that you accept responsibility for that slimy handbill and you retract every word of it, do you understand me? Now, if you're man enough, come downstairs here and take what's coming to you."

"But—but—your nigger's got a pistol! He'll kill me!" McMillan panted, again looking back over his shoulder.

"He won't use it. All I'm going to do is use my fists on you. And I'll give you a fair chance to fight back, fairer than you gave my poor wife. Now come down here and take your medicine, you fat, conniving swine!"

At this moment, Cletus Adams, wearing only his underdrawers, his face lax with sated lust, his arm around a young mulatto girl who could not have been more than sixteen and who wore only a short shift which descended to mid-thigh, appeared at the top of the stairs. "What the hell is all this here noise, Mr. McMillan?" he bawled. "Can't a man enjoy some poontang without all this fuss this late? Who those men you got down there? Hey, you, Verna, come on up and join the fun, 'n bring a bottle with you, you hear, gal?"

"So that's my rival this November, is it?" Luke Bouchard glanced up, his lips curling in scorn. "Your candidate's drunk, Mr. McMillan, you'd best advise him to go

255

back to the bedroom where he belongs. He doesn't need another bottle. You, girl, stay right where you are," he ordered Verna, as the frightened mulatto girl cowered back against the wall.

"Who's 'at there?" Cletus Adams's voice was slurred and thick, and he staggered as he pulled his young partner tightly up against him, squinting down at Luke Bouchard and Marius Thornton.

"Stay out of this, Cletus, you black imbecile!" Barnabas McMillan turned on him with an almost petulant fury. "Take your whore back to bed and stay out of this, I'm telling you! If you want to stay on the Democratic ticket, you'll do what I tell you to!"

"Yessuh, sho will—c'mon Lucille honey, we ain't wanted downstairs. Less' us go back to bed, huh? Only you fellows down there, don't make so much noise, hey?" He turned, stumbled again, then belched, pulled the young mulatto girl to him, and then disappeared.

"Now, get down here before I bring you down, Mr. McMillan!" Luke Bouchard commanded in a voice that trembled with mounting fury.

Barnabas McMillan licked his lips, glanced up at the top of the stairs—now vacant—and then reluctantly descended toward the foyer. "All right. Look, I'll write what you want in the *Advertiser*. I'm sorry Stacey did what she did, but you can't blame me for that, Mr. Bouchard, not rightly." His sweaty face took on a crafty look now. "Look, Mr. Bouchard, I'll level with you. You damned Republicans haven't the chance of a snowball in hell to win this election. Don't forget the Ku Klux Klan is going to ride a lot before election time, and it's going to scare these stupid coons into voting Democratic. We're going to beat you even if I do what you say, I mean about writing that piece for the newspaper."

"At the moment, that doesn't concern me. I'm thinking only of my wife and how you sent that girl to my house to care for my sons and to spy on us so she could report back to you. All right now, put up your fists and try to act like a man for the first time in your life."

McMillan had slowly descended the steps one by one. Now he stood facing Luke, furtively licking his lips and glancing at Marius Thornton, who had pocketed the pistol and stepped back, his arms folded across his chest.

Luke glanced quickly at his foreman. "I don't want you intervening, Marius. If someone tries to stop us, that's where you come in, but that's all, understand?"

"Look out, Mr. Luke!" Marius suddenly cried as McMillan, seizing Luke's momentary distraction as his opportunity, doubled his right fist and swung with all his might at Luke's left cheek. The force of the blow and its unexpectedness made Luke stumble backwards, fight for balance, and then fall heavily onto his side. McMillan triumphantly jeered, "Oh, so it's not so easy as you thought, is it, Mr. Bouchard? I'm going to kill you, yes sir, that's what I'll do! It'll be a proper end for a blackhearted Republican scalawag like you!"

Slowly, painfully, Luke got to all fours, watching his smirking, fat opponent ludicrously prance about, his fists taut in the accepted Marquis of Queensbury pose. Then Luke suddenly launched himself upward and, as he straightened up, he drove with his right fist to the point of the carpetbagger's jaw. With a wail of pain, McMillan stumbled back, lost his balance, and fell heavily, rubbing his jaw gingerly as he eyed Luke with mingled fear and hate. "Get on your feet when you're ready," Luke growled at him, stepping back, his fists clenched and his body tense.

"Hit him a couple good ones for me, Mr. Luke," Marius eagerly urged. Then, contemptuously hawking and spitting on the costly Oriental rug which covered the part of the floor, he added, "On your feet, you oversized barrel of blubber, and take what's coming to you!"

McMillan staggered to his feet, beginning to wheeze from this unaccustomed exertion. His eyes were narrowed, beady, and vengeful. There was a darkening bruise on his jaw from the mark of Luke's fist. Then, with a bellow of rage, he rushed at his opponent, flailing both fists wildly in an attempt to take Luke by surprise, aiming at his midriff. But Luke sidestepped him and drove both fists, first right and then left, into the carpetbagger's side. McMillan emitted a strangled cry of pain and sank down on one knee, panting heavily, his face livid and sweating.

Once again Luke stepped back. "When you're ready," he coldly averred. "And when you've had enough, don't forget you're going to write a letter to the *Advertiser* retracting all those filthy charges against my wife. If you don't within the week, I swear I'll come back here and give you a good deal more of the same. Yes, even if it kills you!"

"You bastard, you goddamned scalawag you, I'll kill you first!" McMillan shrilly cried out as, stumbling to his feet, he lowered his head and charged Luke as a bull might charge a matador, at the same time lunging with his fists toward Luke's groin. But Luke, anticipating just such a maneuver, moved quickly aside and brought up his right fist in a savage uppercut that caught McMillan on the point of his jaw and straightened him to his full height. Then, floundering back, the fat man fell full length on the edge of the huge Oriental rug.

"Have you had enough, sir?" Luke scornfully demanded as he moved forward to stare down at his fallen face.

"For God's sake, yes—I can't get my breath. You've hurt me bad—all right, I'll write your goddamned retraction, sir—now get the hell out of my house!" McMillan groaned. A trickle of blood oozed from his upper lip. As he rolled over onto his side, he wiped his bleeding mouth with the back of his hand and glowered balefully at the man who had bested him. "Get out of here, I said—I've had enough—get out!"

"Gladly. But remember, Mr. McMillan, you've got just a week. If I don't see that retraction in the *Advertiser* by the end of that time, I'll be back here." Luke Bouchard turned to Marius Thornton. "I think that's enough for now. I'm afraid I might have lost my temper and really killed him if this had gone on any longer."

"I know how you feel—for God's sake, Mr. Luke, look out—" Marius suddenly shouted. For McMillan, crawling forward, had suddenly reached up to a little table on which there stood a statuette of a naked nymph in white marble and, seizing it by the head, had suddenly lunged forward at Luke. Marius's warning had made Luke turn to one side, so that the force of the blow struck his upper left arm just above the elbow, fracturing it. With a cry of agony, Luke ground his teeth against the pain, then doubled his right fist and with all his strength drove it into the carpet-bagger's paunch.

Barnabas McMillan uttered a shriek, dropping the statuette. He slumped to the floor and rolled over and over again, both hands clutching his belly. Luke, fighting the sickening waves of pain from his fractured arm, reached for the knob of the door with his good hand and opened it. He breathed in deeply of the cool night air, then stumbled out of the house.

"That son of a bitch, I've a good mind to shoot him for what he just did, Mr. Luke." Marius Thornton's voice was low and shaky. "I'll help you on your horse. It's a good thing you thought of keeping Dr. Medbury back at the house—McMillan must have broken your arm—thank God he didn't kill you. You know, for once in my life I'd like to commit murder!"

"No, Marius, not on my account, not even on my wife's. You're not to be involved in this at all, and that's what I told you. Besides, I think Mr. McMillan begins to understand the consequences of his rascality. God, my arm hurts—let's get back home as fast as we can!"

CHAPTER TWENTY-EIGHT

Lucien Edmond Bouchard stood at the side of the spinet, watching his lovely wife Maxine play a sprightly gigue by Handel. At thirty, Maxine had lost none of her candid wit and keen interest in music and literature which, at his first meeting with her back in 1858 at Windhaven Plantation, had led Lucien Edmond's father Luke to refer to her humorously as a "Baltimore bluestocking." Even then, at eighteen, Maxine had had a decided mind of her own and believed that women should have the right to cast a vote and even to hold public office: the news that both the Wyoming and Utah Territories had agreed to women's suffrage had understandably delighted her. There was not a trace of gray in her tumbling chestnut curls, and her expressive, large hazel eyes and low, vibrant voice still enthralled Lucien Edmond, just as they had done that September day when Ernest Kendall had brought his eighteen-year-old niece to the red-brick chateau.

As she finished the light-hearted piece, Lucien Edmond clapped his hands and bowed low to her. "Bravo, my dearest Maxine!" he exclaimed. "Whenever you play, it brings another world into this dusty old ranch house."

"It's kind of you to flatter me, but I do wish I could take time off and study with a really good teacher, dearest." Maxine rose from the piano seat and came to link her arms around his neck. Almost as tall as he, she leaned forward to kiss him tenderly on the lips, and for an instant both of them forgot they were a staid married couple of twelve years' standing, with three small children.

Flushed and happy, Maxine at last disengaged herself from Lucien's Edmond's fervent embrace, whispering, "My gracious, you're constantly a source of delight and excitement to me, Mr. Bouchard."

"As you are to me, Maxine dearest. Won't you play something else for me?" He sighed regretfully. "One of these days very soon, as you know, I'm going to have to drive the cattle to Abilene, and then I shan't hear any music except the lowing of cows and steers or the howling of the wind."

"I know." A momentary shadow crossed her face, and she gently put her palm to his cheek. "It's always such a long time. And I worry about your getting back safely and what's going to happen to all those good men who ride along with you."

"One of these days, there'll be more settlers here. There'll be law in this part of the country and far less danger. But God has watched over all of us, Maxine, and I'm praying He'll be on our side this year again. Though I'll admit we're later than I had hoped in starting the drive to Abilene—mainly because what our neighbor Robert Caldemare is doing nearby is worrying me."

"Is it really so serious?" She searched his face with a sudden anxiety.

"It might be. The men who work for him are arrogant and hostile, and some of my men have already had some run-ins with them. I've put off going over to see him because legally I suppose he has a right to put up what markers he wants. Also fencing, though in principle I'm opposed to it. If you close part of the range, one day you'll have an end to an open range altogether, and there won't be jobs for the vaqueros. In fact, if the railroads ever extend their lines even as far south as Indian Territory, it'll become a routine business."

"Would that be bad, Lucien Edmond dear?" Again she touched his cheek and added a quick kiss.

His left arm circled her waist as he smiled and shook his head. "No, I suppose not. It'll certainly be more profitable, and I daresay we'll still have to keep a good number of vaqueros on the ranch. But we'll probably have specialists, men who can brand quickly in the pen and then steer cattle into chutes and railroad cars, men who will give more concern to crossbreeding and caring for the calves than it's possible to do in this sort of operation. That's a long way ahead, though. Right now, we must still drive the cattle to market, and I know my riders are impatient to get started. They want to miss that really bad weather in the height of summer. Last year we did very well in that regard."

"Well, I'll say selfishly that I'm not sorry you've stayed a little longer here at home with me, darling. And do you know, I think we're going to have our fourth child. In fact, I'm rather certain of it."

"Maxine!" He dropped his arm and stood back, his eyes wide with delighted surprise.

She tilted back her head and laughed gaily. "Oh my goodness, you may be the toughest range boss in Texas, but right now you're wonderfully, lovably naive. I only just found out last week, so you won't have to treat me as if I'm a Dresden doll. You can still hug and squeeze me— and I wish you would."

"Well, what red-blooded husband could resist an invitation like that from so beautiful a wife?" he murmured as he took her in his arms and kissed her lingeringly and, from Maxine Bouchard's viewpoint, most satisfactorily.

Indeed, they were oblivious to anything else, even to the sudden loud knocking on the door of the ranch house till at last Maxine, breathing quickly, her eyes sparkling and her cheeks a delicious crimson, gasped, "You'd better see who that is, darling!"

Lucien Edmond Bouchard lovingly tweaked his wife's nose, then kissed it, and jauntily strode to the door and opened it. His face sobered the moment he saw Joe Duvray, who stood twisting his sombrero between his hands and scowling. "What's wrong, Joe?"

"Everything, Mr. Bouchard. Ignacio Valdez, Eddie Gentry, and Santiago Miraflores rode out to check on those boundary markers. Just as I told you before, they saw how Caldemare's men are setting up their own posts and wires inside of your land. A bunch of those *pistoleros* came over and the next thing we knew, their foreman, name of Jamie Ruiz, shot poor Ignacio down in cold blood. Claims Ignacio called him a liar—well, he *is* one, by God! Sure, our men had the Spencers along, Mr. Bouchard, but all of them had the draw on our men with their pistols. It wouldn't have been smart to fire. Now, though, I feel I ought to let Ruiz have it no matter what it costs me!"

"No, Joe, you won't do that! I know how you feel, but that'll start a range war. Our men were outnumbersd, they did the right thing to back down. What a damnable thing to happen! He was such a bright young fellow, so eager to work here, and to have his life snuffed out over a stupid quarrel, without even a chance to defend himself—" Lucien Edmond's face contorted with anger. "Well, this calls for a showdown. I guess I've been half afraid something like this was going to happen all along."

"They brought Ignacio back—they figured we ought to bury him on friendly land, Mr. Bouchard," Joe hoarsely interposed.

"Yes. We'll do that. How I wish Friar Bartoloméo were here to read the service. After that, Joe, we'll round up about a dozen men, with weapons, and we're going over there to talk to this Robert Caldemare."

"I just can't make it out, Mr. Bouchard," Joe shook his head. "That daughter of his I told you about, she's such a sweet girl, and she thinks her father's aces. In fact, after I saved her from that runaway mare, she got all-fired mad at me because I happened to say that you were a little annoyed about the posts and the fencing. Why, Mr. Bouchard, you'd have thought I was a rattlesnake all of a sudden, just like the one that made her mare shy, for saying anything against her father. But there's really something wrong there. All the fellows Santiago and Eddie saw on that ranch had guns and knew how to use them, and you could bet they enjoyed doing it. They weren't the type of vaqueros we have here, that's for certain."

"That's another thing that makes me want to find out what Robert Caldemare has in mind. All right, I'll be out with you directly after I've talked to Maxine. I want to help bury that poor fellow. Ask Ramón to find out if Igancio gave him any address of next of kin. I want to send them some money—that's the very least I can do to make things a bit easier for them. I won't enjoy writing a letter to them either, I can tell you. Why, his life was just beginning at twenty-four, and now he's been shot down by a trigger-happy *pistolero* over a fancied insult, without a fair chance at all. He came here looking for a new life, and now it's over, and all for nothing."

"Yes, sir. He's tied to his horse, and I'll just take it around to the bunkhouse, and then I'll get Ramón and the others."

Lucien Edmond nodded, then went back to Maxine,

who stood near the spinet, a hand at her mouth, her eyes wide with alarm. "Maxine darling, there's been a terrible accident," he began.

"I—I could just hear a little of what Joe was saying, darling. Someone was killed? That's terrible! Why would that man who's next to us want to kill our workers?"

"That's exactly what I plan to find out as soon as we've buried poor Ignacio, dear."

"Oh, Lucien Edmond, I'm afraid for you!" Maxine clung to him, tears welling to her hazel eyes. "You and your men are going to ride over there now, aren't you? And you'll take your guns, and there'll be shooting—"

"Maxine, believe me, I didn't want this. But, my God, what am I going to do, back away from it? Caldemare's men would just go on taking more and more of our land with their boundary fence, daring us to protest. There'll be more shootings if we don't tell them here and now we're not going to stand for a range war brought about by his thievery."

"I—I suppose you're right, my dearest. But please take care of yourself. I love you so much, and I've already been consoling myself for the long months you're going to be away on the drive to Abilene—and now this!"

"Don't, sweetheart," he murmured tenderly, stroking her hair and kissing her tear-wet eyelids. "We won't give them a chance to shoot down unarmed men the way they did poor Ignacio. Say a prayer for me, my darling. I'll come back to you, don't worry." He gave her a last kiss, held her close to him for a moment, then resolutely turned and went out of the ranch house.

Jackson Brundiger sprawled lazily in a chair opposite Robert Caldemare's desk in the latter's study, eyeing his partner with a crooked grin. "It's working just the way I planned it, Caldemare," he declared. "Bouchard's so damned worried about our moving his markers around, he's held up his cattle drive."

Caldemare nervously drummed the fingers of his right hand on top of his desk, scowled, and then abruptly rose. "That's all very well, but I didn't want any violence so close to home. Devil take you, Brundiger, couldn't you control your men? Why did you have to let Ruiz kill that cowboy of theirs?"

"Jaime Ruiz is a *pistolero,* which, for your information as an Eastern tenderfoot, Caldemare, means that he's looked on across the border just as I was back in Kansas. We live by the gun, because we have to. There's no law in these parts, except the law we make with these." He suggestively slapped his palms against the butts of his holstered pistols. "And when a man calls you a liar to your face, you don't back down from it."

"But he didn't even draw a gun, from what you told me."

"Perhaps not, but he could have. Besides, his two friends had Spencers, and if we'd given them a chance to use them, we might have lost all five of the men working on the markers. No, it's better this way. I'm sure that Bouchard's going to ride over and have a palaver with you, Caldemare. And you know what I'm going to do? I figure that this is just the time to get a head start on them. He's got to drive his cattle to Abilene in the next couple of weeks, or he might miss the market entirely. There'll be other Texas herds coming up, and Joe McCoy is keeping the buyers from the Midwest and the East around till the big herds come in. Bouchard's stalled long enough so that he might even miss a sale—but of course you and I know he's not going to be the one who makes the sale."

"So you've told me. What do you propose to do now?"

"Well, I figure that I'll just ride ahead of Bouchard and get a good start. I'll take about a dozen of my best men, and they'll all be well armed. We'll wait for them just beyond the Red River. When he crosses it, we'll hit him hard. What with driving the herd—which always takes even the best trail boss a couple of days—he and his cowboys are going to be so damned busy they won't be looking for any bushwhacking. And we'll be there ahead of them to see just where they're crossing and where it's best to hit them when they're least expecting us, savvy?"

"Yes. Only as I told you before, Brundiger, I'm not taking part in any gunplay."

"So you say, Caldemare. Only I've noticed the last week or so you've been wearing a holster. Not a bad idea in these parts. Especially if Bouchard comes riding in hell-bent for leather wanting to make you pay for what happened to that stupid young Mex who shot off his mouth!"

"You talk as if you won't be here when he comes."

"I won't be, *boss*." Jackson Brundiger bared his teeth in a wolfish grin as he lazily rose from the chair and patted his pistols again. "But I'll leave Ruiz here and at least six good men with him so if there's trouble they'll be able to take care of it."

"What about those five hundred head of Mexican cattle? I thought you were going to drive those to Abilene."

"Nope." The Kansan chuckled humorlessly. "They were just there for decoration. Oh, sure, after we latch on to Bouchard's herd over the Red River, the rest of the outfit can always drive them on to join us. But they wouldn't bring top prices at Abilene anyhow, they're too scrubby. No, I thought I made it clear before. The real money is in Bouchard's herd. It's prime beef, Caldemare. He's been crossbreeding, and his stock looks like it'll bring top dollar. Don't forget, too, once we get his herd, we'll have a little chore of branding so that Joe McCoy and his buyers won't get the wind up. Now you just leave this to me. I'm going to pull out right now, before Bouchard and his boys take a notion to ride over. I'll give the orders to Ruiz, he'll know what to do."

"My God, there might be shooting, and Margaret's here—"

"That's easy. Tell her to stay in her room and mind her business and she won't get hurt. From what I've heard about this Bouchard fellow, he doesn't go after women. But I want to even the score with him for what he did to my pal Reedy. And I'm going to make you enough money so you can buy your daughter fancy clothes or whatever you've a mind to. That was part of our bargain, remember?"

"Very well. Only I'm not used to killing."

"It comes easy once you do it the first time, Caldemare." Again the Kansan gave him his wolfish grin, then turned and sauntered out of the room.

Half an hour later, Jackson Brundiger and eleven Mexican *pistoleros,* many with prices on their heads across the border, galloped off toward the northwest, intending to put as much distance as they could between themselves and the Bouchard ranch house. Robert Caldemare came out onto the steps of the house, his face a mask of fear and anger, watching the dust from their horses' hooves rise

266

in a cloud until they disappeared from view. He turned with a start as he felt Margaret touch his arm. "What's the matter, Margaret," he almost snapped at her.

"Why, nothing, Father. I—I just wanted a little fresh air, that's all. And then I saw all those men saddling up and riding off—where are they going?"

"On an errand for me, Margaret. You're not to worry about it."

"But—but I am worried, Father. I—I heard the sound of a gunshot a little while ago. I was resting, and it woke me. I went to the window and looked out. I could see that someone was lying on the ground near his horse, and there were some of your men standing there and watching. Then I saw a man get off his horse and lift that other man's body and tie it onto the horse. Father, somebody was hurt or killed—why did it happen?"

"Margaret," he testily retorted, "it was just an accident, that's all. It doesn't concern you. Now please, I've got a lot on my mind. . . ."

"I don't understand it, Father," she interrupted, intently staring at him. "You know how I've wanted to be with you all these years, how I've missed not having a father when the other girls in school would boast about theirs. And it's an awfully lonely place here. The only ones around are all these rough-looking men, and all of them are wearing guns. That Mr. Brundiger, I don't like him at all. He looks evil, Father. He looks as if he enjoys wearing those guns and knows how to use them."

"Margaret, you came from a girls' finishing school in Boston," he almost explosively interrupted. "Nobody knows what Texas is like, not back there. You wouldn't find it in all the books that Miss Emmons would let you read. There isn't any law and order out here, Margaret. You protect what you have by hiring men who wear guns and know how to use them. You have to, or you'll have your land stolen and your cattle and everything else into the bargain."

"But Mr. Duvray said that your men were moving the boundary markers on his boss's land and putting up posts and fencing beyond them. Wouldn't that mean that your men were taking some of that Mr. Bouchard's land?"

"Who's this Mr. Duvray?"

"Father, didn't I tell you that I was out riding on Belle

267

Etoile, and she ran away when she saw a rattlesnake and almost threw me, and Mr. Duvray was out riding the range and saved me?"

"Oh yes—I—" he passed a hand over his forehead and closed his eyes for a moment. "I've had a lot on my mind lately, Margaret. I guess I did forget that. I'm sorry."

"Well, he works for Mr. Bouchard, and he told me about how your men were putting up fencing and going onto Mr. Bouchard's land by doing it. Isn't that wrong, Father?"

"Now look, honey, you don't understand these things. I bought the land in Austin, that's where the land office is. They give you a map and they show you where the boundaries of your land are in every direction, understand? Well then," he was more glib and assured now, "when I got here, this fellow Bouchard had put up markers because he probably didn't figure he'd have a neighbor so close. As it happens, he got a little generous for himself, that's all. Now please don't fret about it any more."

"If you say so, Father." She lowered her eyes and bit he lips. "Mr. Duvray was very kind to me. He saved my life. Then I got very angry at him because he said what he did about your men moving Mr. Bouchard's markers and putting up their own. I—I was angry at him because he made it sound as if you were doing something wrong, Father. You know that I love you and that I've always believed what you told me all these years. You've worked so hard for me, and I appreciate it, only—only—I don't like what I saw just now, Father, and I feel afraid around all these men with their guns."

"For God's sake, Margaret, I told you that life out here isn't the way it is back in Boston in a fine school where you're protected from what's going on in the world!" Robert Caldemare angrily burst out, the large vein in his temple darkening and throbbing. "Just trust me this once, I'm going to be rich again, and then I can do things for you. I know it's not too comfortable out here for you, but it won't be for much longer, I promise you that. Just trust me, Margaret; I haven't lied to you before, have I?"

She raised her eyes now, again looking at him intently, studying him as if it were the first time she had ever seen him. Greatly troubled, she at last answered in an unsteady voice, "I don't think you've ever lied to me before, Father.

I don't want to think it. I wouldn't have anything left if I did, you know." This last, almost wistfully. "But why did your men shoot down that poor man? Was it because he was asking them about the markers?"

"Margaret, you ask too many questions, and I've got things on my mind. Maybe because he tried to draw a gun and pick a quarrel. I wasn't there, I didn't see it. I hired Jaime Ruiz as a foreman, and Mr. Brundiger, whether you like it or not, is my partner. I trust them, and they're going to make me rich—make us rich, I mean."

"I don't want to be rich, Father, if it means that innocent people have to die."

"That's out of your finishing school for sure," he sarcastically retorted. "Now you stop preaching at me, Margaret, and go back to your room and don't worry about anything. In a few months, if all goes well, we'll be able to leave here and be together and you'll have a comfortable, good life. Just trust me, that's all I ask."

She drew a deep breath, then slowly nodded. "I've no one else to trust, Father." Bowing her head, she went back into the house.

Lovely young Felicidad, five months' pregnant, paid a visit to the little shed right off the bunkhouse to see Coraje, the aplomado falcon whose broken wing she had helped to heal and which she had trained to hunt and to defend her loved ones. Djamba had made a large wooden cage for the falcon, and by now Coraje was so fond of his lovely young mistress that he would utter soft little cries whenever she came into the shed, as indeed he did now.

Felicidad opened the cage and extended her right hand, which was protected by a leather glove. Coraje, cocking his head, uttered the cry again and at once leaped from his perch onto her hand and, with his sharp claws gripping as gently as he knew how, moved onto her shoulder.

"*Halcón pequeño,* how are you feeling this beautiful day?" she softly asked. Affectionately, she reached up with her left hand to stroke the falcon's head, admiring its blue coloring with a dark band across its chest, its pure white throat, brown legs, and barred tail.

Coraje blinked his fierce yellow eyes, uttered the soft little cry again, and playfully nipped at her fingers, then rubbed his head against them.

"*Amorcito*, you are very well behaved today," she commended the falcon. "I shall never forget how you saved us all last year when those two terrible men came with their guns and knives to frighten us while the men were away on the drive. How brave you were, how truly you deserve the name of Coraje—courage!" Her face was momentarily saddened as she sighed. "Alas, *mi esposo* Lucas will be going away soon. It is late for the men to go, Coraje. I am so afraid that my dearest *esposo* will not be back until after I have given him his son—oh, yes, Coraje, I know it will be a son, as strong and brave as he and his father are!"

Once again the falcon uttered its muted cry and rubbed its head against her upheld palm. "But when he is gone, you will stay here to protect me and the little *niño* so that when he comes back, there will be the three of us to love one another, won't you, dear Coraje?"

Now the falcon deftly leaped to the top of her head where it perched, ruffling its feathers, stretching out its wings, and flapping them lightly. This time it uttered a fiercer cry. "Oh, I know, you are hungry, Coraje. Well, I have not forgotten. Yesterday, Pablo caught two mice in the bunkhouse, and I have brought them here for your breakfast. Later this afternoon, I'll take you outside and you can fly with those strong wings. But please, Coraje, do not kill the gentle little doves that perch on our roof and coo so sweetly when it is twilight. I know it is your nature to kill smaller birds, but there are the noisy sparrows, and there are more of them than the doves. It would please me if you would spare the doves, dear Coraje. Now, here is the first mouse. Eat it slowly."

She put her left hand into the pocket of her bright red cotton dress, drew out one of the dead mice by the tail, and lifted it up to the falcon. Coraje seized the rodent in its beak and swiftly devoured it.

"You are greedy, you eat too fast," she playfully scolded. "Just for that, you shall wait a bit for the second one. Oh, it's such a beautiful day outside, but I have duties before I can play with you. I must work in the kitchen, and I must help the señoras Kate and Maybelle to prepare the food for the *patrón* and his family, and then there are the brave vaqueros who are always hungry. You see, Coraje, you are not the only one. But I promise you before the sun

270

sets that we shall go for a walk by the creek, where I first found you, *halcón pequeño,* and I will let you fly and be free."

The falcon again uttered its soft cry and, with a laugh, Felicidad delved into the pocket of her dress to lift the second mouse by its tail, and again Coraje devoured it.

"Now I think that is enough attention for you until I come back late this afternoon," she pretended to scold her pet. "Back into your cage." She extended her left arm and the falcon flew from her head to her wrist, which was covered by an extension of her glove. "That is very good. Maybe I will bring you a treat when I come to let you out of your cage. Here we go now!" She moved back to the cage and Coraje obediently hopped onto his perch, turning at once to fix her with his keen yellow eyes, opening and snapping his beak shut several times as he ruffled his wings once more.

"I know, I know how much you want to fly. You shall have your chance, I promise. And now, *hasta la vista,* Coraje!" she said as she locked the door of the cage and went out of the shed. As she came into the sunlight, she looked up at the sky and sighed again. *"Señor Dios,* You have given a poor little orphan girl such great happiness. At times I do not think I deserve it. *Mi amor* Lucas is such a wonderful man, I am so lucky to have him as my *esposo.* For this I thank You, *Señor Dios,* and also for the little one that I carry." Gently, almost reverently, with an exquisite smile, she touched herself. "I can never thank You enough for all this happiness. I ask You please to watch over Lucas when he rides with the cattle to Abilene. And perhaps, if I am very good and do all my work and say my prayers faithfully, as You know I do, *Señor Dios,* perhaps You will make it happen that he comes back to me in time to see his son."

CHAPTER TWENTY-NINE

Lucien Edmond Bouchard himself had said a prayer over the grave of young Ignacio Valdez, while the vaqueros of Windhaven Range stood silently around, heads bowed, stunned by the realization that the death of this friendly newcomer had taken place only a brief time ago and so near to them. Before the burial, Santiago Miraflores and Eddie Gentry had already told the story of how the arrogant foreman of Robert Caldemare's ranch had shot the young Mexican down without giving him a chance to go for his own gun. As Lucien Edmond concluded and made the sign of the cross, there began a restless murmur of voices as the vaqueros huddled among themselves, their mourning beginning to turn to slow anger against the needless, meaningless killing.

"Hombres," Lucien Edmond called out as he held up his hand for silence, "we've lost a friend, a newcomer to us, but one who already had made friends with his hard work and his eagerness to please. Yet let me caution you against wanting to take the law into your own hands and to avenge his death. That kind of thinking leads to wholesale bloodshed and to the needless deaths of a good many innocent men. What I propose to do now is to ride over to call on this Robert Caldemare. I will ask him why his men are given orders to put up wire fencing and to move our boundaries back and replace them with his own. I'm going to go there armed, and I want men to ride with me, but remember, we're not going in there shooting. We're taking along our guns because we don't want any more of our men shot down in cold blood. It's going to call for self-control and particularly for alertness. We'll be ready if his men want to fight, but we're not going to start one."

"Señor patrón," Santiago Miraflores spoke up, surreptitiously brushing the back of his hand across his eyes,

"Ignacio was my good friend, though I was old enough to be his father. I will ask your permission to stand up against this *capataz* who killed him. I am not bad with a pistol either, and I will make him pay for poor Ignacio."

"No, Santiago," Lucien Edmond shook his head, choosing his words carefully. "There will be no duels of vengence or reprisals, either. I hope I can convince Mr. Caldemare to talk to me and explain what he's doing, and I also hope I can straighten this out without any more bloodshed."

"Lucien Edmond," Ramón Hernandez proffered, "it is possible that we may ride into an ambush. Perhaps they shot Ignacio down to draw us over there, and they may be hiding with their pistols and rifles, ready to pick us off as we ride in."

"What you say is possible, Ramón," Lucien Edmond soberly agreed, "but we'll have to risk that. You told me once you thought they had about twenty-five vaqueros. But if we ride in with a force that strong, we won't have many left to defend the ranch house. Besides, I think ten good men with Spencer carbines and rifles and the new center-fire cartridges and loading cases can surely hold their own against anything Caldemare can throw against us. Joe, you've been close to some of those *pistoleros,* what do you think about the weapons they may have?"

"From what I saw, Mr. Bouchard," the black-haired Georgian promptly responded, "most of them seem to have six-shooters. There are a couple of Belgian rifles, and I caught sight of a Winchester rifle or two. But they don't have any Spencers, that I'm sure of. In fact, I'll stake my life on it."

"We may have to at that, Joe." Lucien Edmond's face was grim as he scanned the tense faces of the vaqueros grouped around him. "Well, I'll call for volunteers. Nine men—but not you, Pablo, or you, Ramón. I don't want any married men with families, that's for certain. No, not you either, Lucas, or you, Djamba," he added as the gray-haired Mandingo and his son raised their hands and moved forward eagerly.

"I want to go with you, Mr. Bouchard," Joe Duvray declared. "Me too," Eddie Gentry, standing beside him, eagerly nodded and lifted his hand.

"All right, Joe and Eddie. You, too, Santiago, but remember, you're not going to seek out that *capataz* of theirs and go looking for trouble, understand? You'll take orders from me. It's going to be a kind of military operation, and discipline is what I mean to have, especially where guns are concerned. I don't think all Caldemare's men are to blame for what Ruiz did, and by the same token I don't want any of you to lose your heads and get yourselves killed just because you're angry about what they did to poor young Ignacio. Is that understood?"

Six other vaqueros had already stepped forward, and Lucien Edmond nodded, then said to Ramón, "Arm these men with Spencer carbines and rifles and plenty of ammunition. Have them saddle up, and we'll ride out in half an hour. It'll be just about twilight then, and it'll be just as hard for them to see us as we ride in, so that ought to minimize the dangers of the ambush you warned me about. We'll ride north and then double back, heading west and then south, so we can ride directly in on them. That way, we'll get a chance to see how many of them are going to be out there to meet us."

"*Señor patrón,*" Santiago Miraflores again interposed, "what if they begin to shoot at us? Do we return their fire?"

"Yes. But only then. We're not the ones who are going in there shooting first and asking questions afterward. Besides, Caldemare has a daughter, and we don't make war on women. She'll doubtless be inside the house, so remember, men, that stray shots may go through windows."

"I sure wish I could get to her first and have her arrange for her daddy to talk to you, Mr. Bouchard," Joe Duvray readjusted his sombrero and scowled. "I've got a powerful hunch she thinks her father's a great man and she doesn't have the foggiest notion in the world what he's really up to. It's going to be a damned shame if she finds out he's just a common, ordinary landgrabber looking for a fight."

"That's true, Joe. I wish I'd been riding out with you that day you saved her from her runaway mare. Maybe I could have convinced her to take me to her father, and then poor Ignacio might still be alive right now," Lucien Edmond answered. He drew a deep breath, then nodded to the nine men who had volunteered. "Get your guns and ammunition, saddle your horses, and I'll wait for you outside the stockade."

274

Among the volunteers was Manuel Rodriguez, whose left wrist still bore the scar of the bullet that had shattered it three years ago, when Bud Larkin's renegades had tried to ambush Lucien Edmond's outfit at the Red River. Also to ride were the half-breed scout Simata and four Mexican vaqueros who had demonstrated their mettle many times against bushwhackers, hostile Indians, and the dangers of a cattle stampede. Armed and ready now, they rode out through the gate in the stockade where Lucien Edmond awaited them on his gray gelding. He rose in his saddle to study them, then nodded and swung his arm in a gesture toward the north. As orange and red began to burnish the sky to herald sunset, the ten men rode out as leisurely as if they were merely inspecting the boundaries of Windhaven Range. If anyone were watching, that maneuver, Lucien Edmond hoped, might lull Caldemare's men into thinking that they intended no reprisal.

Soon the ten riders turned in an easy circle and headed toward the southwest, so that they had a front view of Robert Caldemare's imposing frame house, with the bunkhouse to its left.

Joe Duvray reined in his horse and pointed toward the west as he came up alongside Lucien Edmond Bouchard. "See over there, Mr. Bouchard? Those Mexican cattle I was telling you about, maybe five hundred head, I'd judge. He's got them all penned up in that big enclosure. That's funny in itself, I'd say. You'd expect to see them out grazing till it's time for roundup and the drive."

"Yes, Joe. I'm beginning to wonder if those cattle weren't a decoy to let us think he was just another cattle rancher competing alongside of us," Lucien Edmond observed.

"But what's the decoy for, that's what I want to know," Joe irritatedly retorted, adjusting his sombrero and reaching down to pat his sheathed Spencer carbine beside the saddle. "What's that man up to, anyhow?"

"That's exactly what I hope to find out this evening, Joe. And what's so secret about his operation that his foreman has to go and shoot down poor Ignacio just because of Ignacio's remark about the changed boundary markers. An honest man who had nothing to hide wouldn't tell his foreman to use a gun on somebody asking simple questions, to my way of thinking."

"I go along with that, Mr. Bouchard. Look there—I see a few vaqueros coming out of the bunkhouse. About five or six, looks like from here. Getting pretty hazy now with the sun going down."

"Yes, it is. But there's no sign of any life in the house. You figured they had about twenty-five men in the outfit, didn't you? Well, the rest of them are either in the bunkhouse or in the house. They're not out here putting up any more of their wiring, that's for certain," Lucien Edmond concluded. "Let's ride in slowly. And remember, don't shoot unless they fire on you. I want to have a parley with Caldemare, and that's the main object, not a shootout."

"I told the men just to be careful and have their guns in easy reach, Mr. Bouchard. But I don't rightly fancy being picked off like a sitting duck by any trigger-happy Mex," Joe grumbled.

"I feel the same way, Joe," Lucien Edmond countered. "But from what you and the other riders have reported, Caldemare's men seem mainly to have six-shooters and European pistols. Maybe a few rifles, and those could be either Belgian or French or very possibly some of the old Confederate Whitworths. Which means they'll have to come up close if they want to be accurate, and we'll know their intentions soon enough if they try that."

"There's another thing that doesn't sit right with me, Mr. Bouchard." Joe Duvray squinted toward the distant ranch house, shook his head, then continued his easy pace alongside Lucien Edmond. "The fellow who killed poor Ignacio wasn't the one Eddie Gentry and I had the real trouble with. That one, as I told you, was a real ornery *hombre,* and my guess is that he came out of Indian Territory, maybe Kansas or Missouri. Remember, I told you he wouldn't give us his name. I asked him if he was the top hand of the outfit, and he said he was. But Ruiz said he was the foreman. Now what I want to know is, who is that gunslinger, and what's Caldemare doing hiring a man like that? He's a cold-blooded killer if ever I saw one, Mr. Bouchard."

"Well, that's another thing I hope to find out this evening. Look, I'll tie a white handkerchief to the barrel of my Spencer. As we get closer, I'll ride in holding it up. Even Mexicans know what a white flag means."

"I'll cover you, Mr. Bouchard, right behind you," Joe Duvray emphatically asserted.

Lucien Edmond halted his gelding while he tied the handkerchief to the Spencer, then put the reins in his left hand and rode forward, slowly lifting the repeating rifle. They had come within five hundred yards of the ranch house now, and the young scout Simata leaned forward in his saddle, squinting through the hazy dusk. "I made out six men standing at the door of the bunkhouse, Mr. Bouchard," he called. "They're just standing watching us, and they've got their hands to their holsters."

"So far, so good. I'm going a little ahead of you men," Lucien Edmond announced. Spurring his gelding, he rode forward at a trot, lifting the rifle high so that the white handkerchief could be seen by the watching Mexicans. He could see now that a sturdy wire fence framed off the bunkhouse and the ranch house itself, and that there was a broad, low wooden gate fronting the entrance of the ranch house. He came up to it, waving the rifle slowly back and forth and called, "I want to have a parley with Mr. Caldemare." Then, seeing the half-dozen Mexicans move slowly forward, he repeated his demand in Spanish so that they would understand him, adding the words, *"Vengo como amigo"* (I come as a friend) so that there could be no doubt about his improvised flag of truce.

Jaime Ruiz detached himself from the group of vaqueros standing near the bunkhouse and strode forward toward the gate, his right hand near the butt of his holstered pistol. "A little moment, señor," he drawled. "I am the *capataz* here, and you will talk with me. You bring a great many *hombres* with you, señor, and they have fine new guns that shoot many times without reloading, I can tell that. Why do you ride against my *patrón* like this?"

"Why, you dirty sidewinder—" Joe Duvray muttered under his breath with a ferocious scowl. But Lucien Edmond glanced back, reprovingly shook his head, and then retorted, "Well, it is Señor Ruiz, is it not? I'm told you're the one who shot down one of my vaqueros. Before I ask that you tell your *patrón*, Señor Robert Caldemare, that I wish to talk with him, perhaps you will tell me why you found it necessary to kill a harmless young man."

"Because, señor," Jaime Ruiz replied with malicious

sarcasm as he stared Lucien Edmond up and down, "he made the mistake of calling me a liar. I do not take that from any man—no, not even from you, señor."

"My name is Lucien Edmond Bouchard, and I am the owner of the ranch to the east of you."

"I am glad to see that the *patrón* at last comes to visit us. Up to now, we have seen only your vaqueros. And I know two of your men already—the one who rides alongside you, and that other one," Ruiz gestured toward Eddie Gentry.

"Well, so now you meet me, Señor Ruiz. And you say you killed Ignacio Valdez because he called you a liar. But had he drawn his gun?"

"I do not wait for him to do that. Here in this country, Señor Bouchard, if a man is stupid enough to call one who has *pistolas* at his belt a liar, he must take the consequences."

"I don't agree with your interpretation of the customs of this part of the country, as you call it, Señor Ruiz. But we'll let that pass. Would you be good enough to tell your *patrón* that I wish to talk with him?"

"Very well. It will do you no good, I assure you. But since you say you come in peace and you are all so well armed and we are only poor Mexicans doing the work for which we are paid, Señor Bouchard, I will do as you desire—this once." With heavy sarcasm, Jaime Ruiz slowly finished his phrase and then turned his back and strode nonchalantly toward the door of the ranch house.

"I hope the good Lord'll forgive me for what I'm thinking I'd like to do right now," Joe Duvray hissed as he leaned toward Lucien Edmond. "My hand's just itching to pull that Spencer out and let that dirty killer have it."

"I'm sure He'll forgive you for thinking that, Joe, but you're not going to yield to the temptation, not while I'm running this outfit. Now get your hand away from that Spencer. At least Ruiz understands we've come on a peaceful mission, that we just want to talk. Pass the word for all the men to be careful and to be ready, but remember, there's to be no shooting unless they start the action," Lucien Edmond sternly warned.

Jorge Feliz and Luis Garcia, two of the vaqueros who had ridden to Abilene with Lucien Edmond, sat tensely astride their geldings, eyeing their compatriots who had

278

come closer when their *capataz* had approached Lucién Edmond Bouchard to parley. Luis murmured to Jorge, *"Cuidado, muchacho,* even though those *hombres* are *Mejicanos* like us, I do not trust them. They have the look of men who enjoy killing for sport. Is your gun loaded, *amigo?"*

"Pero sí, mi compadre," Jorge Felix whispered back with a grimace. "Do you think I am a child? I do not like their looks either, Luis. But it's strange that there aren't more men out here. I do not think this *ranchero* is too poor to hire vaqueros for all this land. ¿*Es muy estraño, no es verdad?"*

"There he is, Mr. Bouchard," Joe Duvray said in a low voice, hoarsened by the tension; "that must be Caldemare himself with the *capataz*. And look, there's Margaret, in the doorway. He's telling her to go back into the house!"

Indeed, the young woman had begun to accompany her father, who had angrily turned back, shaken his head, and said something to her in a voice too low for the Bouchard men to hear. She gave him a long, searching look, leaned forward to say something earnestly, and then quickly disappeared. Caldemare scowled, whispered something to Jaime Ruiz, and then came slowly forward toward where Lucien Edmond Bouchard waited at the wide, low wooden gate. Caldemare wore a pair of new riding breeches, glistening black boots with silver spurs, and a ruffled white silk shirt with a flowing cravat through which he had thrust a diamond stickpin, a relic of his earlier financial successes. Jaime Ruiz sauntered along beside him, a condescending sneer on his swarthy face, his hands flexing at his sides. Joe Duvray's eyes narrowed at that sight, watching the Mexican's right hand move menacingly close to his holstered gun.

"Well, sir, my name is Robert Caldemare. My foreman tells me you want to see me. You've disturbed me just when I was about to sit down to supper with my daughter, Mr. Bouchard. I hope you will not keep me from it long. My daughter has only recently joined me from the East, sir, and in this lonely place I welcome her company."

"I'll try not to make you late for supper, Mr. Caldemare," Lucien Edmond Bouchard at once responded with a calm irony to his tone. "Of course, I'd hoped that as soon as you moved in here, you'd have done me the courtesy of paying a visit as my next-door neighbor."

"Not really next door, Mr. Bouchard," Robert Caldemare superciliously replied with a shrug. "There's plenty of land between us, and I really have no interest in your own operation, since I'm busily involved in mine."

"So I'm told. But it seems, Mr. Caldemare, that in the process of making sure that our two land claims don't encroach upon each other's, you've taken it on yourself to put up fences. Unfortunately, some of the posts that your men have driven into what you regard as your land were actually driven into mine. Several of my men have reported over the last few weeks that my own wooden boundary markers have been moved away and that the holes where they were are still visible—inside your newly-fenced boundary."

"Are you trying to imply that I want to steal your land, Bouchard?" Robert Caldemare sneered. He sent Jaime Ruiz a quick smile and shrugged, then turned back to Lucien Edmond. "When I purchased this land in Austin, I had the clerk draw up a map showing the exact boundaries of my property. My feeling is, sir, that since you came here so many years before me, and since perhaps you figured that you wouldn't have a neighbor for quite a while, your men were simply a little more generous than they ought to have been when they put up the markers."

"That's not true at all. I also acquired my land in Austin, and I also procured a very accurate map. Nor was I afraid of having a neighbor. As a matter of fact, there have been two before you, Mr. Caldemare. In neither instance was there a question of boundaries. Nor, indeed, of fencing. There's grazing land enough, and no one objects if another man's cattle sometimes graze over on a few acres of one's own property. That's all sorted out on accounts when it comes time for branding and rounding up for the cattle drive, as you should know."

"Are you trying to teach me how to be a rancher, Bouchard?" Again Robert Caldemare adopted a supercilious look and drew himself up until (as Joe Duvray thought to himself) he looked like a pouter pigeon. "There's no law against putting up fencing, sir, and I simply mean to protect my property."

"It's true there's no law against it, Mr. Caldemare. But what I am most incensed at—and the main reason that I came to call on you this evening—is that one of my young

280

vaqueros was brutally shot down in cold blood by your foreman there." Lucien Edmond pointed with his left hand to Jaime Ruiz.

"Ruiz has told me about the unfortunate incident. I regret it, Mr. Bouchard. But it appears that your vaquero was insulting to my foreman and called him a liar, then made a gesture toward his gun."

"That's a lie if I ever heard one!" Joe Duvray angrily spoke up, glaring at the two men.

"No, Joe, let him say his piece," Lucien Edmond admonished. "As you can see, Mr. Caldemare, the events which you have just described to me don't exactly jibe with those my men observed. Two of my riders, Santiago Miraflores who is behind me and Eddie Gentry who rides that brown gelding, accompanied Ignacio Valdez and saw your foreman kill him. They made it very clear to me that he did not make any gesture toward his gun."

"I'm sorry, Bouchard, I can assure you that I didn't want to see any of your men hurt. But now that you're here, with armed men to back you up, perhaps this is as good a time as any to serve notice on you that I don't expect my fences and my boundaries to be tampered with."

"I think it would be a very good idea, Mr. Caldemare, if you and I sat down and went over our maps in detail. Perhaps then you might discover a perfectly understandable error—because I'm willing to admit that you may not have had any illegal motive in putting up your fences."

"How decent of you, Bouchard! But I'm afraid I can't accommodate you. My men and I are preparing for a cattle drive. There'll be no more such unfortunate incidents, I can assure you, if your men will use a little discretion when they encounter mine."

Lucien Edmond's face was taut with rising anger at the insolent way Caldemare had answered his complaints. "I, too, am preparing for a cattle drive, Mr. Caldemare," he finally answered. "And I'll be frank with you. I've delayed it all this time because I couldn't quite understand what you had in mind. But since you intend to take such a high-handed position and to reject my offer of friendship on this range, I'll serve notice on you also: if any of your men shoot at mine again, sir, you're certain to invite reprisal."

"I mark your warning, Bouchard. And I repeat, sir, that if your men hamper mine in the performance of the orders

I've given them, I can no longer be responsible. I'll say good night to you now." With this, Caldemare turned back toward the house, and Jaime Ruiz followed him.

His lips compressed and white with anger, Lucien Edmond jerked at the reins of his horse to wheel it round and gave the signal to his men to follow him. At that moment, Jaime Ruiz wheeled round, crouched low, drew his pistol from his holster, and snapped off a shot. Joe Duvray uttered a cry, reeled in his saddle, clapped a hand to his left shoulder, and then, drawing his Spencer carbine out of its sheath, steadied the butt against his right shoulder and pulled the trigger. The swarthy Mexican foreman, who was just about to fire another shot, rose to his feet, staggered a few steps backward, and then crumpled to the ground.

"Watch those vaqueros of his, men!" Lucien Edmond cried as he unsheathed his Spencer and trained it on the half-dozen vaqueros who, startled by the unexpected gunplay, had not yet reacted. "Don't any of you draw your guns, or we'll fire!"

Jorge Feliz and Luis Garcia had turned their geldings toward the left side of the gate and had trotted alongside the fence, their Spencers trained on the Mexicans. Luis called "¡Abajo las pistolas, muchachos, pronto!" The other vaqueros who had followed Lucien Edmond echoed his order as they trained their own Spencers on Caldemare's men, who hastened to unbuckle their gunbelts and drop them as they raised their hands and called out for the Bouchard men not to fire.

Joe Duvray was bleeding badly from his shoulder wound. Sheathing his Spencer, he unsteadily dismounted, then leaned his forehead against his saddle as a wave of nauseating pain swept over him. He put his right hand to the wound, while Lucien Edmond, momentarily irresolute as to what further action to take, called out to him, "Joe, do you think you can make it back to the ranch? If the men can hold off Caldemare's outfit, I'll try to bandage that wound of yours."

"It—it's just a flesh wound, Mr. Bouchard. But I'm bleeding like a stuck pig," Joe answered in a hollow voice, fighting the black waves of pain that threatened to engulf him.

"Simata, Santiago, Luis, and Jorge, keep your guns trained on those men and on the house just in case there's more shooting," Lucien Edmond anxiously called as he began to dismount. "I'll try to bandage your wound, Joe, enough to stop the bleeding so we can ride back."

From inside the house, Margaret's voice was heard, tearful and protesting, "No, Father, what are you going to do? Oh, no, not a gun—but it's not their fault! I won't let you, Father!"

There was a cry as Robert Caldemare's voice rose in unreasoning rage, hoarse and vibrant: "Stay out of my way, girl! They've spoiled everything—they're going to pay for it!" At that moment, he came out of the doorway, a six-shooter in each hand. Dropping to one knee, he leveled the gun in his right hand, aimed at Lucien Edmond, and pulled the trigger. Lucien Edmond, in the act of dismounting, uttered a strangled cry of pain as the bullet took him in the fleshy part of his right arm. Dropping down from his gelding, still clutching his Spencer in his right hand, he peered from under the horse's body just as Caldemare, turning swiftly, fired with the other six-shooter. Jorge Feliz swayed back in his saddle, his Spencer dropping to the ground, then slid slowly off his gelding and rolled over, lifeless.

Margaret had come out of the house, her hand at her mouth, tears running down her cheeks, just in time to see Jorge fall dead. "Oh, God! Father, have you gone mad? Stop it! Oh, please, please, why are you trying to kill them?"

Lucien Edmond had flattened himself on the ground. Gritting his teeth against the pain of his wound, he cradled the butt of his Spencer against his left shoulder and squinted down the sight. Robert Caldemare, with surprising agility, turned toward Margaret, then ran back to her. He thrust one of his pistols into the pocket of his breeches and encircled her waist with his left arm, while at the same time lifting the other six-shooter and snapping off a shot at the prostrate Lucien Edmond. The bullet plowed into the ground a foot to Lucien Edmond's left.

"Don't fire, you men, you'll hit the girl!" Lucien Edmond cried out. "Caldemare, throw down your guns, don't involve your daughter! I don't want to hurt you!"

"Go to hell, you goddamned aristocratic Southerner! It's you that wants to steal my land and shoot my men, with all your fine talk of settling things fairly!" Caldemare's face was livid with fury. He raised the six-shooter in his right hand and, wheeling to the left, fired at Simata, nearly grazing the half-breed's shoulder. At the sound of gunfire, several of the geldings whinnied frantically, reared, and pawed the air with their hooves, their riders dragging on the reins to control their restive mounts.

"Caldemare, if you go on shooting at my men, I'll have to kill you," Lucien Edmond cried, keeping his Spencer trained on Margaret's demented father.

"Not before I kill you, Bouchard!" Caldemare bellowed as he pulled his daughter forward with him and at the same time fired his six-shooter at Lucien Edmond's men. This time the bullet whistled harmlessly by Santiago Miraflores.

"No, Father, oh, my God, you've gone mad! Please, if you love me, give this up! They've done nothing, you're in the wrong, Father!" Margaret hysterically cried as she tried to disengage herself. Then, as Caldemare raised his six-shooter again, she reached across him and seized his wrist with her right hand, turning the pistol upward just as he pulled the trigger again.

"You stupid bitch, let me alone! I'll settle this my way!" he screamed at her, giving her a brutal shove with the palm of his left hand which sent her sprawling onto her side at the threshold of the door. Then, dipping his left hand into his breeches pocket, he drew out the other six-shooter and, turning toward the group of vaqueros, fired with both guns. Luis Garcia, trying to control his restive gelding, uttered a strangled oath as a bullet pierced his right thigh, and Manuel Rodriguez winced as the other bullet grazed his right elbow.

"May God forgive me," Lucien Edmond groaned as, steadying himself, disregarding the throbbing pain of his wound, he pulled the trigger of the Spencer. Caldemare stumbled back, his eyes wide with surprise, then stared down at the bright red stain on his white silk shirt. He took a step forward, both six-shooters dropping, then bowed his head and fell lifeless.

Slowly, Lucien Edmond rose to his feet, clapping his left hand to the wound in his right upper arm. Joe Duvray had sunk down on his knees and rolled over onto his side, unconscious from his loss of blood. Slowly, Margaret Caldemare got to her knees, staring incredulously at the sprawled body of her dead father, and then she covered her face with her hands and began to weep with great wracking sobs.

"I had to, Miss Caldemare. Forgive me," Lucien Edmond hoarsely spoke as he approached the weeping young woman. He glanced down at her father's body, then kicked the six-shooters away with the toe of his boot. "Are you hurt?"

"N-no. I—I never dreamed he'd be like this—all these years, he always wrote how hard he worked and the sacrifices he was making—all for me, he said, over and over again—oh, my God, I've no one now—"

"Eddie," Lucien Edmond turned to the friendly young cowhand, "help her back into the house. I've got to bandage Joe's wound before he loses any more blood. You, Simata, go into the house and see what you can find in the way of bandages and please be quick!"

"Yes, at once, Mr. Bouchard!" The half-breed dismounted and hurried toward the house. Eddie Gentry, murmuring soothing words, had helped Margaret to her feet. Her face was pale, and she was trembling violently. She leaned her head against his shoulder as he helped her back into the house.

Simata came out a few moments later with a silk tablecloth which he had pulled from the dining room table, and, drawing out his clasp knife, he began to cut it into strips. Lucien Edmond hurried over to the unconscious Joe Duvray. He nodded to Simata, who knelt beside the young Georgian and swiftly began to apply the improvised bandage, binding it as tightly as he could to halt the bleeding. When he had finished, Simata did the same for Lucien Edmond himself, whose wound, though less serious, still required a temporary bandage until Lucien Edmond could return to his own ranch house.

Santiago Miraflores then came forward to offer a leather flask of *aguardiente,* while Simata and Lucien Edmond lifted Joe into a sitting position. "This is better than water, *señor patrón,*" the genial Mexican explained. "Last time I was in Nuevo Laredo, I bought two bottles of this fine *aguardiente*. Once in a great while, you understand, I permit myself a drop or two—"

"No need to apologize, Santiago," Lucien Edmond grinned. "It's a lucky thing you thought to bring some along today. It's fiery stuff, and it'll help revive him. Not too much, he's still unconscious and I don't want to choke him."

"Just a few drops on the lips, *señor patrón*," Santiago agreed as, removing the stopper of the flask, he very carefully tilted it toward Joe Duvray's mouth, so that a few drops moistened the Georgian's lips.

Joe shivered, then slowly his eyes opened, dazed and dilated with pain. "What—what happened?" he wanly murmured.

"Ah, *bueno,* you have come back to life. May all the saints be praised!" Santiago exclaimed. "Drink a little of this, it will put new life into you, *hombre*! You've lost much blood. But it is all over now." The stocky Mexican carefully held the flask to Joe's lips. "Do not swallow it down too quickly, *amigo,* it has the fire of an angry woman in it. But just a little now, *por favor.*"

"Sure, Santiago." Joe Duvray swallowed a little of the brandy and then coughed, shook his head, his eyes clearing. "Whew! I'll say it's hot, just like *pimentón,* Santiago."

"Well, thank God you're feeling better, Joe. We've got to get you back to the ranch so we can take care of that shoulder. Simata put those bandages on so tightly they'll stop the circulation. I wish we had a doctor in these parts, but don't worry, Joe, we'll all look after you," Lucien Edmond anxiously assured the black-haired Georgian.

"Mr. Duvray, oh, God, I saw him fall down after the shooting—is he all right?" It was Margaret Caldemare's voice, broken with sobs, as she came out of the house with Eddie Gentry behind her. Seeing Joe sitting up, with Lucien Edmond's arm around his shoulders and Simata and Santiago leaning beside him, she uttered a cry and ran toward him. "Are you hurt badly, Mr. Duvray? I'll never forgive myself—I was so rude to you, after you saved my life—oh, please, won't someone tell me, is he going to live?"

"Oh, yes, Miss Caldemare," Lucien Edmond smiled. "It's just a flesh wound. He's lost a good deal of blood, but we'll take him back right now."

"Riding all that way might make the wound bleed again —please, why don't you leave him here in the house? I—I'll look after him. At Miss Emmons's school, we learned a little something about first aid. Besides, I owe him that much—oh, my God, it's been like a nightmare—" She stood looking down at the wan young Georgian, then burst into tears again as she sank down on her knees and put out a trembling hand to touch his cheek. "Please forgive me, Mr. Duvray?"

"There's nothing to forgive, Miss Caldemare. I wouldn't have thought much of you if you hadn't stood up for your father. But my gosh, you need to rest—Santiago, why don't you give her some of that *aguardiente*? You take some, Miss Margaret, it'll steady your nerves." Joe Duvray self-consciously fell silent, and his face, though drawn with pain, suddenly flushed with embarrassment.

"No, no, I'm fine—you're sure you're all right, Mr. Duvray?"

"I'm fine, Miss Margaret. And I have to say I won't mind a bit staying here and being looked after. Right now, I don't much fancy a long ride back." He managed a feeble chuckle, and Lucien Edmond grinned and patted this back.

"Let's help him into the house, Simata, Santiago," Luke's oldest son prompted. The three men gently lifted Joe Duvray to his feet and then, seeing that his steps were weak and stumbling, eyed one another, lifted him in their arms and carried him toward the house. "Hey, put me down, I'm no baby!" he vainly protested.

Margaret Caldemare started to follow them, then she stood for a moment looking down at the body of her dead father. Slowly, she shook her head and then knelt down and hesitantly touched the back of his head. "Why did you do this, Father? You were always talking about being rich and finding a new life for me. All I ever wanted was to be with you, and it wouldn't have mattered whether we had money or not. Now I don't have anyone. Instead of talking things over and settling them, you tried to kill . . . I don't understand . . . I'll never understand."

After a long moment, she rose, stood staring at him for an instant, and then, covering her face with her hands, went back into the house.

In a sorrowing silence, Eddie Gentry and Santiago Miraflores lifted the dead body of Jorge Feliz and tied it to the back of his gelding, and then Lucien Edmond Bouchard and his men rode back to Windhaven Range.

CHAPTER THIRTY

Exactly one week after the scurrilous handbill had been nailed to the door of the red-brick chateau, a statement of retraction was published in the Montgomery *Advertiser*. It was not precisely what Luke Bouchard had expected, since it was signed by his political opponent, Cletus Adams, instead of the true instigator, Barnabas McMillan. However, since it contained phrases that Luke knew had been concocted by the Eastern carpetbagger rather than by the none too well-educated freed black, it was sufficiently acceptable.

Cletus Adams began by disclaiming responsibility

for an unfortunate and erroneously fabricated slander directed against the wife of my Republican opponent. I assure the voters of Montgomery County that it did not come from me and that I deeply regret it. I mean to defeat Mr. Luke Bouchard on the political issues at stake in this election. I repeat, he is, in spite of all his protests to the contrary, a scalawag of the worst stripe who expects to hang onto President Grant's coattails to victory in November. From my knowledge of his wife, I say here and now that she is assuredly beyond reproach—but she is not the candidate, and between now and election day I will prove worthier of your votes than Mr. Luke Bouchard.

Far more satisfying to Luke, however, was the hilarious comment of old Jedidiah Danforth, who himself paid a visit to the chateau the day after Cletus Adams's statement was published and found Luke recuperating from the fracture incurred in the fight with McMillan. Dr. Medbury had set the bone and had urged his restless patient to remain at home for at least several weeks.

In Luke's study, Jedidiah accepted a glass of brandy, lifted it in salute to his host, and chuckled, "It would have done your heart good, Mr. Bouchard, to have laid eyes on that fat carpetbagger who's backing Cletus Adams. I was walking out to have lunch at Moseby's as I usually do, and there he came down the street heading into that pool hall. He was hobbling, sir, and his face was puffy and blotchy from all his contusions. He looked as sour as a man who's bitten into a melon and found a lemon inside of it. Why, sir, he didn't even bother to acknowledge the greetings of several of his carpetbagger friends who came up to him, just brushed them aside and pushed his way into the pool hall as if he couldn't stand the sight of them. I'd have given a year's fees to have seen you thrash him like that, Mr. Bouchard."

"I'm afraid I very nearly killed him—at least, my anger so got the better hand at one time that I really thought I might do exactly that," Luke confessed. "But thank God, Laure is swiftly recovering. I've been seriously debating whether I should have you lodge criminal charges against Stacey Holbrook. She seems to have vanished, at least for the time being."

"I can fill you in on that, too, Mr. Bouchard," the lawyer replied. "I have it on good authority that she's Barnabas McMillan's doxy. More than likely, she's holed up in that fine new house he had built for himself before he visited our conniving assessor to buy the old Williamson land. I shouldn't be surprised but what some greenbacks changed hands, because old Hugo Montrose, the assessor we had before the war, would never have permitted anyone to build a house on land he hadn't first paid for and taken title to."

"At least, so far as the new assessor is concerned, I'm glad you were able to hoodwink him about the old Cavendish land," Luke Bouchard smilingly declared. "Andy Haskins is working out in the fields with those five men he hired, and I almost never see him. Remember, next year some time, I'd like to see you change the title over to Andy. I feel certain he's going to marry Jessica Bambach before very much longer, so it'll be a completely logical transfer."

"You just leave that to me, Mr. Bouchard," Jedidiah shot back with a broad wink. Then, scowling thoughtfully, he pursed his lips and added, "Yes, I guess you'd have cause for legal action against McMillan's bedmate, but it might have some repercussions that would only give you and your wife more trouble ."

"What do you mean by that?"

"Well, Mr. Bouchard, since you've entered politics on the Republican side, I'm sure by now you've studied the history of this country enough to know that the Ku Klux Klan is the weapon these carpetbagging Democrats enjoy using against anybody who gets in their way. I'll draw up charges and turn them over to the county sheriff against that vicious young woman, and I think I can get her a prison term of at least a year for what she did to your wife. But sure as you're born, Mr. Bouchard, Barnabas McMillan will see to it that the Klan harasses you and your workers. You'll wake up one morning and find all your crops plowed under, maybe your cotton gin shed set afire, and they might even try to make off with one of your black workers—the way they did that time with Marius Thornton when you wouldn't join their klavern."

"I hadn't thought of that. I'm afraid you're probably right. Well, then, I'll leave Stacey Holbrook to her eventual punishment by a just Providence. Besides," Luke added with an ironic little laugh, "I should say that being McMillan's mistress would be punishment enough in itself."

"Now there you've hit the nail on the head, Mr. Bouchard," the peppery lawyer exclaimed. "Every now and again, as you may imagine, I hear a choice piece of gossip from one of my old cronies or sometimes even from some of the town's less illustrious citizens whom I got out of straits in the past. It appears that Miss Holbrook expects McMillan to make an honest woman of her if he manages to manipulate Cletus Adams into the state legislature this November."

"Well, they'd make a fitting pair each for the other," Luke concluded. "But now for a more pleasant topic—the young Comanche brave I told you about some weeks ago ought to be arriving very soon. I'll put him up here, and after Laure and I have come to know him well enough, I plan to bring him into town to meet you."

"Fine, Mr. Bouchard! As I told you before, I could certainly use a good, hardworking clerk. And don't you worry, I'll teach him plenty of Blackstone while he's running errands for me and dusting the books in my library. I think I can safely say that within a year I can steer him into passing the examination that Judge Tollefson gives all young aspirants to the bar. You're really serious about adopting him as a son, Mr. Bouchard?"

"It's about the only way he could be admitted into practice here in Alabama, Mr. Danforth. And it'll take Laure's mind off the tragic ordeal of losing our child." Luke Bouchard grinned like a boy. "I can almost hear her now, with that saucy look on her lovely face, asking me if I'm trying to speed her age up to mine by presenting her with a full-grown son!"

It was not until the middle of May that Lopasuta disembarked from the *Alabama Belle* onto the dock at Windhaven Plantation, staring openmouthed at the imposing chateau with its twin towers. Old Captain Tenby had found the young Comanche an exceptionally interesting passenger and had virtually taken him under his wing from the first moment when Lopasuta had boarded at Mobile. He had been intrigued at once when he had seen this strong, coppery-skinned young man wearing a buckskin jacket with gaudy green trousers (which a New Orleans storekeeper had persuaded Lopasuta to buy) and shiny black shoes which obviously pinched the young brave's feet. And when the captain had learned that Lopasuta was going to Lowndesboro to see Luke Bouchard, his excitement had known no bounds. He regaled the young brave with his reminiscences not only of Luke but also of old Lucien, founder of the Bouchard dynasty. And he concluded by saying, as he clapped Lopasuta on the back and himself handed the young Comanche his luggage case, which also had been purchased in the Queen City, "Now you just give Mr. Luke and his lovely missus the very best from Captain Tenby, you mind now, Lopasuta! I tell you this, you'll never find a finer, more honest and Godfearing man than him, you just mark my words."

It was Marius Thornton, busy in the cotton gin shed testing the newly repaired gin, who first spied the stranger. Lopasuta had set down the luggage case and stood staring at the replica of the chateau in which old Lucien Bouchard had been born long before the French Revolution. Amicably, Marius approached the Comanche and said, "You'll be looking for Mr. Luke Bouchard, won't you? He's expecting you. He's in Montgomery right now, but you come right on in and make yourself at home. We've got a room ready for you, and I'll have Hannah fix you a meal—you must be starved after that trip from Mobile."

"You are very kind. My name is Lopasuta."

"And mine's Marius Thornton. Glad to know you!" The young foreman at once extended his hand, and Lopasuta smiled shyly, then shook it warmly. "It is good to have a friend in a new place. Thank you," he said softly.

During Laure's convalescence from the miscarriage caused by Stacey Holbrook's brutal assault, Luke had himself gone to Montgomery to find a replacement nurse who could be trusted and would be devoted to his small sons. Through the help of his lawyer, Jedidiah Danforth, Luke had interviewed a pleasant brown-haired woman in her early thirties, German by birth, who had married a Montgomery veterinarian and had been left a widow during the last year of the Civil War when her husband had died fighting at Shiloh. Her little son had been sickly and died six months after his birth, and she had been supporting herself by sewing and making preserves and jellies which she sold for a modest sum to the greengrocer's shop on Montgomery's main street. He had at once engaged her and brought her back with him to the red-brick chateau. Laure had immediately approved of his choice. Her name was Clara Mathies, and it was obvious from the first that she loved Lucien and Paul as if they had been her own flesh and blood.

Just as Marius led Lopasuta toward the door of the chateau, Laure Bouchard came out for a stroll, having just left the nursery where Paul and Lucien were enjoying their new nurse. Seeing the handsome brave in the striking contrast of buckskin jacket and fashionable, dandy-like trousers, she gasped and regarded him with astonishment until, recollecting what Luke had told her, she exclaimed "Why, you must be Lopasuta, from Sangrodo's stronghold!"

"I am, and you must be the wife of the great *Taiboo Nimiahkana*. Sangrodo has told me much about you both, and it is kind of you to bring me here."

"My husband is in Montgomery, Lopasuta, but he'll be back this evening in time for supper. Please come in, and Marius, you know what room he's to have, don't you?"

"Yes, Mrs. Bouchard," Marius smilingly responded. "And I'll tell Hannah to fix him a little something after that long steamboat ride."

"That's fine! Do please come in! My, you've come a very long way." Laure opened the door to let him enter.

"But each day taught me something new, for I saw how the white-eyes lived and how they walked the streets and talked. And the shops with the beautiful things that most of my people have never seen—and the steamboat and then the ferry from New Orleans to Mobile—these things I must write about to our great chief." Lopasuta's face glowed with enthusiasm.

"My husband and I will want to hear all about your trip this evening, Lopasuta," Laure encouraged the young Comanche. "But tell me, where in the world did you get those trousers?"

For a moment, Lopasuta looked blank, and then, glancing down at himself, gave her a shy, self-conscious grin. "The son of the *Taiboo Nimiahkana* who is in Texas gave me a letter to the man at the bank in New Orleans . . ."

"Yes, that would be Jason Barntry," Laure interrupted.

"Yes, that is his name. I came in buckskin, as my people wear each day, and with moccasins. Mr. Barntry took me to a shop and said that the man there would give me what I should wear here." He glanced down at his shiny new shoes and made a distasteful grimace. "But I am more comfortable in the moccasins of my people. These shoes hurt when I walk."

Laure forced herself not to giggle, so as not to wound his dignity. "That's because they're new. You wait, and a few days after you've walked about here, they'll begin to feel more comfortable."

"I hope that is true," Lopasuta gravely replied. "Otherwise, I shall go back to my moccasins, and I have brought them with me. But I wish to wear the buckskin jacket because, as you can see, one of the squaws in our stronghold has told a story about me in colored beads which she has sewn to the buckskin. It reminds me that I am of the people and that I owe them much and that I must work hard to help them."

"And you will, I know, Lopasuta," Laure said gently. "Now Marius will take you to your room and make you comfortable. Then he'll bring you to the kitchen, and Hannah, our wonderful cook, will give you something good to eat. Then you can rest until suppertime, and you will meet the—how do you say it, Lopasuta?"

"*Taiboo Nimiahkana,*" Lopasuta repeated. "In our language, it means 'the white-eyes who is summoned.' This, Sangrodo told me, was because your man came to help us when we were in need. And this is why also I promise that I will not forget the debt I owe him in bringing me here so that I may learn what the white-eyes know and be of help in my own way to the Comanche."

"You are more than welcome, then, Lopasuta," Laure Bouchard assured him.

That evening, when Luke Bouchard met the young brave and listened to him tell of his journey, he was glad that he had yielded to his impulse not only to help this remarkably intelligent young Indian to a more hopeful niche in life, but also to pay back, even in this small measure, the debt which he himself knew that he owed Sangrodo.

CHAPTER THIRTY-ONE

Porfirio Costado reined in his brown stallion and turned to Jackson Brundiger with a questioning look on his swarthy, bearded face. "I do not understand, Señor Brundiger. Were we not supposed to take the cattle of *mis amigos* to Abilene and join them with the *ganado* from the Bouchard hacienda?"

The Kansas desperado's thin lips scarcely moved in a mocking smile as he replied, "There's no hurry about those scrubby cows, Porfirio. We brought them in so that Bouchard's vaqueros would get the notion we're in the cattle business, too, getting ready for a roundup and a drive. What we're really after is all the prime cattle Bouchard's going to be sending to Abilene."

"*Comprendo*. But then, Señor Brundiger, if you are the real *capataz*, why did you let Jaime Ruiz let the Bouchard men think that he was?"

"Because it'll keep them guessing, Porfirio. Now you and I both know that Bouchard can't afford to hold his cattle back very much longer, not if he wants to get to market when they're prime. If he waits any longer, he'll find that the big buyers have already got their herds and gone on home. No, I'm sure he's going to have to start this week or next, at the very latest. And I'm pretty sure that just about now, Bouchard himself and some of his boys will be riding over to call on Señor Caldemare and raise a ruckus because one of their vaqueros was shot down for shooting off his mouth."

"I understand, Señor Brundiger," Porfirio Costado scratched his forehead and scowled, not fully understanding. "But what if there's gunplay and the *patrón* and the other vaqueros back with him should be killed by Señor Bouchard and his vaqueros?"

Brundiger's cruel smile deepened. "Then, *amigo*, we won't have to split with Caldemare or the rest of the men, will we?"

"*¡Si, es verdad!*" the horse thief chuckled, nodding his head. Then, as a new thought came to him, he scowled again. "Señor Brundiger, it will be many weeks before the *ganado* of Señor Bouchard reach the Red River. What are we to do all that time while we wait for them?"

"Yes, it's over four hundred miles, Porfirio, you're right about that. And I don't think Bouchard's cows will do better than eight or nine miles a day, not with warmer weather coming on. He won't want them to lose too much weight by the time they reach Abilene. So that's about two months. But the time will go quickly, Porfirio. Are we not all brave men with guns and much ammunition?"

"*Seguro*," the Mexican grinned.

"We'll run into a few lonely settlers along the way, and they'll give us hospitality. I'm sure we can persuade them. And there may be some *mujeres lindas* who would welcome men like us, don't you think, Porfirio?"

Porfirio Costado sniggered lewdly at this highly gratifying prospect. "My *compadres* will enjoy *gringa* women, Señor Brundiger. Since we left Durango and Nuevo Laredo to come to work for you and Señor Caldemare, we have not had even so much as a single *puta* to enjoy at night after we have finished our work. And that is not good for a man with real *cojones*, Señor Brundiger."

"Don't worry, Porfirio, you and your *compadres* will have all the women you can take along the way to the Red River. We'll avoid the towns, and we'll get our food from the settlers just outside them. We don't have to worry about the law, not in these parts." His right hand flashed down to his holster as in a single lightning-like maneuver, he drew out his pistol and fired at a jackrabbit running twenty feet away from his horse. The jackrabbit seemed to spring into the air, then rolled over and lay dead.

"*¡Magnífico!*" Porfirio Costado exclaimed. "Señor Brundiger, I begin to think that we shall have much amusement between now and the time we attack Señor Bouchard and his vaqueros at the Red River."

"Of course you will, Porfirio. Now I figure that Bouchard will drive about three or four thousand head to Abilene. The worst part of the drive will be crossing the

Red River. We'll hit him just when he's in the middle of it. If it's night time, so much the better."

"On the other hand, Señor Brundiger," Porfirio Costado doubtfully countered, "he will surely have some twenty-five to thirty vaqueros riding with the herd. And we are only thirteen—I pray to *todos los santos* that we will not be cut down like dogs."

"You worry too much, Porfirio. Leave all that to me. I'm the *jefe* of this oufit, and don't forget it. Even if we hit them in broad daylight, driving all those cattle across, there'll be such confusion and such a stampede that they won't know what hit them. They won't be ready for us, and we'll cut them down before most of them can even go for their guns. I know this country, Porfirio. You've got plenty of scrub trees and bushes and high buffalo grass just past the Red River. We'll come out of there shooting."

"But if all the *ganado* stampede, it will be hard work to round them up again," the horse thief declared.

"You talk like an old woman, Porfirio," Brundiger snapped, his cold gray eyes narrowing. "You men have worked with cattle before and horses, too. That's why I had Caldemare hire you, after I'd hand-picked you myself. There's at least thirty thousand dollars waiting for us at Abilene when we ride in with the Bouchard cows. Plus what gold we can take from the settlers we persuade to put us up for the night. *¿Comprende?* Yes, Porfirio, you'll have to do a little work, you and your *compadres*, to get that gold. But it's better than working for a peon's wages, don't forget that. Now let's ride. I want to put as much distance between myself and Bouchard as I can by sundown so he won't even think of looking for us."

"I take off my sombrero to you, Señor Brundiger," the horse thief grinned as he swept it off with a flourish and inclined his head to the Kansas desperado. "My *compadres* and I will follow your orders. It will be good to have much *dinero* in our pockets once again."

"You're forgetting one thing, Porfirio," the wiry Kansan chuckled mirthlessly. "We're bound to find some guns and pistols in the settlers' homes, that's for certain. Lots of these Johnny Rebs who came out here after they lost the war had some mighty good shooting irons. Like Whitworths —old as they are, you can still pick off a man at a thousand yards if you have good aim."

Porfirio Costado respectfully whistled. "I would give very much to have such a rifle, Señor Brundiger."

"Well, we're bound to find a few. I remember one with that old Davidson scope. It was a lot shorter than the sights they put on Union target rifles, and they mounted in on the side. That means you could use it at close quarters. And don't forget, Porfirio, there'll be all those repeaters, those fine new Spencers the Bouchard men ride with, once we wipe them out. With guns like those, we can do a lot more than poor old Jethro Reedy ever did with his bushwhackers."

The bearded horse thief regarded the Kansas desperado almost with awe, quickly foreseeing the profits to be made by loyalty to so ambitious a leader. "Then after this is over, Señor Brundiger, after we take the Bouchard *ganado* and sell them at Abilene, you would have us go on with you?"

"If you and the other fellows behave yourselves, Porfirio. I've got some plans. It just came to me—not everybody in Texas knows that old Jethro cashed in his chips a year ago, thanks to that meddling Lucien Edmond Bouchard. There's a name for you—faugh!" Brundiger hawked and spat on the ground to show his derisive contempt. "Well, Porfirio, what's to stop us when we pay our little visits to these nice lonesome settlers of an evening, to say that we're the Reedy gang? And we'll wear masks, too, so that they can't identify us—not that we plan to leave too many of them alive, if you take my meaning."

Porfirio Costado showed his snaggly yellow teeth in a cruel grin. "I take your meaning very well, *mi jefe.*"

"Tell your *compadres* how matters stand. Remember, just as you said right now, I'm the boss of this outfit and what I say goes. Now let's put a few more miles between us and the Bouchards!"

Lucien Edmond's wound gave him little pain, and the flow of blood had been staunched by the fairly tight bandage Simata had applied. The bandage would hold at least until he could reach home. But before returning to his own ranch house, Lucien Edmond delegated Simata, Eddie Gentry, Manuel Rodriguez, and Luis Garcia to remain on guard around the Caldemare house, into which the wounded Joe Duvray had been taken. All of them were well armed, but Lucien Edmond was concerned with the possible reprisal of the Mexicans who had come out of the Caldemare bunkhouse and watched the foreman and their *patrón* die in the shootout.

Consequently, he approached the Mexicans, who had dropped their gunbelts and stood with their hands upraised to show that they had no immediate intention of resuming the fight, and questioned them in Spanish. "What will you do now that your *capataz* and your *patrón* are dead?" was his first query.

A short, thickly bearded man in his early forties stepped forward and, with a philosophical shrug, responded, "What is there for us to do, señor? We shall go over the border and try to find work with another *patrón*."

"And these cattle in that enclosure," Lucien Edmond turned to gesture toward the distant cattle pen, "who is to take care of these? Do you not wish to stay and drive them to market?"

"*Pero*, señor, who will pay our wages if we stay? The *hija* of the *patrón* will not do this, it is certain."

Lucien Edmond paused for a moment, deep in thought. Then he declared, "Very well then. I myself will take the cattle and include them in my herd and drive them on to Abilene. The money that I get for them will be paid to the daughter of your dead *patrón*. That is, unless you have an objection?"

The squat Mexican chuckled and shook his head. "Do whatever you wish with them. My *compadres* and I are already weary of this place. We were hired as *pistoleros*, not as vaqueros, but we can see already that your men have better guns. They shoot many more times and they are much more accurate, señor. So, since we do not wish to die without reason or profit, we shall say *adiós*."

"Then, if you wish, *amigo*," Lucien Edmond responded "you might as well take your things and leave now. These four men will remain to make sure that you do not cause trouble."

"There will be no *dinero* for us in trying to pick a fight with your vaqueros, señor," the Mexican shrugged again. "If you will give us a little time, we shall take our horses and ride back to our homes across the Rio Grande."

"You may take what time you need, *hombre*," was Lucien Edmond Bouchard's answer. "But there are only six of you."

"There is Miguel Amangar in the ranch house," the spokesman of these Mexicans interposed. "He was, how would you say, señor, the majordomo for the *patrón* and his *hija*."

"I see." Then, as another thought suddenly struck Lucien Edmond, he pursued, "But my own vaqueros have told me that there are many other men working here. Where are the rest of them?"

"As to that, señor, I do not know. They rode away before you and your men came here to talk to the *patrón*."

Lucien Edmond turned to Simata, vaguely troubled by that answer. In a low voice, he said to the scout, "The question is, will those men return here? Obviously, they can't know what's happened to Caldemare and Ruiz. And one of those men is the gunman whom Joe Duvray told me about, the man who wouldn't give Joe his name."

"The tracks of their horses would still be clear," the young scout answered. "After these men have left, I myself will see if I can find them, and then I will ride back to the ranch house and tell you what I have learned."

"Very good, Simata. It would be wise for one of you to go into the bunkhouse to make sure that there are no other men hiding there. Be very careful."

"I will do that myself," Simata promptly volunteered. Gripping his Spencer carbine at waist-level, he crouched and ran swiftly forward toward the bunkhouse, cautiously opened the door and moved quickly to the left, turning his head to peer in. Then he called back, "It is empty!"

"Thank you, Simata. I'll ride back home then. As soon as you can, tell me if you've found the tracks of those other riders." Lucien Edmond Bouchard mounted his gelding, gestured to the other men who had accompanied him, and rode back to Windhaven Range.

Inside the Caldemare house, Margaret Caldemare, weeping softly, had regained her self-control enough to order the surly-faced servant Miguel to bring a basin of hot water and clean towels to be used as bandages. But Miguel shook his head and stolidly retorted, "I do not take your orders, señorita. Now that the *patrón* is dead, I will go back to my people. There is nothing here for me now."

He turned his back on the astonished young woman and strode out of the house.

Joe Duvray was unconscious, lying on the couch, his head propped up with two pillows. Margaret stood irresolute a moment, then, wringing her hands, hurried outside. Seeing Simata nearest her, she tearfully called, "Oh, please, Miguel won't stay, there's no one to help with Mr. Duvray. All I can do is wash and bandage his wound, but I know nothing about nursing or taking the bullet out."

"I can do that, miss," the half-breed replied. He turned to watch Miguel select a mustang from the corral near the bunkhouse, saddle it, then mount it and ride off without a backward look. Then he said to the distraught young woman, "In New Orleans, I took a bullet out of the arm of a friend of mine when he was shot by a Creole."

"He's unconscious—oh, please, do whatever you can— I'm so worried—it was all my fault—oh, God, if I only hadn't come here!" Margaret broke down, covering her face with her hands, and began to sob uncontrollably.

"It is good to weep," Simata said gently as he came to her: "But I will need you to help me. I do not think it will be too difficult. And it is good that he is unconscious, because then he will feel no pain when I dig for the bullet. I saw the wound, and I think it will not be hard to remove the bullet. Come, you will help me, you are very brave."

Margaret straightened, sniffled, and then uttered a deep sigh. "I will try to be. He mustn't die. He saved my life. The least I can do is to try to save his. Yes, I'm all right now, I'll help you."

Simata turned back to the others who remained on guard. "Make sure those men ride away. Keep your guns on them so that they will not take you by surprise. When this is all over, I know that Mr. Bouchard will want to begin his cattle drive. He has already waited longer than he wished."

Then Simata explained to the young woman, "First, I will heat my hunting knife so that it will be clean when I cut into his shoulder to take out the bullet. You can help by heating more water. I will cut away the cloth of his jacket over his shoulder while you do that."

Margaret Caldemare nodded, sniffling again to hold back her tears, and hurried to the kitchen while Simata went into the living room and squatted down beside the

301

couch on which the black-haired Georgian lay. Taking his hunting knife out of its sheath, Simata carefully inserted the middle fingers of his left hand inside the neck of Joe Duvray's cotton jacket and lifted it from the wound, then swiftly cut away the fabric to expose the shoulder and upper chest of the unconscious man. He studied the wound carefully and concluded that, although the weapon had been fired at relatively close range, there had not been enough force to propel the lead ball deep into the flesh. With luck, he told himself, he should be able to find the ball not more than two inches deep.

Margaret returned with the basin of hot water and more towels and anxiously watched Simata grip the bone handle of the sharp knife with the cut-away piece of cloth he had already removed and dip the blade into the steaming water to sterilize it. Then he leaned over Joe and very gently, spreading the puckered, darkened flesh of the wound apart with left thumb and forefinger, he began to probe with the tip of the knife.

Margaret stood with her hands clasped at her bosom, her eyes wet with tears, her face taut with anxiety. Simata worked very slowly, taking pains not to cut too deeply lest he start a hemorrhage. After about five minutes, he uttered a triumphant cry and drew the knife out slowly, then with the fingers of his left hand plucked out the lead pellet. "It is over," he announced. "Now I will wash the wound with hot water and then bandage it very tightly. There is not as much blood as I feared, and he is strong and young. I thank the Great Spirit that the wound was no deeper nor closer to the chest, or I could not have done this."

"Thank God you've saved him—here, let me wash the wound, I want to help, too!" Margaret declared with a tremulous smile as she sank down on her knees and began to tend the still unconscious man. Simata watched her keenly, a little smile playing about his lips. It was good, he thought to himself. She was a fine woman, very beautiful and young, and she had watched her father die before her eyes. She cared for this man, there could be no doubt of it. That would take away the grief of having lost her father.

"That is very good, miss," he applauded her. "Now if you will hold one end of this towel, we will wrap it under the arm and around the shoulder and then make a knot

302

round the arm—yes, this way. Good, that will stop the bleeding for a time, and then we will change it again and also wash the wound. Now let him rest. When he wakes up, he should have some food."

"I think there is some soup in a pot in the kitchen—" Margaret faltered.

"Good. And perhaps some coffee, if you have any."

"Oh yes, I'll make some fresh coffee right away! Thank you—I—I don't even know your name. . . ."

"It is Simata. My father was Kiowa. I lived with my mother in New Orleans, and the black man who rides on Mr. Lucien Edmond Bouchard's ranch and his friends saved my life when drunken white men tried to kill me. Yes, miss, the man who owns the ranch next to your father's has a good heart, and he speaks with a straight tongue, just as his father does. All of us who work for him respect him."

"I understand," Margaret lowered her eyes, then put out a hand that trembled slightly to feel Joe Duvray's head. "He—he doesn't seem to have very much fever."

"That is good. Bring him soup and coffee and care for him. I will stay here to guard you through the night. But I do not think the other men will come back. Do you know anything about them? One of your father's men outside said that they had ridden away before we came here."

The young woman shook her head. "No, Father didn't say anything about that. I do know he was talking to that awful man—that Jackson Brundiger. I never could quite understand why Father hired him. He acted so—well, so insolently toward Father, as if he were the boss instead."

"Ah," Simata nodded with satisfaction, "that must have been the man Joe Duvray talked about, the man who would not give his name and who threatened him and the other riders when they came to ask about the moving of Mr. Bouchard's markers." He rose and smiled at her. "Now I must look for their tracks to see where they went before it is too dark to see anything at all. But I will come back soon, and by then you will have the soup and the coffee ready."

"Oh, yes—my gracious, I almost forgot. I'll give you supper, too, when you come back—unless you'd like some now?"

"No, I thank you. I will have a little when I come back.

But I must do this for Mr. Bouchard. Let Joe rest now, it is the best thing for him."

"I will—oh, thank you, Simata. I want him to get well— he must get well!" Margaret said, half to herself. Simata nodded, then left the room. He turned back for a last look, in time to see the young woman bend solicitously over Joe Duvray, her soft hand gently stroking his forehead, and he smiled to himself again.

It was dark outside now, and in order to see the hoof marks of the riders' horses, he would need a light. He looked around and saw a piece of brushwood lying on the ground near the porch and retrieved it. Then he went into the kitchen and thrust one end of the stick into the glowing coals till it kindled. Leaving the house, he mounted his gelding and, crouching to one side and with his left arm round the gelding's neck, he extended the improvised torch as close to the ground as he could.

The six Mexicans had by now packed their belongings, mounted their horses, and ridden off. Eddie Gentry called that information to the half-breed scout as he made a slow circle of the terrain beyond the ranch house. A few minutes later, with a cry of satisfaction, Simata observed the marks of many hooves where the grass had been crushed and flattened and, along stretches of the sandier and barren soil, clearly imprinted. There were many of them and they showed a northwestward direction by the riders. He frowned. Why had they not headed south, with those Mexicans who had just left? Where had they gone and why had they not returned in all this time? They certainly had not driven cattle, for the Mexican cattle were still in the pen. Even now he could hear their lowing as they settled themselves for the night. Was it possible that they had ridden to San Antonio for supplies? But certainly not so many, and there were no tracks of wagon wheels, which would be expected if one were journeying to fetch back supplies. It was very strange, indeed.

He turned back to the Bouchard men and told them what he had just seen. "I must ride back to tell Mr. Bouchard," he said to Eddie Gentry. "You and the others should stay here through the night to make sure that nothing happens to Joe Duvray or the girl. I do not like this at all. You should sleep in shifts, so that at least two of you are awake all through the night to guard against an attack.

304

From what you and Joe have told me about the vaqueros of the man who died today, I do not think they are good, honest men who make their living driving cattle as you do. My father used to say to me that when one arms oneself against an enemy, he does not easily fall into a trap. Now I go back to the ranch."

"We'll watch good, Simata, don't you worry," Eddie Gentry assured him. The half-breed scout nodded, waved his hand, and rode back to Windhaven Range.

CHAPTER THIRTY-TWO

Corpulent Matthias Stillman had another quarrel with Dr. Ben Wilson when the former visited the Creek reservation during the first week of March. The crux of it was not only the Quaker's constant censure of the quality of food and clothing that Stillman provided to the villagers, but also the fact that Ben had become incensed enough to write a letter to the Bureau of Indian Affairs in Washington to urge that a man more sympathetic and honest be appointed in Stillman's place.

Glowering, his face flushed and contorted with indignation, Stillman shook his fist in Ben Wilson's face the moment the soldiers had begun to unload the provisions. "You damned squaw-loving meddler you! You've given me a hard time ever since you've come here, and I'm sick of it, do you hear me? I'm doing the job I'm paid to do. The government gives me just so much money every month for these stinking redskins, and it's easy enough for you to sit back here and turn up your fancy nose at what I'm able to buy for the money. I'd just like to see you go out and try to buy food and clothes on the allowance the government gives me for this reservation."

"I've done that already, Mr. Stillman, out of my own money. I've been to Wichita—twice, in fact—and I haven't found the prices particularly high for the quality of merchandise I bought. Perhaps you should do your shopping somewhere else, Mr. Stillman," Ben calmly replied.

The answer seemed to make the Indian agent all the more choleric. "Damn your hide for a busybody! I'll have you know I've been doing this work for three years, and you're the only one that doesn't like the way I handle my job."

"Apparently that's so, because how can poor starving Indians stand up to you, when you're the only one who brings them food and clothing, inferior though those articles generally are?" was the cool answer.

With an oath, Stillman clenched his fists and almost yielded to the impulse to strike the earnest young Quaker doctor. Controlling himself with an effort, he snarled, "Well, I've got friends in Washington, as it happens, Dr. Wilson. So you needn't think that going behind my back and trying to get somebody else there in my place is going to do you any good. I won't forget your meddling, you whippersnapper you. Everybody knows the only reason you're wasting your time here is because you're a damned squaw-lover. Come on, men, we've given them their rations. I won't have to see this lousy place for another month." Turning his back on Ben, Stillman growled an order to the six soldiers who had come with him to distribute the supplies into the village, mounted his horse, and rode off, not without turning back one more time to give Ben a look of undisguised hatred.

Ben had indeed gone to Wichita a second time, to purchase not only more food and clothing for the Creeks, but also a doll for Tisinqua and a dress for Elone. He had already begun to teach Elone English, and it was a delight for him to find how apt and quick a pupil she was. Because she spoke a little Creek, and he had already acquired a passable knowledge of that language, it was relatively simple for him to teach her English by saying the Creek word and then the English equivalent. Many an evening, he found himself raptly listening to the sound of her voice, for there was a gentleness to it and a sweet cadence which inevitably reminded him of his beloved Fleurette. More than that, her gentleness and devotion to the child deeply touched him.

Ben knew her story well and it had won his compassion from the very first: a shy, gentle adolescent girl stolen from a peaceful Indian tribe by a maurauding band of nomadic hunters and wanderers. Then the terrible choice of either submitting to the chief or becoming a virtual concubine to all the braves. She had chosen the lesser evil, to be sure, but it still had been a great evil. Ben was certain that few other mothers would have shown the issue of such a forced and loveless union the intense tenderness that Elone displayed toward her little girl. Now, even in this impoverished reservation, isolated out on the

Great Plains, with little hope of amelioration of their sorrows and deprivations, Elone would speak to him of her gratitude in finding a home for herself and her child, of the friendship which these tragically displaced Creeks accorded to her and Tisinqua. There was to her a gentle humility and, concealed by this, a strength of character which entranced him.

There were times, after the long days and evenings spent in setting up a kind of dispensary using such medicines as he could procure either from the lax and corrupt government agent or from his own purchases in Wichita, where Ben would ponder what would be the eventual fate of people like Elone and little Tisinqua.

The winters were harsh and the summers cruelly hot, and within miles there was no sight of any other human being. Here, within the rickety enclosure which symbolized the government's simultaneous isolation and neglect of the Creeks, there was little hope of any future for any of them, not even the strongest and most energetic young brave. For many an hour, Ben mulled over these problems and then, finding himself absorbed in giving English lessons to Elone, decided that he would open a kind of school for the other young people. It would be good to teach them English. Perhaps, under the aegis of a kindlier and more understanding bureaucracy, the young men of this tribe might have an opportunity for an education and even for work that would give them both dignity and a livelihood.

He mentioned this plan to Emataba, who was highly enthusiastic about the project and spoke that very night about the proposal to the assembled villagers. Almost all of the children showed themselves willing to become pupils of this strange, kindly white-eyes of whom their mothers and fathers spoke with the deepest respect. For many of the Creeks, this was the first time ever that they had spoken the praise of a white man—or, as Elone would have termed it in her own Sioux tongue, a *wasichu*. And many of the young braves, though at first hostile to Ben Wilson's presence as a permanent resident of their village, eagerly volunteered, once they had seen for themselves his kindness and generosity toward the tribe.

The dress that Ben had purchased for Elone in Wichita was a green calico with flouncy hem and puffed sleeves; he had discovered that green was Elone's favorite color. For

Tisinqua, he had found not only a rag doll ingeniously made to look flaxen-haired, but also a tiny cradle in which to rock the doll. When he presented these gifts to Elone, she exclaimed with joy and clapped her hands, then held up the dress against herself and sent him an exquisitely arch look of gratitude. Tisinqua was equally delighted with her doll and little cradle and hugged the doll to her as she stared at him with shining eyes. Awkwardly, he set down the cradle before her, gently took the doll and placed it in the cradle, then began to rock it. With a cry of understanding, the little girl knelt down and imitated him. He laughed with joy at the enchanting scene, and when he looked up, it was to find Elone staring at him with her eyes full of tears. He got to his feet and, in an unsteady voice, trying to sound casual, said, "I hope it will fit you, Elone. The woman at the store said that it should. I know your size and your weight—that is, as a doctor I would know these things, you see."

"You are very kind to us. Tisinqua and I will never forget how much you have done to make our lives happy again. May your God bless you for it, Doc-tor."

"I pray He will bless all of us, Elone," he said, and once again he could not trust himself to speak further. Nodding almost bruskly to her, he opened the flaps of the doorway and went out into the village. He thought to himself that it was a good thing that in a few minutes he would begin another session of his English class, for there would be many questions and many distractions to take his mind off the enchanting, haunting scene he had just left behind him.

The weather was warmer in April and, thanks to the Quaker doctor's conscientious devotion to the old and the ailing as well as the children, the general health of the Creek villagers was better than it had ever been before. There was fresh milk daily for the children from the two cows Ben had brought from Wichita, and by now one of the heifers had calved and would within a week or two be able to furnish a plentiful supply of milk. There was also fresh meat, for Sipanata and two of his friends had ridden out with lances and bows and arrows and, by great good luck, come upon a small herd of buffalo. They had killed a dozen of the shaggy bulls and cows and, as was customary with all the Indians of the Great Plains, the Creek women had followed the men on horseback, carrying travois along so that the slaughtered meat might be taken back to camp for all to enjoy. The hides would help provide warmth for the wigwams when the winter came. There was dried meat and tallow in great quantities in the parfleches, envelopes of waterproof rawhide, slung on packhorses ridden by the squaws or, when these containers were too heavy, lashed to the larger travois. And the chokecherries and berries which had been picked in the fall and dried for winter use would be used to make pemmican, thin slices of buffalo meat which had been dried, cooked, pounded fine, and then mixed with melted fat and either cherries or berries. Thus, for a time, Emataba's tribe feasted and could look forward with more security to the leaner days which would come with the fall and winter.

The monthly governmental allotment of supplies did not arrive until the tenth of April, and when they did, Matthias Stillman rode in, himself driving the wagon and accompanied this time by only four soldiers. They were older men, nearly at the end of their enlistment, and they appeared bored and exhausted from the monotonous duties and long journeys to which they were assigned. When the wagon arrived outside the dilapidated stockade surrounding the Creek reservation, Ben was busy conducting his daily class in English for about thirty children, young men, and women. Emataba had had his braves build a kind of rude lodge made of hewn timbers, grass, and hides, which could house about forty villagers, and this lodge, set at the far end of the village, was used as Ben's classroom.

Elone, this early afternoon, had spied a patch of blackberries and had given little Tisinqua into the keeping of an old childless squaw who occupied the teepee across the way from hers. She carried a basket, and she wore the green calico dress which the Quaker doctor had bought her in Wichita. Though he had somewhat self-consciously indicated that this dress was only for special occasions, Elone was so fond of it that she wore it daily and never failed to take pleasure from it.

Matthias Stillman was in a foul humor. He had just received a letter from Washington curtly informing him that, effective in September, he was to be replaced by a new Creek agent for the territory, Douglas Larrimer. The letter said that Larrimer had been decorated for valor as a captain in the Union Army, but did not say that Larrimer's great-grandfather had married a Cherokee maiden, and that this heritage had given him a kindlier and more compassionate view of Indians than most administrators shared. Dr. Ben Wilson's letter had borne fruit, yet the vindictive Matthias Stillman would still be a prickly thorn to the Creeks until the fall. And, raging at the humiliation of this demotion which he was certain had been brought about by the meddlesome and high-minded Quaker, he was determined before he left his post to settle the score between them.

As he drew the horses to a halt and clambered down from the wagon, puffing and mopping his sweaty forehead from the exertion and the heat of the long journey, he caught sight of Elone. A crafty grin twisted his mouth, and then he peremptorily ordered the four soldiers to unload the wagon and distribute the supplies. Sipanata, recognizing him, opened the gate and, glaring at the soldiers, watched as they toted in the barrels of flour, sacks of beans, salt, and sugar, plus the few articles of clothing and blankets that Matthias Stillman had grudgingly purchased. This time, aware of Ben's critical attitude, Stillman had taken pains to make certain that the supplies were of the best available quality—though he still had been able to siphon a considerable amount of the monthly funds designated for the reservation into his own pocket.

"Guess I'll take me a stroll while you boys are getting rid of this stuff," he nonchalantly remarked to the lantern-jawed, gray-haired corporal who was in charge of the small contingent. "Take your time. It's a long way back, a dry and dusty one. Maybe those redskins have something nice and cool to drink. Ask around. It's the least they can do for you, seeing as how you've brought them such a load."

"We'll take care of it, Mr. Stillman, don't you worry. And we sure could use something cold to drink, that's a fact," the corporal earnestly averred.

Seeing that no one was paying any attention to him, Stillman sidled past the wagon and stealthily made his way toward the west where Elone was busy picking berries, her back turned to him. Near the berry patch were tall, waist-high clumps of buffalo grass, and his eyes glittered at the prospect of amusing himself with this comely young Indian girl.

Holding his breath so as not to make a sound and tiptoeing up behind her, he suddenly whispered, "Now don't you dare yell, gal, or I'll have to shut you up and you won't like that one little bit. Time you redskin squaws had a white man, anyway. You're not bad, and you're nice and young."

Elone had been able to recognize only a few of his words as she froze in terror; the lecherous sound of his low voice made her aware of what he intended. Jubilant over the effect his threat had made on her, he reached around her and clapped his left palm over her mouth while at the same time seizing her by the right shoulder and twisting her round to face him. Elone uttered a stifled cry, and he snarled, "Don't you dare let out a yell, you redskin bitch, or I'll hurt you bad! Now get down there on the grass and pleasure me, or you'll sure wish you had!"

Gripping her by both shoulders, he dragged her down onto her back and flung himself atop her. Elone agilely squirmed away, tried to get to her feet, and uttered a shrill cry of terror. Cursing under his breath, Stillman stumbled to his feet and, lunging out, caught her by her thick braid of black hair and viciously yanked her back, tumbling her down before him. Again she cried out, but he knelt down and clamped his left hand over her mouth while with his right hand he ripped away her calico dress. Elone's eyes bulged with fear and shame as she tried to fight off her corpulent ravisher. Under the dress, she wore only a doe-skin camisole-like garment and a petticoat of the same material. Kicking and twisting, trying to strike at him, she fought to free herself from his odious embrace.

Ben Wilson had concluded the class and had walked outside the lodge when he heard Elone's first faint cry. Looking down toward the gate of the stockade, he saw the soldiers carrying in the supplies and a horrid presentiment seized him.

Again he heard her cry, this time shriller and more agonized, and he began to run toward the gate.

Emataba had heard Elone's cries, too, and had come out of his wigwam. "Who is it, who cries out for help?" he called to Ben.

"It's a woman—I don't know who, but she's in trouble—and I think I know who's causing it—I'm going to help her!" the Quaker doctor called back.

By this time, Matthias Stillman had ripped away the

camisole and was greedily fondling Elone's soft, narrowly spaced breasts with his free hand while he continued to clamp his other over her mouth to silence her outcries. She tried to bite his palm, but could not, for he cruelly mashed his hand down till blood came from her lips as they were forced against her teeth.

Ben Wilson stopped beside the wagon, staring frantically around, and heard her last stifled outcry. Grinding his teeth with anger, he hurried in the direction of the sound and, parting the tall buffalo grass with both hands, stopped suddenly as he saw the Indian agent now plunge his right hand into his britches and begin to unbutton them.

"Let her go, you despicable animal!" he said in a trembling voice.

Dazed with his lust, his face florid and contorted, Stillman turned to look up at him. Then he sniggered, "Aw, come on, Doc, who the hell cares about a little redskin pokemeat? I've got to have me some fun for all the work I do for these lousy red devils—what's it matter to you, anyhow? You've got your squaw, like as not—mebbe quite a few, huh, Doc?"

"Shut your filthy mouth, Stillman! Get away from that girl!" Ben's face was pale with suppressed anger.

"Yeah? Who's going to make me? You, you Bible-slinging Quaker? I hear tell when somebody slaps you in the face, you Quakers turn the other cheek! Now why don't you get the hell out of here and let me have my fun? You've had yours all these months with all the squaws, and you know it, Doc!"

For an instant the earnest young Quaker stared at the Indian agent, the muscles of his jaws contracting as he strove for self-control. But then, as Matthias Stillman turned back to the struggling Elone and cupped one of her bare breasts in his pudgy hand, Ben strode to him, gripped him by the armpits, and pulled him off the girl as he flung him heavily to the ground. Elone uttered a sobbing cry and scrambling to all fours, crawled away with her back to him, then huddled on her knees, her arms crossed over her breasts, as she watched with anxiety and fear mingled in her dark, tear-filled eyes.

"Why, you dirty little pipsqueak!" Stillman bellowed as he got to his feet and lumbered toward the doctor. "I'm going to beat you bloody and teach you not to interfere

313

with Matthias Stillman. You've done enough already, getting me fiired off my cushy job. I owe you this and a lot more, Doc! Now let's see if you'll turn the other cheek—oufff!!" As he spoke, his voice thick with anger, he had launched a swing of his heavy fist at the doctor's head. Ben ducked and drove his own right fist into the Indian agent's belly, doubling the agent over and forcing him to stumble back, his face contorted and livid.

Wheezing as he tried to regain his breath, Stillman straightened and then, with a savage roar, flung himself at Ben, wrapping his arms around Ben's body and pinning him on the ground. With his left hand he tried to throttle his opponent, and with his right, his fingers curved like talons, he sought to gouge out Ben's eyes.

Elone cried out again as she saw this, but Ben gripped Stillman's right wrist and forced it away from his face, twisting it back until the Indian agent uttered a yowl of agony. At the same time, his left hand broke Stillman's grip on his throat and, twisting about, Ben managed to extricate himself from his disadvantageous position and sprang to his feet.

The lantern-jawed corporal had gone back to the wagon for a new armful of supplies and, hearing the struggle, came running forward, drawing his pistol out of its holster. "Hold on there, you!" he called to Ben. "Mr. Stillman, want me to arrest him?"

"You let them fight!" a guttural voice broke in. The corporal whirled to find Sipanata, his bow drawn back to maximum and the arrowhead leveled at the corporal's chest, standing on the other side of the rickety fence, with three other braves beside him, their bows already drawn and arrows notched in readiness.

"All right, you damned redskins, I won't shoot, put those bows down, for God's sake!" the corporal bawled as he holstered his pistol and, shrugging, walked slowly back to the wagon.

"That's right!" the Indian agent jeered as he came forward, his fists clenched, feinting with his right hand toward Ben Wilson's face. "I might have figured you'd get your redskin friends to save you! And I suppose if I hurt you, they'll riddle me with arrows."

"No. They're much more civilized than you give them credit for, Mr. Stillman. If you want to fight, I'll give you all you want and I don't need any help. I don't use weapons, it's true, but this time you've got to be taught a lesson. I'm not going to stand by and see Elone abused by an animal like you."

"Oh ho, so that's the way the wind blows, is it?" Stillman sniggered and glanced quickly back at the cowering, half-naked girl. "So you'll fight this time because that's your squaw. Yeah, now I can see why you're so riled at me, Doc. Well, you know what I'm going to do? I'm going to kill you, and then I'm going to have some fun poking your squaw all I want, see?" With this, he charged the Quaker, his fists flailing. Ben's head snapped back as a wild swing from Stillman's left fist grazed the point of his jaw, but he stood his ground. Retaliating with both fists, he bloodied the agent's nose, and with another vigorous uppercut to the man's corpulent paunch, he made Stillman stumble back, waving his arms with a yell, losing his balance to fall back and sprawl on the ground.

His eyes glassy and narrowed with an almost insane rage, the Indian agent wiped his bloody nose with the back of his sleeve as he slowly got to his feet. "You were just lucky that time, Doc. Now I'm really going to kill you," he hoarsely boasted. He came forward slowly and this time suddenly kicked out with his right foot at Ben's groin. But the agile Quaker, moving about on the soles of his feet and shifting readily, swerved to one side and caught Stillman's upraised ankle in both hands, then swiftly shoved it forward. With another yowl of pain, the Indian agent fell with a heavy thud on the ground, then lay writhing in pain.

Again he slowly got to his feet, breathing heavily, his face a mask of thwarted rage. Then again he rushed at his adversary, swinging his fists with all his strength as he tried by sheer force of superior weight to battle the Quaker to the ground. But his blows were wildly inaccurate, and another jarring punch from Ben closed his left eye and made him topple back to sprawl on the ground. His face streaked with the blood from his wounded nose, Stillman rose more slowly than ever, licking his lips, gingerly testing to see if any of his teeth had been loosened in the encounter.

Then suddenly he drew a clasp knife from the pocket of his vest and, brandishing it in the air, ran at the doctor as he tried to use the weapon as a dagger. Once again Ben was ready for his charge and, stepping to one side, caught Stillman's right wrist with both hands and twisted it so sharply that the knife dropped from his fingers. A shriek of agony attested to his distress. But even as he stumbled back, Ben moved forward and, using both fists, sent short but hard punches against his face and midriff till at last, whimpering in pain and knowing himself beaten, Stillman went down on his knees, bowing his head and shaking it as if to clear it of the dazing shock of his beating. His lips were puffed and swollen, and his chin was almost entirely covered with blood from his battered nose.

"I think you'd better call it quits, Mr. Stillman," Ben calmly said as he moved forward toward the fallen man. "I told you before, I've never used weapons and I never shall. But when I went to school, they taught me how to box. I haven't forgotten it, as you can see. Now then, you'll apologize to Elone and then you'll go back to your wagon and leave here unless you want some more."

"No, no, for God's sake, I've had enough—have your damned squaw for all I care! And I'll give up the job right now—I want no more truck with a conniving bastard like you, you hear?" Stillman got to his feet, groggy and unsteady. Then, pulling out a handkerchief and pressing it against his profusely bleeding nose, he hobbled back to the wagon, painfully clambered into it, and sat there with his head bowed and his other hand rubbing his belly.

"Did he hurt you, Elone?" Ben anxiously asked as he turned to the terrified young Indian girl.

"No, Doc-tor. But I was so afraid for you. He is such a big man, so strong—you have saved me again. My life belongs to you for always now, Doc-tor."

And then, very faintly and very shyly, her cheeks reddening at her own boldness, she murmured, "I would not have minded if it had been you. He called me your squaw. That is what I pray to the Great Spirit to be if you will only have me, Doc-tor."

Ben had turned to one side and removed his coat. "Here, Elone, put this on. I'll get you a new dress—that swine ruined yours."

He had closed his eyes, greatly troubled because the sudden glimpse of her lovely half-nudity had stirred carnal urges he thought had been quelled forever by Fleurette's untimely death. She rose, moving to him proudly, smiling through her tears, as she took the coat and draped it round her. Then, timidly, both hands grasping his left arm, she murmured, "Am I then so ugly to look upon, Doc-tor?"

"No, Elone, oh, no, not ugly ever! You—you're beautiful."

"I am only sorry about the dress because you gave it to me. I loved it so. But you have won me now. In my village when I was a little girl, two braves would fight to decide who should take a maiden as his squaw. You have beaten the man who would have taken me, Doc-tor. I am yours now twice over, ever since you saved my life and that of Tisinqua."

He was trembling now, helpless before the emotions that raged in him. His deeply fervent religious training had taught him that violence was to be shunned at all costs— yet when he had seen Matthias Stillman trying to rape Elone, he had thought only of saving her and punishing that greedy, dissolute, amoral man who had treated the Creeks as if they were wild animals to be shunned and abused and slaughtered. His pent-up grief over gentle Fleurette had found a shattering release in this primitive fight against Stillman, and it had finally purged him of it. Now, in the loneliness of this isolated little village in the midst of a virtual wilderness, he had known the joy of serving others, of being respected for his skill, and finally of having discovered that someone alien to him in every way he had know before was capable of the deepest love and tenderness for him.

For a long moment he could not speak as he took her other hand in his. Then finally he said, "Elone, I will teach you my faith so that you may know what I am and how I think. And when you have learned it, if you still wish it, we will go to Wichita and be married in the Quaker faith. Come now. I will take you back to your tepee. Little Tisinqua will be wanting you."

"Oh yes, Doc-tor Ben! And she will want you, too, as her father. Oh yes, I will gladly learn your faith if that will make you take me," she whispered. Looking up at him with adoration, she pressed against him as, his arm around her shoulders, he led her back to the village.

317

CHAPTER THIRTY-THREE

Lucien Edmond Bouchard had finally made his plans for the drive to Abilene and chosen April 20 as the day to start. During the interim which had followed his call upon Robert Caldemare and the subsequent fatal gunplay, there had been no sign of the riders who had left their tracks heading northwest. After Simata had reported what he had seen that night, Lucien Edmond decided to take twenty-six well-armed men along to Abilene, leaving a dozen to guard the ranch house and eight more to remain on the Caldemare property for the purpose of surveillance. One of these latter would be Joe Duvray, who had recovered from his shoulder wound, thanks to Margaret Caldemare's devoted care. And on the day before the drive was to begin, the young Georgian rode back to confer with Lucien Edmond on a plan for defense in the event that the missing *pistoleros* should suddenly return to take over their dead employer's holdings.

"In my view, those men would hardly be interested in keeping the land and raising cattle on it," Lucien Edmond declared. "And since Caldemare apparently has no other heirs beside his daughter, she would normally stand to inherit it—except that under current law I doubt that the courts would award it to her. As I see it, when we finish selling our own cattle, I may have to go to Austin and talk to the head of the land office there as to the best plan of action. I might even be able to buy the land myself and then, of course, if you're interested, sell it to you on a deferred payment basis." He gave the black-haired Georgian a shrewdly appraising look. "What would you think of that, Joe?"

"But Mr. Bouchard, you know I wouldn't have that kind of money. Sure, I've saved a good part of my pay—there's nothing around here to spend it on—but I can't see myself buying three or four thousand acres even if they went as cheap as fifty cents an acre," Joe worriedly expostulated.

"Look at it this way, Joe. Suppose I bought it in your name, helped you stock it with Herefords and Brahmas, you'd have plenty of acreage for grazing and crossbreeding, wouldn't you?"

"I certainly would, Mr. Bouchard. I think Caldemare's land is even bigger than yours; at least, by the western boundary it looks like it is."

"I have no doubt that's true. Of course, I'll check that when I get to Austin. But then, assuming I handle it that way, you could pay me back every time you sold your cattle. Of course, you'd really be holding the land in trust for Margaret Caldemare."

"Guess I would." Joe looked down at his dusty boots and scowled reflectively.

"Don't look so glum," Lucien Edmond chuckled. "I have a sneaking suspicion that you're as much in love with her as she is with you. And the fact is, Joe, she'll rely on you more than ever now just because her father's dead and she has no one else to help her. From what you've told me of your conversations with her, it appears that she was an only child left in the East to be schooled, and she was rarely visited by her father."

"That's for certain."

"Well, then, there's nowhere else she can go. It appears, also, since she has searched the house to see if there were any letters or papers about stock or bank accounts and has found nothing, that her father must have plunged just about all he had left into buying the land and getting ready for his own cattle drive."

"That also looks to be the way it is, Mr. Bouchard. Only thing I can't figure, those Mexican cattle he's got there won't make very good beef. And I imagine the buyers would complain about their having Texas fever or maybe something worse, seeing as how they come from south of the border."

"Have you taken a good look at them while you've been there, Joe?"

"I have, for a fact, Mr. Bouchard." Joe rose from his chair and scowled again. "I've got a crazy hunch that they might have been rustled all the way from Mexico. Some of them have a brand, but it's blurred. And others look as if there was a brand under the RC they're carrying now."

"You may be right," Lucien Edmond mused. "But why would Robert Caldemare content himself with five hundred head of Mexican cattle? If he came here to be a rancher, he must have had some advice about the territory, the grazing, the breeding, and all the other things you and I know. He couldn't expect to make any money at all on cattle like those."

"No he couldn't, Mr. Bouchard. That's something I just can't figure out. Of course Margaret doesn't know anything about it. She's just glad some of those *pistoleros* of his haven't come back, because she didn't like their looks to start with."

"Including that gunman you described to me who wouldn't give you his name." Lucien Edmond was thinking aloud now as he rose from his desk and stood looking out of the window, his hands clasped behind his back. "Simata told me that he saw the tracks of at least a dozen horses going north. And they left before Caldemare and his *capataz* Jaime Ruiz were killed, so obviously that wasn't their reason for leaving so quickly. Put that together with your suspicions about those cattle having been rustled from across the border, and it gives me some very unpleasant thoughts."

"I'm feeling the same way, Mr. Bouchard," Joe Duvray admitted.

"We've got about thirty-eight hundred head of cattle to drive tomorrow, and I'm picking twenty-six men, all men who've been on the trail with me before. We've got our Spencers and the new ammunition and the cases, so we'll be more than a match for those *pistoleros,* even assuming they have any wild notions about attacking us."

"I thought of that, too, Mr. Bouchard. Only would it make sense for men like that to ride away and spend a couple of months waiting for you to get there with the herd?"

"It wouldn't unless there's more to this scheme than you and I can figure out, Joe," Lucien Edmond ruefully admitted. "Then again, they might have been dissatisfied with the way things were shaping up on the Caldemare ranch and decided to go off on their own, or maybe even join a gang of bushwhackers."

320

"Like that Reedy gang that hit us last year, maybe?" Joe hazarded.

"That could be," Lucien Edmond slowly responded, stroking his chin and frowning as he saw old Jubal chasing his tail just outside the window. Then he grinned. "There's one character on our ranch that doesn't have any worries except maybe getting a tick at the end of his tail. Look at old Jubal having fun out there. What a wonderful old dog he is, and what a watchdog he proved himself to be when the Macaras brothers attacked us."

Joe came to stand beside his employer and chuckled as he watched the lean, long-tailed hound whirl around and nip irritatedly at the tip of his tail. "Still plenty of life in Jubal, that's a fact, Mr. Bouchard. Well, then, you want me to stay on at the Caldemare house, I take it, and you'll have seven of our vaqueros in the bunkhouse there just in case those *pistoleros* take it into their heads to come back and see what was cooking?"

"That's about it, Joe. But you think over what I said to you about Margaret Caldemare. You could do much worse than settle down with a fine girl like her."

"Don't I know it, Mr. Bouchard!" Joe suddenly grew loquacious, while at the same time his sun-bronzed complexion reddened with embarrassment. "But she's way out of my class, and you know it, Mr. Bouchard. Just the same, I care for her a lot, and that's the honest truth."

"I'm sure she feels the same way about you, Joe. After all, you saved her life, and that was the best possible start for a romance."

"Sure, but then I was around when she saw her father killed. And the only good thing about it is that she's beginning to think that maybe he wasn't all that he was cracked up to be. He wrote her a lot of letters and made all sorts of promises, and when she got here, she found that he was a different sort of fellow from what she'd thought or known."

"Then all the more reason why you've got to stand by her. Don't sell yourself short, Joe. You've turned out to be a very valuable friend and worker for Windhaven Range, and you've learned a lot about raising cattle, and you've seen how I sell them at Abilene. You could handle the Caldemare ranch and, when the time comes, as Margaret

Caldemare's husband, you'd have an extra incentive to keep you working at it."

"I sure would, Mr. Bouchard. Gosh, when you met Andy Haskins and me on the wharf in New Orleans, I sure never figured anything like this would happen to me."

"Well, it goes both ways, Joe," Lucien Edmond chuckled. "Father's written me that Andy has taken charge of some land downriver and is just about set to marry a very nice young widow who was living there with her blind old father. I don't think we're going to see Andy around at Windhaven Range from now on. But if you marry Margaret Caldemare, you'll be my next-door neighbor. And I'll be your partner in this deal—if you want it."

"I don't know what to say, Mr. Bouchard." Joe's voice wavered and he coughed to hide his emotion. "Darn it, got a frog in my throat, I guess. Well, anyway, if you think I could swing it, I'd sure like to have a try at it. But I don't even know if Margaret could see me as a husband. It's one thing to save a girl's life, but it's another to have her— well, you know what I'm trying to say, Mr. Bouchard."

Lucien Edmond Bouchard nodded and smilingly clapped Joe Duvray on the back. "Don't rush things, they'll come of their own accord. Well, you look after things there while we're away. And the vaqueros here at the ranch house will ride out every so often just to pay a visit to you and make sure that everything's going smoothly."

"I'll be careful, though in a way I'm sorry I'm not going with you tomorrow, Mr. Bouchard."

"You've a big responsibility, Joe. You're going to look to our defenses, and that's almost as vital as guarding the cattle we're going to drive to Abilene. Maybe even more so, depending on what those *pistoleros* do. Well, I'll see you when I get back. Wish me luck."

"The very best in the world, Mr. Bouchard. And God bless you for all you've done for me." Joe gripped Lucien Edmond's hand and squeezed it hard, then quickly left the ranch house, mounted his gelding, and rode back to Margaret Caldemare.

And so, shortly after dawn on the morning of April 20, the protesting lowing of cattle was heard and the encouraging shouts of the vaqueros, and the rumbling of the wheels of the heavy chuck wagon driven by Tiburcio Caltran. As before, Ramón Hernandez would be in charge of the remuda, and he had already said his farewells to lovely Mara and their two little sons. Lucien Edmond Bouchard had kissed Maxine lovingly and lingeringly, and then hugged Carla and Hugo, lifted two-year-old Edwina in his arms and kissed her and urged her to look after her mother.

Felicidad, big with child, had hurried out to bid farewell to her beloved Lucas, while white-haired Djamba smiled indulgently down at the young couple from astride his black gelding. Celia, who had recovered from a brief cold which she had caught just after returning from her visit to Sangrodo's stronghold and a reunion with her daughter, Prissy, smiled at her son and his Mexican wife, then blew a kiss to the sturdy Mandingo whom she respected and admired as much as she loved for his loyalty to the Bouchards.

Pablo Casares was there to see them off, his black-haired wife Kate standing beside him with her arm around his waist, the two little boys each clinging to his hands. She whispered to him, "Are you sorry you won't be riding with them this time, Pablo dear?"

"No, *mi querida,*" he whispered back, devouring her lovely face with his eyes. "I have here beside me all that I shall ever want in this life, may *el Señor Dios* be praised for His goodness to me."

"A goodness you richly deserve, my darling. And you know, you're going to be a father by the end of this year, dear Pablo," she leaned over to whisper into his ear, then blushed vividly as he started and regarded her with widening eyes.

"What are you saying, *mi corazón?*" he gasped.

"Why, that I'm going to have your baby about November, if my calculations are right, my darling," she teasingly retorted.

Pablo Casares uttered an ecstatic sigh, his eyes shining. "I think sometimes I shall wake up and find all this is a dream, *querida,*" he at last murmured, wonderingly shaking his head. Then, worriedly, "You—you are sure, my sweet one?"

Kate Casares smiled. "A woman should know such things, Pablo. If it is a son, I mean to name him after his father."

"But if it is a girl—and I would like that very much—"

he murmured, "I would like to name her Catarina, after you."

"Well, we shall just have to wait and see, shan't we, my dearest? So now that you know, I hope it will make you content to stay here and look after me and the two little boys and also after this ranch while Mr. Bouchard and the men are gone." She raised her right hand to wave Lucien Edmond goodbye as he gave the signal for the drive to start.

White-haired Sybella stood in the doorway with Maybelle Belcher beside her. Maybelle turned to her. "It's the largest herd of all, isn't it, Mother Sybella?"

"It certainly is. I hope they won't have any trouble handling it. I'm going to pray for them in the chapel this evening. I'll have time, since I won't be looking after Ben's children. I appreciate your having Timmy and Connie take over that responsibility for me. How do they like caring for the children?"

"Oh, Mother Sybella, they get along just wonderfully with them. Poor Ben—I wonder how he's doing out there on that reservation," Maybelle sighed.

"He's working, he's thinking of others, and that will ease his grief over Fleurette, Maybelle. That and the passage of time. When we're young, we don't always realize that, and sometimes we fight against it, but gradually we learn that love and work and family togetherness can ease the deepest griefs," Sybella murmured.

She was thinner than was her wont, having caught Celia's cold and taken to her bed for a week. Today, indeed, was the first day she had been out of bed, and she looked at the sunny sky and smiled as she said to Maybelle, "The air is nice and warm. It's a beautiful day, a good omen for the drive."

"I'm sure it is, Mother Sybella," Maybelle reassured her. "I'll come pray with you this evening."

"And you, Maybelle, are you happy out here?"

"Oh yes!" Maybelle's face brightened. "It took me a long time to get over Mark, as you well know, Mother Sybella. When I came out here, I felt as if everything had gone and there wasn't anything to live for. Then dear old Henry came along, bless his sweet heart, and those wonderful kids of his. And it's as if I'd never been back in Alabama, never met Mark—well, I didn't really mean that—"

"I know what you're trying to say, dear," Sybella gently interposed. "I'm happy for you. I loved Mark, my own flesh and blood, and yet he gave me so much sorrow. I used to pray that somehow he'd realize at last that his headlong way of life would never lead to happiness. But something drove him to it, something I could never reach. Perhaps that's why I've always looked upon Luke almost as if he had been my own, my very own son, Maybelle. He has such a love for life, even now when he's in his fifties, such a zest for it and such a belief in truth and honor, in giving not taking. So you see, I've been blessed and I'm grateful to God. What sorrow I've had has only made me all the more grateful for the love I've known and the love I've been able to give. Well, there they go, Maybelle. May God go with them and watch over them!"

"Amen, Mother Sybella."

CHAPTER THIRTY-FOUR

A week after Lopasuta had arrived at Windhaven Range, Luke Bouchard and the young Comanche rode over to Montgomery and called on old Jedidiah Danforth. The lawyer was much impressed by the twenty-two-year-old brave. He spent an hour talking with Lopasuta, and at the end of the interview he beamed at Luke, saying, "It's been a long time since I saw a young man with so much spunk and good, down-to-earth common sense. I'll be glad to take him on as my clerk. Not only that, since I'm a lonely old man these days, as you know, Mr. Bouchard, I'd be happy to offer him the hospitality of my house. Old Mrs. Cantwell, who's been my housekeeper these past fifteen years, keeps fussing over me like a mother hen. I figure that with Lopasuta around, she'll be outvoted and maybe I can have a little peace."

"That's very kind of you, Mr. Danforth," Luke said. "And you don't think Lopasuta's too young to become a lawyer?"

Jedidiah Danforth glared at him and then indignantly retorted, "Mr. Bouchard, I'll have you know that I got my license to practice law here in Montgomery when I was exactly his age. Don't you worry, by the end of the year I'll have him able to answer questions out of Blackstone and discuss torts and contracts with authority. After that, it'll just be a question of appearing before Judge Henzel or Tollefson and going through the formality of an examination."

"That's wonderful!" Luke exclaimed. Then, turning to the Comanche, he asked, "Will this please you, Lopasuta?"

"I will be grateful all of my life to you, Mr. Bouchard," the tall young Comanche said. Turning to the lawyer, he added, "But I want to earn my keep, especially if I am to live with you, Mr. Danforth."

326

The old lawyer chuckled sardonically and pointed his finger at Lopasuta as he declared, "Don't worry, sir, you'll more than earn your keep. Mr. Bouchard tells me you're a very good horseman, like all Comanches. Well, sir, when we ride from my house to my office, we go in a horse and buggy, and my mare can stand some looking after. I'll be beholden to you if you'll look her over."

"It will be my pleasure, Mr. Danforth," Lopasuta inclined his head.

"Besides that," the lawyer dryly continued, "I'll keep you busy evenings reading law books, and during the day you'll do everything from running my errands to telling clients who walk in unannounced that I'm busy with someone else and they'll just have to wait their turn. Oh, you'll earn your keep right enough, don't you worry about that."

"That is good, Mr. Danforth. I will work very hard to pay you back, you and Mr. Bouchard, for this chance you have given me," Lopasuta avowed.

"And what would you say, Lopasuta, if I were to adopt you as my legal son?" Luke suddenly interposed.

The young Comanche started with surprise, his eyes widening. Then, his face grave, he replied, "You would do this for a Comanche? But I have never heard that a white-eyes has done such a thing. There have been many white-eyes who take Indian squaws and have children by them, but they do not acknowledge them. Sometimes they are even ashamed of them."

"For one thing, Lopasuta, you won't be able to practice law if you're a Comanche and have no sponsors. But I'm sure Mr. Danforth, who knows everything there is to know about Alabama statutes, would tell you that as my son you'll have no such difficulties. Besides, you know how deeply I care about Sangrodo. After what he has done for my family and me, I'd be paying back in a small part the debt I owe, by offering you this alliance."

Lopasuta did not speak for a moment, striving to control his emotions behind his impassive, handsome countenance. At last he said, "Then I, too, have a great debt. It is not only to be able to help my people in return for the chance to study the law of the white-eyes, but I also must prove myself worthy of such an honor. I would be proud to be called your son, Mr. Bouchard. Sangrodo has often told me that you are a true friend to the Comanche and that he

327

trusts your word more than he would trust a treaty signed by your great chief."

"You're not far wrong there, Lopasuta," Jedidiah Danforth broke in with a cackle of amusement. "Our president was a pretty fair general, I'll give him that, but the advisors he's surrounded himself with now that he's in the White House make an old lawyer like me mighty suspicious, yes, sir. Well, then, Mr. Bouchard, do you want me to draw up the adoption papers?"

"At once, Mr. Danforth." Luke walked over to the young Comanche and held out his hand. "I haven't the slightest doubt that you'll more than prove worthy, Lopasuta. Laure and I will be proud to call you son."

Lopasuta gripped Luke Bouchard's hand and stared intently into his eyes. "I swear to you by the Great Spirit that I will never disgrace your name and that I will try to bring as much honor to it as you have in your dealings with my people."

Jackson Brundiger and his eleven *pistoleros* had veered to the north after about ten miles, so as to throw any possible pursuers off their tracks. The Mexicans laughed and joked among themselves, for Porfirio Costado had told them what the *gringo jefe* had proposed. They would live off the land, they would make their way slowly toward the Red River, over four hundred miles away, and lie in wait just beyond it for the Bouchard herd. And there would be plunder and *mujeres* and guns, as well as food and even fresh horses, to be taken from those isolated settlers on the outskirts of towns like San Marcos and Mineral Wells. And the cream of the joke was that the *gringo jefe* Brundiger had intimated that after they had seized the herd and killed all of Bouchard's vaqueros, there would be no need to split the money with the *patrón*. The *jefe* would sell all of the *ganado* in Abilene, split the money with them. Then they could go off on their own and Robert Caldemare would be none the wiser. Nor did they think to doubt the ingenious scheme of the Kansas desperado, for they knew him to be quick of temper and quicker still on the draw. Besides, they understood very well that no cattle buyer in Abilene would transact a sale with men like themselves, whereas the *gringo jefe*, just because he was a *gringo*, would be able to bring it off.

328

Now again they changed directions, heading toward the northeast. Their first destination would be San Marcos, about 150 miles from Carrizo Springs. Five days of hard riding would bring them to the barren outskirts of that little town, and Jackson Brundiger knew that there was no lawman within a radius of fifty miles. The nearest was in San Antonio, and the sheriff there had his hands full enough with drunks and Mexican blood feuds to be quite concerned with what might happen in San Marcos.

On the evening of their fifth day, the twelve men slowed their horses as they neared a large, sturdily constructed cabin made of wood and adobe. Nearby were a barn and a low wooden enclosure which was sectioned off to hold two saddle horses, some cows, a heifer, and a bull. A kerosene lamp cast its soft glow from behind a ragged curtain covering the little window near the door of the house, and Brundiger held up his hand to halt his accomplices. "Porfirio, you go round the back way and tell them your horse broke its leg and that you'd like shelter for the night. You, Diego, and you, Paco," as he pointed to two stocky Mexicans in their early thirties, "knock on the front door and ask if you can have some water for your horses. As soon as they open, rush them. If anyone pulls a gun, kill them, *comprende?*"

"*Si, mi jefe,*" Paco Ruberoso touched his sombrero in token of salute. "We will do as you say."

All of the men dismounted. Jackson Brundiger gripped the butts of his holstered pistols and crouched as he moved to the side of the house, the other eight riders imitating him and waiting nearby for the signal if they should be needed.

Porfirio Costado walked round to the back door and pounded on it with his fist. Presently, a woman's voice was heard, "Just a minute—who is it, this time of night?"

"Señora, my poor *caballo* has broken its leg, and I have nowhere to go. In kindness, will you not give me shelter?"

There was a moment's silence, and then the woman's voice replied, "You can sleep in the barn with the cows, if you've a mind to, and I'm sorry for you, but I'm not letting you in—what's that now, at the front door?" for Diego and Paco had begun to hammer at the front door with their fists.

There was a sound of a wooden bolt being drawn back,

329

and a gray-haired man warily peered out at the two Mexicans. "Who are you and what do you want? Talk fast, I've got a six-shooter in my hand and I know how to use it!"

"But, señor," Paco Ruberoso wheedlingly responded, "we are poor Mexicans who have lost their way. All we ask is a little water for our horses, *por favor.*"

"There's some water in the well near the barn. Take just what you need—water's scarce in these parts. Now beat it, I don't fancy greasers coming to my door this late at night—what the devil—look out, Agnes—no—" For Diego had suddenly flung himself against the door, toppling the gray-haired man to the floor. Before he could level his six-shooter, Paco had stepped in and calmly shot him in the forehead with his own six-shooter. A tall, handsome woman in her mid-forties—the one who had answered the back door—now came into the room, her face a mask of incredulous horror. Beside her was a slim, sweet-faced girl of about sixteen, who had risen from the couch and was now huddled fearfully against her mother, her dark-brown eyes dilated with fright.

"Well, señora, señorita," Paco purred as he calmly lifted the six-shooter and blew away the smoke, "I regret it, but what would you do? He wanted to kill me, *no es verdad,* Diego?"

"*Sí,* Paco," Diego Suarez said with a solemn face as he leveled his own gun at the two cringing women. "Now then, señora, señorita, are there any other men in this house?"

"Only—only my little boy, he's nine," the woman stammered. "Oh, my God, let him be—you've murdered my poor husband—oh please, take what you want but get out of here. Can't you see my daughter's afraid of you?"

"But you are not, I suppose, señora?" Paco sniggered. "We are in no hurry. But first we will make sure you are not telling us a lie. It is very bad to tell us a lie, señora." With this, he pulled open the door and shouted, *"Mi jefe,* come in with the others, there is no trouble here now!"

Jackson Brundiger led the eight men gathered with him into the house, both his guns drawn. After Paco reported what the half-fainting matron had said, he ordered three of his men to search the rest of the house. They soon reported that, indeed, as she had averred, there was only a little boy, wakened by the noise and backed against the corner of the wall of his room tearfully calling for his father.

"*Bueno,*" the Kansan nodded. "Two of you stay in the room with the boy and keep him quiet. Tell him he'll be shot if he makes any noise, *comprende?*" This done, he contemplated the two hysterical women and then demanded of the mother, "Did your husband have a rifle or any other guns besides the six-shooter we found him with?"

"I'll tell you nothing, you dirty murderer!" she sobbed while the young girl clung to her, speechless now with terror.

"If he did, we'll find it for ourselves, no matter. Now, *amigos,* two of you come with me, and we'll see if there are any other guns in this place. As for the rest of you, do you fancy these two *mujeres?*"

Porfirio Costado, who had by now come round to the front and entered through the open door, guffawed and nodded: "*¡Sí, seguro, mi jefe! ¡Son muy lindas!*"

"Then amuse yourselves with them. Come, Augusto, and you, Luis. Let's see what we can find in this place."

The mother and daughter shrieked and tried to struggle as the leering *pistoleros* slowly approached them. Two of them seized the mother and flung her down on the couch, another two seized the daughter and dragged her in front of the fireplace, pulled her down onto the floor and began to strip her. From the couch, there rose the frantic supplication, "Oh, God, not my little girl! Take me, don't touch her, I beg of you—I'll do what you want, just let her be—oh no—stop it—aaaah!"

The lean Kansas desperado glanced cynically toward the two agonized victims, then he and his two cohorts began a methodical search of the house. In the closet of the bedroom, Augusto found an old Henry rifle, and Brundiger ordered, "That's a good one, *hombre.* Go outside and put it near our horses. When you come back, you'll have your turn with them, and you too, Luis." Then to Luis, he said, "Now let's have a looksee in the barn. Maybe we'll find a couple of good horses there. Bouchard isn't the only one who can have a remuda for himself. *¿No es verdad?*"

"*Pero sí, mi jefe,*" Luis Aldemar, a scar-faced former peon from Chihuahua who had murdered his master and fled across the border, grinningly agreed.

Unperturbed by the shrieks and desperate plaints of the two naked, ravished women, Brundiger and Aldeman went out to the barn, where they found two good saddle horses. "Tether them to your own mustang, Luis," Brundiger directed. "This is a good start for our living off the land. And don't forget the cattle in that stall at the end there. We'll have plenty of meat."

"We stay here for a time, then, *jefe?*" Aldemar asked.

"A couple of days, sure. We'll slaughter the heifer and have a feast tomorrow night. We'll take what meat we want with us. It'll do us fine till we find another place like this to hole up in."

"It gives me much pleasure to work for such a *jefe*," Luis Aldemar complimented the Kansan. "Why should we not keep all our horses in this good barn, since we are going to stay the night?" This with a lecherous snigger.

"Not a bad idea, Luis. Keep it up, and you'll earn yourself a little more *dinero* when we hit Abilene. All right. Have some of the men bring in our horses, and don't forget that rifle Augusto put out there. Then you can have your fun."

Before the night was over, the mother and the daughter had been violated by all of the *pistoleros*. The daughter, who had fainted, was carried to the bedroom and rudely tossed onto the bed, while the mother was obliged to go to the kitchen and there prepare a meal for her husband's murderers.

All through the next day, the *pistoleros* worked slaughtering the heifer, the cows, and the bull and preparing some of the meat to be dried for jerky. That night, they had a feast on the fresh beef, washed down with swigs from the bottles of tequila which they had brought with them in their saddle packs. And a second night of agony began for the mother and daughter.

In the morning, Brundiger and his men rode out of the barn. At his order, all three survivors had been shot to death and buried under the ground in the barn, along with the body of the husband. As he peered back to the south whence he had come, the Kansan called, "*¡Adelante, hombres!* Now we'll see what Mineral Wells has to offer."

CHAPTER THIRTY-FIVE

This was by far the largest herd that Lucien Edmond Bouchard had ever driven to market, and he had rightly anticipated that he would do well to average five or six miles a day. From previous experiences, he knew that he must allow time for the inevitable stampedes, dust or wind storms, as well as for the fording of three rivers which he would cross on the trail to Abilene: the placid and shallow San Antonio, the surging Colorado, and the always unpredictable Red River on whose other side Indian Territory began. It was a trail of more than eight hundred arduous miles, with many hazards, some already known from previous encounters, others as yet incalculable. His greatest concern, however, was that with the drive starting so late and with new ranchers offering more competition (especially in the Panhandle region of Texas), his herd might come too late to Joseph McCoy's market to earn the top dollar for which he hoped.

He was already thinking of how that money would be spent. Perhaps Ed Dade, Chicago's buyer for Armour, would give him as much as ten dollars a head. That would be about forty thousand dollars, assuming he did not lose too many cattle in stampedes or, as had happened last year, run into a herd of buffalo to which many of his cows would be attracted and be impossible to round up. Of that sum, he was calculating that five thousand dollars would be needed to buy Robert Caldemare's land in Austin, and he intended to let Joe Duvray manage it for Margaret Caldemare. Eventually Joe would earn title when he repaid the loan. It was a sound investment, Lucien Edmond knew: his western boundaries would be protected by so loyal an ally and neighbor as Joe Duvray. And because Joe thought as he did about cattle, they could interbreed and experiment with continually stronger stock until one day

Windhaven Range might well be one of the richest cattle ranches in all of Texas.

He foresaw that the ranch house itself could be remodeled and strengthened, a necessary step because the last several winters had been more than moderately severe. There could be more comforts for Maxine and the children, and for Mother Sybella—as he always thought of valiant, white-haired Sybella Forsden—one of those new-fangled sewing machines about which she had read in a New Orleans newspaper. The bunkhouse would have to be remodeled, too, since there were now more vaqueros, both on the trail with him and back guarding the ranch house. Better quarters for the hard-working men and some comforts for them, too. Cottages instead of dugouts for Eddie Gentry and Simata, the half-breed scout who now rode ahead of this vast herd of cattle.

Of course more Brahmas would also be needed, perhaps two more bulls and eight heifers, and one of the bulls would go to Joe Duvray along with two of the heifers. A few more Herefords, also, since Lucien Edmond could already see the result of their crossbreeding with the long-horns. There had been no epidemic this spring, not a trace of the ticks which had plagued so many herds and which, indeed, had caused such bloody controversy when the first Texas ranchers tried to drive their cattle to Sedalia or Baxter Springs just after the Civil War. Thinking of the future, Lucien Edmond was certain that the railroads would be extended southward, as they had already been westward. Then the raising and shipping of cattle would be, to some extent, a business with a minimum of hazards and risks. The happy days of the trail, dangerous at times but usually carefree, a life that appealed especially to those who had not known the joy of homes or loved ones, would become a virtual legend of the past. The cattle would be branded and delivered right into the boxcars of the railroad line, perhaps at as short a distance as ten or twenty miles.

Yes, all of this was quite possible, with the tremendous industrial expansion that had begun in the East and the Midwest now slowly spreading South and West. The frontiers were gradually being pushed back. Adventure, triumph over hardship, initiative—these attributes which were so rewarding, so soul-satisfying when a man began humbly

334

on land and toiled to make it prosper, might be consigned to the romantic pages of history. There would be a sadness to this even with the greater profits to be garnered, Lucien Edmond thought to himself. And he knew that his father, with his own keen eye to the future and his understanding of the foibles of his neighbors and his enemies, must think as he did about what the future would hold for the Bouchards.

There would be wealth, perhaps more wealth than old Lucien had ever dreamed of having. With it would come more cares and responsibilities, and also the danger of corruption through wealth and power. Yet Lucien Edmond did not think—knowing his father as he did and how well his father had profited from old Lucien's credo of the rewarding life—that he himself or Luke would ever be tempted by the sin of greed or the lust for power. He guessed that Robert Caldemare had been driven by greed and had paid for it with his life. And he told himself that Carla and Hugo and little Edwina would grow up inculcated with his belief in hard work, honesty, and, above all else, family loyalty. These virtues would withstand the vicissitudes of time.

He did not know why suddenly his mind had turned so intensely to the future, or whether it was merely a vague presentiment of the troubling and still unanswered question that Robert Caldemare's boundary-changing tactics had posed. He had asked Simata to watch for the marks of the horses' hooves which the scout had first seen leading to the northwest, because the hasty departure of Caldemare's main body of *pistoleros* was, he was convinced, tied up with that same singular question. He did not know what all this portended, only that there had been, thus far, the ruthless murder of his newest and youngest vaquero, the death of the foreman who had killed him, and the death of Robert Caldemare himself. But the one thing Lucien Edmond could count on was that Caldemare's land was now being safeguarded by Joe Duvray and some of his most trusted men, and that eventually that land could become a valuable adjunct to Windhaven Range itself.

When the outfit made camp at night, Lucien Edmond spent a good deal of time with his brother-in-law, Ramón Hernandez, as well as with Djamba and Lucas. Ramón had brought a fine remuda along on this drive, having learned much from last year's demands on the trail. The handsome young Mexican had himself broken in and trained a dozen good geldings which could be trusted in work at close quarters with restless, even stampeding cattle. These horses could stop in their tracks at command so that a thrown lariat might bring back a recalcitrant stray. Lives depended on the trustworthiness of the horses and on their ability to follow commands at a moment's notice; Ramón had indeed done his work well.

Lucien Edmond found himself drawn closer to Djamba than he had ever been before. There was a dignity to the white-haired Mandingo, and although he showed unflagging enthusiasm for the long, monotonous days along the trail, he seemed more quiet now, more pensive, as if he were thinking of the past when Henry Bouchard had bought him on the New Orleans auction block from Pierre Lourat. Djamba had been destined to become a boxer who would win his master acclaim and money, but when Henry Bouchard had died of a heart attack, Djamba had been freed by Sybella Bouchard. She had freed Celia, too, the mulatto beauty whom her dissolute husband Henry had also purchased from the Creole slave dealer and intended for his own lustful bed. Djamba and Celia had married with Sybella's enthusiastic sponsorship. Those manumissions had earned the undying devotion and loyalty of the Mandingo and his wife, and they had unhesitatingly volunteered to follow Sybella to Texas after the chateau had been set afire by raiding Union troops. During that raid, Sybella's second husband, Matthew Forsden, first overseer for the widowed Sybella Bouchard and then her husband, had been shot down by one of the Union cavalry. And the son of Sybella and Matthew Forsden, Paul, had died gallantly at the Battle of Shiloh at the tragically early age of twenty-three.

Lucien Edmond found himself thinking a good deal of Sybella this humid May evening as the men made camp. It was as natural for him to call her grandmother as for his father, Luke, to call her mother, even though she had actually been Luke's stepmother. What an amazing woman she was and what a demanding life she had lived, equal to all its challenges! Now sixty-eight, she had married Henry Bouchard when she had been not quite seventeen. She had coped with his infidelities and temper and greed,

336

helped Luke run Windhaven Plantation after Henry's death, known the double tragedy of losing her second husband and their only son. And then, with the radiant optimism of a young woman, she had stood beside Luke and quelled the fears of all the others in urging them to seek a new life in Texas, a new beginning for the Bouchards.

Lucien Edmond remembered how Sybella, on that long wagon trip across Texas to Carrizo Springs, had killed a Mexican guerrilla and wounded two others, including the leader of the band who had sought to ambush the wagon train. And when Carlos Macaras (the brother of that leader under whom Ramón Hernandez had once served in the belief that he was aiding the cause of Benito Juarez), led an attack against Windhaven Range, Sybella Forsden again acquitted herself with the valor of a soldier on the front lines. No wonder Luke adored her, as he himself did. And it was Djamba who was the most devoted of all to her, appreciating what she had done to give him back the freedom he had once known as a young king among his people, betrayed by his weak brother and the latter's evil wife who had arranged to sell him and his bride Itulde into slavery. He put his hand on Djamba's shoulder and said gently, "How goes it, old friend?"

"Not badly at all, Mr. Lucien Edmond," the Mandingo smilingly replied. "You hired a good cook. Even though the men miss Pablo, I think they are quite happy with Tiburcio. He makes a very good stew, and he's learned to ask Simata to look for wild onions the way my wife Celia did that first trip we all made together."

"Yes, three years ago, when we sold our very first cattle in Santa Fe," Lucien Edmond mused. "I'm sorry we had to start so late this year. Because we've so many cattle this time, it might be well into the middle of August or even longer before we reach Abilene."

"That's all right, Mr. Lucien Edmond," Djamba chuckled, "this kind of work makes me young again, keeps my mind sharp. Besides, I've got my boy Lucas along, and his old father has to keep up with him if he's still to respect me and not because of my white hair."

"That's so," Lucien Edmond assented. "Lucas, I'm afraid we won't get back in time for you to see your first child. I'm sorry about that."

"It isn't your fault, Mr. Bouchard," Lucas grinned. "I

337

know Felicidad would want me there, but there's work to be done here. Besides, it'll make me work just that much harder to get these cattle sold for you and then to head home and see my son—I'm sure it's going to be one, she's promised it to me."

"She's a mighty good girl, Mr. Lucien Edmond," Djamba beamed. "She's sweet and she's brave, just like Mrs. Forsden."

"Yes. You know, Djamba, I think it was a wonderful thing for grandmother to give you her name so that you could have that bank account in San Antonio. It was a sign of how much she respected you and wanted to thank you for your loyalty all these years. And I thank you, too, for my own sake; you've been a godsend to us every time you've ridden along."

"That's kind of you to say, Mr. Lucien Edmond," the Mandingo lowered his eyes. "But it's my duty. Your father saved my life once, and you saved it when we were attacked by the Kiowa Apaches. I told you then that I swore to be your man to the end of my days. And I'm your grandmother's man, too, from long ago. She gave me back my freedom, you know."

"Yes, Djamba, I was thinking about it just tonight. It all comes back this evening now, as if all of us suddenly were handed a book with the pages of our days described in them and given a chance to see what we've accomplished up to now," Lucien Edmond slowly said. "Maybe what we learn is that, if we get too proud of ourselves for thinking we've done a lot, we have to remember there are still many unfilled pages ahead of us." He turned and walked back on the chuck wagon where Tiburcio was offering seconds on stew and more steaming hot coffee for anyone who wanted it. "That was a fine stew tonight, Tiburcio," he told the genial cook, who grinned and bobbed his head in pleased acknowledgment of the compliment. "I'll have just a little more coffee, *por favor*."

"*Sí, patrón. ¡Muchas gracias!*"

"*De nada, amigo*," Lucien Edmond nodded his thanks and went back to Djamba and Lucas and Ramón. "Yes, Tiburcio is doing just fine. We took enough supplies along this time. And a little extra for Emataba and his Creeks when we get into Indian Territory. But do you think we

338

should make a stop, say in Mineral Wells, and pick up a few more staples?"

"I think we can manage, Lucien Edmond," Ramón spoke up. "We're likely to find plenty of wild berries, onions, maybe even vegetables this time of year. And we've plenty of beans and molasses and flour for at least the next three or four weeks. Tiburcio took his duties as cook very seriously and made sure that the vaqueros loaded plenty of supplies into that chuck wagon of his."

"That's a good man. Well, I hope we can do better than five miles a day, or we might find the big cattle buyers gone by the time we hit Abilene," Lucien Edmond worried.

"We could always send Simata on ahead of us to let Joseph McCoy know we were coming with the biggest herd we've had so far, Lucien Edmond," Ramón suggested.

"That's a fine idea, Ramón! Yes, we'll do just that. Well, I don't feel sleepy, thanks to this good strong coffee—I'd like to sit and chat—unless you fellows want to hit your blankets."

"Not I," Ramón chuckled.

"I'm in the mood to talk too, Mr. Lucien Edmond," Djamba smiled. Then, with a broad wink at Lucas, "Of course, Mr. Lucien Edmond, this young whippersnapper here is really too young to have much to say, but we'll let him get a word in edgewise between his elders, won't we?"

"Daddy, you can be downright exasperating at times. Here I am a married man and about to be a father, and you think of me still as a little boy," Lucas pretended to complain, and there was laughter all around. Lucien Edmond felt the warm glow of friendship, a strengthening bond that was especially welcome at the start of so arduous a drive.

It took nine days more to reach the Colorado River, and already the weather had become humid and oppressive. Occasionally at night, there would be flashes of heat lightning and the deep rumble of thunder, always a frightening sound to men who had just bedded down a herd of cattle on level ground. Those who had worked with Lucien Edmond for the past three years knew only too well the danger of a stampede and how several of their *compadres* had lost their lives when their horses had thrown them under the pounding hooves of the maddened cattle. And, as before, there was a plague of heel flies which gathered in blackening swarms on the withers of cows, steers, and calves, maddening them into running toward the nearest water. Two cows headed for a shallow creek and were caught in a small bed of quicksand, and it took six vaqueros nearly an hour to free the hind legs of the trapped animals. Such irksome incidents only helped to slow the journey, so that Lucien Edmond found himself still averaging only about five to six miles a day.

Simata, who always rode ahead of the point men by at least a quarter of a mile to survey the terrain, had found an even better crossing than had been used last year. It was about three miles to the east, and shallower there, with good footing for cattle to right themselves as they emerged from the water and headed up the gently sloping bank to the plain beyond. There was thick grass along the bank, too, and after the cattle had drunk their fill, they grazed placidly while Lucien Edmond and his men stopped to enjoy coffee and a biscuit—for the night camp was still at least four hours away.

Once again the bond of comradeship, the reliance of one upon all the others, was vigorously forged by the sharing of hardships and dangers. There could be no petty differences among men who, a few moments later, might be called upon to save their comrades from quicksand or the sudden attack of a bushwhacking gang or the feverish rush of a stampede. It came to Lucien Edmond's mind each night as he made camp that, despite all his yearning for progress and for the railroads to deliver his cattle to market quickly, he would miss the old-fashioned cattle drive. Much of this warmth and closeness would be no more.

Simata continued to look for the tracks of Galdemare's *pistoleros,* but without success. Already Jackson Brundiger and his eleven ruthless companions had crossed the Colorado at a point some fives miles east of where Lucien Edmond had forded his herd and had ridden back and forth, doubling over their trail to avoid detection by any possible pursuers. They had, by this time, come to Mineral Wells where they had found a little frame house occupied by two brothers and their wives, had murdered the two men and then ravished the women, finally killing them and taking along as booty a hidden cache of two thousand dollars in gold and four sturdy horses. They had renewed their supply of meat and also of jerky by slaughtering two cows they found in the nearby barn with the horses, and they acquired the two Henry rifles and ammunition which the brothers had not been able to use in time to defend themselves during the sudden night attack on the little house.

Between the Colorado River, where Lucien Edmond and his men and the herd had crossed, and Mineral Wells lay a distance of almost two hundred miles. It took the Bouchard outfit a month to cross this stretch of the plains. During that month, the men encountered no real difficulties, though during the first week some of the cows ran off to a small herd of buffalo, and it took half a day to track them down and bring them back. The men's spirits were high, for Lucien Edmond had promised them a substantial bonus in Abilene. All those riders who had made the three trips to that bustling Kansas market would be given an additional fifty dollars apart from the general bonus awarded all the vaqueros who safely arrived in Abilene with this record herd. And Lucien Edmond was confident that there would be no encounters with Indian hostiles. The influential and greatly feared word of the Comanche chief Sangrodo had by now traveled like wildfire throughout all of Texas and Indian Territory. And part of that safeguard was Sangrodo's reminder how Luke Bouchard had befriended the mighty, aging Kiowa chief Setangya, who had given him what he had given no other white man: the wampum belt of lasting friendship.

By the end of June, Lucien Edmond and his men reached Mineral Wells and headed northwest toward Wichita Falls, Texas, to replenish their supplies of flour, bacon, beans, molasses, and coffee, to be certain to have plenty during the remainder of the more than four-hundred-mile journey. They had, as was their wont, avoided the towns and thus they had no way of knowing what had happened at San Marcos or Mineral Wells. Moreover, since Jackson Brundiger's desperados had buried their victims without a trace, and since the latter lived well outside of the towns and rarely visited their neighbors, there was no reason to suspect foul play. Indeed, even if foul play had been discovered, there were no lawmen to pursue the malefactors.

Ramón Hernandez was looking forward to Abilene this

time, because in that herd were a hundred of his own cattle—yearlings, steers, heifers, and cows, none older than four years. He himself had cut out of his small but thriving herd all stockers, scrubby calves, and yearlings, as well as older, leaner steers. If, as Lucien Edmond believed, ten dollars a head would be the prevailing rate offered by the Chicago buyer, Ramón could look forward to $500 to spend on gifts for Mara and his two little sons. He thought of her each time they made camp, of what a loving and devoted wife and companion she had become, yet still capable of fierce, youthful passion which was a foil to his own. Their courtship had been stormy, and yet its very hardship and the difference between them in background and race had seemed to solidify their union. What delighted him most was Lucien Edmond's wholehearted acceptance of him as a brother-in-law and a trusted friend in whom he could confide without stint. During these years on Windhaven Range, the young Mexican had come to understand the deep-rooted loyalty of the Bouchards and to prize his entry into that distinguished dynasty.

Out here on the plains, where the grazing land became more abundant as they moved farther north, there was no news of the outside world. These men knew only the long hours in the saddle, requiring constant alertness for the slightest sign of trouble. Meanwhile, back East, Congress had just passed the Enforcement Act whose purpose was to make the Fifteenth Amendment binding, a further evidence of the North's unrelenting suppression of the conquered South. At the same time, the Senate was considering—and would approve—a convention for the suppression of the African slave trade which had just been concluded with Great Britain. President Grant announced in his special message to Congress that the United States would maintain a strict non-intervention policy in the Cuban rebellion. There was also talk that the president was trying to get rid of Attorney General Hoar in an effort to get votes for the annexation of Santo Domingo.

It was a hundred miles from Mineral Wells to Wichita Falls, via the northwest route, but this stretch of the trail seemed easier and there were no delays. Leaving the herd on the eastern outskirts of the thriving little town, Lucien Edmond and five of his men, who drove the extra wagon which had been brought along for the storage of supplies, entered Wichita Falls. Within half a day they completed their purchases and returned to the trail. It had taken ten days to reach Wichita Falls, an average of ten miles per day, which greatly heartened Lucien Edmond. There would be several days lost, he realized, in resuming the original northward trail to Abilene, but with pleasant weather and no stampedes, he hoped to reach the Red River sometime during the first week of July. After the crossing, he intended to send Simata on ahead to Abilene in the hope of either encountering one of Joseph McCoy's circuit riders or, if need be, advising McCoy himself that the Bouchard herd was on the way, the largest yet and of prime quality for the market.

Ten miles north of Wichita Falls, during the second afternoon after the procurement of supplies, Simata galloped back to Lucien Edmond to tell him that the skies to the northeast were ominously black and that the wind for miles around seemed suddenly to have hushed. There was a kind of unearthy calm. Lucien Edmond ordered his vaqueros to bed the cattle in a huge, dry ravine which had long ago been a wide creek. The air was ominously still, and at four in the afternoon the skies beyond them were terrifyingly dark. Djamba and Lucas, working together, raced their geldings alongside fractious steers and cows, turning them down toward the ravine till at last most of the herd milled and lowed in the wide enclosure which would be an asylum against the coming wind.

Lucas uttered a cry and pointed ahead as a dark funnel seemed to grow from the base of the horizon and rise toward them. The men dismounted and flung themselves down on the edge of the ravine, pressing themselves against the ground as flat as they could. Then there was a savage whining noise, and with it driving bits of fine sand which nearly blinded the men who hugged their sombreros over their faces and gulped in as much air as they could to prepare for the sudden onset of this cyclone.

The funnel suddenly veered to the southwest half a mile before it reached the Bouchard men and their cattle. The grass beyond them was flattened, and there were scores of massive tumbleweeds gathering momentum and dashing about helter-skelter. There was a low rumble of thunder, and a sudden flash of lightning zigzagged across the black sky, and then the cyclone swept beyond them. As if by a miracle, the sky to the north of them suddenly cleared, the whistling, biting bits of sand diminished, and there was a quiet to the air such as they hoped for at a calm twilight.

Choking on the dust, Lucien Edmond raised his head and saw Djamba and Lucas a few feet away from him, their arms round each other, and he wanly smiled and said, "That was too close for comfort."

"In my country long ago," the white-haired Mandingo hoarsely called back, "such a storm as this meant that there were evil spirits lurking and waiting for us. Now they have disappeared, and it is a good sign."

"Thank God for that!" Lucien Edmond breathed. "And the herd—I can't believe it, but there hasn't been any panic or a stampede!"

"I know, Mr. Lucien Edmond, it's a miracle," Djamba called back. "If I were a betting man, I wouldn't have a penny left in my wages. The herd is still mighty restless, but they'll calm down pretty soon."

"That's a relief. Djamba, get some of the men to lead them out slowly and to soothe them as much as you can. I can see level ground ahead to the northeast. Let's head for there and make camp. Then have one of the men sing to them. Last year, we quieted them down with some music at night, but so far we haven't had any of that."

"I think Pedro Dornado brought along his guitar, Mr. Lucien Edmond," Lucas volunteered.

"That's exactly what we need right now. See if you can get to him and tell him to sing some of those lullabies. And I'm saying prayers there won't be a repetition of this cyclone. We've been very lucky so far, Lucas," Lucien Edmond exclaimed.

"That's for certain, Mr. Lucien Edmond," Djamba's handsome son retorted with a wry grin. "If we're just as lucky when we get to the Red River, this will be a drive we can tell our grandchildren about."

"And you'll have lots of them, boy, I feel it in my bones," the white-haired Mandingo said to his son as he patted him on the shoulder. "I've got a feeling you'll have a fine son by the time you get back to Windhaven Range, and you'll still be a mighty powerful man by the time that son's ready to take a wife. Only I've got a feeling I won't be around to see all that, Lucas."

"Now look here, don't you go on talking like that," Lucas said. "The way you ride all day long, I get more tuckered out than you do after a hard day, and you know how much younger I am. No, I just bet you'll still be around at the christening of my grandson and a long while after that, too!"

Djamba smiled and, raising himself from the ground, stared at the distant horizon to the north. "No, boy," he said in a low voice after a moment. "I've got a feeling that the good Lord is just about ready to bring me to Him. But He's going to leave you behind for a good long while, Lucas boy. And you'll have lots more sons by that sweet Felicidad of yours, you wait and see if you don't."

Lucas stared curiously at his father, then at Lucien Edmond, then shook his head. "No sense in what you're saying to me. I'm going to pretend I didn't even hear it. Now let's go move those cattle to the camp. Shucks, you're going to be along on a lot more drives with me, and you're going to be telling me what I'm doing wrong each time. You know you always do, Dad."

CHAPTER THIRTY-SIX

After their brutal attack on the isolated family near Mineral Wells, Jackson Brundiger and his eleven *pistoleros* had moved fifty miles northeast near the little town of Graham. From there, after camping out on the prairie for nearly a week, whiling away the time with playing cards and throwing dice and amusing themselves with occasional target practice, they rode northeast in the direction of Bowie, about sixty miles from the Red River.

Brundiger had estimated that Lucien Edmond Bouchard and his vaqueros and the herd would be from five to six weeks behind them, and as part of his original plan to ambush them, he intended to quarter his band of desperados in the house of some isolated settler, then send some of his men southward as scouts to locate the Bouchard outfit. Luck was with him. Ten miles east of Bowie, late one night in the last week of May, he and his men came upon a newly painted frame house built near the base of a gently rolling slope and shaded on each side by a copse of small cedar and live oak trees. Nearby were a barn and a small bunkhouse. It was the property of a fifty-year-old Tennesseean who, as a captain in the Confederate Army, had been wounded several times and decorated for valor. He had moved out to north Texas a month after Appomattox with his wife and two daughters and his hoarded stake of three thousand dollars in gold. He had chosen the vicinity of Bowie because an older cousin of his had moved there before the Civil War and enthusiastically written to him that on this new frontier, there would be no problem with freed blacks or restrictive laws, and that land was cheap and cattle easy to raise.

For the past four years, Anson Ketteridge had driven a herd of cattle to market, beginning with a hundred head.

Just two weeks ago he and his five hardworking and loyal Mexican vaqueros had started for Abilene with over four hundred. Two other vaqueros had been left back in the bunkhouse to guard his forty-three-year-old wife Julia and his daughters, Millicent and Phillippa, nineteen and seventeen.

Jackson Brundiger ordered his *pistoleros* to tether their horses well out of sight and then sent five of them creeping toward the bunkhouse while he and the other six approached the frame house in which no lights were showing. It was a humid night, sultry and without the least stirring of wind, and the silence and darkness benefitted the ambushers. Porfirio Costado, beckoning to Luis Aldemar, cautiously tried the door of the bunkhouse, found it open and crouched low, drawing his six-shooter as did his companion. As the door swung back, it admitted a dim light into the bunkhouse. One of the Mexican vaqueros, hearing the door creek, mumbled in his sleep and raised himself to a sitting position in his bunk. Porfirio at once pulled the trigger. The vaquero slumped back with a bullet in his heart. The other vaquero, roused by the gunshot, uttered a cry and tried to scramble out of bed to reach his rifle, but Luis dropped him with two bullets.

"Bueno, Luis," Porfirio Costado said in a low voice. "This is very good. There are no other *hombres* here. It is my thought that the rest of them have gone to drive the *ganado.* It will be easy for the *jefe* and *mis amigos* to get into the house. Who knows, there may be señoritas there to amuse us while we wait patiently for *el Señor* Bouchard."

"That would be most enjoyable, Porfirio," Luis Aldemar grinned crookedly as he holstered his six-shooter, straightened, and groped his way into the bunkhouse. There was a small table at the very end and a kerosene lamp on it. Taking out his tinder, the swarthy Mexican struck a light and, when the lamp was lit, retrieved the rifle that the second vaquero had tried to reach. "This is a good one, I have seen this kind used in Jalisco and Nuevo Laredo," he proclaimed as he held it up for Porfirio's inspection. "And here is a box of ammunition for it. It is a very good start we have made this evening, *no es verdad,* Porfirio?"

"Sí, hombre," the horse thief chuckled. "But do not also

347

forget to see if the first one I killed has a rifle or a *pistola,* too. The *jefe* has told us that the more extra guns we have when we attack Bouchard at the *Río Rojo,* the easier it will be for us. For, you see, Luis, all these extra guns will be loaded, and we shall not have to waste time reloading ours when we have emptied them."

"Comprendo todo, Porfirio," Luis Aldemar chuckled as he callously rolled the dead vaquero off the bed and, thrusting his hand under the pillow, drew out an old Belgian pistol. "This is not a bad one, either. It kicks like a mule, but it is very accurate even at a good distance."

"You have done well, Luis. I will tell the *jefe* that you have much intelligence. Perhaps," Porfirio sniggered, "he will give you an extra turn with the señoritas in that house, if there are any. Now let us search the rest of this bunkhouse and see if we can find anything that will be to our use. Ah," he turned toward the open door and put a hand to his ear, "the *jefe* is in the house already. Did you not hear that shot? Now it is time for us and our *compadres* to go see what treasures he has found there. *¡Vámanos!"*

The shot which the two *pistoleros* had heard had been fired by Julia Ketteridge. Having warily opened the door to Brundiger's knock, she had been flung back against the wall as he and two *pistoleros* entered. There had been a rifle in the corner near the door, and the tall woman had courageously seized it and fired off a shot. It had gone astray, and Brundiger had dashed the rifle out of her grip with a sweep of his left arm.

At first, Julia Ketteridge valiantly refused to give him any information about her husband and the latter's men who had ridden to Abilene. But when Brundiger had her two daughters dragged out of their beds, brought into the living room wearing only their nightshifts, and threatened with a flogging by his men, Julia admitted that there were no other men to guard the house and that her husband and the others would not return till at least the middle of July.

"That's perfect," Brundiger chuckled. "Well, ma'am, we'll just stay here for a spell then because we've got some time on our hands to kill. This is mighty comfortable, especially seeing that you don't have any nosy neighbors. And you needn't worry about being protected with your

348

man and his vaqueros away from home so long—we'll be on hand to give you all the protection we want."

At this cruel jibe, the Mexican *pistoleros* burst into salacious laughter and began to make lewd appraisals of the two terrified girls whom four of their colleagues held by the wrists.

Thus began six weeks of indescribable wretchedness for Julia Ketteridge and her daughters. The three women were compelled to prepare meals for the *pistoleros* and were forced to submit to their lusts almost without respite. The handsome mother actually went down on her knees before Jackson Brundiger to beg tearfully that her daughters be spared, avowing that she would willingly submit herself in their place. Her frantic plea drew only coarse jeers from the *pistoleros*. At Brundiger's sign, Julia was tied to the chair and compelled to watch her two daughters being stripped naked and violated before her eyes. Then she, in her turn, was stripped and passed from man to man.

When Julia's two young daughters hysterically pleaded to be left alone after several men had already violated them, or, in the nights that followed, sought to minimize their own agony and shame by closing their eyes and offering not the slightest cooperation to their ravishers, they were dragged out to the bunkhouse, there tied by their wrists to a post, and given the quirt until they hysterically promised to do whatever was demanded of them. And, as a further guarantee of their total submission, the vicious Kansan informed Julia that if her daughters did not continue to satisfy his men throughout their stay in the house, they would be killed when the *pistoleros* finally left.

Brundiger was supremely satisfied with the way his plan was working out. The Ketteridge house was a perfect hideout. There was an abundance of food, for there were over twenty calves and some fifteen yearlings which Anson Ketteridge had left behind to fatten when he had taken his herd to Abilene. The presence of three attractive and thoroughly subjugated women further insured that his men would be well satisfied, well rested, and well fed—eager to ambush the weary Bouchard outfit when the latter came in sight of the Red River.

At the end of June, Brundiger sent out three of his *pistoleros* to ride southward to catch sight of the oncoming

349

Bouchard herd. Lucien Edmond Bouchard and his men had turned eastward from Wichita Falls after getting their supplies, and were heading toward the area of Gainesville, which was at about the locale where they had crossed the swelling river three years before. Simata had been sent ahead to learn the river's level at this point and, if it proved to be too high for a safe crossing, to seek a shallower fording.

It was Diego Suarez who rode back on the second day of July, his horse heaving and lathered with foam, with the news that he had seen in the far distance the long line of Bouchard cattle some fifteen miles to the south. Brundiger's eyes blazed with a cold, cruel eagerness as he gave his orders: "We'll pull out tomorrow morning, then cross the river near Dennison. I recall from my old days with Jethro Reedy that there's a big wood about five hundred yards north of the river bank. We'll hole up there and send out scouts to see exactly where Bouchard tries to cross. Wherever he does, we'll be ready for him."

The grinning *pistoleros* hurried to pack their gear and to inspect the rifles and guns they had stolen along their murderous trail. Porfirio Costado and two of his compatriots busied themselves with readying the horses they had stolen. Paco Ruberoso would ride his gelding and lead them. Two others took charge of packing provisions including some fresh meat, flour, coffee, and molasses which they had garnered from the Ketteridge larder.

Julia Ketteridge, black-haired Millicent, and the russet-haired, slim Philippa had been herded into Anson Ketteridge's bedroom. Listless, haggard, all but naked—as they had been forced to remain all these atrocious harrowing weeks—they sobbed softly, believing that at last their ordeal would be at an end. Luis Aldemar guarded the door of the room in which they were incarcerated and, as Jackson Brundiger approached, the Mexican muttered, "It's a shame, *mi jefe*, we can't take them with us. My *compadres* have grown very fond of them."

"They'll only be in the way. And you don't expect me to leave them here to tell the husband what's been happening while he was selling his herd in Abilene, do you?" Brundiger sarcastically retorted. He made a gesture, and Aldemar moved away from the door. The Kansan opened it, drew both his six-shooters and, without a flicker of emotion on his lean face, killed all three with two bullets apiece. Then, turning on his heel, he called back over his shoulder, "Bury them in the barn and make sure the graves can't be seen. As soon as you finish that, we'll ride out."

CHAPTER THIRTY-SEVEN

This June of 1870 had been unbearably hot, the temperature staying well over a hundred degrees till sundown, though the nights were pleasantly cool. There had been only an inch of rain since February, but Windhaven Range did not lack for water, thanks to the underground well and spring and the plentiful supply from both the creek and the slowly moving Nueces River. The mesquite flourished, even more abundantly than it had since the Bouchards had come to Carrizo Springs, and there were many patches of prickly pears and cactus, and thickets of cenizo sage. The bluebonnets and the orange blossoms which perfumed the air had never been more profuse or lovelier, and Maybelle Belcher was ecstatic over her little garden of tomato plants, strawberries, and okra. Felicidad was growing close to her time, and her spirits were bright and eager as she prayed in the little chapel each night that her Lucas might return to her in time to see the birth of his son. And Maxine Bouchard was pregnant, too, a fact she had known two weeks before Lucien Edmond had led his riders out on the long trail to Abilene.

There was news from across the border, too, for one of Sangrodo's braves had ridden up to the stockade just last week with the news that Prissy's baby daughter was doing well, and that Catayuna, the beloved wife of Sangrodo, was with child again. Celia, who had learned enough Comanche to be able to converse understandably, eagerly brought the brave, Mintagre, into the kitchen and stuffed him with beef and biscuits and coffee while she pried from him such tidbits of gossip concerning her daughter as he was able to recall. Amusingly, he spoke of Kitante, Sangrodo's oldest son, now nearly fifteen, and how, seeing the attention given to the little Inokanti, he had begun to feel unimportant. Mintagre, his face solemn but his tone droll, related what Catayuna had said: "But, Kitante, do not be so disappointed. Why, you will be like a wise uncle to your baby brother. You know so much and you are so skillful with a bow and arrow and a lance, that you are almost a warrior now. You see, Kitante, you must help me guide Inokanti to become as fine a young man as you are now." And the brave added, "Aiyee, we did not dare laugh when we saw Kitante walking about the stronghold with his chest puffed out like a bullfrog, feeling himself almost the equal of our mighty Sangrodo. But it is good that a boy takes responsibilities, for one day Kitante may be chief."

Celia had found this Texas summer more oppressive than those in the past, and she had lost weight, but she retained reasonably good health. She was more concerned over Sybella Forsden. At sixty-eight, this white-haired lady was still alert and enthusiastic over the daily events at Windhaven Range. Yet Celia did not like the signs she had perceived in her these past several weeks: an occasional listlessness, even a kind of shortness of breath. Sybella would have indignantly railed at her if such concern had been made obvious, but Celia had always been the very soul of diplomacy and subtle respect for the woman who had given her her freedom.

But Sybella herself was aware that her health was beginning to fail. Two nights ago, she had had a sharp chest pain which had made her sit up in bed, sweating profusely, gritting her teeth against the sudden stab of it. Then it had lulled and finally vanished, but she had lain for more than an hour, unable to go back to sleep till at last sheer exhaustion claimed her. She would not dream of telling Maxine or Celia or Maybelle either; after all, she told herself, at sixty-eight a body's expected to have pains, and there's no reason to go worrying your loved ones every time you have a little annoyance.

She had never feared death, and she did not think of it now. The pain had been swift and, for a moment, excruciating, and then it had passed as if nothing were alien with her body. She remembered the throbbing of the shoulder wound when the renegade buffalo hunters had invaded the ranch house and, just as Maxine had shot the man with the carbine, his errantly thrown knife had pierced her flesh. Her mind went back to her marriage with Henry Bouchard and the anguish of soul it had so often cost her, as she learned to put up with his greed, his selfishness, and above all else, his infidelities. Those last had been condoned by the law of the times, since when a plantation owner coupled with a black or mulatto slave girl, it was considered proper and natural, and in no way destructive to the sanctity of a marriage between whites.

Yet, in a sense, Henry Bouchard's lustful trysts with his black concubines had hurt Sybella more than if he had had an affair with a woman of his own class. For his acts of rapacious conquest of a helpless human, bound by the strictures of slavery, had revealed a self-centered ruthlessness which all her courage and wit and womanliness had not really been able to overcome. Now, alone with her thoughts at night while the rest of the household slept, Sybella Forsden wryly recalled that kind of second honeymoon which she and Henry had had after his own son Mark had fought with him over the possession of young Celia and pushed him down a stairway so that he had broken his leg and been totally dependent upon her. Only then had she known for a brief time the peace and joy of being able to guide and influence her husband.

On this hot evening, hearing the crickets chirp outside her window and the soft chattering of the night birds, she smiled warmly as she thought of Luke and of his oldest son, Lucien Edmond. In many ways, she had felt that Luke was flesh of her very own flesh; he had been and would always be the son she had truly cherished even though she had only been his stepmother. And now, to see the tall, blond Lucien Edmond completely taking over the management of this growing cattle ranch, directing its destinies, and coping with its mounting problems was to feel a warm sense of accomplishment. The encouragement and the love she had shown young Luke Bouchard had, she was sure, guided him toward becoming the steadfast man he was and would always be. She was happy to think that he had found a new life with Laure, with new children to occupy his mind and his energies, so that he would not merely grow old but rather would stay alert and vigorous by giving these young children of his second marriage the same healthy outlook on life that he had given to Lucien, Ramón, and Mara.

There was comfort, too, in thinking of how her saucy, flirtatious daughter Arabella had come finally to the stage of a fulfilled and happy womanhood and motherhood, having learned for herself that a steadfast loyalty and companionable love is so often more rewarding than a brief, fiery passion which has no lasting warmth. And finally, as most frequently she had found herself doing during the past few months, Sybella thought of sweet, gentle Fleurette whose lifespan had been the shortest of all her children's (except, of course, Paul Forsden). In her short life, Fleurette had inspired a devotion and a love that would last all the rest of Dr. Ben Wilson's life and guide him through whatever crises he was destined to face. Fleurette had given the Quaker doctor these two wonderful grandchildren of hers, five-year-old Thomas and the two-year-old little girl whom her daughter had named after her, Sybella.

It had been a rich, good life, and the pain was part of it. It made the love and the knowledge of achievement and fulfillment all the dearer. There were so many memories, and lately they had begun to crowd back upon her, even back to that first day when her lawyer father, Grover Mason, had introduced her to the dynamic, black-haired young man, Henry Bouchard. She smiled to recall their wedding night and how shocked he had been to learn that she was no prim, terrified bride even though she had been a virgin. Even now, so many years after, she could still laugh softly to herself to recall how she had taken him aback and seemed actually to dictate to him the rules of conduct they would follow as man and wife. It had been a small triumph, one to cherish against the bad times. But most of all, there were the children and the knowledge of how they had turned out, with their lives still ahead of them and so many more joys and surprises—and perhaps even more children. It was a wonderful heritage for her to have come into the Bouchard family and herself to have conceived such descendants as Fleurette and Arabella. And yes, even unhappy, tragic Mark, whose hostility to his father had been that of a kind of blood rivalry which even her own wisdom and love had not been enough to overcome. She was glad that she had been able to help Mark's young abandoned wife, Maybelle, to take courage from her own example and to begin a new life here in Texas: now Maybelle Belcher, with her two stepchildren and her elderly but devoted husband was, at fifty, a happy woman who had regained her self-respect and her courage.

By the reckoning of time, Sybella had had a good, full life. What the pain in her chest portended, she did not much care. It would be good to have Ben back to look at her, perhaps, but she was not afraid. Perhaps it would be a good idea, though, to slacken her kitchen chores; she had always shown such industry around the ranch house, quite forgetting her years and her recent slackening of energy. But of course, when Felicidad gave birth to her child, and that would be by August for certain, she would doubtless have to replace Felicidad. So a little rest now would be a good idea.

Sybella Forsden closed her eyes and lay back on her pillow, listening for a moment to the songs of the night birds and to the chirping of the crickets. There was a stillness to the night so that these sounds were magnified as if, indeed, they conveyed all there was of the outside world to her ears. There were sweet sounds, sounds she could recall from the days at Windhaven Plantation when she would lie awake listening to the murmur of the Alabama River. She thought again of all the people she had known there, for she had never considered the blacks as slaves but rather as individuals whose lives were linked with hers: Ben and his son Thomas, wonderful old Mammy Clorinda, their first cook, and then Betty, and old Harry who had loved Betty so. And most of all Celia, who had been surreptitiously brought into the red-brick chateau as Henry Bouchard's fancy girl only to be ravished by precocious young Mark. And she remembered how she herself had entered Celia's room one night and found her husband Henry about to consummate his long-delayed lust for her. She would never forget how Henry, aghast that his own wife would dare interfere with what he considered his rights as a slave owner, had suffered a fatal heart attack and fallen dead upon the very bed on which he had attempted to subjugate the young mulatto girl.

And then there was Djamba, Djamba the powerful Mandingo, ever faithful and loyal, who had saved her life from that runaway horse when she had been so infuriated by Henry's refusal to free Celia that she had run out of the house in a fit of temper. And now Lucas, Djamba's handsome, dependable son, married to sweet Felicidad—oh, yes, she had known so many whose lives had mingled with hers and perhaps even been changed by her influence upon them. It was good to think about these things now. With a sigh of content, she closed her eyes and fell asleep.

Lucien Edmond Bouchard and his men had led the herd to within a mile of the mighty Red River by the late afternoon of July 6. The sun was setting, but they could still see that the waters of this always unpredictable river were at a moderate level. Here and there a white sandbar could be glimpsed. It was a heartening sight, indeed, after their long journey of over two months and more than four hundred miles. Yet thus far, luck had been with them. No rider had been injured, even in the frantic race after the cows which had ambled off to join the buffalo herd. They had seen no hostile Indians anywhere. The herd had been unusually docile with only a balky steer or cow at times upsetting the slowly flowing rhythm of that long processional along the trail.

"We'd best camp here, Ramón," the tall blond trail boss decided. "We took two days to ford with two thousand head of cattle, you'll remember, and this time we've twice as many. We'd best allow four days for it."

"That's very wise, Lucien Edmond. It was a good thing we found that creek this morning so the herd could water. Otherwise, they might be running now, and we'd have the devil's own time rounding them up. Some might even drown," the young Mexican averred.

"Unless Simata can find us a better crossing by tomorrow morning, we'll try this place," Lucien Edmond declared. "We were here three years ago, just at about this very place. It hasn't changed. Lonely and desolate and nothing in sight for miles. But at least there's been better grazing than last year. The cattle have filled out. Even those five hundred head of Mexican cattle we took for Miss Caldemare look better now than they did a few months ago."

"They do at that," Ramón concurred somewhat dubiously, "but don't count on getting a good price from Ed Dade on that lot. He might be a little wary of them because they're from Mexico and might carry the ticks everyone's so afraid of."

"Not this lot. We did a job of currying them before we let them mingle with our cattle, and you remember your-

357

self that we found almost no ticks," Lucien Edmond countered. "Don't you worry, we'll bring back a nice stake for Miss Caldemare and her future."

"With Joe Duvray, if things go as they should," Ramón smilingly added.

"Yes, I'm sure they care for each other. And I'm going to do everything I can to help them, first by buying that land in Austin and then transferring the deed over to Joe—that is, once Miss Caldemare decides to marry him. Ramón, that's an investment for our future on Windhaven Range. We don't have to worry any more about landgrabbers or tricksters like that baron, or a chip-on-the-shoulder sheep man like Andrew Moultrie. We'll be able to expand, to do more and more breeding to develop the very finest quality of beef on the American market. That's my dream, and all of you and Joe and Miss Caldemare will share in it."

"I'll have Simata ride down the bank eastward to see if he can find a shallower crossing for the morning," Ramón promised. "We're just a little past the town of Sherman now. Dennison, where we crossed last year, is about ten miles east. Maybe Simata will see that it's a better place than here. Meanwhile, I'll get the rest of the men to bed down the cattle and tell Tiburcio to start up the evening meal. We really worked today, Lucien Edmond."

"That's why we'll enjoy our supper all the more." Lucien Edmond dismounted from his gelding and stretched himself, glancing up at the sky. "Not a sign of rain or a storm, heaven be praised for that! I don't even want to think of what a stampede would mean where we are now. I'll join you at the chuck wagon in an hour."

Jackson Brundiger had ordered Luis Aldemar to ride east and Porfirio Costado to ride west along the opposite bank of the Red River to pinpoint the location of the Bouchard outfit. Having had the news that the Bouchard herd had left Wichita Falls, he and his men had crossed the river and made their camp in a dense copse of live oak and cedar trees on the northern bank about four miles northeast of where Lucien Edmond now stood conferring with his brother-in-law. Porfirio Costado sighted the bedded herd, saw the chuck wagon's fire and the vaqueros clustering at the back, impatient for the evening meal. With a

358

joyous oath, he galloped his horse back to the copse and reported what he had seen.

"Mi jefe," he excitedly volunteered, "why should we not attack them now while they sleep? We can kill them quickly and then we can round up their cattle."

"That's why you're not the boss of this outfit, Porfirio," the wiry Kansan drawled, his right hand edging toward his holster. "I'll give you a few good reasons right off. In the first place, they'll have lookouts posted during the night shifts. Any cattle man who wasn't born a fool would do that for starters. And they'd hear a splashing as we crossed the river and they'd wake up the rest of the outfit. Don't forget, they've got twice as many men as we do. We've got to take them by surprise. No, let them have tomorrow to drive as many of their cattle as they can across that damned river, because that'll be just that much less work for all of you to do. Then, just about the time the sun's going down, when they're tired from a hard day of fording, we'll move in and hit them. We'll have a stampede, but the cattle will be headed toward Abilene. If you did it now, like as not they'd turn around and go back south or maybe west or east. Cattle haven't got any brains in a stampede. So use yours, Porfirio, and we'll do just fine."

"Sí, mi jefe."

"We'll have a good feed and a good sleep and we'll be ready by tomorrow at sundown," Brundiger grimly repeated, slapping his holstered gun. "And what you do first off tomorrow after breakfast, Porfirio, is to get all your *amigos* to carry rifles, with the six-shooters shared with all the men, understand? We've picked up plenty of holsters, and you'll have your *amigos* strap on at least a pair apiece, and keep the rest in your saddlebags so when you're out of ammunition on a rifle or a six-shooter, you won't waste any time reloading. And just you make sure that all those guns have as many bullets as they'll take."

"Understood, *mi jefe*." Porfirio gave him a respectful salute with the back of his hand to his head and hurried off to his compatriots.

The sun was pitiless all that next day, and Lucien Edmond Bouchard's vaqueros were bone-weary as they forded the huge herd. Simata had found a crossing two miles east which seemed even shallower, and it had been an excellent choice. The men rode carefully, calling out and waving their sombreros to keep the herd in formation. Now and again a young cow or a steer would panic and flounder, and it would take the skill of the mounted vaqueros to guide the errant animal across to the waiting bank. The slope there was not excessive, and the cattle had good footing to reach the top where there was abundant grass to graze. As the sun began to set, Lucien Edmond turned to Ramón and exclaimed, "It's gone better than I'd hoped, Ramón. I'd say we've forded fifteen hundred head already. Maybe we can do the job in three days instead of four. That'll be a blessing indeed. And don't forget we want to spend a day at Emataba's village. I'm anxious to see Dr. Ben Wilson again and tell him how well his children are doing and how we all wish him the very best in his fine work."

"I, also, Lucien Edmond. Well, I'll tell the other vaqueros to hold back the rest of the herd and to try to bed them down. We'll keep ten men on this side of the bank and the rest of them with the balance of the herd, do you agree?"

"That should do," Lucien Edmond slowly conceded, glancing up and down the river in the hazy twilight. "The sky still promises good weather for the rest of our crossing. I'm grateful for that. Well, as to supper, the men on the northern bank will just have to wait until the others here with the cattle and the chuck wagon have their meal, and then these men will cross over to replace them. We'd best explain it to them so there's no grumbling. I know how tired and hungry everybody is by now. I am, myself."

"And I, too," Ramón grinned. "I'll ride across and tell them. Djamba and Lucas are over there, and for once Djamba really looks done in."

"He's got the strength of five ordinary men, even at his age," Lucien Edmond smilingly chuckled. "And he knows what it is to go hungry." His face clouded a moment. "I'm afraid that poor Lucas won't be able to see his child until after its birth. We'll never get back in time, not with the late start we got because of that fool Caldemare."

"Yes, it's a pity. Well, I'll cross now, Lucien Edmond. The remuda horses are tethered for the night in a rope corral."

"Good work!" The tall blond trail boss nodded and waved to Ramón as he trotted his horse toward the river

360

and then, glancing back to wave in return, crossed to the other side and up to the bank to tell the waiting vaqueros what had been decided.

It was darker now, and the trees lit by the setting sun cast long, grotesque shadows along the buffalo grass and the water itself. A stillness had come upon the air, and there was not even a hint of a cooling night to relieve the scorching heat of the day. The vaqueros on the southern bank of the Red River had dismounted and were working now to bed down the cattle, almost desperately impatient for their own repose and the comfort of a good meal. Ramón, having informed the men on the northern bank of Lucien Edmond's plan, returned to aid the men on the south side of the river.

Jackson Brundiger had killed an ex-Confederate officer in a tavern brawl in Laredo two years ago and taken the dead man's powerful field glasses. He had brought them along in a shiny new leather case for this ambush and deployed his men after riding within a mile and a half of the Bouchard camp. The *pistoleros'* horses were tethered to thick mesquite bushes or small scrub trees along the river bank, and Brundiger himself and five of his men crept forward till, even in the darkness, he could see with the field glasses the cheery fires at the back of the chuck wagon and, spotted here and there on the southern bank of the river, the occasional small fires which Lucien Edmond's men had made to give themselves light to see by in the event of any untoward incident.

With him were Porfirio Costado, Diego Suarez, Paco Ruberoso, Luis, and Augusto, all armed with rifles and with holstered pistols at each side, each man holding in his left hand another set of holstered six-shooters fully loaded. His other six *pistoleros,* still on horseback, waited to cross to the southern bank of the Red River on his signal, which would be the first shot fired. As he and his five Mexicans came within range of the smaller part of the herd and the ten men whom Lucien Edmond Bouchard had stationed on the northern bank, they began to crawl on their bellies to keep out of sight. The verdant buffalo grass shielded them from view, and the moon had suddenly disappeared behind a mass of fleecy clouds.

Though he preferred pistols because of his lightning-fast draw, the Kansan carried a rifle also, one of the fine old

Confederate Whitworths with its special scope for accurate shooting at long range. Cradling the butt against his shoulder, he squinted down the sight and made out the vague outline of a tall, wiry man who was chatting with one of the other vaqueros and standing on the edge of the northern bank. Sucking in his breath, he pulled the trigger. Manuel Rodriguez uttered a choking cry, spun around, and fell with a bullet in his right shoulder. At the same time, he had presence of mind enough to cry out as loudly as he could, *"¡Bandidos, guardese!"* And, rolling over onto his stomach, he groped for the Spencer carbine which he had dropped when he had been struck.

The other six Mexican *pistoleros,* on horseback, hearing the sound of the rifle shot, descended the gentle slope of the bank and crossed over to the other side, agilely reining in their swimming horses with their left hands while, with their right, the rifle butts pressed hard against their right shoulders, they opened fire on the men who were camping with Lucien Edmond and Ramón.

Manuel Rodriguez, grinding his teeth against the throbbing agony of the leaden ball imbedded deep in his shoulder, squinted along the sight of his carbine and opened fire. Paco Ruberoso, who had got to his feet and begun to lope in a half-crouching posture, dropped his rifle and fell backwards, his arms sprawled in a cross and his dead eyes staring up at the darkened sky. With a violent oath, his best friend, Diego Suarez, seeing the flash of fire from the carbine, knelt down, took careful aim and pulled the trigger of his Henry rifle. Manuel Rodriguez slumped forward and did not move, a bullet through his head.

There was confusion and panic now, and the bellowing of the frightened cattle on both sides of the river as the fifteen hundred on the northern bank got to their feet and began a pellmell run toward the northwest. Djamba and Lucas, who at the first moment of the attack had dismounted from their geldings and flung themselves on the ground, now triggered their carbines at the shadowy figures beyond them, wounding Diego Suarez in the left calf. Drawing both his six-shooters, the *pistolero* snapped off a shot from each gun, killing one of Lucien Edmond's men and wounding another in the fleshy part of his right arm.

Lucien Edmond and Ramón called out a warning to their men, hurrying to the supply wagon to take shelter, Lucien

Edmond crouching at the back while his brother-in-law lay under the wagon with his repeating rifle trained on the galloping *pistoleros* who had boldly circled the herd and were firing at the vaqueros they could see in the darkness and at the cattle to increase the maddened tumult of the stampede in which, outnumbered as they were, their chances would be infinitely heightened.

The amiable chuck wagon cook, Tiburcio, sustained a minor flesh wound in the side, but valiantly returned the fire of his assailant and, with three quick shots from his Spencer carbine, toppled the *pistolero* from his galloping horse. The horse went down under the sudden veering of a group of maddened steers.

But the surprise attack by the mounted *pistoleros* proved murderously effective at the start: the small campfires which Lucien Edmond's men had lighted marked them out as targets for men who could shoot quickly and accurately at close range, and four of Lucien Edmond's vaqueros were killed or seriously wounded before they could regroup, seize their carbines or rifles, and return the first withering volley of the bushwhackers. Two of Jackson Brundiger's men were shot off their horses and fell under the thundering hooves of the stampeding cattle. A third, with a bullet in the spine, slumped unconscious over the neck of his horse which, in its terror of the milling cattle, managed to ride off toward the southeast and to safety for itself. The rider toppled to the ground a mile farther and died there.

As part of his plan to be mistaken for the old Reedy gang, Jackson Brundiger, himself, and all of his *pistoleros* had worn bandanas over the lower part of their faces, a characteristic of that infamous bushwhacker band. Discarding the Whitworth now, Brundiger drew his six-shooters and, still concealed on his belly near a small clump of mesquite, fired at whatever targets he could see. Ramón took careful aim with his carbine and fired at Brundiger. His shot missed the Kansas desperado, but killed Luis Aldemar who had moved up alongside his leader.

Porfirio Costado had moved off toward the north and taken shelter behind a lightning-stunted cedar tree. His quick rifle shot killed one of the younger vaqueros, and he quickly drew both six-shooters, firing twice above the heads of the panicky cattle to continue their stampede, and then watched his chance to aim at one of Lucien Edmond's men.

Djamba and Lucas, still lying flat on the ground, continued to fire their Spencers in the direction of the gunfire toward them. They lay by the edge of a grassy knoll about fifty yards from the northern river bank, a small mesquite bush slightly to their left and helping to comouflage them. Augusto, swearing a malediction at the death of his companion Luis Aldemar, had run in a crouching posture in a wide arc toward the north in order to take some of the vaqueros by surprise. Now, crouching behind a live oak tree, he wounded another vaquero with a shot from his rifle, then blazed away with both six-shooters till they were emptied, grazing the arm of another vaquero but inflicting no further damage. Lucas, attracted by the rapid fusillade, turned, aimed his Spencer, and triggered off a volley of shots. One of them caught Augusto in the temple and stretched him lifeless beside the tree, his empty guns still clutched in both nerveless hands.

Ramón and Lucien Edmond kept up their fire, but Porfirio Costado and Jackson Brundiger had imitated Augusto and made an even wider circle round this segment of the Bouchard outfit. The wild lowing and bellowing of the cattle and the thundering of hooves filled the night now, with the cries of the wounded and the dying, the staccato reports of rifle and pistol shots. The moon still remained hidden, and the darkness had swallowed up this side of the Red River.

The Kansas desperado and the swarthy horse thief lay side by side now, concealed by a thicket of purple sage. They could hear the shouts and the shots across the river, but could only conjecture how the other part of their marauding force was faring. Cautiously, Brundiger drew out his field glasses and leveled them, then muttered to Porfirio, "They've got two niggers with them, see, over there, on this side of the river, Porfirio? They've got Spencers, damn their souls to hell! See if you can draw their fire while I get over to that little ravine close to them. I'll crawl there while you fire in the air. Keep hidden, so they don't see where the shots are coming from, and don't fire too quickly or they'll for damn sure see the powder flashes!"

"¡Sí mi jefe!" Cautiously, the Mexican horse thief lifted one of his six-shooters into the air and pulled the trigger, then flung himself flat on his belly as Lucien Edmond, espying the sudden flash, fired his Spencer in that direction. The bullets whined harmlessly over Porfirio Costado's head, and he swore under his breath, calling on all the saints to let him kill these accursed *gringos*.

Taking advantage of the darkness and the direction of Lucien Edmond's returning volley, Brundiger swiftly crawled into the shallow ravine and grinned wolfishly as he pulled the other pair of six-shooters from the holster which he wore about his neck. Twelve shots, each enough to down a man if properly aimed. First the niggers, then that son of a bitch across the river who ran the outfit. And that greaser with him, who had to be more than just a vaquero to be so chummy with the trail boss. Once again he trained his field glasses, and now he could see Lucas and Djamba about a hundred feet away from him. Licking his lips in anticipation, his cold blue eyes squinting along the sight of his six-shooter, he leveled the gun in his right hand and pulled the trigger. Lucas uttered a yelp as the leaded ball pierced his upper left arm and clapped a hand to the wound, momentarily dropping his Spencer. Djamba, with an angry growl, took careful aim with his Spencer and pulled the trigger, but the gun jammed. Working at it desperately, the Mandingo was unable to clear the misspent bullet and flung it down as he reached for his son's weapon.

At the same moment, Brundiger broke into a run, crouching as low to the ground as he could, his six-shooters blazing. Lucas was hit in the left shoulder. By the time Lucien Edmond could shift his position on the ground and level his Spencer at Brundiger's running figure and blazing guns, the Kansas desperado suddenly had a clear view of the wounded Lucas. His teeth bared in a savage grin, Brundiger leveled the six-shooter in his left hand and prepared to fire. Djamba, off balance, leaning across his son's body to retrieve the latter's weapon, saw that it would be too late to prevent the Kansan from firing a fatal shot.

Without an instant's hesitation, he flung himself in front of his son and, raising the Spencer, fired at exactly the same moment Jackson Brundiger's finger pulled the trigger of the six-shooter.

The white-haired Mandingo uttered a strangled cry, his eyes rolling to the whites as the Kansan's bullet took him in the throat. But Brundiger staggered back, both six-shooters dropping to the ground, as the bullet from Djamba's Spencer drilled a bloody hole in the center of his forehead.

Porfirio Costado had seen this, and now, terrified and believing indeed that all was lost, turned to flee. The moon now emerged from behind the clouds, and Ramón Hernandez saw his running figure clearly. Aiming his Spencer, he killed the desperado with a well-placed shot.

Lucien Edmond's vaqueros on the south bank had stood their ground despite their first heavy losses, and the six *pistoleros* who had ridden across the river were dead or dying. Now the moon cast a ghostly light upon the twisted, sprawled bodies on both sides of the river, on the fleeing herd of cattle.

Sybella Forsden had gone to bed early this July evening. It had been terribly humid and she had felt her energy waning, even with the few kitchen chores she had forced herself to undertake. She had begun to dream.

She was riding her mare, Dulcy, because she had just insisted that her husband Henry Bouchard free Celia, and he had refused. She had been unable to reason with him, and she had told him that a ride in the fresh air would clear her thoughts about him and that he'd best do some soul-searching on his own while she was gone.

The sky had turned an ominous gray, and the wind was rising, tugging at her long flowing skirt, at the ruffles at her bodice, but she paid it no heed. The Kru stableboy Jimmy came out of the stable, and she ordered him to saddle Dulcy as quickly as he could. She had taken her riding crop with her. And then, her forehead creased with exasperation, she was directing the mare toward the narrow, cleared path which led to a clump of thickets, emerging beyond it into a wild stretch of grassy field as yet uncultivated. Her mind was filled with the rift that had grown between Henry and herself, with her awareness of how much her young son, Mark, was emulating his father. She was thirty-three again, still vital and attractive, with her deep underlying needs which Henry Bouchard so often ignored.

Suddenly she heard thunder growling and the sky was dark and there was a sudden spatter of rain. Dulcy had become skittish. Now there was the shaft of jagged lightning, and the mare bolted. In her dream, Sybella uttered a

366

cry of fear and strove with all her strength to draw in the reins, but Dulcy had taken her head and would not stop.

"Oh, my God!" she groaned as, in her reckless gait, Dulcy brushed her against the overhanging branch of a small oak tree which tore the crop from Sybella's hand. Now her lips were moving in prayer and she closed her eyes and she could almost hear herself say, as she had thirty-five years ago, "Please, God, let it be quick!"

Then suddenly there was a shout beside her, and it was Djamba, the powerful Mandingo, riding the black stallion Midnight, reaching out with both hands and seizing her by the waist and lifting her free. Then he set her down in front of him as he called out a command she could not understand, and the great stallion obediently slackened its pace and came to a halt.

"Oh, thank God—oh Djamba—you—you've saved my life!" she gasped, her arms clinging around his dusky, sweating body.

"Missy safe now. Dulcy, she run herself out, she be quiet soon," he consoled her. Now he gently disengaged her arms, slid from the stallion, and helped her down. Sybella tottered, suddenly weak. There was a flash of lightning, and she uttered a terrified cry and clung to him.

"We hide down here from the lightnin', Missy," he urged, guiding her down into a deep, wide ravine whose overhanging sides gave shelter from the storm. She huddled against him, and she knew that although he was a slave, he had once been the chief of his tribe, and still a man of indomitable courage and strength.

"Djamba—Djamba!" Sybella said aloud as her eyes opened. And then there was a terrible stabbing pain, and her eyes remained open but unseeing.

CHAPTER THIRTY-EIGHT

Under the bright sun of the hot July morning, Lucien Edmond Bouchard, Ramón Hernandez, and the sorrowing vaqueros buried their dead. They had lost seven men in all, and they mourned Djamba the most deeply. Over these past years on the cattle trail, the stout-hearted Mandingo had cheerfully shared their hardships, and there was not a man among them who did not think of him as a friend and a comrade. His last act, that of saving his son, of taking the bullet Brundiger meant for Lucas, moved them to furtive tears, each vaquero seeking to hide his emotions from his *compadres,* yet all of them understanding why it was they were so deeply moved.

Lucas, his wounds bandaged, weak yet insistent on participating in this memorial to his courageous father, had taken an axe and hewn a cross out of pieces of timber, bound it with rawhide thongs, and planted it on the northern bank of the Red River to mark his father's grave. He had knelt there, unashamedly weeping, murmuring his promise to remember his father's precepts all the rest of his life and to take special care of his mother, Celia, now that Djamba was no longer there to love and cherish her. He pledged to the Mandingo that if Felicidad gave him a son, he would call him Djamba so that this proud name which had once been that of a king of the Mopti would never die.

This done, there was the exhausting and seemingly endless work of pursuing the stampeding herd and rounding up the two segments which had fled in opposite directions. It took three days to accomplish that and two and a half more days to complete the crossing of the river and to head toward the Creek reservations.

Of his nearly four thousand head of cattle, together with the five hundred Mexican cattle from the Caldemare ranch,

Lucien Edmond tallied a loss of nearly four hundred head. In spite of the loss, when he came to the Creek village and greeted Emataba as a blood brother, he directed his men to lead five steers, four cows, and six heifers into the cattle pen as his gift to the villagers.

His reunion with Dr. Ben Wilson was joyous, and he and Ramón were warm in their congratulations when the Quaker doctor somewhat shyly informed them that he and Elone would be going to Wichita next month, where she would be presented to the Quaker pastor and his deacons as a preface to the announcement of their intended marriage.

"When we come back from Abilene, Ben," Lucien Edmond smilingly suggested, "would you and Elone like to ride back with us so that she can meet your little boy and girl and introduce them to Tisinqua?"

"I'd like that very much, yes, and I know Elone would, too. When do you think you'll be back, Lucien Edmond?"

"At this rate," Luke's oldest son ruefully admitted, "we won't get to Abilene much before early September. But the return trip should be very quick. We should be back here by mid-September. Then we can ride the rest of the way to Windhaven Range in a month, maybe even less."

"We'll certainly be married by September," Ben avowed, with a quick, loving glance at the slim young girl in buckskin who stood beside him. "But I want to stay here with the Creeks for a time after we're married. I'm sure Mother Sybella won't mind looking after Thomas and her namesake."

"I'm sure too, Ben. It'll be good to get back home again, though," Lucien Edmond sighed. "Well, tomorrow we'll hit the trail again. God bless you and Elone and her little girl. Emataba has already told me how many lives you've saved and how much happiness you've brought to his people. I'm proud that you're one of us. Ramón and I wish you and your wife and children long life and all the happiness there is."

"If we have that in our hearts, Lucien Edmond, and we believe in the justice of God, your wish will come true. I'm blessed by Elone, and I shall remember Fleurette always because there is so much of Fleurette's goodness and kindness and gentleness in Elone." Then he turned to take

Elone's hand while he extended the other to Lucien Edmond and Ramón, who each shook it warmly.

Simata rode ahead to Abilene to tell Joseph McCoy that the Bouchard herd was on the way, and when Lucien Edmond and his vaqueros drove their herd into the cattle pens near the railroad, the exuberant Irishman with his familiar bowler hat and cigar was there to greet them, as was Ed Dade of Armour. The 500 Mexican cattle were sold for $2,500, a good beginning stake for Margaret Caldemare. Lucien Edmond's herd of some 3,600 head went for $37,000. As usual, Lucien Edmond asked Ed Dade to give him part of the money in gold, so that he could pay off his vaqueros and give them their promised bonus. And there would be money to the families of the six dead vaqueros as soon as he returned to Windhaven Range.

This time, because of the delays along the trail and the tragedy which had befallen them at the Red River, Lucien Edmond and all of his men rode back to Texas the very next day. They did not even care to celebrate the drive in the now more than a score of noisy, bustling saloons where professional gamblers and gaudily painted women of easy virtue waited to fleece them of their wages.

They rode home, averaging thirty miles a day, stopping only at the Creek village where Dr. Ben Wilson, his lovely young wife, Elone, and the baby Tisinqua joined them, riding in the extra supply wagon. They returned to Windhaven Range on the tenth of October. During their time on the trail, many important events occurred in the young nation's history: Georgia had been readmitted to representation in Congress for the second time, the last state to be so readmitted; the first through railroad car from the Pacific coast reached New York City on July 24, 1870; and a strict neutrality in the Franco-Prussian War had been proclaimed by President Grant. At about the same time, the first editorial attacking the profiteering and the corrupt rule of Boss Tweed in New York City appeared in the *New York Times*. But all these events were far removed from the vaqueros' world, as they made their way back to Windhaven Range. Their thoughts were on the sad events at the Red River. And when they reached the ranch house, they found still further sadness and mourning.

Sybella Forsden had been buried at the base of the oak

370

tree in which Felicidad had found her *aplomado* falcon, Coraje. Lucas's young wife had herself proposed this to Maxine Bouchard when, that morning after the ambush at the Red River, she and Maxine had entered Sybella's room to find out why the white-haired woman had not come into the kitchen to prepare breakfast as had been her wont. As she had said to the sobbing Maxine, "I think, Señora Bouchard, she would like that. My *halcón's* name means courage, and that was what she had so much of—how I respected and loved her!" Maxine had nodded and clung to Felicidad as the two young women tried to comfort each other after their irreparable loss.

Felicidad had indeed given birth to a son, and when the vaqueros were approaching the gate around the ranch house, she ran to them and sought out Lucas, holding her baby in her arms, her eyes shining with joy and pride. But when she saw his solemn young face and when he kissed her and softly said, "My daddy's gone," she burst into tears and breathed, "Oh, *Dios mi amor,* what are we going to tell your mother? She had been very sick the last few weeks, with the river fever."

And she and Lucas went into Celia's room, and the mulatto woman sat up from her pillows, her face emaciated from the fever, her eyes anguished as she saw the grave look on her son's face. "Where is Djamba, boy?" she had asked in a faltering voice.

Lucas was unable to speak; he could only bow his head and stifle his sobs. Celia uttered a heart-rending groan and fell back on her pillows. Her eyes closed. Her lips moved in a kind of prayer, repeating Djamba's name, and then there was the sound of a soft, sighing breath as she joined him, her spirit free at last.

Lucas buried his mother near valiant Sybella Forsden, for he knew how closely their lives had been interwoven since that fateful evening when Henry Bouchard had tried to smuggle Celia into the red-brick chateau after having bought her on Pierre Lourat's auction block in New Orleans. Lucas also knew that he was free because his mother and father had been set free by that indomitable white-haired woman who detested slavery as much as old Lucien and Luke Bouchard.

Lucien Edmond, meanwhile, was deeply grieved by the news of Sybella's death, and he went at once to pay a respectful visit to her grave. His sorrow was mitigated, at least, by the fact that Maxine was in excellent health and eagerly awaiting the birth of their fourth child. And when he rode over to the Caldemare house to bring Margaret the twenty five hundred dollars from the sale of the Mexican cattle in Abilene, Joe and Margaret met him at the gate, smiling radiantly, to tell him that they planned to be married by the end of the month.

Ben Wilson and Elone knelt before Sybella's grave, where he told her what he knew of his mother-in-law's kindness and goodness and heroism.

A week later, Ben, Elone, Tisinqua, and little Sybella and Thomas left in the wagon for the Creek village. He had promised his young wife that he would remain there with her until he was sure that the new Indian agent would provide not only adequate supplies for the villagers, but also see to their medical needs.

The news of his stepmother's death did not reach Luke Bouchard until mid-August, in the form of a letter from his son's wife, Maxine. When Marius Thornton brought him the letter and two others from Jason Barntry in New Orleans from Captain Horace Tenby, after the *Alabama Belle* had docked at the wharf, Luke went to his study and, locking the door, seated himself at the escritoire to reread Maxine's letter. Then, covering his face with his hands, he wept—hoarse, racking sobs of deepest anguish at the loss. Sybella had been a true mother to him, a guide and inspiration. Her valor had heartened him many a time when he had chafed under his father's contempt and indifference. He knew what his grandfather, old Lucien, had thought of her, and he knew the positive influence for good she had had on Maybelle Belcher and on her own daughters, Arabella and Fleurette. She would be, Luke thought to himself, a living legend just as old Lucien had become: a branch of the Bouchard family that would be eternally in flower and remind each new generation of the love of family, of the deep-seated beliefs in honor and justice, and the faith in the future which Sybella had possessed.

Dimarte would have been like her, he was certain, if the beautiful young Creek wife of old Lucien Bouchard had lived. In them both there had been the same fervent honesty and candor. Both women had been tolerant of the foibles of men and had loyally offered to overcome them. He only wished that Sybella had met Laure, so that she could have understood what it was that had made him decide to go back to New Orleans after Lucy's death and to start a new life with Laure beside him. He knew, with a warming comfort even as he wept, that he would commune with her spirit just as old Lucien had done for so many years with his beloved Dimarte. The spirits of those two indomitable women would, he prayed, continue throughout time to guide the destinies of the Bouchards who would come after him. For they were women who, without sentimental glorification or poetic fantasies, represented the very epitome of all that was inspiring and rewarding and heartening in women.

He lamented the fact that he could not have been present at Sybella's funeral. There was no purpose now in going back to Carrizo Springs, though he silently pledged that he would pay a visit to her grave before Christmas. The crops were within a month of harvest at Windhaven Plantation, and there had already been two raids by the robed white marauders who called themselves the Ku Klux Klan. The second of them had come only last week, at two in the morning, when Hughie Mendicott, Hannah's new husband, had been wakened by the sound of sepulchral groans and had peered out of his cottage to see the flaming cross of the infamous night riders. They had set fire to a dozen acres of cotton, and Hughie had fired his pistol at one of them and wounded the man. Moses Turner, Dan Munroe, and Buford Phelps, wakened by the sound of the shot, had hurried out of their cottages with their own weapons and had driven the Klansmen off, then extinguished the fire. Luke Bouchard knew very well who had directed both of those attacks: the Eastern carpetbagger Barnabas McMillan. After the first one, Luke had made a speech in front of the Montgomery courthouse, declaring that peace could not be obtained by terrorism and that so long as free and decent men allowed the evils of fear and tyranny to exist, they had no right to expect to be able to decide their own destinies. He had appealed to all Republicans to overcome their fears of the Klan and to vote according to their heartfelt convictions.

That same day, he wrote a letter to Jason Barntry asking the manager of the Brunton & Barntry Bank to have a silver cross engraved with the name of Sybella Forsden and the dates 1802–1870, to be charged to his account and shipped by the best possible way to Windhaven Range, for the chapel there. And that night he went into his chapel and knelt in prayer, communing with the woman who had truly been mother to him and the source of all his admiration for and respect of the opposite sex. When he emerged from the chapel, he stood looking up at the towering bluff where his grandfather and the beloved woman were buried, and he murmured again a prayer for their spirits and for the spirit of Sybella Forsden to join with theirs in watching over the Bouchards wherever they might be.

This day was memorable also for him, since it marked the formal adoption of Lopasuta. That very morning, Jedidiah Danforth had appeared in the courtroom of Judge Hugo Tollefson to present the legal documents petitioning for adoption. It took only a few moments, and then Lopasuta turned, his face radiant, as he held out his hands to his legal parents, Luke and Laure Bouchard. "I promise both of you that I shall live my life to be worthy of you and your trust in me. I thank you for giving me your name, and I will never dishonor it. This I swear by the code of my people and by the Great Spirit," the young Comanche solemnly avowed.

There would be more work for Jedidiah Danforth in the future, because Andy Haskins and Jessica Bambach had been married in the little Baptist church on the outskirts of Montgomery on the first day of August, and the lawyer himself was present at the ceremony. When it was over, he, Luke, and Laure approached the happy couple, and Luke said softly to the one-armed Tennesseean, "Next year, if it's possible, Mr. Danforth is going to transfer the title of the land over to you, Andy, so that you and your wife and father-in-law will never have to worry about its being taken away from you. A long and happy life to you both is the sincerest wish of Laure and myself."

CHAPTER THIRTY-NINE

By October, 1870, a month before the election, it was evident that the Republicans would face a gruelling battle, not only to re-elect Governor Smith in Alabama but also to maintain presidential prestige. On the third of October, Secretary of the Interior Jacob D. Cox, under the pressure of spoilsmen and unsupported by Grant himself, resigned. The president's cabinet had already been greatly weakened, and the rumors of booty and corruption threatened the popularity of the "winningest" Union general who had been catapulted into the White House primarily on the strength of his crushing victories over the South.

Luke Bouchard was well aware of the national debits of the party which he supported, but his idealistic concern in achieving a sensible balance of governmental activity in his own native state made him tenaciously determined to defeat his opponent. Nonetheless, in spite of his frequent campaign speeches around the county, appearing at schools and black churches and even at farm homes in the poorer sections of Montgomery County, he did not neglect his stewardship of Windhaven Plantation. Indeed, he spent many a morning and afternoon out in the fields, working side by side with the black co-owners in this unusual commune—that was what Luke Bouchard considered his experiment in raising crops, produce, and cattle to show that men of all races could work together if they pursued a communal goal.

Every weekend through these summer and early fall months, Lopasuta rode in from Montgomery to spend Saturdays and Sundays with his adoptive parents. Luke savored these meetings, which led to many an animated discussion of politics and law and even sociological trends over the lunch and supper table. Laure, too, contributed much to the discussions, and it was evident that she admired the tall young Comanche for his industry and devotion.

Nevertheless, she had mixed feelings about Luke's debut into the devious world of politics. If he did succeed in being elected to the legislature, would that victory encourage him to seek higher office and to alter his life totally in the service of the many rather than of the few? Now that she had shared crises with him, given him two sons and lost another child through the miscarriage caused by Stacey Holbrook's attack on her, Laure Bouchard had come to appreciate her husband as well as to love him as deeply as she could ever love any man. She could look back now and understand that her marriage to John Brunton had been motivated almost solely by gratitude in return for the help he had given her to rebuild her life after her father's suicide and her violation by the Union corporal in her own father's bank. She knew Luke to be capable of heroism and self-denial, of almost pitiless self-searching as a perfectionist who tried to give the very best of himself and yet who could be aware of his own flaws. He had shown physical courage, much more than even she had believed he could do as an intellectual man instinctively opposed to violence and ungovernable passion.

Now that she had been able to cast aside the sophisticated veneer which she had had to adopt in New Orleans in order to survive, Laure knew that she was serenely content with Luke and that the difference in their ages mattered not one whit. No woman, she often told herself with a secret smile, could have wished for a more gentle and considerate and yet passionate lover, a man who sought first and foremost to let her exult in her womanliness without being selfishly possessive of it. In a word, she had achieved that perfect balance of sharing which steadies a marriage and provides its own romantic solaces, once the blazing ardors of physical union are banked. Yet it would be a long time, she whimsically assured herself, before Luke would show disinterest in her as her lover—and she meant to keep his interest constant for all their days.

But the glaring spotlight upon an official in public office —especially one who might seek to take a more important part in politics—could conceivably alter the happiness each had gained with the other. That, perhaps, was what Laure most feared.

376

Yet Luke, for all his idealism, was also practical. His experiences in life had already taught him how to temper his dreams with hard common sense. He had seen how his own father, Henry, had tried by bluff and trickery, greed and ego, to gain land and to outmaneuver his neighbors; he had seen the serene life of Windhaven Plantation come to an abrupt and tragic end when Union troops had set fire to the chateau and shot down his stepfather, Matthew Forsden. He had had to cope with the Northerners' hatred of a Southern-born gentleman who had never been either a rebel or a slaveholder when he had come to New Orleans to prepare for the journey to Windhaven Range. He had had to fight for his very life in two duels against the embittered Cournier brothers, whose feud against the Bouchards had threatened to topple the foundation on which Windhaven Plantation itself had been so gloriously erected. And finally, after the death of his wife Lucy, he had had to retrench and to rebuild a new life at an age when most men would have preferred to rest on their laurels. He had thus been seasoned by life's vicissitudes, and even though he was the veriest tyro in politics, he had an extremely clear picture of what was happening, both in the entire state of Alabama and in the county which he hoped to represent.

As he himself had pointed out to William Blount, one of his three principal supporters, what was hurting the re-election of Governor William Hugh Smith was the appearance on the Republican ticket of James T. Rapier, who had been nominated for secretary of state. Rapier was the son of a wealthy, free black businessman, tutored privately in Nashville before attending school in Canada for seven years. He had studied law and had been admitted to the bar, though he never practiced. When he returned home to Florence at the end of the Civil War, he became one of the most successful cotton planters in the Tennessee Valley. Luke had already observed that Governor Smith was not canvassing with Rapier or even acknowledging him in speeches in white counties, although he was endorsing the entire Republican ticket in the Black Belt counties of Dallas, Perry, and Marengo, as well as Madison in the Tennessee Valley.

Moreover, white Republicans themselves did not give Rapier a warm reception as he canvassed throughout the state, and John C. Stanton, general superintendent of New Alabama and Chattanooga Railroad Company, had already been accused of offering ten thousand dollars to Rapier if he would resign from the ticket. "It's evident from this," Luke had told Blount, "that white Republicans believe that if Rapier's defeated, other blacks will be afraid to run for office. This is one of the terrible injustices that decent men must stamp out, so that men of merit and ability, regardless of whether they are white or black, shall have a chance to represent the people."

"You and I both see the difficulties, Mr. Bouchard," Blount had gloomily declared. "The simple fact is that whites are just not going to vote for blacks as matters stand right now, no matter what party they represent. You can call it bigotry or lack of education or whatever you will, sir, but my view is that the people of this state for generations have been used to seeing blacks as inferiors and slaves, and they resent finding out that a black man can run for public office. What they think is that the Northern carpetbaggers are just trying to rub dirt in their faces—if you'll pardon the expression."

"I'm well aware of that, Mr. Blount," Luke gravely nodded. "And Rapier's even been called a carpetbagger, which is probably just as unjust as their calling me a scalawag. I've met him and I think he's a brilliantly educated man and a sound one. I wonder if we'll ever live to see the day when people will forget color and judge a man by whether he's a decent man or an evil one. At any rate, I'm going to campaign as hard as I can, if only to protest against the abuses of the Klan and the Knights of the White Camellia."

"You're a brave man, Mr. Bouchard. That's one reason we wanted you to be on our ticket. And you remember that I warned you in advance you might expect reprisals— you've already had two visits from the Klan, I understand."

"Yes, Mr. Blount. They destroyed some of my cotton, but it's been a good year all the same. Produce and cattle and dairy products and even chickens have given my little commune a very reasonable profit in this Reconstruction era. The co-owners of the land are quite satisfied with my stewardship and that of my foreman, Marius Thornton."

"I see you had an article in the *Advertiser* last week relating how well whites and blacks can get along as exem-

378

plified by your own experience at Windhaven Plantation, Mr. Bouchard," Blount observed.

"Yes. I wanted to do that on my own, anyway, regardless of the political issue. You see, Mr. Blount, in June, three ex-Confederate soldiers came by looking for work, and I offered them a chance to earn a piece of land, build a little house on it, get their fair share of food and also some profits. What we did was to have three of my black co-owners, Moses Turner and Hughie Mendicott and Dan Munroe, lease part of their own holdings to these men, you see. Then, when we pooled our profits, a part of them went to these three new workers, and with some of that money they paid back their share of the lease. It sounds a bit complicated, but the basic idea is that everyone works together for the greatest good of all. It's like a team, and it's been very successful."

"You've already been called everything from a scalawag to a nigger-lover to a gentleman crackpot, Mr. Bouchard," Blount commiseratingly smiled.

"I expect to be called a great deal worse than that before I die," was Luke's humorous comment. "Besides, I know where most of that venom originates: from none other than Barnabas McMillan. I'm sure he's the one who had the Klansmen visit the land. But my men are all armed, and if they try anything in this last month before the election, we'll be ready for them."

When Luke Bouchard returned home from that meeting with William Blount, he had supper with Laure, the two little boys, and Lopasuta. He and Laure listened with great enjoyment to the tall young Comanche's description of his experiences as an embryo law clerk with Jedidiah Danforth. By now, Lopasuta had been persuaded to wear not only the store-bought shoes—though from time to time he ruefully admitted that they still pinched a little—but also a jacket, shirt, and cravat. He had become even more personable and eloquent since he had begun his apprenticeship in the old lawyer's office. He had a thirst for knowledge which never failed to delight Luke, and on many an evening the two had animated discussions in Luke's library as Lopasuta earnestly argued how the white man's law could, if interpreted justly, provide ample recourse for the neglected Indians of all tribes driven from their homes and living in poverty and neglect on reservations such as Emataba's.

379

The young Comanche found it amusing that most of the white men in Montgomery whom he met while running errands for Jedidiah Danforth considered him a mulatto and not an Indian at all. Laughingly, Luke countered, "I think it would be a shock to most of them to discover that perhaps for the first time in the history of Alabama a real Comanche is not only now our foster son but also has a very good chance of being admitted to the Alabama state bar."

"Yes, that is not without its humor," Lopasuta conceded. "The only trouble is, once I'm admitted to practice here, there will be no Indians at all for me to defend." His face grew grave. "But then perhaps I shall defend black men who are still oppressed even though they are called free."

"That would be an admirable way to show that you believe in honesty and decency, Lopasuta," Luke earnestly concurred.

Early in October, Luke seated himself in his study with Marius Thornton and went over the accounts of sales and expenditures. Windhaven Plantation was showing a decided profit in comparison with last year. Despite the loss of a dozen acres of cotton, the dairy products, the cattle, and the chickens had more than compensated, and each of the workers would receive a handsome share of profits. Even the three new white "leaseholders," as Luke humorously called them, would do well in the short time they had come to work on the rich land.

Two weeks before the election, Laure went walking in the fields with her husband. Hand in hand, like young lovers, they smiled and stopped to chat with the workers. From time to time, in a kind of spiritual unison, they looked up at the towering bluff where old Lucien and his Dimarte lay. As they neared the gentle slope which both had so often ascended to reach those all but obliterated graves, Laure turned to Luke and gently asked, "If you win the election, my darling, will you give up this bucolic life for that of a politician?"

"Heavens, no," he laughingly retorted. "I've no political ambitions whatsoever beyond this immediate appointment. I accepted having my name placed on the ticket only because I wanted to raise my voice against the terrorism of the Klan and the usurpation of Southern rights by the

380

Northern victors. What I want most, and not only for this state but throughout all of the South, is to see men of good will working side by side again, just as they do here in our own fields, my darling. I want them to forget the war. This country is too great, this land is too rich, to tolerate the renewal of bigotry and hatred and feuds. If I had thought one good thing about the Civil War at all, it was that we might be able to end our differences and that the North would be able to understand the agricultural nature of the South. I had hoped, too, that the South would have learned from the North that you can't give all your land to cotton and tobacco and expect to maintain a growing and prosperous economy. We have so much to learn from them and they from us—and yet the lesson hasn't been learned at all, it seems. That's why I'm running for the legislature this time. But even if I win next month, you may be certain that I won't give up my responsibilities here—and certainly never to you, my dear one."

She turned to him, her face radiant. "I wanted to hear you say that, Luke. I've been thinking—and I've kept it from you all these months—that perhaps I might lose you, that you might be too ambitious. You're so good, you've such a quick mind, you stand head and shoulders above all these other men in politics, I was afraid that you might want to become governor and then . . ."

"No. Don't forget, I'm an intellectual, and that damns me from the very start. The majority of people are always suspicious of a man who speaks too well and seems better educated than they. They're afraid he may become a tyrant or a dictator. That I could never be. Well, my sweetheart, I'm realistic enough to see now that I may well be defeated. We Republicans don't have the Klan on our side, you know. And they're conducting such a reign of terror in the black communities that I'm afraid we may lose the entire state ticket."

"Is it really as bad as that, Luke?" Laure worriedly asked.

"Oh, yes. William Blount tells me that the Klan has maintained a systematic campaign of degradation and violence against Republicans in Greene and Sumter Counties for over a year. And just the other day, Democrats staged a riot at a Republican rally at Eutaw, the county seat of Greene. All the blacks were driven from the courthouse

381

square, and when they rallied in return, they were stopped by Federal troops."

"That's shameful and dreadful!"

"It is, indeed. Tomorrow the *Advertiser* will print my letter of indignation of this kind of harrassment. If we continue to treat the blacks with oppression and violence, just as many slaveholders did through the lash and the branding iron, how can we ever expect the blacks to trust us? I pray God we don't wind up trying to drive them out as we did the unfortunate Creeks."

"Amen to that, my darling."

On the night before the election, Luke Bouchard made an impassioned speech on the steps of the Montgomery courthouse, reiterating his plea for tolerance and honesty, urging voters to reject the terror of the Klan by voting in a bloc as Republicans. For if the Republicans should win, it would be an answer to the intimidation and violence and serve notice on the Klan that men of earnest convictions would represent the state. The new Republican state would also oppose the oppressive Reconstruction measures which the North still sought to force on the South.

That speech won him many supporters, but not enough to defeat Cletus Adams, who was elected to the legislature from Montgomery County by the narrow margin of 119 votes. Luke Bouchard took his defeat philosophically, but that next evening, at the dinner table, Laure smilingly announced, "Well, I for one am glad it's over, Luke dear. And from the number of votes you got on your first try, it appears that you've made many friends who think as you do. That should hearten you."

"My only try, Laure dear," Luke gently corrected. "But I don't intend to give up my principles, and I'll still go on sending letters to the *Advertiser* attacking injustice and political corruption. Perhaps if others like myself constantly give battle against evil, some part of it may be wiped out in our lifetime—that's all any man of honor could expect."

"I think," Laure archly murmured, since Lopasuta had excused himself and gone out for a walk along the river, "that a man of honor deserves something else. You're going to be a father again, I should say next May if Dr. Medbury's observations are at all accurate."

"Laure darling!" Luke sprang up from his chair and

382

hurried over to her, held her by the shoulders and kissed her ardently. "That's certainly better news than winning an election."

"I'm very glad you feel that way, my dearest," his wife whispered back as she returned his kiss, "because I was almost certain of it when we had that little talk out in the fields. I was asking myself whether, if you were really ambitious for political office, you would think of being burdened with another child."

"Burdened?" he echoed, then shook his head. "Blessed, rather. It's the most beautiful proof you could give me that you love me and are content with me. And certainly another child will keep me from growing old. I can remember how you used to chide me about being such an old sobersides."

She linked her arms around his neck and laughed softly, her green eyes glowing with joy at his pleasure and his happiness with her. "I do wish you'd forget that word. I know I have, Luke. Since the day I agreed to marry you, I've never once thought of you as that, and that's the honest truth. Would you like another boy, my darling?"

"No, since this seems to be an evening for honesty," he laughed exultantly, "I'd very much like a girl, as beautiful as you."

"I shall try my best, Mr. Bouchard," she said with such a saucy primness that he laughed uproariously and, lifting her to her feet, smothered her with kisses.

Robert Burns Lindsay, the Democratic gubernatorial candidate, arrived in Montgomery on November 19th to begin his administration. The election returns showed that he had received 79,670 votes against incumbent Governor Smith's total of 77,760, a margin of victory which was less than 2,000 votes. From the black counties, Lindsay had received 34,721, an increase of nearly 4,000 from the total that the Democrats had registered in the 1868 Presidential election. Governor Smith had received 55,379, an increase of only about 1,000 from 1868. But in the white counties, Lindsay garnered 18,315 votes, while Governor Smith was able to earn only 7,215. Violence, intimidation, fraud, and the strength of the Ku Klux Klan had caused the Republican defeat.

But the Republicans were not willing to surrender Alabama to the Democrats without a fight, and they encouraged Governor Smith in a desperate protest that he, and not Lindsay, was the lawfully elected governor, claiming that fraudulent election returns had been reported. An injunction prevented the Republican president of the senate from opening and counting the returns for governor and treasurer, but the returns for lieutenant governor, secretary of state, and attorney general were counted and Democrats declared elected to all three positions.

The new lieutenant governor, Edward H. Moren, was escorted to the speaker's stand and sworn in, then announced that Robert Burns Lindsay had defeated William Hugh Smith for governor and that J.F. Grant had won over Chester Arthur Bingham for treasurer. But Smith refused to concede defeat and, with Republican Treasurer Bingham, barricaded himself in his office, then called in U.S. troops who took possession of the capitol.

The two men remained barricaded in the governor's office for two weeks, sustained by food handed in through the windows till a scalawag judge and old enemy of Governor Smith, James Q. Smith, arrived in Montgomery and ordered the incumbent to appear before him within half an hour. Thus it was that on December 10, 1870, Lindsay became the twenty-second governor of Alabama.

It was evident that Senator Spencer had maneuvered well to defeat his Republican senatorial colleague, and that now this man, a carpetbagger, exercised sole control over the federal patronage for Alabama, except for the power held by the scalawags in the state judiciary who had influence on nominations for state offices. President Grant would need the electoral vote of Alabama in 1872 to secure his re-election, and Spencer's re-election would be by the legislature elected in that forthcoming year. For the immediate future, only carpetbaggers would be appointed to federal positions in Alabama. But there would still be political feuding for years to come.

On the evening of the day that Governor Lindsay formally took possession of his new office, Barnabas McMillan gave a victory party at his elegant new house downriver from Luke Bouchard. Stacey Holbrook was not invited, but she came after midnight and confronted her carpetbagger lover, demanding that he keep his promise to marry her. She reminded him that he had made her that promise if

384

she would help defeat Luke Bouchard, and she had indeed done that.

The corpulent Easterner stared at her and then guffawed. "You're really more stupid than I thought, Stacey girl," he replied as he drew a pretty mulatto girl down on his lap and began to fondle her. "Marry a whore like you? Oh, don't look at me like that, honey. Sure, we've had good times together, but you really didn't think a man of my influence in this state would lower himself to take a piece of soiled goods like you as a wife, now did you? I'll see that you get a nice piece of change, though—you deserve that much, I'll admit. Look out now—what're you doing— no, my God—"

For Stacey had taken a small pearl-handled derringer out of her reticule, aimed it at McMillan while the mulatto girl with a shriek of terror flung herself onto the floor, and pulled the trigger. His mouth agape, his eyes incredulously staring at her, Barnabas McMillan died instantly.

Stacey Holbrook turned and ran out of the house. In the uproar that followed, she escaped and was never heard from again.

CHAPTER FORTY

Once again, as he had pledged to himself to do each year that he remained on Windhaven Plantation, Luke Bouchard ascended the gently rising slope to the high bluff overlooking the Alabama River, to pay tribute to his grandfather and Dimarte on this anniversary of old Lucien's birth, December 18, 1870. This time he went alone, for Laure, now four months pregnant, had caught a lingering cold and he had insisted that she stay in bed and rest till she had completely recovered.

It had been a year of singular eventfulness, and he wondered, as he knelt before the now almost unrecognizable graves of his grandfather and the beloved woman, whether this augured an even more unpredictable year ahead. Just yesterday morning, old Horatio Bambach had been found dead in his bed by his daughter, Jessica; he had apparently died of a sudden heart attack, peacefully and in his sleep. Luke had already prayed in the chapel this morning for the soul of that kindly man who had come here to become his neighbor and friend, as he and Jessica sought to reshape their lives after the tragedies the Civil War had inflicted upon them. At least, he thought to himself, Jessica's grief was eased by her husband's devotion: Andy Haskins would help her toward a happier life.

There was in all this a kind of comfort, in knowing that the eternal cycle could not be broken by violence or evil or even war. There was always a new beginning, always a new goal to set one's sights for, and there was always a kind of Providential compensation for loss. Laure and he had lost their unborn child through an act of violence engendered by a man who represented the very worst sort of evil that was abroad in the South today. Yet Laure would bear another child, and the man who had used a weak, vulner-

386

able young woman as his tool had perished by that same young woman's hand. Somehow, even if one were an atheist, Luke thought to himself, one could not help seeing that the scales of life and death were in remarkable balance; there was a design, by whatever name one chose to call it. For Luke it was another proof of the eternal awareness of the God to whom he now prayed, the same God whom the Creeks called Ibofanaga, the Giver of Breath.

He spoke to old Lucien and Dimarte now with an eloquence and a tenderness that was evoked by his mystic mood, a mood which looked back to the past, saw the present, and eagerly welcomed the future. Yes, assuredly there was eternal balance. For Dr. Ben Wilson, who had lost his sweet Fleurette, there were the Indian girl Elone and her little child, Tisinqua. Sybella was dead, and yet the deaths of Djamba and Celia might well be linked to hers; all three of them had been brought together in the turmoil of the old slavery days, and Sybella had withstood the corruptive influence of slavery by freeing them both and encouraging them to marry. And all three of them had gone on to Windhaven Range, and their freedom and courage had helped make this new home of the Bouchards a place of love and trust and loyalty. Even in death, they would long be remembered.

Yes, all was well with the Bouchards. Luke had just received a letter from Arabella announcing the marriage of young Melinda. He had smiled wryly to himself and then shown Laure the letter, remarking, "And when Melinda presents Arabella with her first grandson or granddaughter, Arabella will be brought up rather short, I think, and begin to realize how very much time has mellowed her and strengthened her nature through a steadfast marriage to a man who brooks no nonsense from her, yet loves her devotedly."

There had been a letter from Laurette last week, too, a chatty, rambling letter in which she detailed at great length her husband's innovations in his Chicago department store. The children were flourishing like weeds, she wrote, and they had a jewel of a nursemaid in Polly Behting. Their new house was very comfortable, and there was a big yard and her own garden and at the back a little carriage house with horse and buggy. The only fly in the ointment of

Laurette Douglas's serene happiness was that Carrie Melton Haines had become her neighbor and, despite rebuffs, still tried to become friends with her and the children.

Two months ago, Laurette had written, that audacious, brazen creature had actually dared to send over by her butler a basket of fruit and cheeses and a package of toys and dolls for the Douglas children. Laurette simply could not understand how thick-skinned this cunning little adventuress must be, when she had already made it very clear that she wanted no part of Carrie Melton Haines. Luke had chuckled as he had read this to Laure, adding, "Laurette's temper is well come by, and it's expected from a red-haired female, don't you think?" To which Laure had made a saucy face and retorted, "That's one of those old wives' tales, my darling. I have a temper, too, though happily you've never really provoked it."

"And I never shall, I hope," he had gallantly responded and then taken her into his arms and kissed her soundly.

This week, a letter had arrived from Luke's daughter, Mara Hernandez. Mara wrote that Lucien Edmond's wife, Maxine, had just given birth to a girl, whom Maxine had named Diane after her own mother. Kate Casares had also had a baby in November, Mara added, a daughter, and she had yielded to Pablo Casares's fervent wish that the girl be named Catarina. And finally, Mara said, she herself was expecting a child by next summer.

Yes, the Bouchard family was growing, as were the other families connected with Windhaven, and it delighted Luke to conjecture where and how these new descendants would take up useful lives to benefit not only their eventual families but the communities where they would dwell. He touched the earth beneath which old Lucien lay, and said softly, "Grandfather, now you are a part of our history, the pioneer of all of us. And from you there has come, often by strange and unexpected turns, a family whose roots are strong and deep in the soil of freedom and honor. You will watch all of them as they make their mark, just as you made yours. I revere you as I revere her who first shared your life in this young country. Perhaps with the coming year, we shall be closer to the peace you foresaw could come when men of all creeds and races worked together as brothers. And I think today, on your birthday, you are pleased that my foster son, Lopasuta, in whose

veins there runs the strong Comanche blood, will become
a lawyer next year and can defend the oppressed and the
needy just as you yourself did so long ago. He has come
already to visit you by himself, as was his wish, after I told
him the story of your life. He is eager for knowledge and
dedicated to truth and tolerance. Those were virtues you
yourself possessed, Grandfather, and how well you inculcated them in me. What I am now, I owe to you and
to Mother Sybella—your spirit and hers are together now
for all time. God bless you, Grandfather. Sleep and dream
and guide us in the days ahead."

Luke Bouchard's prayer for peace seemed to have evoked
one augury of encouragement for the future: in this same
month, the third session of the Forty-First Congress con-
vened and every state in the Union was represented for the
first time since 1860. Also, President Grant, in his annual
message to Congress, called for civil service reform, acknowledging that he had discovered corruption in his own
administration. Now that the seceding Southern states had
once more been returned to voice their demands in a unified
Congress, there was the faint light of hope that the tyrannical Reconstruction program initiated by such vengeful
men as Thaddeus Stevens might be eased.

In March of 1871, the Civil Service Commission was
formally authorized by Congress, and George William Cur-
tis was appointed its first commissioner by President Grant.
On the same day, Congress authorized the Centennial Ex-
position, to celebrate the first hundred years of the growth
of this new nation, to be held in Philadelphia in 1876. But,
much more ominously, Congress passed, again on this same
day, the Indian Appropriation Act, which made Indians
national wards and ended all Indian treaties. Luke Bouchard saw in this a denial of the original rights of these
first settlers, whose land had been taken from them by
treaties. Now the treaties had been scrapped, and the Indians would be little better than neglected orphans patron-
izingly supervised by governmental agencies. He said as
much to his adopted son, Lopasuta, when the news of this
act appeared in the Montgomery *Advertiser*.

"That is why, Mr. Bouchard," the quick-witted young
Comanche replied, "I must excel in my studies of the law
with Mr. Danforth, so that I can apply the white man's

law to the advantage of my people when the opportunity presents itself."

Since his adoption, Lopasuta's attitude toward Luke was one of the greatest respect and gratitude. He invariably addressed him as "Mr. Bouchard" rather than as "father." Yet by his open admiration for his adopted father and his increasing zest for acquiring knowledge, Lopasuta gratified Luke far more than had he paid him the lip service of calling him "father." Indeed, Luke often told Laure that when he and the young Comanche exchanged ideas, it was rewardingly stimulating for him and that he admired the intensity of Lopasuta's study of the law.

By early spring, Luke and Marius Thornton (who had just become the father of a girl who was almost exactly the image of her mother, Clementine) conferred to plan for the spring planting of crops. Once again, as was his firm belief, Luke Bouchard insisted upon a diversity of crops, not only to nurture the rich soil without taxing it, but also to derive the largest potential profits for the co-owners and himself. Yams, okra, snap beans, squash, melons, and tomatoes as well as an acre of watermelons would be planted on the acreage which had been devoted to cotton the previous year. Fifteen acres of cotton would be planted in soil which had formerly nourished vegetables and fruits. The chicken flock would be increased, and Luke had bought five milk cows so that cream and milk and butter could be sold to the stores in Lowndesboro and Montgomery, along with an estimated thousand pounds of beef.

Andy Haskins brought his wife, Jessica, to the chateau in March to introduce her formally to Luke and Laure, and also to participate in Luke's conference with Marius Thornton. He readily agreed with Luke that concentration on cotton would be ill-advised and that vegetables and fruits would be easy to cultivate and harvest and yield a most rewarding profit. Andy proudly declared that he had paid a visit to Dalbert Sattersfield at the latter's store in Lowndesboro and received a tentative order for his intended crops. The two men had become good friends. Each of them had lost an arm in the war; each respected the other for having rehabilitated himself and having begun a new life through his own energetic optimism.

Mitzi Sattersfield had already paid several visits to the

chateau to see her former employer, Laure, and last week she had declared that she and Dalbert Sattersfield were expecting a child in the summer. Laure urged her to bring her husband to dinner soon, and Mitzi promised that she would. It was obvious that she was head over heels in love with him, and when Mitzi observed that her former mistress was pregnant also, the two women clung to each other and wept tears of joy.

On April 20 of this new year of 1871, Congress passed the Ku Klux Act, to enforce the Fourteenth Amendment. It authorized the President to suspend the writ of habeas corpus and use military force to suppress disturbances in Southern states. Interestingly enough, Governor Smith had been castigated by his opponents and the newspapers for his failure to call out federal troops to suppress the violence of the Klan, because he had logically shown that martial law could only be invoked under Alabama's constitution in case of invasion or rebellion and that even then such power lay with the legislature. For this he had been called a coward and even a criminal, yet Governor Smith had urged that harassed citizens should screw up their courage, swear out an affidavit, and join a posse to aid the local sheriff. He had also urged local civil authorities to act more aggressively, to get statements, obtain warrants, make arrests, and to raise a posse and report any who refused to join. It was his belief that so long as a community tolerated violence without punishing the offenders, just so long would the violence worsen. Also, he had understood that forming a black militia in the state would have been worse than useless to stand against the power of a totally white Klan. Yet now, through this Act of Congress, there existed a new tool to abrogate the rights of the individual Southern state. This, Luke believed, was but a further indication that the era of vindictiveness had not yet come to an end. On the other hand, this new Act, at least in theory, had the power of suppressing the Klan's activities; Luke hoped that the good gained from such suppression might outweigh the dangers of usurpation of states' rights.

But at least, Luke wryly reflected to himself, there were no more visitations from the Klansmen; his political defeat had apparently bought him immunity from their depradations. Besides, since the Democrats had won the election, they had no real reason to terrorize Montgomery County, though throughout this year there were sporadic reports of occasional lynchings and whippings carried out against freed blacks in other counties of the state. It was Luke's fervent hope that these men, who were certainly no better than criminals, would soon be outlawed: what they accomplished was only the augmentation of hostility between the races, and this in itself would be a deplorable deterrent to a lasting peace.

On May 8, the day on which the Treaty of Washington with Great Britain was signed, Luke and Laure went to the Montgomery courthouse to witness the admission of their adopted son, Lopasuta, to the Alabama state bar. Elderly Judge Tollefson administered the oath, to which the handsome Comanche eagerly assented, and then came down from the judicial bench to shake Lopasuta's hand and to welcome him as an attorney who henceforth could plead his clients' cases before any court in the state of Alabama. What he said to Luke Bouchard pleased the latter mightily: "I am in the twilight of my years, Mr. Bouchard, and when I was a boy I knew of the Creeks and how wrongly they were driven out of the state because Andy Jackson hated Indians. Maybe it's poetic justice that today I should be here to swear in your adopted son, who has Comanche blood in his veins. They are a tribe whose courage and horsemanship I privately admire, because until my infirmities a decade ago, I liked nothing better than a good canter on horseback of an early morning before I ascended the bench. Yes, Mr. Bouchard, today is a kind of landmark for the state, and you've had a great hand in it. I admire your fortitude and humanity. What a pity there aren't more men like you in Congress—we'd have an end to petty squabbling and bigotry, and we'd be able to get on with the business at hand. My congratulations, sir."

Thanks to his partnership with Joe Duvray, Lucien Edmond was able to start the driving of his herd to Abilene as early as the second day of April in this year of 1871. Three weeks before the drive began, Luke's oldest son had ridden to Austin to investigate the status of the Caldemare land. As he had suspected, there was no provision for the legal inheritance by a sole surviving female. He therefore conferred with the chief land clerk, who was none other than Tobias Jennings, the same clerk whom Durwood Mc-

Cambridge had so ingeniously flimflammed by plying him with food and drink and introducing him to the dance-hall girl Lily Mellers. In this way, Jennings had been tricked into furnishing maps, which were used to create fraudulent land grants. Jennings had been promoted as the result of his conscientious work, and he had married Lily Mellers after having been deluded into believing that she was Durwood McCambridge's ward. The marriage had turned out well; Lily Jennings had made her husband a happy, contented man, no longer morose and cynical, with a zest for his work.

As the result of his discussion with Jennings of the status of the Caldemare property, Lucien Edmond Bouchard made a formal bid of five thousand dollars, which was duly registered and accepted a month later. By then, to be sure, Lucien Edmond had already left with twenty-eight vaqueros and Simata for the Abilene market with a total of forty-one hundred head of cattle and another fifteen hundred from the Caldemare ranch. He had purchased Herefords and Brahmas, and the men he had sent to stay with Joe Duvray and work on the Caldemare ranch had rounded up a thousand Texas longhorns. Through interbreeding with the stronger stock, Joe was able to send a quite acceptable herd of prime quality along with Lucien Edmond's.

When the letter of acceptance of Lucien Edmond's bid to transfer the Caldemare ranch to himself was received at Windhaven Range. Maxine sent Pablo Casares to ride over to Joe to inform him that the partnership had been consumated. The black-haired young Georgian had remained on the ranch with Margaret, because she was expecting their first child.

On this drive, Lucien Edmond and his men encountered not a single hazard, apart from a minor stampede which cost them only half a day and was caused by a dust storm just before they reached the Red River. They made their usual stop at the Creek village of Emataba, and Lucien Edmond's gift to the villagers comprised a dozen heifers, five steers, and a bull. There Lucien Edmond visited Ben Wilson and his young wife, Elone, who was with child also. Thomas and Sybella were thriving and wore the buckskin garb of the Creeks, playing with the Creek children as enthusiastically as if they had been born on the reservation.

With Eddie Gentry riding point, Lucien Edmond and

his men and the cattle arrived in Abilene on the last day of August. It would be the last time they would come to this market. During Abilene's five-year reign as king of the cow towns, small farmers—or nesters, as the cowmen called them—had been pushing steadily westward along the Kansas Pacific railroad line until most of the free range was gone. The natural emnity between farmers and cattlemen would lead even so enterprising a man as Joseph McCoy to order cattlemen to stay away from Abilene—and with this the boom would collapse. In addition, another westward-moving railroad, the Atchison, Topeka and Santa Fe, was preparing to share in the cattle trade. By the spring of this year of 1871, the Santa Fe had reached Newton, sixty-five miles to the south of Abilene.

When he arrived with his herd, Lucien Edmond learned from several other ranchers of the development of new markets and heard also their speculations that the high prices which they had previously enjoyed here in Abilene were certain to be curtailed because the farmers had been bringing a great deal of produce into this Kansas town and diverting its bounteous commerce to their own side of the ledger. This news confirmed Lucien Edmond's own prediction that the advent of new railroads would change the prevailing pattern of preparing cattle for the market. As he told Ramón Hernandez, "It might pay us to leave one of our men here in Abilene during the winter to let us know exactly what's going to happen. If this Santa Fe town of Newton is booming the way I've just heard, we might go there next year."

It was not Ed Dade of Armour and Company who bought the Bouchard herd this time as he had done in the past. Instead, a new buyer from St. Louis, Henry Trowbridge, came out to see Lucien Edmond's cattle and promptly offered him a flat price of $10.75 per head. Thus, with Lucien Edmond's 4,000 and Joe Duvray's 1,500, the total sale amounted to $59,125—the largest amount Lucien Edmond had made from his cattle ranching. At once he began to plan the expansion of the combined range which had been effected by the combination of his own holdings and those of the late Robert Caldemare.

Moreover, since Joe's 1,500 head of cattle had netted $16,125, this piece of good fortune would allow the black-haired Georgian to pay Lucien Edmond immediately back for the land. Out of the balance of some $11,000, Lucien Edmond proposed to deduct another $5,000 for his own cost in furnishing some of the Herefords and Brahmas which he had allocated the Caldemare range. Thus Joe would net about $6,000 clear profit from his first year as a rancher. The final touch, a mere formality, was the transfer of title to the Caldemare range from Lucien Edmond to Joe, in return for one dollar and "other valuable consideration." Lucien Edmond felt a warm sense of satisfaction in being able to offer so loyal a man this superb wedding present.

During his short stay in Abilene, Lucien Edmond met James Butler (Wild Bill) Hickock, who had fought against the Confederates as a scout and a spy in Missouri and Arkansas and who had become Abilene's marshal early this year. Hickock was a tall, graceful man and a spectacular gunfighter, popular with most of the cowboys. His first act as marshal was to ordain that cowboys could wear their revolvers wherever and whenever they pleased, a welcome change from the rules established by his late predecessor, Bear River Tom Smith.

Hickock patrolled the main street of Abilene, Texas Street, by walking in the center. His long auburn hair, which hung in ringlets over his shoulders, and his small, finely formed hands and feet gave him a feminine appearance, but that was to belie his expert ability as a gunfighter. Invariably, he wore a pair of ivory-hilted and silver-mounted pistols thrust into a richly embroidered sash, wore shirts of the finest linen and boots of the thinnest kid leather. His salary was extremely small, but he augmented his earnings by frequent gambling. Lucien Edmond found him candid in speech and manner and admired his bravado.

Ramón and Lucien Edmond remained in Abilene only two days, fearing the multiple temptations that this booming cow town offered the vaqueros and cowboy. By now it had beer gardens, dance halls, and over a dozen saloons, with such colorful names as "Applejack," "Old Fruit," and "The Pearl." The "Alamo," obviously christened to appeal to Texans, was the most resplendent of the drinking houses. The Alamo boasted three sets of double-glass doors and a bar with carefully polished brass fixtures and rails. All along the walls were huge paintings, nudes done in imitation of the Italian Renaissance painters. There was constant music from pianos, raucous horns, and bull fiddles, and there were dance hall girls, painted and gaudy, to induce the exuberant cowboys and vaqueros to part with their pay. Many of those girls had come from Mexico, either kidnapped, lured by grandiose promises of fabulous earnings, or in many tragic instances, sold by impoverished fathers to white-slavers who brought them to ply the most ancient of all trades in this now unsavory Kansas town.

On their way back to Windhaven Range, Lucien Edmond and Ramón broke their journey once again to visit Emataba and his Creeks. To their great delight, they saw a nearly bald, portly man in a brown cassock and robe standing beside the tall Creek *mico,* and they both exclaimed simultaneously, "Friar Bartoloméo!"

"How good it is to see you again, my sons," the Franciscan friar beamed as he hurried forward to shake their hands. "You and your men have always been in my thoughts since I dedicated your chapel. And you, Mr. Bouchard, what has happened to that wonderful father of yours?"

"A good many things, Friar Bartoloméo," Lucien Edmond smilingly responded. "He's run for the state legislature in Alabama, but unhappily was defeated by a narrow margin. And he and his wife will have another child soon. I only wish he could be here with us today to see you again, for he's never forgotten your kindness and humanity."

"Please send him my blessing and my very best wishes to him and his wife, Mr. Bouchard." The plump little man sighed and shook his head. "Since you last saw me, I have been in Arizona and the panhandle part of Texas, helping the needy Indians and some of the farming communities too isolated and too poor to have a priest. I have found men of good will everywhere, despite my failing strength— alas, you see that the good Lord has justly punished me for my gluttony." He dolefully patted his paunch, and Lucien Edmond and Ramón had all they could do to keep from bursting out laughing. "But, as I was about to say, my reward for all my travail was in coming here and meeting again that wonderful Dr. Ben Wilson. He has such compassion that I think he would have made a magnificent priest if he had chosen such a vocation. He is more than a

396

doctor, he is a friend and confidant to those unable to voice their wants and their grievances. I think our own blessed founder, Saint Francis of Assisi, would have loved him as I do. I am truly happy to know that he has been blessed with a young wife and that even now she is with child. Truly, our Lord moves in wondrous ways to show His compassion and love for men of good will!"

"Will you stay here long, Friar Bartoloméo?" Lucien Edmond asked.

"No, my son. I shall go where the good Lord sends me, and I leave tomorrow for another Indian village on the border of Indian Territory, near Kansas from which you have just come. They are Kiowas, once proud and free and now forced to live in a village far shabbier than this one. I learned this from one of the soldiers—a man of surprisingly kind feelings toward these abandoned people —when he helped bring the supplies to Emataba at the beginning of this month."

"May God go with you, then, Friar Bartoloméo." Lucien Edmond warmly shook hands with the Franciscan. "I pray that you will one day come back to Windhaven Range and hold a service for all of us in the chapel which you dedicated. And you will want to know that my father kept his promise—that of building his own chapel in Alabama to give thanks unto God for the restoration of his son Lucien."

Friar Bartoloméo Alicante made a sign of the cross as both Lucien Edmond and Ramón bowed their heads. His face was radiant as he looked up at the sky and said, in a voice that trembled with fervor, "Oh, dear Lord, hearken unto this blessed news which has just been given me. How comforting it is to know that Thy servants on this earth do honor to Thee and remember the promises they made in their hour of need to thank Thee. Surely, with men like this, most gracious Lord, Thou wilt remember how in ages past Thou saidst that Thou wouldst spare the cities of Sodom and Gomorrah if there could be but a few men of honor and goodness dwelling in them. And surely now, seeing how this son and his father do constant homage to Thee, Thou wilt bless them for their good deeds upon this earth and assure them a place in heaven. Amen."

Deeply moved, Lucien Edmond and Ramón crossed

themselves and echoed his last word. Then, after talking with the *mico,* they went to greet Ben and Elone and Tisinqua.

"I was going to ask you, Lucien Edmond," the Quaker doctor declared after he had exchanged greetings with the two men, "if you could take us back with you. I should like to pray at Fleurette's mother's grave, and Elone wishes to do this with me."

"Thank you, Ben," Lucien Edmond said, his voice choking with emotion. "I'd be proud to have you. But perhaps you'd like to stay with us for a longer spell than just to visit?"

"No, Lucien Edmond," Ben shook his head. "I'm needed here. It was here that I met Elone and little Tisinqua. Thomas and Sybella have made many friends here, and I'm teaching them both Creek and English. They'll be very wise children and they'll grow up to be useful because of this experience. Besides, I couldn't think of the comfort of staying at a place like yours for any length of time— I've work to do as a doctor, and these people have no other one but me to look after them. They regard me as their shaman, their medicine man." He smiled gently. "It's the finest tribute I could ever be paid by anyone. When someone needs you and is grateful that you're there, it's the best reward any doctor could have."

"But do you actually think of spending the rest of your life here, Ben?" Lucien Edmond anxiously asked.

Ben shrugged. "That's in the hands of God, Lucien Edmond. All I know is that so long as I'm needed here, I'll stay. Elone is four months away from her time, and she wishes our child to be born here, where we first met. So she can easily make the journey with me, and Tisinqua and Sybella and Thomas will go with us, if you've room."

"Of course. There is the extra supply wagon. We'll leave when you're ready, Ben."

"It won't take us long, Lucien Edmond. We've only ourselves to pack," the Quaker doctor whimsically retorted as he shook hands with the tall blond trail boss.

The men of Windhaven Range returned to Carrizo Springs by the fourth week of September. It was an especially joyous homecoming for Ramón Hernandez, since he found himself a father again. Felicidad and Maybelle, who had helped at the accouchement of Maxine the previous

November, had helped Mara in July. Mara had presented her husband with a girl, and to Ramón's great pleasure, she had named her daughter Dolores, after Ramón's mother.

It seemed, indeed, that the cycle of life was felicitously renewing and advancing itself, for in Sangrodo's stronghold across the border, his beautiful wife, Catayuna, had given him a daughter just this past January, and Prissy's daughter was now well over a year old.

On the warm September evening of the day of his return to Windhaven Range, Lucien Edmond rode over to visit Joe Duvray to hand him the check for six thousand dollars. He also gave Joe the gratifying news that the rest of the money paid for the Georgian's herd had been enough to pay off the cost of the land and the cattle which had been procured in order to strengthen the stock of Joe's herd. Joe let out a whoop of joy and declared, "You'd better pinch me to make sure I'm not dreaming, Mr. Bouchard. Because I don't mind telling you it's just like a dream, having all this good luck piling on top of itself. This money's going to come in mighty handy, Mr. Bouchard— especially with Margaret's baby due in a couple of months. I swear, I'm a mite afraid I might just wake up and find out that all this had been a dream."

"No, Joe, it's real and I don't have to pinch you," Lucien Edmond chuckled. "You've earned it. And now you're going to be my partner. With your help on this range to go along with my land, we'll be able to build a ranch that will be far ahead of our competition. Good stock, fine crossbreeding, and best of all a partner like you whom I can depend on."

"You sure can, Mr. Bouchard." Joe shook Lucien Edmond's hand, and there was a suspicious mistiness in his eyes. "I guess Andy and I must have done something right to have been on that wharf in New Orleans at the time you and your family came there on your way to Carrizo Springs. I'll never be able to thank you enough, Mr. Bouchard."

"You already have, Joe. I'm happy for you. Well, good evening, Mrs. Duvray," this last as Margaret, flushed from her kitchen chore of preparing supper, came into the room to tell her husband that it was ready.

"Good evening, Mr. Bouchard. My, what a very nice surprise! Do please stay for supper, won't you?"

"I've already had supper, Mrs. Duvray, but I'd very gladly enjoy a cup of coffee and visit with you, if it's no bother," Lucien Edmond countered.

"Oh, my gracious, of course it's not a bother, Mr. Bouchard!" Margaret happily declared as she came to stand beside her husband and give him an affectionate look. "But now that you're back from the cattle drive, Mr. Bouchard, I insist that you come over here often and have a real supper with us. You know, I'm not a bad cook."

"You're too modest, honey," Joe grinned and put his arm around her waist. "If we didn't have this ranch, and I couldn't get a job, I'd go back to New Orleans with you and start a restaurant. With your cooking, we'd make a fortune."

"Oh, get along with you, Joe Duvray!" Margaret giggled, her cheeks coloring with pleasure at this flattery.

"Well, honey, I'm not out of a job and I'm not broke. Look at this check Mr. Bouchard just handed me, from the sale of my cattle up in Abilene." He unfolded the bank draft which the St. Louis buyer had made out in his name and given to Lucien Edmond, and Margaret gasped and clapped her hands with joy: "But that's wonderful, Joe! And we should put a little of that aside for the baby so he'll have—" She suddenly stopped, turning scarlet with a delicious confusion, then clung to him, stammering, "Oh my gracious, I didn't mean to be so rude and talk about family matters in front of Mr. Bouchard!"

"But I feel I'm part of the family, Margaret," Lucien Edmond said to put her at her ease. "After all, when I ran across Joe that time in New Orleans, he made himself so handy and dependable that I thought of him that way."

"Oh dear!" Margaret Duvray gasped again and hid her face against her husband's chest while he patted her shoulder and kissed her hair, then grinned somewhat self-consciously at Lucien Edmond.

Taking his cue, Lucien Edmond broke in with, "You know, I could really use that cup of coffee—that is, if you're sure I'm not intruding on you both?"

"Intruding? What a word to use! The very idea—I'll get the coffee right away!" Margaret turned, her eyes bright. "Supper's just about ready anyway, so, Joe dear, you take Mr. Bouchard into the dining room and make him comfortable, you hear?"

"Yes ma'am, I'll do just that," the black-haired Georgian chuckled with a broad wink at his smiling former employer.

In Galveston, on this very evening, Arabella's lovely daughter Melinda Davis was delivered of a son, and Arabella was at her bedside as the nurse smilingly displayed the new-born infant. Melinda turned her head on the pillow and held out her hand to her mother: "Are you mad 'cause I made you a grandmother so fast, dear Mama?"

Arabella shook her head and smiling through her tears, retorted, "Of course I'm not mad, you silly goose! I'm so very proud of you and I wish you and Lawrence a wonderful, long lifetime of happiness." Then, taking a handkerchief out of her reticule and swiftly dabbing at her eyes, she said somewhat wistfully, "Honey, you're off to a much better start than I had, I'll tell you the truth. Land sakes, when I was your age, I set my cap at just about every handsome man there was because I didn't know anything about love with the right man. But you see, you found him early in your life, and you've both so many wonderful years ahead of you to keep on making new discoveries. No, Melinda, I envy you, if you want to know something. Now give me a nice sweet kiss, and then I'll go back and tell your father what a wonderful girl you are. And you get some sleep, you hear me?"

"Yes, Mama darling. I love you so!"

Luke Bouchard had no real cause for regret over having lost the election of his political debut. Everything else in his life was working out for the best. The rich soil of Windhaven Plantation was yielding more abundant and profitable crops than had been realized in many a year, and Luke's adopted son, Lopasuta, had already begun his legal career by appearing before old Judge Henley three times and winning all three of his cases. Though all of them involved simple contracts between two individuals, the eloquence and persuasiveness that the young Comanche exhibited in the courtroom made Luke prouder than ever of his adopted son. The harmonious relationship between Luke and the other members of this enterprising and original commune was strengthened; Luke believed that he had truly reached the very pinnacle of all of his ambitions.

Best of all, Laure had given birth last May to a little girl, golden-haired like herself, whom she named Celestine after her mother.

The state's economy, however, was in turmoil. The Alabama and Chattanooga Railroad had failed to meet the interest due on its bonds, and Governor Lindsay ineffectively sought to persuade the company to convey its property to the state of Alabama. That railroad line had been Republican-controlled, but now the Democratic-controlled South and North railroad was also in financial trouble. In the end, Governor Lindsay's compromise decision to stand behind some of the questionable bonds of the Alabama and Chattanooga and to make three of the interest payments satisfied no one, and his own party began to denounce the new governor as a man who lacked "nerve, backbone, and the great mainspring of common sense." The Republicans saw in this a great chance to gain victory in 1872, but two bitter squabbles over distribution of federal patronage (scalawag officeholders had been ousted for carpetbaggers at the Mobile post office and customhouse) began to dim their chances. Luke Bouchard was impatient with these machinations behind the scene: in his view, the state sorely needed to concentrate on diversified crops and enterprising industry to overcome its poverty. Meanwhile, as he philosophically said to Laure, "All I can do now is set by my own example a standard which I hope others will see and adopt. That's why it's so important that Windhaven Plantation remain solvent with its balance of free whites and blacks working together."

Dalbert Sattersfield's Lowndesboro store was flourishing, and Luke saw to it that the former Conferderate officer had first choice of quality produce and dairy products. His prices were fair and his dealings with people admirably courteous and considerate. His wife, Mitzi, who had given birth to twin sons during the summer, had had dinner with Luke and Laure two weeks ago to show the twins off with pardonable maternal pride.

There would be more money to expand the growing commune of Windhaven Plantation, too, quite apart from the satisfying profits which this year's farming had procured. During the last week of September, Luke received a letter from Jason Barntry, informing him that some of his investments in land which the bank manager had ar-

402

ranged would be paying handsome dividends by early next spring. And, the same week, Luke received a gossipy, cheerful letter from Laurette Douglas in Chicago. Charles, it appeared, was growing more ambitious every day. Now he was talking about opening a chain of department stores and had tentatively selected St. Louis, New Orleans, and San Antonio as ideal bases for this expansion. The children were wonderful, and Laurette hoped that Laure had been able to find a nurse as loving and attentive as her own Polly Behting.

In Laurette's opinion, however, Charles was working much too hard, and both of them really needed a vacation. The heat was mainly responsible for Charles's fatigue; all summer long the entire Midwest and large parts of the West had been afflicted with drought. Leaves had started dropping as early as July; only one inch of rain had fallen between July and October; and there was a clipping in the *Tribune* which she enclosed with the letter declaring that livestock by the thousands had perished near dry mudholes. There had also been an unusual number of fires consuming pinewood homes, rickety shanties, and flimsy buildings, especially in the slum areas of the Windy City. Of course, Laurette declared, fires like that could never start in a neighborhood like hers. Just the same, it was all very alarming.

CHAPTER FORTY-ONE

Even for this strange season, the Chicago wind was unusually hot and crisp on the evening of October 8, 1871. The dryness of this unusual summer had continued through the fall, and in this first week of October alone thirty fires had sprung up, the fiercest only the night before on the West Side. That fire had involved all of Chicago's two hundred exhausted firemen before it finally spent itself in wiping out four square blocks and causing $750,000 in damages. Yet it was only the harbinger of a disaster more immense and terrible than even the most pessimistic could conjecture.

In the sky, throughout the evening, there had been flashes of lightning, heat lightning, the natural concomitant of this prolonged drought. There was a small stable behind the frame house of Patrick and Catherine O'Leary at 137 DeKoven Street, a muddy tract near Halsted and Twelfth Streets. Far in the southwest there was a low rumble of thunder and then another even nearer like the clap of doom and with it a jagged flash whose tip seemed to dart down against the stable.

For a few minutes there seemed to have been no effect from that eerie bolt from the heavens, but soon there was smoke, and swiftly flames streaked out of the structure. At the same time, the wind, traveling at thirty miles an hour from the southwest, tore from the structure burning brands and sticks and sent them hurtling into other barns and dwellings, all of these made of quick-burning pine.

Although the flames were seen as early as nine o'clock, it was at least half an hour before an alarm was sounded and the first fire company dispatched. Delays, confusion, and tragic inefficiency hampered the firemen, and most of their equipment broke down. They cursed and wept, but they were powerless against the spreading fire. The fire itself whipped up a kind of vicious wind, comprised of self-generating whirls of flame and heated air—historians would call these "fire devils"—capable of carrying blazing brands, sparks, and masses of flame through the air for nearly half a mile.

Scarcely an hour after the haystack fire in the O'Leary stable began, flames hundreds of yards wide and a hundred feet high surged toward the heart of Chicago. Hour after hour they continued, and nothing seemed to stop them. Hope that the river would be a natural barrier vanished as the hungry flames swept by the wind leaped across the south branch into the wholesale business district, where it razed factories and warehouses, and then on through the squalid cribs and brothels and hovels of Conley's Patch. There was no class distinction in this fire: it reached out swiftly for such sumptuous and newly-built hotels as the Palmer House and the Grand Pacific, the Sherman House and the Tremont House, as well as the elegant dwellings on Terrace Row.

By one-thirty in the morning, the courthouse itself was ablaze and, within thirty minutes, its great bell still clanging as it had done since the very first hour of this conflagration, down fell the cupola and most of the famous structure itself.

Laurette Douglas had heard the clanging of the courthouse bell. She had gone quickly out of the frame house and stared down the street, but could see nothing—the fire had not yet neared the river. Charles had gone to Indianapolis on Thursday to meet the owner of a furniture factory whose merchandise he wanted to carry exclusively in his department store. The six-year-old twins, Kenneth and Arthur, and even two-year-old Howard had been awakened by the clanging courthouse bell, and it was all that Polly Behting could do to keep them in their rooms and urge them to go back to sleep, that everything would be all right.

But on every street leading toward the main branch of the river and to the lake shore, terrified masses of people fled for safety. Particularly on Lake Street, a street of merchants, and along Randolph Street, whose bridge was still intact and offered egress to parts as yet not reached by the fire, there was a suffocatingly close press of men, women, and children. All of them carried boxes and packages, bundles, babies, chairs, picture frames, toys, and housewares. They crashed through fences and they ripped down awnings in their headlong flight away from the flames. Many were trampled. Here and there one saw a man or a woman, eyes glazed and face streaked with the grime of smoke, crying out solemnly, "Chicago is doomed! God is punishing us all!"

On the other streets leading away from the center of the fire, there were men with coaches, omnibuses, and wagons offering to carry anyone who could pay. Those who had $150 in cash might board these vehicles toward the lake shore or over the river bridges to the city limits beyond Lincoln Park. Some of these men, even in the midst of such tragedy and terror, showed their greed: they would be ready in an instant to dump their passengers if others offered them more money.

Already, looting and widespread thievery had broken out, and no one could control it, for even the police were fleeing to safety. As flames leaped through the department stores on State Street and Wabash Avenue, vandals broke in and ran out with bolts of cloth, suits, dresses, and silks. From the windows of dry-goods stores, boasting and laughing thieves tossed silks and fabrics to their accomplices on the crackling sidewalks. Mayor Roswell Mason had already issued the first of many emergency proclamations, ordering that all saloons be closed. But there was no need for such precautions: already many of the saloons in the burning sections had been invaded by looters who smashed bottles and guzzled liquor and overturned whiskey barrels. Private homes were broken into. Down the cobblestones of State Street a woman staggered, her bony arms laden with stolen dresses, cackling a repetitive nonsense rhythm of "Chickey chickey craney crow! I went to the well to wash my toe!" At the foot of the Clark Street Bridge, a dead boy sprawled beneath the marble slab. On his hands were two white kid gloves, and his pockets were stuffed with dozens of gold-plated sleeve buttons.

A sallow, black-haired young lawyer peered out of the window of his apartment on 250 Fifth Avenue (now the west side of Wells Street at Lake), saw the flames, gathered what belongings he could in a suitcase, and ran like one possessed toward the nearest bridge across the river. His name was Charles Guiteau, and on July 2, 1881, a frustrated office-seeker, he would assassinate President James A. Garfield.

In the precious minutes before the flames reached the new Palmer House, its builder and Chicago's pioneer architect, John Mills Van Osdel, gathered together all his construction plans and record books, went to the hotel's basement, and dug a pit into which he placed the documents. He covered the hole with two feet of sand and a thick layer of damp clay, thus not only saving important blueprints and other papers from destruction, but also devising, through this impromptu method, a way of fireproofing with clay tile that would be extensively used for years to come.

Theodore Thomas of Cincinnati, two decades away from becoming a permanent Chicagoan and the first director of the Chicago Symphony Orchestra, was in town this Sunday evening for a concert with his orchestra. He called his musicians together in their quarters at the St. James Hotel and coolly directed them to gather up their instruments and belongings, then led them to safety.

Laurette Douglas had finally managed, with Polly Behting's help, to get her three little boys to go back to sleep and had spent a fitful evening. At midnight, she had gone out into the street and seen a man driving a carriage with two horses. "How bad is it?" she had called. "It's all hell broken loose, lady! It might jump the river—and then we're all in for it!" he called back over his shoulder as he urged the horses on to greater speed. Laurette stood frowning, not certain what to do. If only Charles were here! But there was no reason to panic; their house was far across the river and to the north, and the quality of structures in this part of the city could hardly be compared with the flimsy hovels and shanties on the south side of the river. Besides, she had her own horse and buggy and would use it. She looked apprehensively at the sky, and it seemed to her that she could see, far in the distance, a dreadful pall of smoke and tongues of black and red leaping among it. The dry wind fanned her cheeks and tugged at her skirts. Worried, she slowly went back into the house, lay down on the couch, and tried to doze in order to rest so that she would be ready for the emergency if it should come.

With early morning, the fire showed little sign of slackening and continued its northerly route. Furiously, it made its destructive way in the areas extending from the north side of the river. Warehouses on the river bank flared up and then toppled, their sparks showering the ships docked nearby and being borne continually northward by the "fire devils." The huge McCormick works at Pine Street crumpled into burning ashes as easily as did McCormick's own luxurious mansion on Rush Street. Half a mile north of the river, the waterworks and adjoining stone water tower were set aflame and appeared to be doomed—yet survived to become the landmark known as Water Tower.

By six in the morning, the hubbub in the streets and the actual smell of smoke determined Laurette Douglas to action. She went into the twins' room and found Polly Behting standing there, sobbing and wringing her hands. "Get the boys dressed, Polly dear—don't be frightened. We've a horse and buggy in the back, and we'll just go north until we're safe," she encouraged the terrified nurse. "Thank God the children were able to get some sleep on this awful night."

"Why—yes, m-ma'am," Polly Behting sobbed, sniffling and drying her eyes with her sleeve. "I'm sorry, ma'am— it's just so awfully scarey. I'll dress the twins right now, I'm sorry—"

"No reason to apologize for being afraid of fire, Polly dear," Laurette uttered a nervous little laugh. "We'd better get moving now. The news isn't good. Last night a man driving by in a carriage said that the fire was sure to jump the river and head this way. I can smell the smoke now and there are lots of people on the street. You get the twins ready, I'll dress Howard, and then I'll go out back and get the buggy ready."

She went into Howard's room, lifted him up from his crib and soothed and hugged him, then swiftly dressed him. Holding him in her arms, she went out of the back door of the house and toward the stable. Then she stopped short and uttered a cry of dismay: the door had been broken down and the horse and buggy were gone.

Little Howard began to cry, recalling Laurette's dazed thoughts to reality. "Don't fret, Howie baby," she consoled him, "we'll get away from here, we won't let the fire hurt us." She ran back into the house to find Polly Behting finishing dressing Arthur. Kenneth, the sturdier twin, had disdainfully declined her help and was finishing by him-

408

self. "Someone's stolen the horse and buggy, Polly!" she exclaimed. "We'll have to go on foot."

"Mrs. Douglas, now I can hear all the yelling and screaming, and look"—the young German nurse drew aside the curtain and pointed—"Why, the street's just jammed with people, pushing and running and crowding—oh, look, some man knocked down that poor old gray-haired woman! Oh, the brute, the selfish brute! Oh, I'm scared, Mrs. Douglas, I can't help it, I'm just so scared!"

"Get a grip on yourself, Polly. Panic won't help any of us," Laurette tried to maintain her poise and to fight the sudden growing hysteria that welled up in her, deepened by her husband's absence. "I'll see if I can find some money in the house. Charles never likes to keep very much, you know. Maybe somebody will have a wagon or a carriage, and if we offer him money, he'll take us to safety."

"Why, that's a wonderful idea, ma'am!" Polly Behting brightened. "Here now, Kenneth and Arthur, each of you hold my hands. Be good boys now. Don't get scared."

"I'm not scared, you are," Arthur stoutly and sulkily countered, glaring at the frightened young woman. "But I'll hold your hand if you want. There."

"Be nice, Arthur," Laurette Douglas gently chided. "All of us have to stick together now. We'll go outside now and see if we can get someone to take us north."

"Yes, ma'am."

Carrie Melton Haines had dined late with her elderly husband last night and had drunk more champagne than she should have. When she woke, it was with a splitting headache and a queasy stomach, and the cries of the people running down the sidewalks and the street only partly roused her. Slowly, she sat up on the edge of her bed and rubbed her knuckles over her head as hard as she could, a trick she had learned when she was a young girl and had drunk too much wine or whiskey. Then, as she felt more revived, she turned to look at the other bed where Dalton Haines lay. Her eyes widened and she put her hand to her mouth. He was on his back, his mouth open, and his eyes wide and fixed on the ceiling. He had tried to make love to her last night, but they had both had too much champagne, and it hadn't been very good—poor old Dalton had been drinking a lot more lately than was really good for him, and she knew why. It was all because she couldn't give him a child. When he got the least bit high, he'd start mumbling and crying like a kid about how much he'd always wanted to be a father and to hold his own little son in his arms, and it made her feel just terrible. He'd been so good to her, though, you couldn't gainsay that.

Now fully awake and with a chilling presentiment, Carrie walked over to the bed and felt for her husband's heartbeat. There was none, and when she tried to take his pulse, she detected nothing. "Oh my God, my God!" she said hoarsely. "Whatever am I going to do now?" For a moment she stood, nonplussed, paralyzed into inaction, till again the renewed din on the streets drew her from her black and dismal thoughts. "For God's sake, what's going on anyway?" she said aloud, and, fearfully glancing back at her husband's body, made her way to the door and opened it. The butler had been given the weekend off and the old cook had gone home to Wisconsin for her week's vacation. There wasn't anyone else left in the house. She opened the door, and the dry, hot wind made her cough. She could smell the smoke, and as she turned to the south to look, she said again in an awed tone of voice, "Oh Jesus God save us! Fire—and it's heading this way!"

She slammed the door shut, leaned back against it, closing her eyes. She had to think and think quickly. Poor Dalton—he'd made a will leaving her everything, that was for sure, but that was in the bank. Right now, he was dead and she had to get out of this house before it burned. And she'd need money. Money to buy food and a place to sleep in till the fire was out and she could find out from Dalton's lawyer exactly where she stood. One thing, she'd never go back to Bridgewater again, no matter what happened to her.

She went back into the bedroom, opened the closet, and took out her reticule. There was a sheaf of greenbacks, about a thousand dollars. She always kept that much in what she called "mad money." After all her years in the slums and living by her wits, Carrie firmly believed that if you had money in your purse, you could stave off most disasters. Maybe Dalton had some in his trousers pocket, in his wallet. She went into the other closet, rummaged through several pairs of trousers until she found the wallet, and breathed a sigh of relief. There was at least another

410

thousand dollars in it. Well, that would take care of her for a good long while until all this business could be straightened out.

Splashing some water on her face and patting it dry with a towel, she put on her bonnet, tucked the wallet into her reticule, and cautiously opened the door. There seemed to be a never-ending exodus of people from all walks of life, some calm, some laughing and joking, others babbling with terror and looking back over their shoulders as if the devil were behind them. In the street there were carriages and wagons and men with bowler hats driving the horses with carriage whips and cursing as people ran up to them and begged to be taken to safety.

She saw one wagon driver rein in his horse and bend over to bawl at a trembling fat man who was waving some greenbacks in his hand, "Cost you two hundred, friend, not a cent less. And if you haven't got it, there's plenty who do—well, make up your mind, I'm not staying here any longer!"

Carrie ran out to the curb of the street and, holding up Dalton Haines's wallet, screamed out at the driver, "I'll give you five hundred!"

"Step right in then, lady. Back away, mister—back away, I said, or I'll give you a taste of this whip, you hear me? Come on, lady, let's see the color of your money!" the driver, a red-faced burly Irishman, yelled at her.

At this moment, Laurette Douglas, carrying little Howard in her arms, and Polly Behting, leading Kenneth and Arthur, emerged from the house across the street. As she moved toward the wagon, Carrie saw them. "All right, driver, here's your five hundred!" she exclaimed, opening the wallet and taking out the crisp new greenbacks. "Now just don't drive off this second, there's a neighbor of mine over there with three kids and a nurse, you'll take them, too."

"Cost you more than that, lady! This is an old wagon, and my horse has got spavins."

"All right, you bastard, here's another two hundred!" Carrie impatiently pulled out some more greenbacks and thrust them into his sweaty palm.

"Now that's more like it. Tell the dame to hurry with her brats, though, can't you feel the heat? Fire's getting too close for comfort!"

411

"Over here, Mrs. Douglas, over here! I've got a wagon for you and your boys—hurry!" Carrie cupped a hand to her mouth and yelled as loud as she could, then waved her hand to attract Laurette's attention.

"Look, Mrs. Douglas," Polly Behting cried, "that's the woman from the park—she's got a wagon there for us!"

"I—" Laurette Douglas was about to refuse indignantly, but then she looked at the scene of terror before her: the jostling of the crowd, the smell of the smoke, and lurid brightness in the sky, all of which combined to make Chicago an inferno worthy of Dante. This, together with her maternal instinct, swiftly pushed from her mind all thoughts of her dislike of Carrie Melton Haines. "Let's see if we can get across there, Polly. Hold on to Polly's hands tightly, Kenneth and Arthur! Now, let's make a run for it!"

"Fer God's sake, lady, get a move on! I can't stay here all morning!" the Irishman bawled, glancing nervously back over his shoulder as patches of smoke began to float overhead. The fire was now a block and a half away and the heat was stifling. Still the wind kept pushing it forward to the north.

Polly Behting helped the two little boys into the wagon and then took Howard in her arms and climbed in beside the driver while Laurette got into the back with Kenneth and Arthur. "Come on, Carrie, there's room enough for you," she urged, as tears ran down her cheeks.

But the driver would wait no longer. "We're too full already, lady! Come on, Corky!" He drew back his carriage whip and directed a stinging flick against the old horse's side. With a snort of pain, the horse lunged forward and Laurette was thrown back, righting herself and clutching Kenneth and Arthur to her. Carrie stood, then shrugged. Well, she'd hoof it. After all, she was still young and healthy, and she could outrun a fire any day.

She hadn't seen three stocky, shabbily dressed men idling near the Haines house just at the sidewalk and watching her all this time. They had been following the transaction with the driver, and the oldest one of them muttered, "That bitch is loaded for bear. Let's just grab her kale. If she gives us any trouble, use your jawbreaker, Fred."

The man just named, in his early thirties, with thick sideburns and a shaggy beard, grinned evilly and adjusted a pair of brass knuckles onto his right hand, balled his fingers into a heavy fist as the three men started toward the unsuspecting young woman.

"Now, you won't be needin' this, I'm thinkin'," the leader of the trio muttered as he made a grab at her reticule. Carrie uttered a cry, twisted round, and tried to tug the reticule away. But Fred drew back his fist and smashed it against her temples as the third man pulled the reticule out of her nerveless hand. Then the three ran down the street northward without looking back behind them.

Carrie's skull had been fractured by that savage blow. She lay sprawled, and as the fire neared, the scores of terrified, frenzied people running down the street paid no attention to her inert body, stepping on her, kicking her, in their maddened race against the approaching flames.

Laurette had turned back now to look, as she knelt in the back of the wagon, her arms tightly encircling Kenneth and Arthur. She saw the man drive his fist against Carrie's forehead, and she uttered a heart-rending groan: "Oh, that poor woman! May God forgive me all the wicked things I've thought and said about her—she saved our lives—God, have mercy on her, don't let her die for this—"

The wagon turned down a side street and, mouthing foul oaths in his own fright, the driver pitilessly used the carriage whip till he had reached the city limits at Fullerton Avenue.

By Monday night, some twenty-seven hours after the first tongues of flame had sprung out of the O'Leary stable, rain fell and continued for over an hour. The worst calamity in Chicago's lifetime was over. The known dead numbered 250, with as many or more never accounted for; there were at least 100,000 homeless. The full property loss was over two hundred million dollars, and the entire business district was destroyed. All that was left was a mass of twisted girders, fallen columns of iron and stone, huge piles of bricks and rocks and cornices, reminding many learned observers of the destruction of Pompeii. And yet in some sectors of the devastated areas there were incredible sights: a row of houses untouched and yet completely surrounded by whole blocks that had been totally ruined; intact church towers looming high above gutted buildings and crumpled walls. And, as the fire's final irony, the O'Leary stable and house stood almost whole in a patch of land that looked as if a vast cauldron had spilled its contents upon it.

As the wagon reached safety, Laurette, hysterical and dazed by what had taken place and what she had witnessed, began suddenly to laugh. Polly Behting stared incredulously at her employer. "I—I just can't help it, Polly," Laurette half-sobbed, half-laughed. "Just before my husband went away, he was talking so proudly about the stores he wanted to build in other cities, part of his chain. Well, it looks very much now as if he's going to have to go to another city, because this one's burned for sure." Then she buried her face in her hands and said a prayer for the soul of Carrie Haines.

CHAPTER FORTY-TWO

The month of October, 1871, was noteworthy for much more than the devastating Chicago fire. On October 2, the Mormon leader Brigham Young was arrested at Salt Lake City, Utah, on the charge of polygamy. Three weeks later, there was a race riot in Los Angeles and fifteen Chinese laborers were lynched. Several days later, the corrupt rein of "Boss" William Tweed came to an abrupt end when he was arrested after looting New York City of between thirty and two hundred million dollars. Jay Gould, who had tried to corner the gold market and brought about the infamous "Black Friday," provided most of the politician's million-dollar bail bond. But on November 7, the election of reform candidates in New York City marked the overthrow of the Tweed ring and its stranglehold on Tammany Hall.

Laurette Douglas and her husband, Charles, the three little boys and Polly Behting were visiting the red-brick chateau. They had arrived at the end of October and were on their way to Carrizo Springs for the long-delayed reunion between Laurette and her mother, Maybelle Belcher.

Charles Douglas had returned from Indianapolis on the Wednesday after the great Chicago fire and had found Laurette and the children and the nurse in a temporary shelter erected for the homeless on the city's northern limits. Laurette had wept as she clung to him, believing that all was lost, but Charles Douglas had shaken his head. "Honey," he told her, "I got a copy of Joseph Medill's *Tribune* today, and he's got an editorial in there saying that Chicago will rise again. I believe it, and I've got a hunch that Medill is going to be our next mayor. Sure, my department store burned to the ground, but I've already gone around to see my banker, and he says that within a week there'll be at least a dozen banks ready to make full payments to depositors. And they've already set up shops for real estate men, and half the merchants I know are already setting up temporary shops—why, one of them is using an old horse barn at State and Twentieth that escaped the flames. So you see, Laurette honey, we're not wiped out at all."

"But our home—where shall we go?" Laurette had sobbed.

"Why, honey, it'll take maybe six months before my store's rebuilt—I've already arranged with my banker to float a loan to do just that. And you've always wanted to go see your mother in Texas, so this is a perfect time to do it. It'll be a kind of vacation for us. Besides, didn't I tell you that I had ideas for a department store somewhere in Texas, maybe San Antonio? It's a golden opportunity to kill a couple of birds with one stone. That's the way you've got to look at it, Laurette. Come on now, you fiery red-head you, weren't you the one that always showed the most spunk, especially when you took a horsewhip to that Carrie Melton?"

But this joking attempt to cheer Laurette up had had exactly the opposite effect. She had burst into hysterical tears, clinging to him, burying her face against his chest, and finally blurted out what had happened to Carrie. Charles Douglas's handsome young face sobered and shadowed at once. "Forgive me, Laurette, I didn't know. God rest her soul. She redeemed everything by doing what she did—and I'll never forget her, because she got you and the boys here to safety. I'll think of a way to have her name remembered with the honor due her—I know, I'll put in a new line of beauty products for women, and I'll name them after her. That way, we'll always remember what she did for us."

The Douglases and their nurse spent two weeks with Luke and Laure Bouchard and then took the *Alabama Belle* to Mobile, whence they would take the ferry to New Orleans, then the steamer *William Wallace* to Corpus Christi. Luke sent a telegram from Montgomery to Jason Barntry, asking him to arrange transportation and escort for the Douglas family from Corpus Christi on to Wind-haven Range.

A week after the Douglases had boarded the *Alabama Belle,* Luke and Laure went with Marius Thornton to Montgomery to hear their adopted son, Lopasuta, defend a freed black who had contracted with a rich carpetbagger to do some carpentry work and to build a little chapel in a small room of the carpetbagger's house, the latter and his wife being of the Catholic faith. The carpetbagger, ten days after having inspected and verbally approved the work, had sent a note to the black saying that the work was shoddy and incompetent and he would not pay the fee agreed upon.

The black was Joseph Trenton, a man in his late sixties, tall and wiry and almost illiterate. He had been a slave for over fifty years on his master's plantation about sixty miles upriver from Lowndesboro, and since his master's name had been Trenton, he had adopted that name when he had been freed by the Emancipation Act. The work involved had been billed at a cost of $125, which Luke Bouchard himself regarded as about one-fifth of what it was really worth. Old Joseph Trenton had come to Montgomery to buy some tools from a friendly storekeeper and had been told that Lopasuta was a new young lawyer who believed in justice and did not charge exorbitant fees. He had been directed to the young Comanche's quarters, for Jedidiah Danforth, Lopasuta's sponsor, had rented another room adjacent to his own office and installed him there.

The case was to go before a jury, and the carpetbagger's lawyer, a dapper Easterner who had settled in Montgomery six years ago, used as many challenges as he was allowed to reject jurors whom he felt would favor Joseph Trenton simply because he was black. Lopasuta, somewhat to Luke's surprise, protested very few of these challenges, and when the jury was finally selected, there were ten white men and two blacks in the panel before Judge Henley.

The carpetbagger, a florid-faced, bearded man in his mid-fifties, Clarence Mathewson, regarded the young Comanche with a sneering curl of his upper lip and leaned back in his chair to exhibit the diamond stickpin in his ruffled cravat. He listened to Lopasuta making the opening argument that a contract had been established, a fair price had been agreed upon by both parties, and that now the buyer had arbitrarily and wrongfully rejected the work which he had at first approved and refused to pay the agreed-upon sum. He leaned over to whisper to his own lawyer, and the latter rose to answer Lopasuta with the

417

claim that there had been nothing in writing, that his highly reputable and well-known client had made it very clear that the work had to be satisfactory or else it would be rejected and not paid for.

Lopasuta called Joseph Trenton to the stand, and after the elderly black had been sworn in, gently questioned him, step by step, from the time when the work had been commissioned to its delivery and to Clarence Mathewson's verbal approval. At this point, the defendant's attorney rose and objected, on the grounds that Joseph Trenton, being an uneducated man, might not have understood the connotation of the words which his client had used.

When Judge Henley had ruled that he would decide on this objection after a further development of the proceedings, Lopasuta requested that Clarence Mathewson take the stand. The carpetbagger swaggered over to the chair, raised his hand, and repeated the clerk's oath, then seated himself, crossed his legs, adjusted his cravat so everyone would see the diamond stickpin, and again regarded the young Comanche with obvious contempt. "Mr. Mathewson, I should like to know exactly what you said to my client after you inspected the work," Lopasuta began.

"Well, you understand after all this time, I don't remember every single word, but I just told him that it looked fine at first glance, but I'd want to test it and see if the joints were sound and the wood first-rate. You know, appearances are deceiving."

"Indeed they are, Mr. Mathewson," Lopasuta suavely interpolated. "Now, would you mind telling this Court and me why you object to it now and do not wish to pay my client?"

"Because it's very shoddy—the workmanship is poor, very poor. My wife doesn't like the cross at all. And it wasn't put together properly."

"I see. Your Honor," turning to the bench, "may I request that you and the jurors be permitted to see the work my client did in Mr. Mathewson's home? It is obvious that this is a case of judgment, and I should go so far as to say artistic judgment."

"I object, Your Honor! My young opponent is trying to throw a red herring across the trail, to use a phrase," the dapper attorney had sprung to his feet. "This is a matter strictly between my client and his, and my client is a judge of such matters."

"I think in this case I shall allow Counsellor Bouchard's request. This court will be adjourned, and this afternoon the jurors and I will visit Mr. Mathewson's house to inspect the work," the old judge declared with a whack of his gavel.

That afternoon, the jurors and the judge went into the chapel room, and one of the white jurors, himself an expert carpenter, exclaimed, "There's nothing wrong with this job at all! It's as sound as a dollar—a Northern dollar, that is!" which drew a burst of laughter from the others.

When the case was resumed in the courtroom the next morning, Judge Henley directed the jury to retire to bring in a verdict. The foreman, who was the carpenter, rose and said, "Your Honor, that won't be necessary. We've already found for the plaintiff, and we think the defendant ought to pay the court costs, too."

"Gentlemen, I congratulate you on your conscientious service to this county. The defendant will pay the plaintiff, Joseph Trenton, the sum of $125 together with all court costs and attorneys' fees," Judge Henley declared with an emphatic whack of his gavel.

The elderly black had tears in his eyes as he gripped Lopasuta's hand. "You done real good for me, real good, Mistah Bouchard, sir. Jist the same, even if I'd lost, I'd have paid you, that's for certain. You're a fine man, and you stand up for poor folks that don't have any education like me or don't know their rights."

"That was why I became a lawyer, Mr. Trenton," Lopasuta gravely answered. "And I'm proud to have you as a client. One of these days, when I have my own home, I want you to do some work for me, and I assure you I'll pay you a good deal more than Mr. Mathewson tried to weasel out of. Good luck to you, and keep in touch with me."

It was December 18, 1871, the birthday of old Lucien Bouchard. Luke Bouchard, with little Celestine in his arms and Laure beside him, climbed the gentle slope to the top of the towering bluff to keep their annual rendezvous with the founder of Windhaven.

With them had come also their adopted son, Lopasuta Bouchard, and he had brought with him a special token sent by Sangrodo, a token he had kept all this time until the proper moment to pay tribute to Luke's grandfather, whose valor and compassionate humanity had impressed the Comanche chief.

It was a bracelet made of tiny turquoises, and in the center were the claw and the great front tooth of a brown bear which Sangrodo himself had killed with a lance many years ago.

After Luke and Laure had prayed at the graves of Dimarte and old Lucien, Lopasuta turned to them and drew out the bracelet and explained, "You remember that you told the leader of our people how your grandfather killed a bear on his way to the village of Econchate and how he took the claws to prove to the Creeks that he was without fear in this strange new land. When you sent for me, Sangrodo ordered me to bring this token of respect and honor to your grandfather and to give it to you when I believed the time had come to do this. It is now, on the anniversary of your grandfather's birth, and thanks to you, I can speak for my people as well as for all those who are oppressed and scorned. Take it, and bury it so that your grandfather will know that another great chief of a great people, as mighty as the Creeks in their own land, salutes him and his spirit."

Luke took the bracelet reverently from the young Comanche, showed it to Laure, then knelt down before old Lucien's grave. With his bare hands, he scooped up the earth and then buried the bracelet and covered it. Then, looking up at the serene, cloudless sky, he said, "Grandfather, this is the living proof that your spirit will never die. For those in far distant lands who know how you lived with honor and truth and justice revere you as Sangrodo does, as I do, as do all of our family and all of those who have heard your story. You will never be forgotten so long as there are men in this world who cry out against evil. I pray to God to cherish your heritage always and to pass it on to our children and our children's children."

When he had finished, he turned to Laure, who knelt beside him, and said, "I remember the prayer of Friar Bartoloméo Alicante, and I think grandfather would like to hear it now." As she nodded raptly, he raised his face to the sky and said, "Lord, make me an instrument of Thy peace. Where there is hatred, let me sow love; where there is injury, pardon; where there is doubt, faith; where there is despair, hope; where there is darkness, light; and where there is sadness, joy. It is in giving that we receive; it is in pardoning that we are pardoned. We seek not so much to be loved, as to love. Almighty God, hearken to my prayer and grant Your blessing upon all men and women of good will wherever they may be. Amen."

SPECIAL PREVIEW

The Oklahomans

The following is an excerpt edited from *The Oklahomans*, by Whitney Stine,* a towering epic of an extraordinary family—the Herons—who challenged a primitive land and spawned an empire. Driven by pride and ambition to wrest their fortune from the dark riches that lay deep beneath the earth, theirs is a saga of struggle and strife . . . a gripping story of courage and conquest. But, most of all, it is a triumphant testament to human endurance in one of the most turbulent chapters in American and Indian history. Watch for *The Oklahomans,* to be published by Pinnacle Books in August 1980.

Hardship

There was an enormous crowd lined up at the Land Office in Enid, Oklahoma.

Opposite the square, a tent sported the sign POST OFFICE, written in what seemed to be shoe polish. In the midst of hundreds of tents of all sizes and shapes, a group of peddlers had set up displays on the backs of wagons, offering for sale lugs of vegetables and fruits, alongside everyday kitchen staples —all the worse for wear, having made the land run, which opened the Cherokee Strip on September 16, 1893. Potatoes, Letty Heron noted with dismay, were one dollar each, and one overripe brown pineapple, covered with flies, was marked down from ten dollars to eight-fifty! Even white navy beans, obviously old crop, the bane of cowhands the country over, were offered for eighty-five cents a pound. Women were queuing up in front of an old man in a mackinaw pitching water at five cents a cup!

While children played hopscotch and marbles in the dusty road, clusters of men, in assorted attire ranging from celluloid collars to cowboy hats, chaps, and boots, sat on their haunches swapping stories that must have had a vulgar tinge, judging from the raucous laughter that frequently poured out from the group.

"Look around, ladies," Edward Heron, Letty's brother-in-law, exclaimed. "You may never see such a sight again." He glanced slyly at the mushrooming tents. "This is a historic time . . . the beginnings of a town. . . ."

"Yep," neighbor John Dice agreed. "This mornin' there warn't nothin' cher except a lot of soldiers keepin' the peace over a passel of prairie dogs!" Dusk was falling as he looked out over the prairie with wonder. Campfires and white tents marked the countryside for miles around; each section hosted four families. Suddenly, he did not feel so alone nor his former home in Texas so remote. In the spring, Dice's wife, Fontine, whom they called Fourteen, would join them about the same time that they would start to break the prairie with Jack Rabbit plows. . . .

As night fell on Enid, hundreds of tents and even a few Indian teepees were illuminated by flickering coal-oil lanterns. A man with two barrels of kerosene sold fuel at "fifteen cents a fill-up," and a lad in cap and short pants, blowing into a harmonica, was joined by another lad in overalls, who sang in a clear soprano:

"From this valley, they say we are going
Going back to the fields and bright stars. . . .

Valley indeed, thought Edward, as he closed the canvas wagon flap against the slight, cool breeze that had swept down over the prairie after nightfall. At the end of an exhausting day, the campfires had been banked early, and most of the settlers were snug in their pallets. At nine o'clock there was not even a baby's cry.

Edward's wife, half sat, half lay on a pile of comforters placed on the bottom of the wagon, which they had divided into two sleeping areas with a quilt. She was combing her long black hair with quick stabs of the comb, and her olive complexion gleamed in the flickering light of the coal-oil lantern, which also threw her green eyes into dark shadows. Her long, cotton flannel nightgown, high-necked and long-sleeved, successfully hid the magnificently proportioned body that Edward had tried to take again and again during their courting days. But she had stood firm against his onslaught with surprising tenacity. Although very much in love with him, she was not to be possessed until the wedding ring encircled her finger! Now, in their third year of marriage, their bodies still responded as if they were both eighteen instead of twenty-two.

Looking at her, with the exhaustion of the day behind him, and the shocking murder of his brother, Luke, still fresh in his mind, Edward was disgusted with himself to discover that he was physically aroused.

Somewhere in the wagon, probably in the collection of foodstuffs, a lone cricket began an evensong. On the other side of the partition, Letty listened to the chirping and wondered if the little fellow had traveled all the way from Texas or had come into crickethood in Indian Territory. Luke, her late husband, would be at her side now if they had not made the land run. She ran her hands over her body. Her stomach was still flat. She had been with child for six weeks, but she had decided not to break the news until the claim had been staked. Now Luke had died not even knowing that she was pregnant.

Pent-up emotions surged in her breast. She prayed for the torrent to burst, but the tide of tears was mysteriously held back. And, still wide awake, she became aware of the intimate sounds that filtered through the thin guilt.

Edward blew out the coal-oil lantern and modestly removed his clothing in the darkness, which was not easy in the confines of the wagon. Putting on his nightshirt, he crawled into the pallet; every limb was numbed with weariness, yet he was filled with an exciting tension. He took Priscilla in his arms and adjusted his position so that the rough boards seemed more hospitable to their lean bodies.

Priscilla responded to his kisses, although she was surprised that he wanted to make love to her with Letty so near. Somewhere close a baby started to fret but was hushed as a teat was shoved into its mouth. She could hear the contented gurgling just as clearly as if they shared space with mother and child. *What would Letty think?*

Priscilla dutifully raised her nightgown to her chin, making her body accessible. They would have to be very quiet. Ordinarily, under the circumstances, she would have whispered no into his ear. But in some strange way, she understood his need, which did not wholly concern passion but had something to do with the terrible loss of his brother. As Edward's rough, callused hands caressed her body, which usually responded quickly to his ministrations, she felt nothing—only an inward insensitivity. To get it over quickly, she breathed into his ear, but she could not sigh or utter the other intimate sounds of love that she knew always heightened his own feelings of desire.

Confined to the close quarters of the pallet, she turned on her side and opened herself to him. She thanked God for the noisy cricket who, at the moment, was joined by the chirping of a soulmate. She tried to emulate quick movements of passion for Edward's sake.

It did not matter now whether or not she was aroused as he began to plunge into her, numbing her solar plexus. She bit her lip as the delicate area of her inner thighs pulsed with a chafing burn. In a way she understood that he was somehow avenging Luke's death. But because he was very, very tired, she knew it would take him a long time to achieve relief. She steeled herself for the ordeal ahead.

Letty lay very still, listening both to the sounds of the crickets and of her brother-in-law making love to Priscilla. It was the first time she had ever shared such intimacy with other human beings, and she suddenly felt alone and abandoned. With Luke dead, how long would it be before she experienced lovemaking again? Then she was horrified that she had thought such a thing. There would never be anyone like Luke, as tender, as aware of her needs and her desires, as right for her in every way. And as she thought about those intimate moments, which would never occur again, the horror and the pain of the afternoon came back, and her eyes burned with scalding tears.

Underneath the wagon, John Dice adjusted to a new position. The damp, cold ground was as hard as his own body at the moment. Aroused by the slight movements of the planks above as Edward made love to Priscilla, he could not sleep. His own body cried out for release; he had been on the trail for twenty days without the comforting embraces of his wife, Fontine, still in Santone. Picturing the scene taking place in the wagon, he ran his hands over his wide chest. Then he reached lower, and for one long, pleasurably agonizing moment, became Edward and felt the soft, moist warmth of Priscilla.

Mentally, he was with his wife. He wanted to tell her how much he loved her, tell her how beautiful her eyes were, how he gravitated to her every movement. But he had never been able to speak to her in this intimate way, utter the feelings in his heart because, again, he could not put his thoughts into words. He was cursed because of his ignorance. If he could only speak about what he felt inside. . . .

At last, Priscilla felt Edward's body tense. She waited as long as she dared, then whispered, "*Now!*" He withdrew and spilled his seed on her thigh. They did not yet want a child, and there were only a few days during the month when they could stay with each other until the very end. Panting heavily, he lay next to her and, thankfully, the sounds of his quick breathing were covered by the intermitten chirping of the crickets.

Tears ran down Letty's cheeks, wetting the neck of her nightgown. Afraid of crying out in agony, she buried her face deep in the eiderdown pillow. The painful sounds of muffled sobs came through the canvas.

"You must go to her," Edward whispered.

"No," Priscilla whispered back. "She must have privacy." *How little men knew about the feelings of women!*

After Letty's emotions were completely spent, she lay staring at the dark shadows, silhouetted by the moon, that played on the covered wagon. Only toward morning, when the sky turned the canvas a deep pink, did she feel secure enough to sleep.

By the time John Dice drove the wagon onto the Heron claim, located sixteen miles east of Enid, a long, golden twilight touched the prairie. The landscape, thought Letty, looked like a rich medieval tapestry viewed through a piece of amber-tinted glass. "I've never seen anything so beautiful," she said.

John Dice clicked his tongue. "I seed this ever' time after a prairie fire. The smoke gits up in the air and it just stays up yonder. Miz Heron, the sun tries to shine through and it cain't make it. . . . It's a kind of . . ." He worked his mouth.

"Reflection?" Priscilla put in quickly. Oh, the man was a dullard!

"Yeah, that's it!" John smiled to himself. She was a bright woman, all right, and she and Edward were perfectly matched. He liked to be in the company of intelligent women, even though he always felt inferior. Fourteen had no formal education either, yet she was smart in her own way, and she was certainly wonderful between the covers. Thank God, he reflected, it didn't take brains to fuck.

Up ahead, a small crowd of settlers gathered in God's Acre over four mounds of red, freshly dug earth. "What's this, Poppa?" John Dice called as he reined in the team.

His father came forward. "We been busy burying four fellers. Three got trampled in The Run and one had a heart attack when he staked his claim. Seems word got out that we'd set up a gravey'ard and people begin cartin' in their dead. One of the widders even rounded up a preacher, Reverend Haskell. He's over there now spoutin' verses." He paused. "Git your claimin' done, Edward?"

"No," Edward replied. "People are lined up for city blocks around the Land Office, and the Post Office is about the size of an outhouse."

"Edward!" Priscilla admonished.

"All right." He threw her a sharp look. "Privy."

"That's just as bad!" She turned up her nose, then smiled sweetly at Poppa Dice. "Would you help us down, please?"

He held out his callused hands to support Priscilla and Letty, taking the opportunity to glance at their ankles as they descended from the wagon. Although he felt few stirrings below his belt buckle these days, he still admired a well-turned calf.

"We jest mailed in our papers," John Dice said.

"We'll be notified as soon as they git through that pile o' claims."

Poppa Dice spoke in a low tone. "The preacher rode in about four o'clock yestidy, according to the widder Barrett. Seems as though he got confused, thought he was near Enid, and ended up out here after all the land was claimed. Guess he's pretty pore with a horse."

Priscilla smiled weakly. "Let's hope," she said wryly, "that he preaches better than he rides!"

Letty took Edward's arm. "I'd be willing to contribute an acre of ground for the church and the parsonage."

He nodded. "With Luke buried here, it seems fitting, Letty."

Poppa Dice clicked his tongue. "Some of these settlers have been talkin' about formin' a little community. One fella is a blacksmith, another used to own a provision store and says he'll apply for a fourth-class postal permit." He paused. "I guess if we got a church 'n a gravey'ard, we got the makin's of a town!"

Letty frowned. "I can't possibly farm this land by myself. Leasing out a few acres for cash might be the answer."

Priscilla threw Edward an icy look. "I don't see why we can't have a town on *our* property, Edward."

"No, Prissy, our claim is too far back," he explained with more patience than he felt. "Eventually, a county road will run right along here, because this is the section line. Besides, we've got a lot of timber that has to be cleared and not much open pasture."

As the Heron family joined the other mourners around the graves, an Indian squaw and her small son stood in the golden dusk that splattered over a nearby hill. She and a few others of her tribe had been on their way to Osage country when the news of The Run spread throughout the Territory. In the old days when the Cherokee Nation leased these lands to cattlemen for pasture, Indians passing through had been shot on sight. But when the government bought the lands from the Cherokee to make way for white settler's, and surveyors swarmed over the area, Indians were once more allowed free entry as long as they had permission.

The old woman's face was creased with the passage of many sun-drenched summers. She had not embraced the white man's religion as most of her tribe had done, although she treated missionaries and Indian agents with deference. But now as she observed the ceremony below, she clicked her tongue and drew the boy protectively to her side. The Cherokee were foolish, she thought. They had adopted the ways of the white man for over two hundred years and dressed and behaved as he did. They had forgotten their real heritage and had made no use of this hunting ground that the government had given them. She smiled bitterly. They had forgotten how to hunt. The Cherokee were content to stay in the Council House in Tallequah in their white collars and suits and negotiate endlessly with Washington.

As the sounds of a kind of chant filtered up from below, she turned her ear to the wind to catch the meaning: *shepherd . . . green pastures . . . still waters . . .* She had been told that the Christian priest could lift up the spirits of the dead. She waited patiently, waiting to see the graves open and the souls drift upward. But nothing happened. She clicked her tongue again. Another example of the white man's duplicity!

With the spirits of the dead still in their mounds, she turned back to her people below. Then the little group crept along the creek to find the special place where the mass of running-rock was to be found. Each carried an earthenware vessel. They knelt near the bank, and while there was still enough light in the sky, before the golden glow at the horizon turned dark, they scooped up the thick black mixture that oozed from the ground and filled the pots. They would not be back by this spot again for a very long time, and enough running-rock had to be gathered to waterproof the bottoms of many wicker baskets and to provide curative medicines and to be burned to chase away insects from their homes.

Reverend Haskell, a small man with a sparse red mustache that hid his thin mouth none to well, and his wife, Thelma, who was short and fat and round as a butter ball, shook hands solemnly with the group. It was strange, indeed, the minister thought, looking at the brave settlers, that a catastrophe had brought them all together on the lonely prairie.

Poppa Dice introduced the Herons and his son.

"What is your calling?" Letty asked quietly.

"Methodist," Reverend Haskell replied just as quietly.

"We're Baptists," Priscilla put in quickly, her dark eyes flashing.

"And you, sir?" The minister turned to Poppa Dice, who exchanged glances with his son.

"Nothin' much, Rev. We always go wherever it's handy—'bout twice a year—Easter 'n Christmas. John's missus is a Dunkard. I s'pose you, being out here in the middle of nowhere, ain't gonna be strick to Methodist ways."

The Reverend smiled tightly. "I believe, of course, in Wesleyan principles, but I do think that a nondenominational approach would be best. I'll build a church and parsonage if I can barter some land."

Letty nodded, her blue eyes very deep. "It's already been decided," she said kindly, pressing his arm. "I'll be pleased to give you space beside God's Acre."

He looked at her in wonder. "I'll be much obliged." His eyes were suspiciously bright. "I'd be much obliged indeed." He turned to the group. "Before we disperse, let's all recite the Lord's Prayer."

As the familiar words echoed out over the claim, the three widows drew closer together. All wore borrowed dark hats and veils. There had been no time to hunt through trunks and packing crates after the remains of their husbands had been sewn into the canvas sacks ready for burial.

Leona Barrett, whose husband had died of a

heart attack, was already pondering the future. Before she had met Lawrence, at the age of thirty, she had been a businesswoman in Detroit, with her own millinery shop. She had banked the money when the business was sold, and she knew that her husband had a five hundred-dollar insurance policy in her name. She was not one to look at the past, nor to grieve unduly. Life should be a total experience. She knew that her modern views would make little headway among women of her age group. Yet she had never met a man with whom she did not feel equal.

The second widow, Mary Darth, smothered a sob with her handkerchief. She was not as delicate however, as her five-foot-three, ninety-eight-pound frame would indicate. Having been raised in a family of twelve, she was certain to find employment as a hired girl.

Liza Galbraith, the third widow, was a tall, buxom blonde of nineteen. Married only ten days, she felt foolishly lost and abandoned. She could not think of the future because she could not think about the present.

Reverend Haskell intoned the last lines of the prayer, and as a chorus of "amen's" resounded over the prairie, he glanced up into the sky, drew in his breath sharply, and cried, "Look!"

Across the heavens stretched a startling cloud formation, highlighted by the glow of sunset. "A sign," he exclaimed breathlessly. "A sign!"

The silhouette of a divine being, wings unfolded, head surrounded with a halo, and garments flowing to the horizon, was exquisitely formed by the clouds.

"If that ain't a perfect sight!" Poppa Dice cried, awestruck.

Letty stepped forward dramatically. "If a town is to spring up here," she proclaimed, "let's call it *Angel*."